JANELLE TAYLOR

Golden Torment

ZEBRA BOOKS
KENSINGTON PUBLISHING CORP.

ZEBRA BOOKS

are published by

Kensington Publishing Corp.
475 Park Avenue South
New York, NY 10016

Eleventh printing: August, 1992

Printed in the United States of America

LOVE'S DEEPEST DESIRE

"I know this area better than any other man. But I'm not for hire by you," Landis stated crisply.

"I see," Kathy murmured thoughtfully. "I guess that means you'll be leaving soon and won't be back for a long time?" she speculated.

"I'm not sure yet," he lied convincingly.

"Where can I reach you?" she innocently pressed.

"I move around a lot," he parried.

"But I might need you! Where can I find you?" she insisted.

To prevent any further questions, his mouth came down on hers. He kissed her deeply and hungrily. In her agitated state, Kathy clung to him and artlessly responded with intense yearnings, totally unprepared to deal with this fiery reality. Her head spun wildly at his nearness and manly smell. He invaded her senses—entrapped them in a world of heady desire. . . .

FOR

KATHRYN FALK,
a "Leading Lady" in romance . . .

&

BERTRICE SMALL,
my "Mentor" and "Guardian Angel" . . .

&

TOM (JENNIFER WILDE) HUFF,
whose wit and charm surpasses that of
his delightful characters . . .

A special dedication
to romance readers,
who have known golden dreams or
shared in golden torments
in books or reality . . .

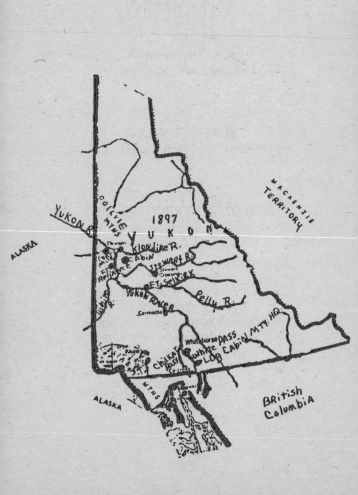

GOLDEN TORMENT

Many are the hardships in a vast, bitter land;
Suffering and strife, close companions to man.
Challenging Fate to control my own destiny;
Alaska boldly offered her golden prosperity.

My elusive search began, conquering frozen earth;
I discovered a treasure, a nugget of rare worth.
With eyes of richest sapphire, complexion of pearl;
Yet, commitment had no place in my carefree world.

Adventure my first love, danger controlling my day;
Like gold, Love charms a dreamer, taking his freedom away.
Love accepted this challenge, my strong will to tame;
Though I must forgive her changes, for I am to blame.

A woman was molded from hardship and despair;
Even knowing me well, offered her heart with a dare.
Defeat glazes her eyes, her tears and dreams all spent;
Without even knowing, she became my Golden Torment.

Now the moment has come when I must choose;
Which of these treasures I will recklessly lose.
My heart's not as frozen as this glacial frontier;
Will freedom be as golden when Kat's no longer here?

Penny Moxley Thomas and Janelle Taylor
April, 1982

One

September, 1897

The steamship *Victoria* was sailing a hazardous course from Seattle to Skagway. As with most ships which made this voyage up the Inside Passage to that beckoning land of golden promise, the vessel was packed with gold-obsessed men. The *Victoria* crew was experienced, pleased with a leader who knew these treacherous waters as well as the lines on his weather-crinkled hands. But this particular voyage included two passengers who inspired amusement and intrigue: two lovely and daring females, a young widow with vivid red hair and a striking blonde of eighteen.

Captain Cyrus Shurling had taken the women under his wing for protection from the rowdy men who flooded his lower decks with their piles of gear. But Shurling's motive was hardly unselfish; he wished to avoid any trouble which might stain his presently spotless record.

To Captain Shurling, it seemed absurd for two women to be heading for Alaska, especially since they were not going there to become saloon girls. Everyone wondered what two attractive and gentle females could do in that lonely, perilous location. Shurling had decided it was not

9

his place to judge their motives or to prevent their trip. But after last night's fiasco, he wished he had refused them passage! A smart captain should have realized two single women aboard a ship of tense and bored men spelled trouble!

It was beyond the duty-minded, reserved Shurling to comprehend why men would turn their backs on civilization and their families to blindly rush to this land of golden torment. Shurling labelled them idiots to believe that hogwash in the newspapers which colorfully painted an idealistic image of Alaska. The men he transported to this frozen Hades sounded as if they expected to fill their empty pockets on the first day! Shurling sneered, if they knew only the half of it!

The stories cruelly and deceptively omitted the bleak realities of the rigorous conditions there: the frustrations, the tragedies, the disillusionments, the backbreaking work, and the meager triumphs. None seemed aware of the ultimate price for willfully seeking that golden illusion. None admitted to the unspeakable horrors which these jaundice-eyed men would soon confront and endure. None spoke of the thousands who lost all hope and withered away or eventually returned home haggard and embittered men. Alaska did not honestly sing out for brave and hardy men; she provocatively trilled her mesmerizing song to fools and dreamers too enchanted to resist it.

Harriet Pullen's eyes scanned the comfortable stateroom she was sharing with the striking female who was asleep. This particular cabin had allowed them to travel in relative safety and serenity, along with the eagle eye of the captain. A smile tugged at the corners of her wide mouth as she studied Kathryn Hammond, recalling how this vivacious and charming creature had generously tricked her into accepting a five-hundred-dollar cabin for one-hundred-fifty dollars.

The smile was quickly replaced by a worried scowl as Harriet wondered how she would ever repay her, for surely Kathy realized she was not a person to accept charity. Harriet was proud and stubborn, a woman quickly learning to take care of her own problems and to control her own destiny.

Harriet walked over to Kathy's bunk and glanced down at her silky head. Kathy had no relatives; she had left no close friends in Seattle. Sadness gripped Harriet's heart as she prayed it would not take long to earn enough money to send for her precious children, left behind out of necessity. Now, the future of this vulnerable, green girl was also in her workworn hands; these responsibilities weighed heavily as Harriet bravely sought to earn more than a meager existence in America.

Harriet's mind was trapped in a vicious turmoil. Did she have the right to lead a mourning girl into danger? Harriet wished she knew the truth about Jake Hammond, Kathy's father. How could a father walk away from his property and child and never glance back? She couldn't imagine her departed husband diseased with gold fever.

Suspicions teased at Harriet's mind concerning the many things Dorothy Hammond had insinuated during their brief friendship. Why had Dory unwittingly mentioned her sable-haired love with dark eyes, when Kathy dreamed of seeing her father's golden head and blue eyes? Harriet shook her head to halt her mental meandering.

Harriet's solace was in the fact Kathy would have her friendship, protection, and guidance. Protection, she mentally scoffed. She had been of no help during Kathy's recent encounter with that lecherous Marc Slavin, first mate on this ship bulging with gold-crazed men.

Harriet's hand stretched out to stroke Kathy's tawny head as she sighed heavily in despair. Annoyance and remorse filled Harriet as she recalled how Kathy had rushed to their cabin in near hysterics after that man had assailed her on the upper deck last night. But to have Captain Shurling imply Kathy had misled him was an outrage, even if Kathy was a beautiful stranger and Marc an officer!

"Kathy . . . Kathy, it's time to get up," Harriet called her from her deep slumber, gently shaking her shoulder. "The bell will sound any moment for breakfast, dear. We'll be arriving today," she blurted out excitedly, hardly able to control her tension and suspense.

Kathy rubbed heavy lids which drooped sleepily over cornflower blue eyes. She sat up groggily, confused. As her sight touched on the flaming-haired woman towering over her, reality promptly returned.

Was she actually on a steamship heading for the wilds of Alaska in search of a father she couldn't even recall? Kathy gazed at the handsome woman poised near her bunk. Whatever would she have done without Harriet Pullen? No fate could be worse than hers: to be left widowed and destitute with four small children to raise. But Harriet was a stout-hearted woman who possessed the courage to head to another land at age thirty-seven with only seven dollars in her pocket! When compared to Harriet, her troubles were scant. That is, if Kathy didn't include Marc Slavin on her list!

"You go on ahead, Harriet. I can't face that scoundrel again," Kathy declined, shaking her head.

"Don't be silly, child. I doubt he'll even be present this morning. The captain won't take kindly to trouble this close to his destination. Besides, Shurling said food was scarce and expensive. We'd better fill up on this free fare before we dock," Harriet coaxed to lighten the anxiety in this delightful girl with entreating eyes and a trusting air.

"You honestly don't think Marc Slavin will be present this morning?" she watched Harriet closely.

"You said Shurling ordered him to steer clear of you for the rest of this voyage. Even if he's as mad as a wet hen, he'll obey the captain's orders," Harriet gently reasoned, although unsure of her own confidence in the captain's power over that persistent man.

"I don't know . . . ," Kathy replied hesitantly. "Marc Slavin has a mind of his own, an evil one!" she added. "The captain told him to be my guard and escort. I don't understand. He's been such a gentleman. Did you know he's married? I couldn't believe my hearing last night; he suddenly vowed he loved me and wanted to marry me. When I rebuffed him, he tried to ravish me! He's cruel and dangerous!"

From her own observations, Harriet knew Kathy was not exaggerating. Marc Slavin was handsome and wealthy; he was devious and arrogant. Men like Marc were beguiling and courteous until they were ready to strike at some unsuspecting and susceptible female who had caught their fancy. Harriet thought it best not to overly worry Kathy with her concerns. Slavin's proposal had been a cunning ruse, since he had attacked her and even threatened to trap her below at the mercy and lust of those rough men: many of them fleeing criminals! But this precarious situation would be over soon . . .

"Just let him say one word to you and I'll box his ears!" the older woman shrieked, aware of her own fiery temper and resolve.

"If anyone can put him in his place, it's you, Harriet. Why should I let that fiend imprison me in our cabin?" she vowed, her shaky voice and wary expression belying her brave words.

Kathy threw the covers aside and stood up, yawning and stretching her shapely frame like a graceful feline awakening from a catnap. Harriet jested playfully, "If I had your beautiful face and figure, I wouldn't have to worry about earning a living; I could find droves of men eager to support us. Use them wisely, dear; they're powerful weapons," she advised as Kathy hurriedly dressed.

"You aren't sorry you came along with me, are you?" Harriet unexpectedly inquired, her expression and mood serious. "I did take advantage of you in a moment of weakness and distress," she added, nervously pushing some straying curls from her flushed face.

Kathy smiled at her. "How else can I discover the truth if I don't track it down? If not for you, I couldn't have survived these last weeks. You didn't twist my arm, Harriet," she asserted, a spark of her old spirit returning.

As Harriet mulled over those words, Kathy's gaze wandered over her from flaming head to foot. Harriet wasn't a hefty female, but she was large and firm. Her skin was very pale, as was natural for a woman with her coloring. Kathy cheerfully concluded, if anyone could survive and prosper in intimidating Alaska, it was Harriet.

As Kathy completed her task, images from the past flashed before her. She could not forget the art exhibit she had viewed in San Francisco two years ago which had shown the dangers and hardships of this dreamland. She envisioned the blond-haired friend who had shared that impressive moment with her, who was intensely infatuated with her beautiful mother. She should write him with the news of her mother's death. For two years, his letters had arrived, his affections for her mother increasing with time. She wondered how this fatal news would affect Jack London. They had shared so many good times; he was the brother she never had. She missed him and wondered where the carefree wanderer was; his last letter months ago had sounded sad and mysterious. But this wasn't the time to handle that problem. Soon, she would be viewing those frightening sites in person. Alaska . . . even the sound of that word was intimidating—but strangely compelling.

Kathy closed the trunk which held most of her possessions and the heavy clothing she had purchased for the North Country. Being the point from which most people left for "Seward's Icebox," Seattle was well stocked with the necessary garments and supplies for the severely cold climate of the glacial frontier. Between the storekeeper and Harriet, Kathy had bought and packed everything she would need for a lengthy voyage and an indeterminable sojourn in Skagway. Kathy's plans called for her to allow two months to locate her errant father, then to return to the United States before the worst weather arrived, or her money ran out. The thought of being stranded in that awesome territory until spring didn't suit Kathryn Leigh Hammond at all.

Jake Hammond . . . no matter how many times Kathy had vowed to hate him and to ignore his existence, she desperately needed to meet him and to speak with him at least once. Until she heard his side of this tormenting tale, she could never find peace of mind. Fresh waves of anguish washed over Kathy as she wondered what her life and personality would be like if her father had never left home. Why was she truly heading for Alaska?

15

Revenge? Justice? Truth? She was so confused that she honestly didn't know.

Harriet locked their door before they headed for their last breakfast on the *Victoria*. Sure enough, Marc Slavin was noticably absent. Kathy still remained apprehensive during the meal, fully expecting him to swagger in at any moment, wearing a taunting smirk. She hardly noticed the fragrant coffee, the cat's-head biscuits, the country ham, or the deep red gravy.

Kathy ate as quickly as she could. Afterwards, the two women returned to their cabin to pack. Taking a last bath and pulling on warmer clothing, the morning passed swiftly and uneventfully. When the luncheon bell rang out, it was two hours to docking time. Excitement wafted over the ship like a strong breeze from the nearby mountains which lined the Inside Passage. Noises from the boisterous group below gained volume as they neared their destination.

Marc Slavin did not appear at the captain's table. Kathy halted before thanking Shurling, wisely concluding it would be best to ignore the offensive affair. As did Harriet, the captain suggested they eat hardily. This last meal was delicious. They slowly devoured the baked ham with its honey glaze, the steaming corn-sticks, the black-eyed peas, the fluffy rice, and the apple cobbler.

The voyage nearly over, Captain Shurling was in high spirits, savoring his new accomplishment. He served a heady red wine to toast their success, stating, "To the prettiest ladies I've ever transported to Seward's Icebox. May all your dreams be shiny ones, and may you never experience any golden torments."

Both women thanked him, beaming with anticipation. Shurling invited them to join him in the wheelhouse to witness the impressive sights and to hear his informative narration. He thought it best not to tell them he simply wanted them safely out of the way when they docked. The men below were getting raucous and anxious. Crude talk was flowing as swiftly as the Lynn Canal. In the greenhorns' eagerness to get ashore, the ladies could get in their way and be injured, so Captain Shurling had decided to keep them aboard until all of the men had departed. He turned to Harriet and asked to speak privately with her in his cabin.

The two women exchanged wary looks. "Is it important, sir? I should accompany Kathy back to our cabin," Harriet remarked softly, clearly alluding to last night's trouble.

Annoyed at this reminder, Shurling asserted, "We'll walk her to the door. There's a matter I must discuss with you before you leave the ship." He sounded persistent.

"Kathy? Is that all right with you?" Harriet inquired. Her eyes and tone of voice revealed concern for her youthful companion.

"Certainly. I still have some things to do," Kathy replied uneasily, pondering Shurling's curious behavior.

Waiting just down the hallway, Harriet and Shurling lingered until the door was opened and Kathy turned to wave them goodbye.

Kathy entered the square room and closed the door, locking it. Just as she leaned against the door to sigh in relief, a large hand clamped over her mouth. She found herself imprisoned in the steely embrace of Marc Slavin. Pressed tightly against the sealed entrance, she stared at him through terror-filled eyes.

Marc's green eyes were brittle and piercing. His jaw was taut; his teeth were clenched. A savage sneer curled up the corners of his full mouth. His body was hard and

17

lean; there was no hope for escape.

Kathy was in a panic; she could not think clearly or reason calmly. She strained to breathe, for his hand was almost blocking her nose. Never had she been this frightened or helpless, not even when her life changed so drastically with her mother's sudden death.

Marc's sardonic gaze slipped to her throat and watched her throbbing pulse as it revealed her terror. His glacial eyes fused with hers, his salacious intent clearly displayed there. He exuded a soul-chilling aura as he asserted, "The captain sends his regards, love. He said I was to bid you farewell while he does the same with your friend. Surely you didn't think we could allow your insult to pass unpunished? We simply didn't want any interference from the other passengers who are presently too preoccupied to notice anything happening aboard this ship. Nice to have privacy," he informed the rigid girl in a frosty tone.

She struggled, trying vainly to pull free or at least to reason with him. He would permit neither. "Time is very short, love; I'll be needed top-side soon. Shall we finish what we began last night?" he calmly suggested, leering at her.

Kathy futilely struggled again as Slavin merely laughed. Pinning her against the hard surface at her back, he gagged her. Just as she was about to claw his taunting face, he cruelly seized her wrists and squeezed them. Kathy grimaced and moaned; tears sprang to her eyes. Marc grabbed her trembling chin and put pressure on it, causing her to wince in pain.

Marc warned in an icy tone, "Behave yourself or you might get hurt! You owe me, Kathy; and I fully intend to be paid before you leave this ship. No woman rejects me or humiliates me!"

18

As he pulled her resisting body toward the bunk, she tried to stall. He chuckled devilishly as he easily lifted her and carried her the short distance. She squirmed as he casually tossed her on the bunk, then fell atop her before she could roll off the other side.

Slavin captured Kathy's thrashing head between his hands and held it motionless. "Such a little tigress," he murmured huskily, as he rolled her to her side and fumbled with the zipper down the back of her dress.

Once down, Marc began to yank the dress over her shoulders, exposing their creamy texture and her stark white undergarments. Kathy desperately wiggled and made muffled noises which drew amused chuckles from him. He pulled the dark green ribbon from her tawny hair and bound her hands with it. He was quickly out of his shirt, tossing it to the floor beside the bunk. He slipped her bound hands over his head and shoulders. "That should hold you for a while," he lightly remarked, savoring the contact of their naked flesh. "I assume you've never made love to a man; so, be good, love, if you want me to be gentle with you."

Kathy moved her hands to dig her nails into the smooth muscles of his back. Caught by surprise, Marc cried out in pain. Seizing her hair, he yanked forcefully, calling an instant halt to her brave attack. "You little spitfire!" he snarled, teeth bared like a wild animal and eyes blazing in fury. "You'll regret that. If it's pain you want, I can certainly oblige you," he threatened ominously.

Too late, Kathy realized the danger in her desperate action. Where are you, Harriet? she silently questioned. Had Shurling lured Harriet away to assist this terrible crime? God, help us both . . .

Angered and rushed, Marc jerked savagely at her

19

clothing. Suddenly a loud knock shattered the silence of the stateroom. Her frantic gaze riveted in that direction. Marc clamped his hand over her mouth. He softly growled a warning, "Stay silent, Kathy, or you'll be fatally sorry."

The knocking became louder and more insistent. Kathy felt new hope. Then, doubting she could be heard even if she dared defy this violent man, she closed her eyes and wept. Help was so close, and yet so far away. Whoever was there would soon leave when she failed to answer, and she never doubted Marc would carry out his threat.

Without warning, the door was kicked open. In stormed an enraged Captain Shurling, several startled crewmen, and a furious Harriet. Kathy felt confusion and relief as she stared blankly at the group, gaping incredulously at her and Marc.

Witnessing what had taken place, Harriet rushed past the astonished men and angrily attacked Marc Slavin. She beat on his back and pulled his brown hair; she pinched his arms and cheeks. She screamed at him, "You filthy animal! You rutting beast! How dare you assault an innocent child! You should be horse-whipped!"

One man pulled Harriet from the stunned Marc and restrained her. Shurling glared at his blatantly guilty first officer and the bound girl. "You filthy scum! I'll have you disgraced for this offense! Untie her, Hiram. See if she requires the doctor's attentions. Tim, you and Pete take this slime to the brig. I'll deal with him shortly. Just get him out of my sight before I toss him overboard to the sharks!"

Kathy was freed and then comforted by Harriet. The two men led the rebellious and sullen Marc out of the congested room. "Miss?" the freckle-faced Hiram inquired hesitantly of the half-dressed girl. "Are you injured, Miss? Should I fetch Doc Tanner?"

Harriet glared at Shurling. "Wait outside while I calm her and check her! She's too upset to answer. If justice is to be done this time, Captain, you will throw that creature overboard!" she declared.

"I'm sorry this happened, ladies. I swear this is the first such disgrace on my ship. I'll deal out a severe punishment to Mister Slavin. He'll never sail on my ship or any other ship again," he vowed.

"If you had heeded Miss Hammond's words the first time, this new insult might have been prevented, sir. There is no excuse for allowing such an offense to take place a second time. I gravely question the safety of your ship and the wisdom of your command." The nettled man in his crisp white uniform shifted from foot to foot. "I certainly hope he isn't permitted to lie his way out of this vile episode. Surely it's clear she is totally blameless. In my opinion, you owe Kathy an apology for doubting her yesterday."

"You're correct, Mrs. Pullen. I sincerely apologize for the unnecessary danger and embarrassing position I placed her in. I can promise this will never happen aboard my ship again." 'Cause I'll never allow another troublesome female along, he added to himself.

Harriet focused her attention on the distressed girl as Shurling waited in the corridor. Before Harriet could soothe Kathy's jumpy nerves, a man came to notify Shurling he was needed in the pilot-house. He stuck his head inside the room and stated briskly, "Sorry, Mrs. Pullen, but I must see to my ship and her course. These channels are highly treacherous. I'll post a guard at your door. Send word if you require anything. Oh, yes," he added as an afterthought, "stay here until I come back for

21

you. Those greenhorns get rambunctious."

The damaged door was pulled to as far as possible. The older woman looked down at Kathy. "Kathy, you must get control of yourself, child. We'll be docking soon. Are you all right?" Harriet hoped the tone of her voice would calm her; it did not.

"I want to go home," Kathy sobbed uncontrollably.

"You can't, child. Your mother's gone and your home was sold. You must find your father; he'll protect you," she encouraged the distraught girl.

"What does he care about me? I could be dead for all he knows! He doesn't want me or need me!" she cried.

"But you need him, Kathy. Find him and listen to his side. How could he possibly deny such a lovely daughter who's all alone now?" Harriet reasoned, hoping to soothe Kathy's torment.

Kathy lifted tearful eyes to gaze at the concerned woman. "Do you honestly believe he might have some logical reason for what he did?" The hope in her eyes and voice touched Harriet deeply.

"Perhaps he does, Kathy. Learn the truth, then decide how you feel about him. He is your father, Kathy, good or bad," she stated.

Kathy's eyes scanned her scrapes and bruises, shuddering. "I said Marc Slavin was dangerous. How did he get into a locked room? How did he know I was alone?" she questioned, brushing away her tears.

"A crewman told Shurling that Slavin wasn't in his cabin as ordered. Shurling discovered his master keys missing. He knew where the keys and Slavin would be. We came as quickly as we could," she explained.

"Why did Shurling want to see you? Marc said the captain knew he was here with me. He even told me the captain was also taking his pleasure with you. If you hadn't knocked the door down . . ."

Harriet placed her finger on Kathy's quavering lips and shushed her. "Don't dwell on this dreadful event. Shurling has him confined in the brig. He wanted to discuss what happened last night," she replied to Kathy's prior question. "He suspected Slavin had exaggerated the truth, but he didn't wish to press the matter without proof. He wanted to know what you had confided to me," Harriet replied reluctantly.

"I told you he didn't believe me! Did you tell him everything?"

"After what he witnessed, he doesn't have to question me! He was also concerned about our safety and welfare in Alaska," she added.

"I hope you told him we'll certainly be as safe there as on board his miserable ship!" she shrieked, her breathing ragged.

"Slavin gave him the proof he needed. The beast! I could strangle him myself! It's a fact of nature, Kathy; a woman's strength cannot compare to a man's brute power. We must depend on our wits and courage." She abruptly asked, "Do you know how to fire a pistol?"

Bewildered, Kathy replied, "Yes, but why?"

"I have two in my trunk. They belonged to my husband. I thought it wise to bring along some protection. I'll give you one. It's small and has its own holster. You can wear it under your parka."

"Carry a gun on my person?" she questioned in astonishment.

"This is a wild and savage area. From what Shurling told me, very little law exists. Marc just proved how powerless we are against a man with superior strength and evil intent. A gun will even the odds. Another thing to consider: what about the protection of your money

23

and property? Shurling said theft is quite common," she blurted out before thinking, then wished she hadn't spoken so bluntly.

"You make it sound so uncivilized, like straying into a den of wolves. I wish I were still in Seattle," Kathy murmured.

"I'm sorry, Kathy. I shouldn't have persuaded you to come with me. This isn't a place for a young lady. If I had known anything like this would happen to you . . ." Tears clouded her eyes.

"No, Harriet," she injected. "Please don't blame yourself for this trouble. I'll be fine after we dock. You'll see," she wistfully promised, forcing a smile. "We'll both be fine," she added.

"In a way, Kathy, I did trick you. I pounced on you like an old tomcat on a fieldmouse. I used your father as an excuse to entice you. I tried to make you feel obligated to find him. I'm truly sorry."

"I hope you'll be just as devious and successful in Alaska as you were in getting me here," she jested to ease Harriet's anguish. "Life is so complicated. I've always felt happy and safe. Now, I'm responsible for my existence and happiness; it's petrifying. How could I blame you for not wanting to face this new challenge alone? We'll make it, Harriet," she vowed, defiance and pride filling her eyes.

Harriet concurred, then her tone became grave. "It's really happening; we'll be there before dark. It sounds crazy, but I'm happy and sad; I want to laugh and cry. Imagine, riches . . . a new life . . ."

Kathy tittered in suspense. "That's how I feel. It's such a drastic change. If we don't like it, there's another ship going home."

"If it isn't winter," she refuted. "The channels and

rivers are frozen solid. It's make it by December, or be stranded until spring."

"You'll make it; have no doubts," she complimented her friend.

"My poor babies . . . I wonder if they're all right," she fretted miserably.

"Just missing their mother and anticipating the day they can join her."

Kathy bolted up straight. She cocked her head sideways and strained to hear. "Listen, Harriet! What's all the shouting about?"

"Land!" Harriet squealed. "We're here, Kathy! Alaska!"

In the contagious exuberance which surrounded her, Kathy conquered her doubts and fears. A heady sense of adventure ensnared her as Harriet coaxed, "Hurry, or we'll miss the first view of Skagway!"

Kathy reminded, "Captain Shurling said to wait here. He'll be angry if we disobey." Soon, she would be safe from Marc . . .

The older woman scanned Kathy's appearance and remarked softly, "Your hair and clothes are mussed, Kathy. We best get you fixed up a bit. Who knows, the first man you meet could be Jake Hammond . . . or your future husband,'" she hinted to lighten the gravity of this moment.

New life washed over Kathy's unblemished face and settled within her eyes. "You're right. I must look my very best for this momentous occasion." She changed clothes, pulling on a dress of lightweight wool in a rich sapphire shade, one which made her eyes appear even bluer. She brushed her hair and secured it with a matching blue ribbon.

Harriet placed the last item in Kathy's valise and closed it. She looked up and smiled warmly, taking in her radiant appearance and striking beauty. "Stunning. He'll be so very proud of you, Kathy."

"If I can find him, you mean," Kathy absently corrected her older friend, pulling on black gloves to conceal the scratches on her hands.

"Ready?" Harriet inquired.

Kathy wavered, then decided, why not; Marc was in the brig.

Harriet pulled on the door and confronted the guard. "We want to go out on the deck and see the docking. Can you escort us?"

"The captain said to remain here, ladies," he courteously replied.

"I know, but we'll miss all the excitement. Please," she wheedled. "We'll have you to protect us," she added to sway him.

"Only if you tell the captain I couldn't stop you," he reluctantly consented, wanting to please them and enjoy a last view of Kathy.

"Done! Let's go," Harriet exclaimed before he could think twice.

They walked down the lengthy hallway. "You mean it's already nippy here in early September?" Harriet commented in astonishment.

"About forty-five degrees, ma'am. Once the sun goes down, the temperature drops fast. Up in the mountains there, it snows and freezes all year long. You have someone meeting you ashore?"

"No," Harriet replied.

"What about a place to stay?" he fired another question at her.

"Not yet," she responded, not the least disturbed.

He gaped at the two women in utter disbelief. He impertinently said before thinking, "Are you crazy? You came to a place like this without family or preparations? You'll never survive!"

Kathy frowned at him. "You forget your place, sir!" she hastily admonished him. "Our personal affairs are none of your concern. You will kindly keep such opinions to yourself."

"Sorry, miss. I was just shocked. Two ladies alone in a settlement like that," he stressed, pointing toward the coastline. "Thousands of men and only a few tents! What food you can find costs a fortune! Where will you stay? Who's gonna take care of you and protect you?"

"You mean there's no hotel or boarding house?" Kathy asked.

"Nothing but tents and makeshift huts. Only three log cabins and they belong to wealthy men. No law to speak of either! The Yukon's owned by Canada; that's where most of the gold is found. Those men can't pan until spring. They ain't seen nothing yet until they discover they've got to fight their way over those glaciers! There's days when the temperature doesn't get above twenty below zero. Those arctic winds get so cold that it hurts to breathe. It'll kill you!"

Stunned by his vivid description of this treacherous new land, Kathy disregarded his last remark to storm Harriet with questions, "Did you hear him? Did you know how terrible the conditions were up here?"

Harriet was mutely staring at the dismal shore. The young man went on, "It's a hardship on most men, but two women alone . . . there's fighting, stealing, people dying from hunger and cold, and tragedy at every turn. The only females around work in them fancy saloons in Dawson and Whitehorse, stealing the earnings of miners. You planning to live in Skagway or head on up into the Yukon Territory?'"

"Stay here," Kathy murmured, without realizing she had spoken.

"That's too bad. At least the Yukon has some form of law and order because of those Canadian Mounties. But this area's still wild and unsettled! If you ever get into trouble, see if you can locate one of those Mounties. You can recognize them by their blue pants and bright red jackets. From what I hear, they fear no man and no danger," he stated.

Kathy observed the awesome sight before her astonished eyes. The steamship was drifting almost silently through the royal blue water whose untroubled surface reflected the primitive landscape like a gigantic mirror. Skagway was snuggled between towering, snow-capped mountains on three sides and strikingly separated from those awesome mounds by a massive timberline of spruces, pines, and hemlocks. The Lynn Canal appeared a liquid blue street flowing to the only open angle to this impressive area. Portions of those steep slopes revealed obsidian rock formations which were a majestic blending of imposing gorges and tall peaks. It was a rugged and perilous region which would demand all the endurance and courage any man—or woman—had to offer.

The little settlement appeared dwarfed by its lofty surroundings; it sat before the snow-covered escarpments like a small, dark splotch of humanity boldly challenging blue-white Nature. The air was brisk, a noticeable dampness lacing it. Smoke curled from obscure campfires. Dense fog and a misty blue haze attested to the high humidity. But for the verdant evergreens, the area was harsh and desolate. Kathy's wide gaze scanned the rock-bound strip of beach which was coming into sight.

The ship slowed, stopped, and dropped anchor. Three

shrill blasts of her horn announced their arrival. Boats of varying sizes and descriptions dotted the shoreline. There was no landing dock. The area between the trees and water was cluttered with boxes, supplies, equipment of all kinds and sizes, men in tattered clothing, countless small tents, and three log cabins. The mass of humanity was a strange and disturbing sight. One haggard and dejected group sat around small fires as if utterly listless or totally exhausted. Many men looked weakened and emaciated, their faces and bearings revealing despair and desperation.

Yet, another smaller group was scurrying around as if the town was ablaze. They were warmly dressed and appeared healthy and happy. Kathy wondered at this startling contrast. Who were these men? What wretched existence had many faced here? How many wished they had never heard the words "gold" and "Alaska"?

The steamship was now bustling with excitement and ear-splitting noise. Men on the shore were waving and shouting to those on the ship, as if selfishly delighted to have others come and share their misery. The men on the ship were responding with overwhelming enthusiasm. Boats were forced into the deep blue water to head their way. Pushing and shoving for first place in line began immediately. Gear and supplies now cluttered the decks.

Suddenly a deathly silence settled over the entire ship. The men could not believe their eyes and senses as they realized what they were actually viewing: their final destination. They gaped at the tent-town, the frost-tipped ridges, the awesome summits, the harshness of the land, and the pitiful men on the rocky strand. The only invasion of beauty on this intimidating setting was the pink reflection of the snow-capped mountains on the pearly surface of the water.

One tenderfoot furiously shouted, "There's thousands of men here afore us! Won't be no gold left! Look at them mountains and all that snow! Surely this ain't where we land!"

Captain Shurling walked up, his annoyance with the two willful females visible. "This here's the gateway to the Yukon, the end of the earth: Skagway. See that tallest peak up there," he directed impassively, pointing to the White Pass. "That's the trail over the mountains and glaciers to the Yukon Territory and the Klondike. If you're after gold, that's where it is."

"You mean we don't pan for gold here? We gotta go somewhere else? I been cheated!" one greedy man snarled.

Weary of this rough lot of men, Shurling irritably snapped, "Pan anywhere you please! But the gold strike is on the other side of those mountains, down the raging rapids of the Yukon River, and over about Dawson area. That's where the claims office Fortymile is located and that's where the Klondike is. It takes a lot of walking, some boating, and some mountain climbing. If you got the money and luck, you might find a dogsled or a boat. If not, it's walking and building your own boats. Skagway is the entrance to the gold fields, not the termination point of your journey," he declared.

Holding their full attention, Shurling continued with his narration. "There's two ways to get to the Yukon Territory, which is part of Canada, not American Alaska," he smugly informed the ignorant men. "You can take the northwesterly route over Chilkat Pass or you can take the northeasterly route over the White Pass. Both end up in Whitehorse and the distance is about the same. Both of 'em are dangerous and rugged. It's a narrow path only wide enough for one man to walk at a time. To one side you got a slope of ice and on the other, a sheer drop into nowhere. A few hours up there and your feet won't move and your hands can freeze. But if you don't move on, you die right there. Lots of men don't ever see White-horse or Dawson. I'll be back in several weeks if any of you change your minds." With that statement, he glanced at the two females nearby and smiled expectantly.

"This damn place is no more'n a dung heap!" One infuriated man growled, stomping the deck with a booted foot.

"It's a freezing hell-hole if you asked me!" another stormed.

The talk and remarks quickly became crude and vulgar. Several men were swearing in disappointment and vexation. Another was spouting off angrily, "I spent my good money on a joke like this? Ain't even fittin' to piss on!" He balled a fist and shook it at Skagway.

"Cease this foul talk! Can't you men see we have two ladies present?" the ruddy-faced captain shouted harshly above the noise.

"Ladies, Hell! Wouldn't no ladies come to a stink-hole like this!" the first man snapped, nerves and patience frayed by the bleak reality before him, the monstrous cruelty of his tarnished golden dream.

"Silence, man, or you'll be thrown in the brig until this ship is empty! The boats will be here soon to take you ashore. Line up in an orderly fashion," he sternly commanded, his temper strained.

Rope ladders were tossed over the rails as the boats brushed along side the ship's hull. Men dashed to be the first aboard, irritating the boatmen with their precarious attempts to overload their crafts. Gear and assorted goods were handed down and men scrambled over the rail into bobbing crafts. Before everyone could reach shore, it began to rain, a steady mist which soon dampened clothes and hair. The sun was dropping low on the distant horizon, casting picturesque shadows on the water. The breeze was gusting briskly; it yanked at the women's clothing and played carelessly with their hair. What a contrasting pair of females they made standing there: a flaming-haired woman and a tawny-haired beauty. Time passed snailishly in the flurry of activity.

The two women stood in the doorway, apprehensively awaiting their turns. Both shivered, from fear and the increasing chill. The dampness caused their noses to glow and their cheeks to flush. They remained still and silent, not even conversing with each other. This awesome moment in time was assailing their senses and mesmerizing them with its implications.

Eventually, Captain Shurling approached them and smiled regretfully. "Sorry, ladies. Men with gold fever are a reckless and rude bunch. I can't imagine why they rush ashore like frenzied jackals over a carcass; they can't head inland until morning." He chuckled, "They're frantically searching for a place to sleep and affordable victuals to fill their bellies. See that log cabin to the left of the settlement?" he inquired, pointing in its direction.

When the two women nodded yes, he continued, "A man named Drayton Cardone lives there. He's a reliable and pleasant fellow; he buys and sells equipment and supplies. If anyone can help you, it's Dray. If not, that largest tent belongs to Moore, a lumberman. If there's a problem or any trouble, see him. He's a friendly and kind sort. Lumberjacks, trappers, and some of the more fortunate miners eat at his place. He might have some

32

work for you. As to where you'll live, or even sleep tonight, God only knows. Pardon the candor, but it's the bare-faced truth. Are you sure you two want to get off the ship? I'll return you to Seattle for free," he offered, hoping his generosity would appease any lingering hostility toward him.

Harriet smiled at him and stated, "You're a fine man, sir. Thank you, but we'll be staying. Right, Kathy?" she probed.

Kathy didn't even hear her or answer her. She stood transfixed by the railing, her eyes on that gruesome vista and her damp curls blowing around her head in wild abandonment. "Kathy?'" Harriet called out to her. "Are you sure you want to remain here with me? The captain said he would take you back to Seattle without charge."

Kathy met her imploring gaze. "If my father's here, I'll find him. .

"It's a shocking sight. Where will we stay? What about our things?"

"Captain Shurling gave me the names of two men to see. I'll take care of everything, child," Harriet announced with false bravado.

"Let's go then. It's getting late," Kathy whispered. Facing any unknown was better than remaining within Marc's violent reach.

The final decision made, they gingerly approached the rope ladder. Harriet agilely went over the side and settled herself in the boat. Their belongings were passed over to a sturdy man in the craft. Kathy dropped her cape and drawstring purse over to the man to give to Harriet, fearing they would entangle her during this terrifying descent.

As modestly as possible, Kathy placed her leg over the railing and put her foot on the limp rung. The ladder swayed precariously as her entire weight was placed on it. She clung on for dear life, having been cautioned about the temperature of the water and the unlikely chance of finding a private place to dry off and change clothes. Thankfully the distance was only a few feet, although it seemed more like twenty to the girl dangling in mid-air. The wind whipped at her skirt-tail and threatened to entangle her shaky legs. The boat rocked as her feet touched its wooden bottom. She wavered and would have tumbled into the gelid blue water if the burly man hadn't caught her and steadied her. She flashed him a wan smile of appreciation and relief.

The smaller boat headed for shore, leaving behind the larger steamship. They turned to wave to Shurling as the captain called out, "Don't forget; I sail at dawn. If you change your mind, come back before then."

The two women waved and smiled again. As the craft neared shore, the man at Shurling's side asked, "Why didn't you tell them Slavin will be put ashore before we sail? I doubt Skagway is big enough for Miss Hammond and Mister Slavin."

"After getting a good look at that place, maybe they'll change their minds. If not, that's too bad. But I want that scum off my ship; I can't stomach him a minute longer. It'll teach him a good lesson to be stranded here! In a camp with no other females and scores of husky men, they'll find somebody to protect them," he declared, watching the little boat land on the shore. "That Pullen woman is quite a female, but that sandy-haired lass has much to learn," he muttered as he walked off, caught up in his own cares and interests.

The snaggle-toothed, snub-nosed man stepped out and dragged his boat onto the loose rocks to beach her. A lopsided grin claimed his broad mouth, looking odd amidst the heavy beard which sorely needed a good trimming. In spite of the harsh conditions, his light blue eyes revealed a kindness and a gentleness which pleased both women. He was a giant of a man when he stood up, his frame robust and hard.

"Who gonna meetcha here?" he asked in a strange accent which neither female could place, tugging habitually on his wiry beard.

"No one," Harriet calmly replied, smiling brightly and confidently. "We came to work and to earn a pouch of gold."

"Ya ain't got no man or family?" he asked in a booming voice.

Kathy's face and eyes glowed. "I do!" she blurted. "I've come to find my father and join him," she perkily announced to the startled man who was eying them critically by this time.

"What be his name?" the dark-haired giant inquired instantly.

"Jake Hammond," she replied, lifting her chin proudly.

"Jake Hammond . . . ," he echoed, mulling the unfamiliar name over in his mind. "No man hereabouts with that name. I knows most of 'em. No Hammonds," he declared with finality, twisting some long hairs around his index finger.

"But I was told he came here two years ago! He must be here!" she argued, alarmed by his assured air.

"Lots come. Some leave quickly. Some head inland. Some die. Some makes their fortunes and gets out before another winter sets in," he announced.

Kathy whitened and swayed. Griff, the boat man, reached out to catch her, thinking she was about to faint at that distressing news. Kathy clutched at his thick arm and held it tightly until her head cleared.

35

"Not to worry. If there be a Hammond in this territory, Old Griff'll find 'em for ye," he gallantly exclaimed, puffing up with self-confidence, smiling amicably, wanting to return a smile to her face.

"Thank you, Mister . . ." she faltered in ignorance of his identity, then said, "I don't know your name, sir."

Griff beamed in pleasure and cheerfulness. "Griffin Carter, but I be called Griff. Where ya wants this stuff?" he genially asked.

"I don't rightly know, Griff," Harriet confessed uncomfortably, presuming friendliness might encourage his assistance. "No one mentioned there weren't any boarding houses or such. What do you suggest, Griff?" she entreated, her eyes imploring him for help.

Griff sighed heavily and scratched his head of thick, bushy hair as he gave this puzzle some serious consideration. He finally shook his head. "Don't get many females over this way. Most of 'em which comes here heads for Dawson the next morning. They don't exactly needs any special place to stay that one night," he innocently alerted them to the meaning of his words, then actually blushed when Kathy enlightened him to his crude implication with her sudden inhalation of air. "I meant, there ain't no place for ladies here, ma'am."

"We're here, so we'll make the best of it," Harriet stated to ease his embarrassment. Griff gave a good impression; they might have use of a strong, proud, and genial man like this. "We had no idea things were this rough. My husband died and left me penniless; I couldn't find a good job down in Seattle. When I read about the gold rush and how much money could be made here with hard work and a cunning mind, we packed up and here we are. We don't have enough money to buy passage back to America. So, we'll just have to stay here and find some work and a place to live. You've been kind and helpful, Griff; thank you."

Flustered by this novel feminine attention and their friendliness to him, he grinned and stammered, "Ain't no need to thank me. I'll help you two all I can. I can't rightly allow two defenseless women to go roaming around a place like this."

The captain's words flashed across Harriet's frantic mind. "What about a man called Drayton Cardone? Captain Shurling said he might assist us," she optimistically offered.

"He might if he was here, but he ain't. He's gone to Dawson for a few weeks on business. Be there at least six to seven more days."

"What now, Harriet?" Kathy asked in rising panic.

Before Harriet could reply, another burly man approached them. "Any problem here, Griff?" he asked in a raspy but courteous tone.

"They ain't got no family or a place to live, Mr. Moore. I don't rightly know what to do with 'em," he replied in a respectful tone.

"Moore!" Harriet exclaimed in renewed excitement and hope. "You must be the man Captain Shurling mentioned to us. He said to check with a Drayton Cardone or Mr. Moore. Would that be you, sir?" she asked, eagerly awaiting his response.

Two

"Probably," Moore hesitantly mumbled, amazed by the presence of ladies. "Why'd you two come to a secluded and wild place like this?" he probed.

Harriet nervously repeated her tale.

"Children!" Moore snapped irritably, glancing around in anger. "Surely you didn't bring little ones with you?"

"Not with me. A friend is keeping them until I can send for them. From what I read, the miners pay hefty for chores. I'm strong and dependable. Surely there's plenty of cooking, sewing, cleaning, and doctoring to be done. But Kathy came to search for her father," she hastily added to lessen his lingering annoyance.

"You're Kathy?" Moore asked the younger woman, boldly observing the demure female with eyes which were a lovely mixture of sapphire and amber. He curiously scanned her expensive, almost elegant, dress which seemed absurd in this crude setting.

"Kathryn Hammond, sir," she softly answered him, then related her explanation. Kathy noted the way Moore was scrutinizing her; yet his keen study was not offensive.

He mused over the unfamiliar name, then shrugged. Glancing around, Kathy said frantically, "There are countless men here! Surely you can't know all of them!" she poured out her fear on the roughly dressed man. Abashed, she lowered her head and whispered, "I'm sorry, Mr. Moore. Please forgive my outburst."

"I understand, miss. You came a long way under bad conditions to discover worse. This isn't what you two expected, is it? Alaska's a big territory. We're sitting on a small tip; this here's the Panhandle area. He could be hundreds of miles from Skagway," he ventured.

"But his last letter said Skagway, Alaska," she softly disputed. Lingering suspicions about her mother's motive for keeping that momentous letter a secret returned to plague her. Had it been the only word from her father over the years? She pushed her mental probings aside to listen to Moore's reply.

"When did she receive that letter?" Moore quizzed, intrigued by the mystery which had compelled this delicate girl to Alaska.

"Mama said about two years," she quickly replied, embarrassed by her lack of knowledge about her own father.

"A lot can happen in two years in a place like this. I've been here years, and I've never met him or heard of him. I'll ask around if you want me to. I've got men who travel to Dawson and Whitehorse. They can check around there for you," he kindly offered.

"You are most thoughtful, sir. Any help would be appreciated."

"Since you two are alone, I can let you bunk in my supply tent for a while. I need a cook or two if you're interested. I have eighteen to twenty-five men to feed every day. I'll pay four dollars a day, and the men might toss you a gold nugget once in a while. Plus, there's other ways to earn gold, those you mentioned earlier, Mrs. Pullen."

"Is there some place to purchase one of these tents?" Kathy asked, reluctant to depend on a strange man for her accommodations.

"I'm afraid not. Wood's being cut and sawed for cabins. But for now, that's the best I can do for you."

"I wish we had known about the harsh conditions here," Kathy remarked dejectedly. "If not for you, sir, I don't know what would happen to us," she offered their gratitude.

Moore smiled jovially and nodded his thanks. "Might be nice to have some decent womenfolk and good food for a change. You two ladies come with me." Noting their luggage, he halted and said, "We can't leave this stuff here. It'd be gone time we turned our backs." He called two strapping lumberjacks over and ordered them to collect the baggage. With the help of the four husky men, their possessions were escorted along with them to the supply tent.

"Put your things in here. I always keep a guard on duty. It rotates between Griff and Lewis Johnson. Lots of stealing in a place like this. Too many poor folks. You want the jobs as cooks for me?"

Harriet quickly accepted, "I do, Mr. Moore. Kathy?"

Kathy felt trapped into accepting. "Until I decide how to locate my father, I'll help Harriet." Where and how did she begin her quest?

"Great! See that long tent? You cook and serve each morning and night. Unless I say otherwise, plan on twenty hungry men. Feed 'em good, but don't waste supplies. Right now, that place is a pigsty. I ain't had the time to clean it up for days. When it's dirty, the men don't take care with keeping it picked up. Once you get it in order, they'll keep it that way. They're good men, just messy and tired at night," he remarked as the women exchanged guarded looks.

He chortled ruefully and went on, "You got three hours to wash up and cook the evening meal. I was just about to start it when I saw you two standing there with Griff. I been leaving my crew early to get supper. My last cook got gold fever. Sure gonna be nice not to slave over that wood stove; I ain't no cook anyway. If you need anything before I come back, ask Griff. The guard ain't allowed to leave his post for any reason." As Moore headed off, he stopped and looked back to add, "If you need any privacy, there's a new chamber pot in the supply tent and there's an outhouse near the last tent. Just for safety, better take Griff if you leave my area," he cautioned.

Both women fused a deep scarlet at the mention of such a personal chore; they glanced at the stony ground in modesty. "See you later," Moore tossed over his shoulder and walked off.

The two women stared at each other, then smiled faintly. "Well," Harriet murmured, "let's get moving."

They entered the supper tent and came to an abrupt halt. Moore hadn't exaggerated. The wooden tables were littered with filthy dishes and hardened bits of food. Trash was everywhere. Sticky spots stood out like brazen invitations for hungry bugs to come and eat hardy. The air was stuffy and offensive. From the chill, there was no fire.

"Who eats here, men or animals?" Kathy sneered in disgust. "How could anyone have an appetite surrounded by such stench and filth? Pigsty is a compliment compared to this place!"

"It definitely lacks a woman's touch and care," Harriet agreed, then laughed nervously. "If there was time, I would tear my hair and cry like a baby. Where to start?" she murmured to herself in utter despair, fighting back tears of frustration.

"Burn the whole place and start from scratch! We'll never get this place cleaned, aired, and filled with food for twenty men in only three measly hours. Two whole weeks wouldn't even see it ready for service. It's utterly impossible, Harriet! Does he think we're magicians or simply desperate fools?" she said in exasperation.

"I know, Kathy. But it's the only job available, and four dollars a day is very good money. We are accepting his hospitality, and food is outrageously high. With potatoes at thirty dollars a bushel, canned milk at four dollars, eggs at twenty dollars a dozen, and sugar at over one hundred dollars a bag—how could we possibly survive for long? Even your money could run out soon. Please don't feel obligated to help me; I'll make out all right," she bravely declared; yet, her voice was shaky and her face ashen. Embarrassed by her vivid show of disappoint- ment and sadness, Harriet angrily brushed at the telltale tears which sparkled brightly on her rusty lashes. Unable to prevent it, she sat on the nearest bench and wept openly and bitterly.

Kathy was moved. Harriet had been good to her. It was only fair to help her in this vile predicament. Calling on all of her inner strength, Kathy removed her cape and tossed it over a solitary chair near the stove. She stuffed her velvet purse into a pocket on her dress. She gingerly touched the stove; it was slightly warm. Checking inside, she found glowing embers. It was get busy or . . .

"We're in luck, Harriet," she sang out cheerfully. "There's a tiny fire; let's work on it before it dies. Let's see . . ." She looked around, mentally noting each impending chore. "First, we need lots of hot water. We can sweep the floor and scrub the tables while the dishes soak. We need to pull back every flap and air out this place. Then, while one of us washes that pile of dirty tin, the other one can start dinner. Since I'm not a good cook, how about if I do the chores?"

Harriet rushed to her side and hugged her affectionately. "Thank God for you, Kathryn Hammond. I'm so glad you're here with me."

Kathy smiled. With hard labor and determination, they vigorously attacked the tent with washcloths, brush broom, strong and nimble backs, industrious hands, obstinate minds, and dreamy hearts. Kathy hauled in wood from the towering stack outside. Harriet worked until new flames were licking greedily at the added pieces of fuel. Kathy went all around the tent securing back each flap to produce an air-flow to dispel the repulsive odors.

Harriet filled a large pot on the stove to supply them with boiling water. She then stacked the dishes in a round basin to be covered with the water when it was hot enough to perform its difficult task. Kathy took a thick cloth and brushed the loose remains from the tables and benches. Later, she took a brush-broom in hand and started to work on the floor debris.

"Kathy, I'm going to see what supplies they have to work with while I'm waiting for the water to boil."

"Good idea. I can cook, but I sorely hate to plan meals and the amounts to prepare. I don't even know how much food one ravenous man can consume, much less twenty starving males," she jested lightly, winking at the grinning Harriet.

"I've had plenty of experience in that line. My husband, God rest his soul, was a hardy eater. Now I have three growing boys with very healthy appetites. I'm so glad you're here, Kathy. I'm not as tough as you think. I have just as many fears and doubts as you do. But I have others depending on me to be strong and successful. I just pretend to be tough and brave to keep others from taking advantage of a poor widow." With that unexpected confession, Harriet left for the supply tent. She nodded at the amicable guard and disappeared inside.

It required some back muscle and time, but finally the dirt floor was clean. Fresh air, tinged with the delightful scent of spruce, wafted through the oblong tent and cleared away the stagnant odors. Steam started to rise from the rolling water on the stove. Kathy went to pour it over the metal dishes and utensils. Taking two thick pads, she struggled to lift the heavy pot. Her sore body and depleted energy rebelled at her strain on them.

"Drats!" she fretted in annoyance. "I'll never finish!"

A masculine voice spoke behind her, "Need some help, miss?"

Startled, she whirled around at the sound of the unfamiliar voice. Her forearm brushed against the hot stove, searing the flesh. Before taking note of her company, she winced and cried out. Her eyes flew to the smarting injury, ignoring him completely.

The tall stranger rushed forward, seizing her arm and pouring cold water over the gradually reddening area. "I didn't mean to scare you, miss. I heard we had a new cook and I just wanted to see for myself if rumor could be trusted. Looks like you been mighty busy," he casually remarked in a vital tone which she found warming. He dunked her arm in a bucket of cold water. "This'll stop the pain and lessen the damage. Pardon me for barging in on you."

Kathy watched him closely, stunned into silence by the compelling creature. He eventually glanced at her, his devastating smile slipping from his handsome face as he gazed at the beautiful girl of eighteen who was staring back at him. Without awareness, she assessed his looks as he simultaneously catalogued hers.

He was very tall, muscular and virile. The rolled-up sleeves on his flannel shirt revealed arms of smooth, firm iron. Kathy couldn't decide if he was in his late twenties or early thirties. His hands were strong, but slightly rough due to work and the harsh Alaskan weather. His mane of sooty black hair was full and nearly straight; it fell casually to his nape and there it curled under. Thick, dark brows perched over eyes which were so deeply brown that they looked almost black. His upper lip was full and wide, the lower one even fuller. He had that kind of mouth which invited kisses, whose smiles could be beguiling and heart-fluttering. His firm jaw was squared and angled enticingly upwards to prominent cheekbones. His towering height and broad shoulders made him appear massive, almost intimidating. Yet, his eyes and expression were warm and tender, sensually seductive. He evinced a prowess which Kathy found overpowering and appealing. A commanding aura emanated from him, charming and tempting even at first glance.

Mesmerized, she stared at him, oblivious to the pain in her arm. How could she possibly notice such a minor injury when his touch and nearness enflamed her entire body? Her heart raced wildly and her eyes softened noticably. When he spoke again, his deep voice caused her to shiver and to listen enthralled.

"Is that any better?" he murmured, his mahogany eyes never leaving her enchanting face. "Who are you?"

When she failed to answer him, he waved his hand before her entranced eyes and teased, "Anybody home in there?" He grinned as she flushed apple red.

She promptly recovered her wits and poise. She hastily jerked her arm free of his gentle grasp. To cover her discomfiture and attraction to him, she snapped, "Don't ever sneak up on me like that again!" She absently studied the burn on the underside of her arm. Who was this magnetic man who had held her hypnotized until she felt foolish and forward?

"I didn't sneak in," he mildly corrected her accusation. "You were just busy and didn't hear me. Might have been due to all that chattering to yourself," he mischievously hinted, playfully mocking her.

She angrily glared at this formidable stranger with twinkling eyes, a daring manner, and an engaging smile. She almost returned it, but controlled that impulse. "Dinner won't be ready for another hour. Come back then. I have chores to do." Kathy turned to struggle with the weighty pot, unable to lift it.

Dinner? he mirthfully speculated. "Here, let me do that," he offered, taking the pads from her before she could object or agree. "Next time, don't put so much water in it. You're much too fragile and small to lift this much weight," he chided her.

Reprimanded like a child and thoroughly unsettled, Kathy stated, "My chores are none of your concern, sir!" As he calmly and carefully poured the steaming liquid over the dishes, she added tersely, "And I'm stronger than I look! Besides, I'm tall for most women; I'm five-seven," she snippily divulged, troubled by his effect upon her.

"No need to spread your wings of warning, my Golden Duckling; everybody is short to me. You didn't say; what's your name?" He glanced at her, his eyes warming and lingering as they fused with her sapphire ones. Spitting beads of water called his attention back to the overflowing dish basin. He set the pot down and turned to face her. "Well?" he practically demanded as she suppressed her amused giggles with a hand clamped over her mouth, her sparkling eyes mocking him.

"Well, what?" she chirped saucily, enjoying his nettled plight.

"Your name, my fair-haired cook?" he stressed in annoyance.

"You may call me Cook. I don't give my name to strangers, especially not sneaky ones who cause accidents."

"I'm Landis Jurrell. I eat here when I'm in Skagway," he introduced himself, extending his hand, calmly anticipating her reply.

She looked at his outstretched hand as if it were some coiled viper about to strike her. She looked up at him, sticking out her pert chin in defiance of his simple request.

His probing gaze slipped over her golden tresses, the small, slender nose, the unmarked complexion, the full lips, and her exquisite bone structure which added up to the most beautiful picture he had ever seen. His appreciative gaze went back to her striking and stormy eyes. They were like liquid topaz surrounded by igneous blue sapphire. Her thin brows arched nicely over provocative lids. Her eyes were bright and impressive, eyes which bravely defied him and his intense scrutiny, eyes which displayed an innocence and vitality which intrigued and bewitched him.

He grinned, concluding, a body and face to drive a man crazy. Irrational jealousy flooded him as images of a husband or anxious fiancé stormed him.

"If you've quite memorized my face and figure, Mr. Jurrell, would you mind clearing out so I won't lose my job on the first day! Mr. Moore wants dinner served in one hour," she sassily informed him.

Landis scanned the brazen temptation which she presented without even trying. What sexual torture she could inflict on a man! He unexpectedly inquired, "Are you married or engaged?"

Kathy stared at him in disbelief. How dare a total stranger question her this way! "I hardly feel that's any of your business, sir!"

"I just assumed you came here with your husband or to meet your fiancé," he insouciantly suggested, hoping she would respond.

"Well, you assumed wrong!" she announced.

He chuckled and murmured in a sensual tone, "I shall see you again at . . . dinner, my little Golden Torment." He turned to swagger out, his carriage and fluid movements suggesting immense self-confidence and agility, flavored with great pride and roguish arrogance.

Kathy ran forward and blocked his path. She stared into his handsome, expectant face. She demanded, "What did you call me?"

Amused and baffled, he chuckled at her inexplicable anger. "My little Golden Torment," he lazily replied. A strange look filled her muted eyes before she turned away.

"It was meant as a compliment, miss; no offense intended," he murmured from behind her, shrewdly aware of the odd mood his words had inspired. He wondered why, but didn't ask.

She slowly turned and stared up at him, then brushed past him to return to her work. Just above a whisper she threw over her shoulder, "The name's Kathryn Hammond, Mr. Jurrell."

Before he could respond, Harriet came back, lugging

two heavy bags. Landis quickly took one from her and placed it on the last table which was closest to the cooking area. Harriet smiled and thanked him.

He nodded and bowed slightly. "Landis Jurrell at your service, ma'am. I've already met your lovely daughter, Mrs. Hammond. We'll look forward to some good food and lovely faces for a change."

Harriet laughed merrily at his mistaken impression. "The name is Mrs. Harriet Pullen. Kathy is my good friend, not my daughter."

Landis glanced in Kathy's direction, a curious look on his arresting face. He shrugged, smiled, and left. Harriet watched him until he was out of sight. "Who was that?" she asked, charmed.

"He said Landis Jurrell," Kathy replied, hoping to conceal her disquiet and interest in him.

"I caught his name, Kathy; but what does he do here?" Harriet pressed, an odd inflection lacing her voice.

"Why, Harriet Pullen," Kathy teased impishly. "I do believe he caught your eye. He didn't say, and I didn't ask. He only mentioned that he eats here when he's in Skagway."

"That means he doesn't live here. What a shame! He's the closest thing to a perfect man I've ever seen. His size and manner say he would make a fine . . . protector for you. He was most charming and pleasant, didn't you think? Why the cold shoulder?" she persisted.

"He crept up on me and made me burn my arm," Kathy foolishly snapped. Instantly sorry, she apologized for her curtness, "I'm just tired and tense, Harriet. Don't pay any attention to me. He filled the basin for me; the pot was to heavy to lift."

"Since he's not from here, did you ask him about your father?" she tried another approach to interest Kathy in this vital man.

Kathy gasped in irritation. "I didn't even think about it," she confessed. "I will at dinner," she hastily resolved.

"I can see how a man like that could drive a female to distraction," Harriet jested, cackling mirthfully.

Kathy flashed her a reproving look. "Harriet Pullen, you simply won't do. Behave yourself. We have work to finish."

"You didn't think he was appealing?" she probed as she unpacked the supplies, watching Kathy from the corner of her eye.

Kathy sighed wearily and admitted, "Yes, Mother. In fact, he is *too* handsome and disarming. Now, can we finish here? I'm exhausted."

"I'd bet my first earnings he won't be the only man chasing your skirts before this night's over," Harriet mirthfully teased.

"If one of those ruffians dares to touch me or insult me, I'll claw his eyes out!" she vowed, recalling her dreadful episode with Marc Slavin.

"Then you'll be fighting most of the time. Ignoring their stares and remarks is the best way to handle them," Harriet advised calmly.

"Do my ears deceive me, Harriet Pullen! Surely you don't mean to allow such insulting behavior?" she seriously protested.

"A cold shoulder is far more acceptable than a slap in the face, especially in public. Men feel we should be honored by their attention. Don't rashly make a refusal appear a challenge. I'm serious, Kathy; it'd be spoiling for trouble to slap countless faces every day," her friend gravely warned.

"If you say so, Mother," Kathy teased in return.

Within minutes, cured ham was frying and potatoes

were boiling to be creamed. Four pots of coffee were brewing, sending their heady odor into the tent. The dishes were all washed, and Kathy was placing them on the wooden tables as she dried them. Harriet was busy with biscuits and red-eye gravy. The tantalizing smells filled the tent and floated outside. It was just before dark; the despondent men around the other campfires were getting raucous as they prepared their own meager fares, mouths watering at the fragrant odors from Moore's tent.

Harriet commented, "It's a good thing we ran into Mr. Moore and got these jobs. Now, we have a place to live, a job, and his protection."

Kathy merrily speculated, "I could always go to work as one of those fancy saloon girls and earn barrels of money. At a dollar a twirl, I could amass a few eagles each night. Who knows, those gold-diggers might enjoy a singer and pianist for a change."

"And what about the chores expected of such brassy females?"

"If I have to help wash dishes and clean-up, I'll charge extra. I've certainly had plenty of practice today!" she saucily announced with a purity of mind which Harriet delighted in, but hastily corrected.

"I meant the chores upstairs," the red-haired woman clarified, her own modesty still clouding her real meaning.

"If you mean change linens and do personal laundry for strange men, never!" she protested, turning up her pert nose in disgust.

Harriet's amused laughter filled the tent. "My innocent girl, I was referring to serving the miner's physical needs."

"Physical needs?" she echoed. "You mean care for

51

sick men?"

Harriet could not suppress her humorous giggles. "I'm sorry, Kathy, but I can't help it." She shook her head of rusty locks and sighed in sympathy. She gently chided the naive girl, "I mean sex. That's the main task for saloon girls. Dancing and merry-making are for men who cannot afford a visit upstairs to relieve those carnal urges."

Appalled, Kathy's large eyes widened even more, diminishing the topaz circles around her black pupils to a narrow band. She paled in embarrassment, then fused a livid red which quickly danced down her slender neck. "They have . . . sex with perfect strangers?" she blurted out in disbelief when her speech and wits finally returned.

"Strangers, yes; but perfect, hardly," Harriet teased the shocked girl. "Surely you know what goes on in those bawdy houses? Didn't your mother ever tell you the facts of life?" she asked seriously.

"Some of them, but she was too timid or reluctant to say very much. She claimed a husband taught his wife all she needed to know."

"In a wild frontier like Alaska, most of the females who come here do so for only one reason. In all fairness, Kathy, many of those girls have no other way to earn a living. They become ensnared in a golden trap of their own making and don't know how to break free. How can they change when people won't allow it?"

Shocked, Kathy clamored, "Surely they know we're not here to earn money in such a repulsive manner!"

"If they don't, they soon will. Ladies are recognized by their actions and speech," Harriet ventured her opinion.

Kathy became silent and thoughtful, reflecting on this news. "I'm sure you're right; you know more about life and men than I do. I certainly hope we don't meet any more Marc Slavins!"

"I'm sorry to say, but there's plenty more like him. But with a man like Mr. Jurrell around, there's little to fret over," Harriet slyly inserted his name into their conversation.

Kathy eyed her. "You really liked him, didn't you? You two are about the same age. Why not pursue him?" she suggested to test the depth of her friend's interest, but dreaded her reply.

Astonished, Harriet stared at her. "Me?" she exclaimed, as if a romantic interest in a man was absolutely impossible. "Child, you flatter me. Men don't chase a woman like me. My size and red hair scares 'em off. Perhaps some old codger might compliment me with his attentions, but I'm quite safe," she assured the girl whose face was glowing with admiration and mischief. "Mr. Jurrell isn't for me."

"You underrate yourself, Harriet. You're a very attractive and charming woman. You have endless good qualities."

Harriet smiled in amusement and pleasure. "Thanks, but I know my own looks and quirks. I might get a few proposals from love-starved men, but offers to go romping in the snow . . . ," she playfully hinted, then burst into jovial laughter as Kathy flushed.

"We're either the two smartest women alive or the dumbest. I seriously wonder if Alaska is prepared for us," Kathy quipped, bringing more laughter from her amicable companion.

Harriet agreed. "Things are looking better every minute."

"Want me to mash the potatoes, Harriet?"

"Not yet. They might get cold." Harriet glanced

around. Moore should be surprised and pleased when he returned, at any time.

"I'll let down the flaps; it's getting chilly," Kathy said. She tossed the cloth aside and walked into the night air. She made her way around the oblong tent, untying the strings and dropping the flaps.

At the back of the canvas tent, strong arms imprisoned her, cutting off her breath. A hand clamped tightly over her mouth before she could scream for help. Not again, she prayed in fearful silence. She began to stomp the booted feet of her unknown assailant.

"Let her go!" came an icy order from the impenetrable shadows. Kathy recognized the stirring tone of Landis Jurrell. Her terrified gaze flew in the direction of his voice. Without thinking to question his sudden arrival, she struggled, but her captor would not release her.

She froze in dread, recognizing the sinister voice of the man attacking her. "Stay out of it, mister. This is between me and Kathy," clearly informing Landis this intruder was no stranger to the intoxicating creature who was being forcefully held captive in his terrifying embrace.

The girl had denied a husband or fiancé; therefore, the stranger didn't have a rightful claim. Even if he were a discarded sweetheart, he had no excuse to treat her so harshly. A novel urge to protect her filled Landis, as did fury at her savage treatment. Besides, she had revealed an attraction to him, one which strangely pleased him. . . .

Three

Landis's voice was deceptively calm as he stated, "Since that's my woman you're handling so roughly, Sailor Boy, it is my business. You all right, Kat?" he asked in a mellow tone, guilefully inserting familiarity and tenderness into his query.

"She isn't your woman!" Marc Slavin growled in reckless dispute. "She got off my ship today! We have some unfinished business, so get lost!"

As Kathy futilely tried to free herself once more, Landis stiffened unnoticably in the shadows. "Is this the fellow who gave you so much trouble on the voyage, Kat?" he asked. "I hate to disappoint you, Sailor Boy, but she came here to meet me. If you care to add another year to your miserable life, let her go . . . now!" The last word of his demand fired from his taut lips like a gunshot, startling both Marc and Kathy.

Landis stepped into the fading light, his stalwart size and intrepid stance sending chills over Marc. Never had Marc viewed such overwhelming prowess in a man. Alarmed, he quickly released Kathy.

"Come here, Kat," Landis called tenderly to her, opening his arms in an inviting manner which she could not resist, the sheer force of his voice compelling her to obey him instantly. She ran into his protective embrace, encircling his narrow waist with her trembling arms. She buried her face against the flannel shirt which concealed his hard chest. His arms instinctively eased around her and held her possessively. She was shaking and crying from the physical and emotional demands of this nerve-racking day. Desire and fury flooded him.

Watching the enviable scene, Marc sarcastically sneered, "She ain't worth fighting over, the little tease! From the way she carried on with me, she didn't act like she had a man waiting for her! Does this mean our engagement and marriage are off, Kathy?" he caustically taunted her. "Tell me, Kathy, why did you ask me to meet you tonight if you were expecting lover-boy? What a sly and fickle woman you are! You best teach your woman some manners and some caution or she'll get into lots of trouble with this many men around. She'll have you rescuing her three times a day!"

"You vile bastard!" Kathy ranted at him. "I did not tease you nor lead you on! Stop lying about me! I don't have the slightest interest in you. I despise you! I wouldn't marry you if you were the only man in the entire world!" she flung her stinging insults into Marc's leering face.

Kathy lifted misty eyes to Landis and vowed, "I didn't, Landis; I swear it! He broke into my stateroom this morning and attacked me. He even tried to force himself on me last night. Look at these scratches and bruises!" she cried, holding up her hands for Landis to view. "Do they indicate I was willing and eager to attract Mr. Slavin? I fought him tooth and nail, and he knows it! He . . ." Suddenly aware of her humiliating confessions, she halted her flurry of words and lowered her eyes. Even in the dimness, Landis could make out the fiery patches on her cheeks. His keen, deadly gaze shifted to Marc.

"Kat never lies, Sailor Boy. Consider yourself lucky I don't tear you limb from limb. But if you ever come near her again, I'll kill you. And if you want that face to remain pretty, you'd better keep your lying mouth shut about her. I won't have you soiling my future wife's good name. I can't blame you for desiring her; Kat's the most beautiful woman alive. But I won't allow any man to harm her."

Kathy stiffened in his arms at those disturbing statements. Was she actually allowing a total stranger to comfort and to defend her?

"It's all right, love," he whispered softly. "This scum won't ever bother you again. Right, Sailor Boy?" he challenged.

When Marc remained silent and rigid, Landis persisted icily, "I insist on your word of honor, my good fellow. Will you leave Kat alone?"

Afraid to press this puissant giant, Marc growled, "Yes! Just make sure you order her to leave me alone, too."

Ignoring Marc's last words, Landis calmly continued, "Now, I believe you also owe her an apology for your insults and lies. Spit it out quickly; my supper's getting cold; else I'll beat it out of you."

"I'm . . . sorry, Miss Hammond," Slavin sputtered in a voice laced with hostility and venom.

"Now, be on your way. But remember my warning. You won't get a second chance to test my patience and temper."

Marc hurried off into the gathering night. Landis leaned away from Kathy and asked seriously, "You all right, Kathy?"

She questioned, "How did you know what happened

57

on the ship?" Who was this arresting, perceptive, fear-less man?

He chuckled and replied smoothly without a trace of guile or arrogance in his tone. "Those sailor whites gave him away; he stands out like a cloud against a black sky. His violent treatment suggested it wasn't the first time he had besieged you. I would imagine he hotly pursued you the entire trip, right?" he probed.

"Yes. But he's married," she added.

"Was that why you refused his amorous attentions?" Landis couldn't help but ask, watching her closely.

"Heavens, no! He's an animal. I wouldn't care for him, married or not. I apologize for my outburst; mother would have washed my mouth out with strong soap if she had heard me say something like that."

He laughed mirthfully, then inquired, "He wasn't your type?"

"Definitely not!" she angrily informed him. Why was she amiably conversing with this charming rogue she had met tonight?

"What is?" he leisurely went on with this intriguing topic.

She stared at him in puzzlement. "I really don't know," she answered candidly for some unknown reason. "I've never met any man who stands out before all other males. I . . ." She faltered in her foolish ramblings and looked away from his gaze. Why did this physical contact feel so natural and pleasant? Why was she unwilling to end it?

"Not even one?" he playfully challenged.

Shifting nervously in his intoxicating embrace, Kathy did not answer him. "I'm awfully glad you showed up when you did. He frightens me," she murmured softly, dropping the explosive subject he had begun. "Thanks for your help, Mr. Jurrell. It was very chivalrous of you, considering my earlier rudeness. I'm just overly tired and distressed by this place. This isn't what I expected to find. And I certainly didn't expect to see Marc Slavin again." She felt she should move away, but she didn't. Indebted and relieved, she was helplessly susceptible to this dynamic and stirring creature.

"He's dangerous, Kathy; watch out around him. Nothing is more unpredictable than a man with an obsession."

"I haven't encouraged him in the slightest way, Landis. I just wish he would leave me alone. Why would a man chase a woman who can't stand him? Doesn't he have any pride? You'd think he'd be too embarrassed to pursue me. I don't understand men at all. Perforce he'll be sailing with the morning tide and be out of my life for good," she asserted, unaware of Marc's dismissal by the furious Shurling.

"Good riddance, if you ask me. We've got too many like him here now," he said.

"I fully agree. Too bad there aren't more like you around," she murmured dreamily, then quickly moved away from him. "I better finish letting down the flaps and get inside. Harriet probably thinks I'm lost by now." Why had she made such a statement?

"Here, I'll help you," he offered, but did it for her as she tagged along behind him. He was so masterful and virile; he seemed qualified to take command of any situation.

At the last flap, Kathy smiled and thanked him again. "See you at dinner." Confused by her brassy behavior, she needed to put some distance and time between them.

"Think I can wrangle a cup of coffee while I wait?" he asked with an engaging grin, his sensual eyes appearing as rare mahogany, readily flustering her.

"Would it be all right with Mr. Moore?" she asked, doubtful of the rules here, having difficulty thinking and speaking.

"I'm paid up for the month. And we're good friends," he added.

"Come along; I'll get it for you." She smiled and murmured, "Thanks for everything, Landis." His name was spoken like a silky caress, bringing a handsome grin to his lips.

As he followed her inside, Harriet glanced up, concern clouding her eyes. "Where have you been?" she asked hurriedly, then noticed Landis behind her. "I see," she added with a jolly grin.

"Marc was here," Kathy quickly corrected Harriet's false impression of her tardiness. "Landis . . . I mean, Mr. Jurrell, was kind enough to send him on his way. If you think he was mad on the ship, you should see him now," she added.

"What was he doing ashore? That black-hearted demon! Doesn't he ever learn his lessons? Thank you, Mr. Jurrell," Harriet promptly added her own gratitude to Kathy's. "That snake is determined to . . ."

"Harriet!" Kathy cried in alarm, slicing off the rest of her revealing words. Harriet's head jerked up as the reality of her slip flooded her mind. "The matter is settled now. Mr. Jurrell warned him to stay away from me. From the way Marc looked, I doubt he'll challenge that threat," she confidently stated, smiling at Landis.

"Captain Shurling also ordered him to leave you alone, for all the good it did! He frightens me, Kathy," Harriet readily admitted. "Don't let him find you alone or unprotected again."

"Thanks to La . . . Mister Jurrell, Marc is the one terrified now. He would be a fool to cross a man like . . ."

She groaned in annoyance. "I'm so tired I can't even think straight. I hope I never see another day like this one." What was wrong with her? Why was she talking and behaving in this forward manner?

Harriet smiled comfortingly. "I know, dear. It has been rough on you lately. But things'll get better soon. Why don't you eat and turn in? I can clean up after supper. The way you've got this place looking, it won't require much time or work."

"I'm not going to that supply tent alone! Besides, you're just as tired as I am. When everything is done, we'll both go to bed. Maybe some hot coffee will lift me up. Coffee!" she exclaimed. "I completely forgot about your coffee, Landis. Pardon me." She hurried to fix it as Harriet left to bring in more wood. "Milk or sugar?" she asked, eyes glowing as they fused with his.

He grinned playfully. "No milk. Sugar, if it's the right kind," he teased, devilish lights dancing in his eyes, a mirthful grin tugging provocatively at the corners of his lips.

Kathy blushed. "Stop teasing me; I'm too tired to defend myself," she chided him, then laughed herself.

"Who was teasing?" Landis boldly ventured, his igneous eyes warming her. He came to stand within inches of her to accept the coffee cup. "Surely three good deeds deserve just one little taste of sweetness?" he entreated huskily.

Senses intoxicated, Kathy helplessly returned his smoldering gaze. He leaned forward and kissed her briefly, but pervasively. The mischievous kiss held surprises for both Landis and Kathy; a magical fire sparked and passed between them. Confusion and pleasure settled within her softened eyes, as in his. Entrapped in a dreamy world, Kathy never thought to

61

refuse him or to scold him.

His hand came up to caress her satiny cheek. His touch was stirring and tantalizing. She traced her finger over her tingling lips, then over his sensual ones. She had the strangest desire to throw her arms around his neck and kiss him again! Such bewildering and unfamiliar emotions washed over her, irresistibly drawing her to his magnetic aura. He was everything a man should be. She ached to feel his arms around her again and to experience the delights of his kisses.

Hopelessly attracted to her seductive innocence and enchanted by her ravishing beauty and gentleness, Landis couldn't take his eyes off of her. He unknowingly captured the hand which had boldly touched his lips and had sent sparks throughout his entire body; he placed a warm, moist kiss in the palm of her hand, keenly aware of the tremors which his action inspired within her. Forgetting all reality, he was about to lean forward and kiss her again, really kiss her this time!

Loud talk and jovial laughter from outside broke the powerful spell between them. Alarmed by her uncontrollable behavior and his potent hold over her, Kathy fled to a safe distance just before Harriet's return. Landis's molten eyes remained on her slender back and tawny head for a long time, unsettled by her effect on him. No female had ever bewitched him like this; she had a powerful magic which was dangerous to an unsuspecting man who loved his freedom as much as his life! He had positively pegged her right: a golden dream which couldn't be permitted in his carefree and perilous life was definitely a golden torment! He cautioned himself against staking a claim on this golden treasure, unaware she was already invading his life.

The congenial lumberjacks poured into the tent,

stopping abruptly and bumping into each other in their shared astonishment. The tent was clean; delectable odors filled the air. Two lovely females were poised at the cook stove. The booming voice of Moore invaded the cozy atmosphere, "Surprise, men! Home cooking from now on! This here's Mrs. Harriet Pullen and Miss Kathryn Hammond. Let's get something clear right now; these are ladies, not saloon girls. I demand each of you treat them with respect and kindness. The first man who disobeys this order is fired. If that's clear, let's chow down."

Moore pushed his way through the cheerful group and took his seat at the back table, nearest the stove. The others quickly took their seats. Kathy and Harriet served the delicious fare, topping it off with apple pie. The men were so pleased by the excellent food and service, the clean tent, and the two lovely ladies responsible for them that they behaved respectfully without another word from Moore. They laughed at tall tales and chatted about their day's work in the nearby mountains. It was arduous labor under difficult conditions, but they obviously loved it. One thing for sure, the sourdoughs didn't fool around with these burly lumbermen.

Compliments and laughter flowed as freely as the steaming black coffee. The men seemed reluctant to leave this pleasant atmosphere after finishing their pie, dessert which had delighted them and had disappeared without a trace. As they talked, Moore gave his instructions for the next day's work, telling the men which groups to form and which treeline to work.

It was Moore to the rescue. He called out, "Men, I know we're savoring every minute of this great food, warm tent, and nice company; but our two cooks have endured a very busy day. I think we should leave now and let them wash up and get to bed. This clean tent and tasty food were a lot of work in only a few hours' time. What about a show of appreciation?" He began to clap.

Landis stood up, nimbly stretching and yawning: an action which drew Kathy's eyes to his virile physique and arresting face. He grinned and winked at her as he followed Moore's lead. She flushed and looked away. The entire group came to their feet and greeted the two women with roaring applause. When it finally ceased, Harriet thanked them with misty eyes and a radiant smile, then Kathy added her appreciation. To the women's surprise, most of the men wiped their plates and put them in the wash basin. When the tent was emptied of all men except Moore and Jurrell, they also noticed how tidy the tables and floors were. They exchanged smiles.

Kathy remarked, "You were right, Mr. Moore; clean inspires clean. That should teach us to keep things in order to lessen our work."

Harriet laughed merrily and agreed. As Harriet filled the dish basin with hot water, Kathy busied herself wiping off the tables and benches. She collected the metal salt and pepper dispensers and returned them to their waterproof tin. She took the brush broom to sweep away the few scraps of dropped food. The only thing left to save was three biscuits. Moore stepped up to compliment them on their wisdom and planning, "That was the best meal I've ever eaten, Mrs. Pullen. You prepared plenty, but wasted nothing. I made a very wise choice in cooks. You two worked hard this afternoon; this place's never been cleaner. As for that apple pie, where'd it come from?"

"I found some dried apples in the supply tent. I hope it was all right to use them?" she asked.

"You're the boss now. You can use anything there, ma'am."

"I'll save the leftover biscuits to make bread pudding later this week. I don't believe in throwing away good food. You're a fine man to work for, sir; thank you."

"I tell you what, Mrs. Pullen; if you learn how to check over the supplies and how to order them yourself, I'll pay you three extra dollars a month. As for the other chores mentioned this afternoon, the cooking comes first. If you have the time and energy, you can do whatever you please on your own time. You can also set your own prices for extra tasks. Just don't get too tired doing them," he teased. "I like this homey touch; you two give my place an air of respect and warmth." They talked on about Skagway and its lumber trade.

Landis spoke to Kathy as she was sweeping the trash outside. "Will you be all right in that supply tent?" he asked in an odd tone.

"Since there isn't a hotel or boarding house in this town, it'll have to do. What good is money when there's nothing to spend it on? There isn't a tent or cabin to purchase," she sadly replied. "I can't believe this place. I've never seen any area so lacking or so savage. Under the circumstances, I suppose I should be grateful for the loan of the supply tent." Yet, she craved Landis's protective arms and presence. How was it possible to feel this way about someone she'd just met?

"If you do have money with you, Kathy, you'd best keep that news to yourself and hide the money safely. There's great hunger and desperation living right out there on that beach. Maybe it would be wise to let Moore keep it for you. He's about the most honest man I've met. I know you're exhausted, but I wanted to say how good it is to have you and Mrs. Pullen here with us. It isn't much of a town yet, but it will be. Moore's crew is cutting timber for cabins and buildings. With luck, you'll have your boarding house within two or three months."

"I'll definitely be gone in two months," she declared confidently.

"Can't say as I blame you; this isn't a place for a lady like you. But I do hope we become good friends before you leave. 'Night, miss," he murmured hastily and walked off, leaving her staring after him, hoping she hadn't read the disappointment in his eyes and voice.

Something vital stormed her whirling mind: her reason for being here in the first place and for leaving before winter. That news had seemed to annoy him in a most pleasing way. She smiled at that delightful speculation, concluding Alaska wasn't so bad after all.

"Landis! Wait up a minute. I have something important to ask you." She covered the distance which his lengthy strides had created.

She stopped before him, catching her breath for a moment. An inquisitive expression shone brightly within his dark eyes, or was it only the moon's reflection? Her silvery-yellow light danced on his features, revealing the strong planes and angles of a face filled with strong character and irresistible charm.

"Yes?" he asked, wanting to reach out and pull her into his arms, fiercely restraining that impulse.

"What?" she replied in temporary confusion. He so easily stripped away her poise and thoughts that she forgot herself. In truth, she could gaze into his face and eyes for hours on end!

"You wanted to ask me something important?" he prompted, trying to control his pleased and amused grin. How could a female surrounded by numerous men behave as if she'd never seen one before? She was observing him as if he was some unknown or rare species. A female this beautiful and ravishing could have any man she set her eyes on or her mind to possessing That reality goaded him, nettling feelings which gleamed in his eyes and tensed his jawline.

Misreading his look, she stammered, "Never mind," and turned to leave. She scolded herself for appearing to chase this vital creature with a disarming way of making her forget he was indeed a stranger!

Astutely guessing the reason for her change in mood and expression, he gently halted her departure. "Sorry, Kathy; my mind was somewhere else. There's a nasty problem I'm trying to settle. What did you want to ask?" he coaxed, hoping his explanation had relaxed her enough to reveal what was distressing her.

She hesitantly faced him once more, deliberating whether or not to speak with him or to trust him. It would be foolish to allow her pride to interfere with her search for her father, so she relented. "I've already talked with Mr. Moore and Griff Carter about why I'm in Skagway. They couldn't help me, but perhaps you can since you live somewhere else," she began. She inhaled deeply, then slowly released it as she pondered just how much to tell this intrepid creature.

"How do you know I live somewhere else?" he inquired warily.

"You told me. At least you gave me that impression. You said you ate at Moore's tent when you were in Skagway. Why?" she asked, perplexed by his odd reaction to her statement.

He chuckled merrily to dispel his groundless suspicions. "I was hoping you had been asking about me," he jested with a roguish grin. Perhaps she was just as distressed by his imminent departure as he was about hers! For certain, she wasn't a female easily ignored or resisted!

"I haven't discussed you with anyone. Why should I?" she asked, chafed by his playful accusation. "I need some information from someone who lives around Dawson, or perhaps Whitehorse," she hinted. "I have a critical, pressing matter to settle so I can leave here before winter."

"Go on," he entreated.

"My mother died recently, and I . . ." Waves of fresh pain and loneliness crashed against her and jolted her in this fatigued state. Tears glimmered in her somber eyes. "Perhaps we should discuss this another time; I'm really very tired," she murmured in a strained voice, so many conflicting emotions storming her weary mind and body.

"I'm sorry, Kathy; I didn't know. Did you just pull up stakes and come here on an impulse?" he asked, attempting to distract her.

"In a way," she confessed wretchedly.

"Now you're sorry and want to return home?" he concluded aloud.

"That's only a minor part of the problem. Besides, I don't have a home or family. Before my mother died, we were searching for my father. When she became seriously ill, she made me promise to come here and locate him. You see, he's the only family I have now."

She swallowed to clear the lump in her throat before going on with her explanation and request, "You might have met him or heard his name. I must find him, Landis; can you help me?" she beseeched.

"You mean that's why you came here alone?" When she nodded yes, he went on, "What's his name?" Elated by that news, he forced himself to conceal his satisfaction and relief, knowing how grave the situation was for her. So, the only man in her life was a missing father!

"Jake Hammond," she responded, eyes filling with new hope, innocently placing her hands on his muscled chest as if to draw comfort from him or to steady her balance.

Watching those childlike eyes pleading with him, he hated to crush her hopes and dreams, "I'm afraid not, Kathy. But Alaska's a big territory; just because I don't know him doesn't mean he isn't here somewhere," he candidly stated, covering her cold hands with his warm ones, wondering if she could detect the rapid thud of his racing heart.

"I've been told that, by Moore and Carter. But Papa said Skagway, here!" she emphatically stressed. "And please don't say a lot can happen to a man in two years," she added in dismay.

He smiled in comprehension and parried, "Then I won't. What does he look like? Men often change their names after coming here."

"Why would anyone deny his rightful identity? That's absurd," she innocently reasoned, pulling her hands from beneath his, fearing he might observe her tremors and erratic respiration.

In a mysterious tone he casually stated, "There are many reasons to lose your name around here. Some of these prospectors and sourdoughs are fleeing the law somewhere else. Others are too ashamed to let their families see them again. Others have deserted their wives and children to follow a golden illusion. Some . . ."

She heatedly interrupted him, feeling tense and defensive, "My father isn't like that! He has nothing to hide! He would never . . ." Her lips and chin quivered as the truth was painfully mirrored in her misty blue gaze. "Good-night, Mr. Jurrell," she murmured, needing to be left alone after this new disappointment.

"If I'm to locate Jake Hammond, I have to know what he looks like, Kathy. He could have a good reason for using another name here. Certain problems and businesses call for secrecy," Landis hinted, knowing full well how true that statement was!

"Forget it! I'll look for him myself," Kathy fiercely declared, ashamed to confess the whole truth. She was hurting, but she was proud.

Tears were easing down her cheeks when he pulled her around to face him. "This place is nothing compared with the interior, Kathy; there's no way you can go looking for him in there. Why not give me his description and I'll look for him?" he softly demanded. "If he's still around here, I'll find him for you."

"I can't," she miserably replied, touched by his promise.

"Why not?" he retorted impatiently, unaccustomed to resistance. "I can't help you without his description."

Flustered, she shouted at him, "Because I don't know! I haven't seen him since I was two! Satisfied?"

Enlightenment filled his eyes. "Do you have any idea what he looks like? Something your mother told you? A picture?"

"He's supposed to be tall and muscular with blond hair and eyes the color of mine. There weren't any pictures; Papa took their wedding picture when he left. As far as I know, there hasn't been any word from him until that letter two years ago from this terrible place. Is that sufficient?" she demanded, wishing she didn't have to reveal so much about herself to this particular man.

"That description could fit numerous men, Kathy. But I'll ask around in Whitehorse, Dawson, and a few other smaller settlements. Is he a miner or fur trapper?" he gently continued his interrogation.

She coughed to clear her constricted throat and chest. He brushed away her tears. "I don't know. Mama refused to say much about him after he . . . walked out on us. She was trying to explain things to me when she died." Humiliated, she looked away.

"Do you know why he left home? That might give some hint as what he might be doing here or to his location."

She drew in a ragged breath of air. "Until I was thirteen, I was told he was away. When I discovered the truth, she would only say he was a good man. She begged me to forgive him and to find him. I don't even know why I came here; I hate him! Why should I care?"

"If that were true, you wouldn't be here right now. Perhaps your mother was right; maybe he did have good cause to leave home." Landis tried to comfort the distraught girl who was playing havoc with his concentration and wisdom.

"Good cause? How could a decent man just pick up his belongings and leave his wife and baby to never return? What kind of a man is he? Could you do something wicked and cruel like that?" she challenged.

"Never been married and probably never will be, so I can't rightly accuse or defend the feelings of a married man. Still, it sounds strange to take your wife's picture when you abandon her."

That disheartening news about himself caught Kathy's full attention, pulling her thoughts from her own worries. "You never want to marry?"

He chuckled devilishly. "Marriage isn't for me. I'm constantly on the move. My life's full of freedom, excitement, and danger. A home and family would demand too much of my time and energy. I've got too much to see and do to settle down. Marriage means commitment; and there isn't any room in my life," he stated with dismaying finality.

"Don't you ever get lonely?" she probed.

"I would make a terrible husband and an even worse father. I couldn't be saddled with heavy responsibilities or corralled by wedlock. Those chains give me the shudders! No woman would accept me like I am, and I won't change. I like myself, and I love my way of life. Why tamper with perfection?" he jested—yet, Kathy sensed he was utterly serious.

"Surely you get lonesome once in a while?" she disputed, wondering how any female could resist him or wish to change him.

"Wouldn't know about such feelings; never had 'em. Been on my own since twelve and plan to stay that way. Loneliness is like love, Kathy, only a foolish state of mind. I have good friends to spend time with when the mood strikes me. Frankly, I'm a loner and I prefer it that way," he calmly stated opinions which Kathy found disconcerting.

"You've never loved any woman? There's none of your type around?" she questioned intently, wanting to comprehend this mysterious man.

Robust laughter came forth. "Love?" He laughed again. "Love is like gold fever, Kathy; it's for fools and dreamers," he stated.

"You're awfully cynical for a young man," she reproached him.

"Young man?" he laughingly refuted her assessment. "I'm thirty-one years old, Kathy. That's hardly young."

"It's hardly ancient either," she retorted.

He laughed mirthfully. "I can see you're one of those dreamy-eyed romantics. You're in the right place. When you choose a husband, be smart and pick a rich one," he

72

teased mischievously, a roguish grin taunting her. "I doubt you'll remain single long."

To wipe that smug smile off his handsome face, Kathy haughtily stated, insulted, "No way, Landis. Like you said, marriage and love are for dreamers and fools; I don't intend to become either one. I have plenty of money and I cherish my freedom as much as you do. Marriage isn't the great life it's proclaimed to be, unless you're the husband! From my observations, a wife is nothing more than a husband's legal possession who can be treated in any manner he chooses. A wife is nothing more than a dutiful slave and a brood mare. I don't care for any of those demeaning roles. I'd rather be free and happy."

He studied her in pensive silence. "If you feel the same way I do, then why did you accuse me of being hard and cynical?"

She laughed saucily. "Because I don't feel the way you do. Marriage and enthrallment, no way; but denying all feelings and contacts? I should think a life without ever experiencing such special emotions would be cold and miserable," she rashly spouted.

"What about children?" he instantly pressed.

"Why does everyone feel because you're a woman you should instinctively want or bear them? What's so great about being a wife and mother, Landis? Talk about commitment and heavy responsibilities, that's exactly what children and marriage are! As for a husband, who could possibly give me anything of value in exchange for what I would sacrifice to marry him? Look at my father; he had everything, but did it satisfy him? If a man decides he wants his freedom again, all he has to do is pick up and leave. But a woman, how can she leave when she has children hanging around her skirts, children she can't ignore as easily as he can! Just like you, I have too much

73

to see and to do. I don't intend to spend my life and energy on menial labor and self-sacrifice. As you so aptly put it, why tamper with perfection?"

"Then why did you come looking for your father?"

"Perhaps I want to punish him, to humiliate him, to have the pleasure of showing him I don't care about him either . . . I honestly don't know. But when I meet him, I will."

"Don't let your childhood embitter you like this, Kathy. You've allowed your past to distort your views on marriage. I can't imagine any man lucky enough to marry you treating you like you just described. He'd be a bloody fool if he did. I think you're deceiving me, maybe even yourself. I doubt you really feel like that at all."

"Look who's expounding the virtures of marriage and love! The man who doesn't even believe in them. I recall your saying you didn't know anything about such feelings and situations. But, you're partially accurate; I was exaggerating, part of the time," she saucily admitted.

"Which part?" he asked, his gaze probing hers.

"Most of it, except for the part about marriage," she oddly fenced with him, wanting him to be just as confused as she was.

"Most of it was about marriage," he parried her cunning move.

"Since you're perceptive and cunning, you figure it out. As to my father, I must see him once, to learn why he left and what he's like. Afterwards, I'll get on with my life . . . alone, Mr. Jurrell."

"You would make a fine wife and mother, Kathy; give it some serious thought." His expression and tone clearly excluded himself from his strange suggestion, provoking her to rashness.

"And you, Landis Jurrell, have more to offer a wife and

74

children than you realize. Where could a woman find a stronger, more attractive, more valuable man? Even so, such enviable traits do not compel you toward stifling wedlock. Why should I be any different?" With that daring statement, she left him staring after her.

She passed Moore at the tent entrance as he was leaving. They briefly exchanged congenial words. Kathy looked around in amazement; everything had been done while she was debating with Landis. She rushed forward and apologized. Harriet fondly patted her shoulder. "Don't worry. Mr. Moore helped me clean up the dishes. I told him you were asking Mr. Jurrell to help you locate your father."

"What did he say?"

"He said if anyone could discover Jake's location, it was Mr. Jurrell. Besides, he makes a nice friend for you. With him around, the other men will leave you alone," she hinted optimistically.

"Him as a friend? I think not, Harriet. There's something mysterious and intimidating about him. He isn't a man to be taken lightly or to be used by some wily female."

"Certainly not. But his friendship could be valuable to you. The others respect him. No one would harass his friend."

"Respect, yes; but they also fear him. With just reason I might add. You should have seen him bluffing Marc, rather terrifying him. It was like confronting the devil himself. He's a most formidable and changeable man. I wouldn't be surprised if he's as dangerous and unpredictable as Marc Slavin was. I don't trust him, Harriet."

"Is it Mr. Jurrell you fear and mistrust, or is it the way he makes you feel that frightens and baffles you?" Harriet asked, confused by this abrupt change in

Kathy's attitude.

Guilt and modesty lightly dusted her face a glowing red. Harriet laughed. "I see," she murmured suspiciously. "The path to true love is never smooth or tranquil," she absently muttered.

"That's silly, Harriet. I just met him," Kathy debated, as if that fact prevented her ridiculous feelings. Odd, in some ways he was a provoking stranger; in others, it seemed she had known him . . .

"Time has nothing whatsoever to do with love, Kathy dear. As with a flower, it can take months to blossom, or it can strike you instantly as a bolt of lightning," she averred dramatically.

"Love?" she exclaimed. "What do I know about love?"

"That's the point, young lady; you don't even comprehend your own emotions. Each time you look at him, it's written all over your face," she carelessly announced.

Unnerved, Kathy paled. "I'll admit he's the most handsome man I've met to date; and he's most charming and valiant, but love him? That's too silly to even consider. You're just imagining things, Harriet."

"Have it your way, my stubborn and blind friend; but don't say I didn't warn you. Anyway, what's wrong with falling in love with a stimulating man like that?" she challenged.

Kathy already knew the plaguing answer to that question, but didn't voice it aloud. She wondered if Landis had also misinterpreted her attraction to him. Did he think she was brazenly pursuing him and enticing him? Was that why he had loudly proclaimed his views and feelings about love and marriage? Of all the nerve and gall! Admittedly she was deeply affected by him; what woman wouldn't be? But brazenly pursue him? Fall in love with him? Marry him? None of those things had even entered her mind! She scolded herself for acting an idiot and a flirt. No doubt Landis could have any female he desired!

They walked to the supply tent after dousing the hanging lanterns and sealing the flaps. "Let's turn in," Harriet suggested. They bid the guard good-night and sealed the flap to the supply tent from the inside. Harriet showed her the thick bear skins Moore had said they could use for bedding. She tossed Kathy two heavy blankets.

"Until we can manage a cabin or tent of our own, Kathy, I think it best if we sleep in our garments. In case of some problem, we don't want to dash outside in our petticoats or flannel gowns."

They spread the skins between the U-shaped arrangement of crates and boxes. Removing their shoes and loosening their buttons and belts, they lay down and pulled the blankets over them. Within moments, both were sound asleep, ending the first day of their new existence.

"Mrs. Pullen, time to wake up, ma'am," the voice of Lewis Johnson called through the thick canvas walls. "The men will arrive for breakfast in a little over an hour. You ladies awake?" he asked.

Harriet stirred and answered him, "Yes, Mr. Johnson. Thank you." She shook Kathy's shoulder and called her name several times.

Kathy moaned and snuggled deeper into the warm covers. Harriet was tempted to let the girl sleep on, but didn't. Gradually she roused Kathy. The younger woman sighed heavily. Her lids fluttered and opened. "What time is it?" she groggily murmured.

"Six. Breakfast must be ready at seven. Up, sleepy-head."

"Six o'clock! No one gets up this early. It's still night." Kathy rolled over and closed her eyes again.

"Why not tell Mr. Moore you don't want this job. Once I get the hang of things, I can manage. I'm used to hard work; you aren't."

Kathy turned over to rest on her aching back. She pushed the blanket down and looked up at Harriet. "Every inch of my body hurts, and I feel as if my head just touched his pillow," she groaned, boxing the rolled up cape which had been her makeshift headrest. "Mama always said that idle hands and too much leisure time get a person into mischief. What could I possibly do all day if I give up this backbreaking job? I suppose I'll get used to the hard work and ungodly hours. Just give me a minute to clear my head and eyes."

The water in the pail was very cold. Kathy shuddered as she washed her face and hands. Harriet was dressed first and was selecting the things needed for breakfast. "While you dress, Kathy, I'll get the fire started in the stove." She left.

Kathy struggled with her trunk. She opened it and withdrew a long, heavy skirt in muted greens and reds. She searched for the dark green blouse to match it. Finding it, she quickly pulled them on. Next, she drew on her ankle-length, laced shoes in shiny black leather. She brushed her hair and secured it at the nape of her neck with a green ribbon. Ready at last, she hurried to the cook tent.

The fire was going good by then, but the tent was still chilly. "Kathy, you need a shawl, dear. It's nippy this morning."

"Once I get moving, I'll warm up. A shawl's cumbersome." She lifted stacks of clean dishes and placed them on the wooden tables. She added cups and utensils. "What's next, boss?" she cheerfully asked.

Harriet was frying smoked bacon and storing it in the warming holders. "You could mix up the pancake ingredients for me."

"How much flour?" she began, reaching for the sack and tin cup.

Harriet mentally tallied the amount needed for twenty men, then answered her. "Lard?" came Kathy's next question, continuing until the sandy-colored mixture was ready. Kathy placed the two wooden bowls near the stove on the working table.

The coffee was perking and filling the tent with its heady aroma. Harriet said, "I'll start the johnnycakes while you fetch the crate of syrup in the supply tent. It's next to the entrance on the left side."

Kathy returned to the supply tent. She found the box mentioned and pulled out several metal cans. It was too awkward to carry them all at once, so she picked up a few and turned to leave. Landis Jurrell was there. "Need any help?" he asked, observing her loaded arms.

Gathering her wits and courage, Kathy smiled and replied sweetly, "There are three more cans, if you don't mind."

He quickly retrieved them and followed after her swaying skirt-tail. The sight was most provocative and unnerving. Kathy turned to find him watching her intently. Her fine brow lifted quizzically. For a man uninterested in women or love, his look was most appreciative! He hastily glanced away from her sensual body. "Put them down at the end of each table, please." She did the same with her load, setting the two extra ones on the working board.

"Anything else, Harriet, besides milk and sugar for the coffee?"

Harriet said good morning to Landis first, then answered Kathy's last question. Kathy took the large tin box down and passed out the sugar containers, then poured several cups of milk to join them. "All done, boss lady." She turned to Landis and politely offered, "Would you like some coffee, Mr. Jurrell?"

He grinned roguishly at her cool formality this morning. She was as fresh and crisp as the morning air. "If it's no bother, Miss Hammond," he smoothly replied; yet, he seemed tense and cautious.

She smiled brilliantly and retorted, "None at all, sir. A gallant knight surely deserves special attention," she merrily teased him, enjoying his disquiet for a change. Neither mentioned the night before.

He sat down at the table nearest to the cooking area. Kathy poured his coffe and handed the cup to him, not daring to meet those taunting mahogany eyes. She turned to face Harriet. "All finished," she announced calmly. "Do you want me to take over the other skillet?"

"No need, dear. Good morning, Mr. Moore," she promptly stated as their boss swept into the tent, sniffing the air.

"Hum-m-m," he murmured, smiling in pleasure. "What's that tempting smell? Morning, Landis," he nodded to his friend.

"Pancakes, coffee, and bacon, sir," she answered in a tremulous tone, still unsure of herself. "I found the syrup in the tent. You did say to use anything there, didn't you?" she asked anxiously.

He grinned. "Right. I can't even recall eating proper pancakes. I never was any good at 'em," he confessed, then chuckled happily.

"Coffee?" Kathy inquired, offering a steaming cup to him.

"Thank you, Miss Hammond. You two work wonders here. I surely hope you like Skagway and stay forever."

Kathy smiled, as did Harriet. "Perhaps it isn't as bad as we first thought," Kathy admitted, for Landis was keenly observing her.

"Then you might be staying on?" Moore ventured, grinning.

Without glancing at Landis, Kathy murmured, "I don't know yet. Perhaps . . ." Landis's face remained impassive, but his dark eyes gleamed with some imperceptible reaction. "Will the other men be here soon?" she inquired when he refused her bait.

"They're on their way now."

"Harriet, shall I pour the coffee and set out the food?"

Catching the noise of the approaching men, Harriet nodded yes and returned her concentration to her task. Kathy placed the bacon and pancakes on tin plates and set them on the tables, then she poured the cups of boiling black liquid. The men entered with much the same reaction as the night before. To live and to work under such harsh conditions, they were certainly a jocular bunch for such an early hour. Kathy halted at the front table to refill Moore's cup and then Landis's.

"Be careful, Mr. Jurrell," she cautioned in a near whisper. "That black gold is very hot and dangerous," she teased.

He chuckled and replied for her ears alone, "Anything of value is dangerous to attain, Miss Hammond."

Their gazes locked for a brief moment, before she smiled and audaciously agreed, "You should know."

For the next hour, she rushed around serving hot pancakes and pouring countless cups of coffee. Finally

81

the men were leaving, but not before profusely thanking both women. The two women sank down wearily on the back bench to catch their breaths before eating. "They're a grateful lot," Kathy said, then laughingly added, "and a ravenous one!"

As they were eating, Moore returned to say there would be only nineteen men for dinner. "Someone quit?" Harriet innocently asked.

"Landis left a while ago. Probably be back in six weeks."

Kathy's bright smile faded instantly. Gone? Without even saying a word to her? She lowered her head to hide her reaction to this unexpected and disturbing news. Harriet quickly spoke with Moore to hold his attention away from Kathy until she could compose herself.

After his departure, Harriet softly asked, "He didn't tell you he was leaving this morning?"

"Why should he? Besides, that's one less greedy appetite to satisfy." Yet, her expression and tone belied her flippancy.

"I'm truly sorry, Kathy. Men are such thoughtless fools at times. He'll be back soon. I'm sure he was just in a hurry."

"I don't care if he ever shows his face in here again. He doesn't owe me anything; nor I, him. He arrived early for breakfast; he had plenty of time to tell me he was leaving. So don't play Cupid with me. I'm looking for my father, not some inconsiderate husband. If that's what he thinks, too, he's got another thought coming!"

Kathy began to gather the dishes, calling a halt to the conversation. Harriet watched her for a time, then shook her head. What a fine pair they could make. Too bad neither of them realized it!

While Kathy relaxed that afternoon, Harriet checked

over the supplies available, making a list of their quantities to ascertain how much she used and how quickly. That extra money could come in handy. About three o'clock, they headed for the large tent to begin supper preparations. Kathy worked diligently, but in a trance. Knowing the reason behind her melancholy mood, Harriet wisely ignored her.

It seemed forever before supper was served and the tent was cleared and cleaned once more. Yet, Kathy eventually found herself lying restlessly on her bedroll. "Can't sleep?" Harriet inquired into the darkness, conscious of the young woman's tossing and turning. The poor child, one disappointment after another, she mused sadly.

"Am I keeping you awake, Harriet? I think I'm too tired to relax," she excused her inexplicable mood.

There was some fumbling around in the blackness. "Here, maybe this will help," the older woman offered.

Kathy accepted the cup and sniffed it. "Brandy? You're giving me bad habits, friend. I might become a drunk," she jested, slowly draining the cup. The biting liquid warmed and relaxed her. "Thanks," she whispered later, but there was no reply; Harriet was sound asleep. She smiled to herself and closed her eyes, drifting into peaceful slumber.

Four

The women's schedule was much the same that next day. Kathy continuously found herself wondering about Landis; but refused to ask questions. Would she see him before her departure, whether she went inland to search for her father or returned to America? Why was an arresting stranger haunting her when she needed her energy and concentration to plan her quest for her father, even though she had no idea where to begin?

About noon, Kathy and Harriet scrubbed vegetables and cut chunks of beef. While the stew was simmering, Kathy left to catch a breath of fresh air. Harriet remained in the tent, concocting a surprise dessert for the men. Kathy strolled over to the big spruce near the side of the tent. Leaning against it, she gazed out across the choppy Lynn Canal. The body of murky, white-tipped water was empty; the *Victoria* had sailed yesterday at dawn, and Landis had departed shortly afterwards. Yesterday? It seemed more like years ago since she had docked. She sighed in relief, then her traitorous thoughts drifted back to the distressing subject: Landis Jurrell.

Why had he left without a word? Was he punishing her silly conduct? Was he trying to show disinterest? He was such an enigma. Why had he switched from fire to ice? That first night, he had definitely acted interested! Or had it merely been a mischievous game? If only she hadn't mentioned love and marriage. Evidently he felt intimidated by both!

A scrawny man approached her. She inwardly grimaced at his drawn face and cadaverous frame. His beard was scraggly, tinged with white. His wiry hair was dirty and shaggy. His age was indeterminable. The harsh life he led was emblazoned on his deathly face and skeletal frame. She hoped he wasn't going to beg for food; Moore had forbidden handouts. Since the supplies were his, she could not give them away. Her heart filled with sympathy for him.

"Miss 'ammond?" he hinted, squinting against the bright light.

She nodded. "Lan'is Jurrell wants ta see ye. He said fur ye ta meet 'im o'er in Cardone's cabin. Says it's impo'ant."

Elation and suspense flooded her. He was back! But why did he want to see her alone? News of her father? To apologize for his chilly rudeness? Probably about her father, she instantly decided. Had he discovered some information this quickly? Tension and eagerness rushed through her.

"Thank you," she tossed over her shoulder as she hurried across the cluttered area between the tent and cabin. She knocked timidly. It opened and she almost ran inside. "Did you learn . . ." She whirled around as the door was slammed and locked.

She paled and her eyes widened as she stared at the cruel lines etched on the face of none other than Marc Slavin. She inhaled sharply and shivered. He was leaning against the only exit, blocking any escape. "I hear your sweetheart's gone. What a crying shame. Who's gonna

85

look after sweet Kathy?" he maliciously taunted her.

"What are you doing here?" she nervously demanded. "The *Victoria* sailed yesterday. Don't tell me you missed your ship while harassing me," she sneered contemptuously.

"Old Shurling kicked me off. Seems I have to wait for the next one, thanks to you. Wonder how I'll occupy my time for three weeks and use up all this abundant energy," he conjectured in an ominous tone.

"If you're blaming me for your misfortunes, the shoe's on the wrong foot, Marc. You brought this trouble on yourself," she rebuked him. He was stranded here with her!

"We have plenty of privacy; so let's discuss it without any intrusions from the mountain man," he stated banefully.

"We have nothing to say to each other! I'm leaving," she announced, but didn't move.

He snorted coldly, an evil and glacial sound. "I think not, love. This cabin has very thick walls and the owner's gone for another few weeks. There's plenty of noise outside, if anyone dared to interfere. And, this is the only exit," he said, tapping the door behind him.

Kathy's mind was working fast. Harriet and Lewis were of no help here. The wretched souls along the beach couldn't care less about her precarious position. She was trapped once more by this evil villain who refused to leave her in peace. Even Landis's warning had obviously had no effect on him, and he would be gone for weeks!

Landis! "That old man told me Landis wanted to see me," she blurted out, stalling for time to think and to plan.

"I knew you would come running to your lover's side! I

paid him several good coins to deliver that message," he smugly announced.

"You're despicable! Say what you must so I can leave. I have chores to do," she snapped irritably to hide her fear.

"It isn't talking I want. Your chores will just have to wait."

"Someone will come looking for me," she warned.

"Not until supper time. By then, you can leave any time you wish." He savored her terror and helplessness.

Kathy summoned her lagging courage and bluffed, "Landis warned you to stay clear of me, Marc. He isn't a man to cross."

Marc threw back his head and filled the stuffy air with freezing laughter. "It won't work, Kathy. At the parting of a few more coins, I've learned a great deal about your Landis. You two just met. He isn't due for thirty days or more. By then, our disagreement will be nicely settled and I'll be gone. Just imagine a month or longer without his strong arm of protection . . . This here's a dangerous place for such a beautiful woman all alone. Seems to me you need a better guardian. Landis is awfully careless. For the same fringe benefits you give him for his services, I'll eagerly accept his position."

"Benefits? I didn't hire Landis as my bodyguard," Kathy naively argued. "We're to be married," she boldly declared.

"Come now, Kathy; how else does a female pay the man who guards her life and property? You denied me on the ship; this time you won't. There's no Shurling or Jurrell here now, just you and me."

His lecherous intentions now were clear and she shouted at him, "You filthy-minded beast! I won't listen to such vulgar talk! When Landis comes back, he'll cut out your vile tongue and your black heart!"

"Even if he objects to sharing the lovely spoils of Kathryn Hammond with me, I'll be in Seattle before he returns and discovers your little run of bad luck," he scoffed, nonplused by her threat. He knew she was terrified. "But I doubt he'll get a soiled bride."

Her trembling hand delivered a stinging slap. Slavin grabbed her offending weapon and crushed it as she winced in pain. He rubbed his smarting face with his other hand. "You'll regret that," he vowed coldly.

Capturing her other flailing hand which was boxing his right ear, he pinned them behind her, forcing her quivering body against his hard one. He began to back her into the next room. Kathy stumbled and his grip tightened. Despite his prior claims everyone would ignore her screams, she yelled as loudly as she could.

Slavin hooked his leg around hers and tripped her. She toppled to the bed, sending the air rushing from her lungs, silencing her screams.

Landing atop her, Marc forcefully drove his knee between her thighs. Kathy couldn't move or battle him with any success. Winded, she could not call out. He grinned, anticipating her total capitulation.

He pinned her hands above her head, then leisurely unbuttoned her dress down the front. Rolling her imprisoned and writhing body from side to side, he eventually had her dress lying on the floor beside them. Still struggling, she fused a deep scarlet in shame. No man had ever viewed her body. He fumbled until he had her white petticoats lying with her dress. She opened her mouth to scream again.

He chuckled satanically. "If your screams are successful, Kathy, look how those miners will find you. Half-naked, your rescue will be forgotten. I don't relish sharing you with numerous lusty men."

Petrified by his statement, Kathy suppressed her outcry until she could clear her wits. "That's the same threat you used on the ship. What makes you so sure they won't help me?"

He laughed and exclaimed, "You think men who haven't had a woman in months or years will rush in and rescue you without some charge? The moment they lay eyes on you they will be fighting over who is going to rape you first! Those men are like wild savages out there. If it comes to a choice between sex and manners, which do you think they'll choose?"

She paled in uncertainty and panic. "Landis will kill you, Marc," was the only reply she could think of to frighten him.

His head came down and he nibbled at her earlobe, his erratic respiration sending chills through her. He ground his hardened manhood into her tender groin. "Be nice or you could be hurt badly."

"Never!" she yelled, gritting her teeth and narrowing her eyes.

"If it's the last thing I do, I'm going to have you at least once."

"I would rather die first!" she sneered in disgust.

"If you cause me any more trouble, that can be arranged . . . afterwards, of course. People do have fatal accidents around here."

"I hate you! I'll fight you all the way," she vowed earnestly.

"If you submit, I'll be just as gentle as old Landis is," he scoffed.

"You're nothing like him! You can't even walk in his shadow!"

"Zat a fact?" he taunted.

"He'll kill you for this! No man touches his woman."

"In a few minutes, you won't be able to say that."

"Damn you, Marc Slavin! Get off of me this instant! He'll be back very soon, and he'll make you pay dearly for this."

"Landis, my ass! I'm not afraid of that conceited rake."

"If I were you, I would be. He's the bravest and most powerful man alive. Are you forgetting how he made you squirm like a scared rabbit the other night?" she reminded him.

"I'll have my revenge. After I'm finished with you, no man will want you. A few slices here and there and you'll be a hideous sight. Even Landis won't be able to look at you."

"You're a mighty tough man when your enemy is a defenseless female. If Landis was here right now, you would be cowering . . ."

"Shut up, you slut! Don't mention his name to me again, or I'll cut out your tongue before I take you!"

Marc leaned over and sucked repulsively on her earlobe as he yanked at her chemise. Disgust and nausea swept over Kathy. As she thrashed her head to avoid his mouth, her terror-filled eyes touched on the stormy face of Landis Jurrell. His forefinger on his sensual, taut lips signalled her to silence. Tears of relief and joy greeted him. He smiled tenderly. Kathy was no longer afraid as she lost herself in the fathomless depths of Landis's molten eyes. The tautness within her body faded, giving Marc the wrong impression.

Marc leaned back and said, "See, I knew you could relax with a little effort. Yield to me, Kathy, and I won't hurt you."

She glared him in the eye and stated rashly, "The only man I'll ever yield to is Landis. You'll soon regret this day, Marc."

"I'll die before I allow that stinking gold miner to stop me!"

"That sounds fine to me, Sailor Boy," Landis snarled from behind Slavin, making his intrepid presence known to Marc.

Marc instantly rolled off the bed to lunge at him. Seeing the wide, flat blade of the hunting knife in Landis's grip stopped him. "Seems to me you like to live dangerously or stupidly. I was sure I made myself clear; Kat is mine. Mine, Sailor Boy! Every time my back's turned, you try to harm her. Now what should I do about it this time?" His burning gaze seared away any courage Marc had.

"I was told you were gone. She was teasing me and taunting me. I was only gonna scare her," Marc declared in visible fear. "She thought you'd deserted her and she wanted a new protector. She came over here playing up to me. What was I supposed to do? I'm only a man!"

"Landis, I didn't. I was told you wanted to see me, but Marc was here waiting for . . ."

Landis injected, "Hush, love. Let me handle this fool. I know you had nothing to do with this." He turned to Slavin. "What would Kat possibly want with you when she has me? Fact is, you chose the wrong place to carry out your revenge; this is my cabin and that's my bed you're attacking my woman on. That's three errors: my cabin, my bedroll, and my woman," he glacially emphasized, increasing Marc's terror.

"But I didn't harm her!" Marc shouted in panic.

"But you did. You frightened her; you abused her and you insulted her. If I hadn't come home, you would have ravished her, and we all know it. You've pressed the wrong man once too often. It's past time I teach you some manners. I said I'd kill you if you touched her

91

again." Landis's body was taut with rage and surges of inexplicable possessiveness stormed him.

Being a coward, Marc pleaded—but he couldn't deceive this vital man. Landis laughed in his whining face. He seized Marc's collar and yanked him to his feet. With a few lightning movements, he had landed three blows into Marc's gut and four across his jaw. Blood eased from a cut near Marc's mouth. Marc could hardly breathe following the rain of heavy blows.

He sank to his knees. "I won't come . . . near her . . . again. I . . . swear it," he stammered in pain.

"You liar! The moment I leave again, you'll be after her! You can't be trusted." Several more blows followed those words.

Marc rolled on the floor, gripping his abdomen and groaning.

Landis challenged, "Get up and fight me like a man, if you are one! You prey on helpless females and grovel before a man. Get up! I ain't through with you yet!"

"I can't. I'm hurt bad. My ribs are broken; my jaw feels busted. No more, please . . ."

Landis drew back his fist, but Kathy surged forward and caught his powerful bicep. "Enough, Landis. He's really hurt. I don't think he'll bother me again. Please don't beat him anymore," she pleaded, frightened by this vivid show of violence which she had never witnessed before. Landis's eyes burned with a ruthlessness which alarmed her. He could actually kill Marc if he continued this potent attack. She couldn't be responsible for a man's death, not even Marc's.

"Don't you understand, Kat? He was going to brutalize you! If I hadn't returned, he would have. This isn't the first time he's tried this! There's only one way to prevent him from ever raping any defenseless woman!"

he gravely threatened. The unleashed fury which flowed from him stunned her. Why had Marc's attack infuriated him this much? She wasn't actually his woman or his responsibility.

Marc's face lost all color at Landis's hint. "No! Please! I won't touch her again. I promise. The law won't let you get away with this. You can't just butcher a man."

"He's right, Landis. You can't; he could die," Kathy shrieked in panic. The thought of seeing Landis jailed or executed for protecting her from this brute was unbearable. Vividly, wilderness law was made and ruled by the strongest man or force; Landis was such a force.

"There isn't any law in Skagway! It's make your own! There isn't a man in this settlement who would stop me from punishing this scum!"

"What about the Mounties? What will they do to you?" she cried, recalling the crewman's mention of them.

Landis focused his full attention on her. "What did you say?" he demanded in a fierce tone. His eyes darkened and narrowed with a strange glow. He watched her closely. "Why would the Mounties be interested in me or what happens over here?"

"You appear to be the authority in this camp. Men here respect you and fear you; they obey you. You're the only one who's helped me. But if you kill Marc or injure him so badly that he dies, the law might arrest you and take you away from me. I would die if anything happened to you because of me," she voiced her fears.

Still, he observed her warily. "Listen to me, Kat; I can't permit him to strip you like this and assault you every time I leave camp! He can't be trusted to keep his word. He's proven that to both of us. I say fix him so he can't ever desire you or harm you again."

As Landis's concentration was on her, Slavin was inching towards the cabin door. Near it, he dashed for it and fled outside. Landis started after him, but Kathy prevented it. "Please don't leave me alone," she cried in fear, and began to sob.

Landis glanced outside. Marc was frantically heading for the nearest treeline to hide. Landis looked at the dishevelled and nearly naked Kathy who was in tears and shaking violently. He slammed the door and locked it. He came back to where she had sank to the bed, weeping.

He sat and pulled her into his arms. "Sh-h-h, love; it's all right now. He's gone, and I'm here. Don't be afraid anymore."

She innocently flung her arms around his neck and clung to him for comfort. "Don't leave me again, Landis. I'm so afraid when you're not here. Where did you go? Why didn't you say anything about leaving? I didn't even know when or if you'd come back," she shamelessly blurted out, clad only in lacy cambric drawers and matching chemise.

He was brushing kisses on her hair, forehead, and cheeks. "I had some business to see about," he muttered huskily, telling her nothing. "I was worried about you when Slavin didn't get on his ship."

"Where? What kind? You didn't even say goodbye," she anxiously exclaimed, wanting to know what had taken him from her side for nearly two days, sounding as if she had some rightful hold on him.

He tensed at her questions, then cautiously murmured, "Forget it, love. I'm here now." Twinges of suspicion and wariness chewed at him. Why had she mentioned the law? The Mounties? Strange . . .

"Will you be leaving soon?" she asked, praying he would say no.

"I'm not sure yet," he lied convincingly.

"Where can I reach you?" she innocently pressed.

"I move around a lot," he parried.

"But I might need you! Where can I find you?" she insisted.

To prevent any further questions, his mouth came down on hers. He kissed her deeply and hungrily. In her agitated state, Kathy clung to him and artlessly responded with intense yearnings, totally unprepared to deal with this fiery reality. Her head spun wildly at his nearness and manly smell. He invaded her senses and entrapped them in a world of heady desire, the reason for his hasty return forgotten.

He continued his quest of her tasty mouth and they inevitably sank into the softness of the bed, clinging feverishly. Kathy's hands wandered over his sinewy back, relishing the feel of his hard muscles. He was so warm and inviting. His kisses carried her mind away on waves of stormy passion. Eventually, the only thing she wanted and needed was for his magical and gentle assault to go on forever.

It had been a long time since Landis had taken a woman. His body flamed and ached. His seeking hands began to explore her virginal territory, mentally mapping it. His mouth willfully invaded hers with great skill and intensity. His flames were quickly spread to her smoldering body, igniting dangerous wildfires which she could not control or extinguish, searing away any defense against this compelling trespasser.

Unknown emotions called out to her and ensnared her. Instinctive longings plagued her. She had no desire or strength to prevent this heady tune from playing its sensual song on her taut and responsive body. She loved him and wanted him.

Tantalizing kisses played over her lips and face; intoxicating nibbles attacked her ears and shoulders. Her remaining two under-garments were removed. Caught up in a swirling and torrid vortex of passion, she could not resist him. Without pulling his lips from hers, he deftly came out of his own clothes and knee boots. Kathy moaned against his mouth as Landis's hand teased at her taut breasts. Such intense and bittersweet agony fused through her, a blissful agony he was increasing and stimulating.

His hand slipped down her flat stomach and found a secret place which brought forth more hunger and moans of desire. He moved between her thighs; yet, she did nothing to stop him. She was mindless with overpowering desire and greedily accepted his loving torment.

"Love me, Kat," he huskily whispered into her ear, causing tremors to sweep over her with his warm breath and tender, but urgent, plea. He was beyond thinking or halting, his mission here forgotten.

He gently probed her resistive maidenhead, then gradually severed it. Kathy cried out at the searing pain and a feeling of fullness. His pervasive kisses gradually removed her awareness and brought new tremors to her fiery body. He tensely waited for the burning sensation to lessen before beginning to move rhythmically within her. Between his devouring mouth, tantalizing hands, and stimulating movements, Kathy was once again transported beyond reality.

Landis struggled to master his rising passion until she was aquiver with need. "My beautiful Kat, I want you. Yield to me, love . . ."

Hopelessly enchanted, Kathy surrendered to the novel and powerful emotions which were storming her senses

96

and betraying her. Golden lights danced before her hazy vision as sweet rapture consumed her. Exquisite pleasures attacked her mind and eternally enslaved her. Landis hadn't planned to seduce her; yet, it was too late to restrain his passion or to heed duty. The probing letter about Kathy and Jake he had sent to America was forgotten in the furnace of blazing passion.

As they gradually eased down the conquered spiral of their explosive union, satisfaction and contentment filled them. They relaxed in each other's arms. He held her possessively; she snuggled peacefully against him. Time passed as they savored this unique moment: the forging of two bodies into one and the fusing of two hearts for all time.

Clasping her to his sated body, reality drifted back to him. He was confounded by these unknown stirrings of affection and tenderness which consumed him. He had taken lots of women, but never with such intense need and utter completeness. Kathy had come to him and had shaken the core of his being. No woman had stripped away his reason and control. He felt he could lie here entwined with her forever, possessing her and loving her time and time again. Why, he didn't understand. What should he do now? How could he stake a claim on a female he had been ordered to investigate!

He propped on his elbow and gazed down at her serene face. Such softness and warmth could be viewed within her eyes. He couldn't explain it or even comprehend it, but he wanted her again! "You're mine now, Kat, all mine. I've wanted you since the first moment I gazed into those lovely eyes," he murmured huskily, his eyes tenderly relishing her beauty, branding her with his ownership.

Strangely feeling no shame or modesty, she smiled and

whispered, "It would appear that way, my love. I didn't know it could be like this between a man and a woman," she demurely confessed, lost in the wonder of love. The first time she had seen him, she had known he was different from other men. He had made her feel and think things she didn't understand, until moments ago.

"Nor I," he readily agreed, smiling provocatively. "You're quite a unique woman, Kathryn Hammond. Stay here; don't leave. I want you," he carelessly admitted, as he lovingly stroked her silky hair.

Her hand came up to trace the proud lines of his arresting face, then moved seductively over his full lips which had driven her wild with desire for him. "I could never leave you, Landis. You're everything a woman could ever want or need."

His mouth came down on hers as her arms encircled his neck. This time, their lovemaking was deliberate. He whispered instructions into her ears which she eagerly and willingly obeyed. He was so gentle, and yet so demanding. He claimed her mouth, skillfully and hungrily ravaging it. He trailed consuming kisses over her closed eyes and face, utterly intoxicating her. His deft hands leisurely roamed her pliant body which burned for his possession. When he nibbled at her taut breasts, she moaned in rising need to end this blissful torture. Her body trembled as he gently moved his probing hands over it, exciting her and increasing her desire. He discovered every inch of her body, enticing it to quivering hunger. His sexual prowess rewarded them with wave after wave of undeniable pleasure. Later, they lay exhausted within the peaceful aura of sublime tranquility.

When Landis began to seductively tease at her breasts with his moist tongue, Kathy murmured happily, "Do all men possess such stamina, or is your appetite greedy? As you've learned, this is new to me," she jested, her molten blood singing within her veins. How she wished she knew what to say and do in such an intimate and tender moment. In spite of her strict upbringing and purity of mind and body, she felt this loving encounter with Landis seemed so right, so perfectly natural, so utterly beautiful.

"You don't need any more skills than you already possess, my golden Kat. I am hopelessly enchanted by you, and I'll never have enough of you. I sorely missed you these past two days. I could hardly keep my mind where it should have been. I didn't realize what I was missing. Perhaps my heart and life have been as barren and glacial as the Yukon," he whispered, though Kathy interpreted more from his words and mood than he intended. He didn't know which path to follow, his emotions or assignment, especially since such emotions were new and he always carried out his missions. Somehow, he had to keep her out of the line of his duty.

"If the Yukon is as cold and empty as they say, perhaps you need something to keep you warm or something to keep you entertained," she teased in return, laughing contentedly as lovely dreams flooded her ecstatic mind and heart. He could fill so many voids in her life.

"Not something, Kat, someone," he playfully corrected her, unintentionally misleading her. Could this be the woman he had waited for all his life? Did he dare carry out his orders now? God, what if he and Bill were wrong? If she discovered the reason for his hasty return, she would despise him. He had to find some way to halt her trip inland, to entice the truth from her. He resisted this demanding task. She was alone and in danger. He must protect her until . . .

"Not someone, but Kathryn Hammond," she clarified. Sighing peacefully, she glanced above her head, the ceiling in the cabin returning her to full awareness. She looked at him and asked, "Is this your cabin? I thought it belonged to Cardone."

He chuckled heartily, shaking his head to her first question and nodded yes to her second one. She paled, then blushed. "You mean we're lying here like this in another man's home? What if he walked in on us?" Horror flooded her; she shuddered in dismay.

Assuming she was only chilled, he pulled a blanket over them. "He won't, love; he's in Dawson for another week or so. He lets me use his cabin when I'm in Skagway. I have a key."

"But what if he returned earlier than planned? I would die if someone caught us in such a ... compromising position. Not to mention how my name and reputation would suffer," she added.

"Relax, Kat. He won't be back for at least seven days. I've missed you terribly. Stay a while longer," he coaxed, grinning enticingly. There was so much he needed to learn, but dared not birth suspicions in her. Besides, he was enjoying this unexpected situation.

"I really should go, Landis. It must be late. Harriet is probably frantic wondering where I am. Besides, wouldn't that be placing too many demands on your time and energy," she reminded him of his past words, then smiled. "You're a carefree loner, remember?"

His igneous eyes danced merrily as her words hit home. "Perhaps before I met my Golden Torment ... don't go yet, love. I'll explain things to Moore. You said you have plenty of money, so you don't need his job. You work too hard over there. And I don't like those lumberjacks gaping at my woman everyday," he confessed to stirring jealousy.

She laughed. "Since I am so obviously your woman, you have nothing to fear. I would never look at another man with you in my life. But I did promise Harriet I would help her until she gets things under control. She's been such a good friend to me. I would feel terrible if I deserted her. The work is hard, but I can handle it for a while longer. Besides, the men seem so appreciative of what we're doing for them; they're warm and friendly, and so kind and courteous. Another thing, with the outrageous prices here, my money won't last very long. Worst of all, Mr. Jurrell, if I spent all of my time in here with you, people would gossip. How many vulgar tongues can you silence like you just did Marc's?"

"I would cripple the first man who opened his mouth against you," he fiercely vowed, rekindling her qualms about a ruthless and stormy streak within him. "Who cares about the idle chatter of dreamers and fools?" he scoffed. It wasn't like him to be so indecisive and tense. As to jealousy, this was their first introduction; and Landis didn't like the green monster at all. For a man accustomed to governing himself and his destiny, he fretted over the loss of his control.

"I do. I wouldn't want them chasing around my skirts every time you leave on your mysterious business ventures. What kind of business do you have? I know so little about you."

"A little bit of everything: gold, furs, and supplies. Sometimes I hire out as a guide," he lazily and smoothly deceived her.

"A guide? Doesn't that take a long time?" she fretted.

"Sometimes," he nonchalantly replied. "Perhaps not as long now that you're here in Skagway," he ventured with a devilish grin.

101

"How long do you normally remain here?" she inquired.

"A day or two every five to six weeks," came the unwanted reply.

"I won't see you for over a month at a time!" she exclaimed miserably. "Can I go with you?" she boldly implored, dreading such a lengthy separation from him, needing to search for her father.

He stiffened slightly and altered his mood most noticably. "No, Kat. It's too dangerous out there. It's no place for a gentle girl." To distract her, he began to fondle her breasts, bending forward to tease them with tantalizing kisses and light nibbles. His lips moved up to her ear. She shuddered and moaned. He made his unwitting mistake when he huskily murmured, "This is the place for you, my golden torment, safe in my arms, torturing me with desire."

"You're a sneaky devil, Landis Jurrell! Do you mean I'm supposed to sit here patiently waiting for you to show up every month or so?" she anxiously demanded, sounding possessive and petulant.

"I'll come to visit you every chance I get," he lightly promised, caressing her cheek, bristling slightly at her attitude. After all, she had willingly surrendered to him.

His tone and words panicked her. Visit me? she mentally echoed. She suddenly realized he had not mentioned love, commitments, or marriage. He had only spoken of companionship and desire. Anxiety and alarm raced through her mind and body. Was she so naive and gullible that she believed such an intimate and total submission revealed and expressed love and permanence? Yes, she positively felt that way! She had trustingly assumed he felt the same, but did he?

In heart-stopping dread, she forced herself to say, "But

102

what about us, Landis? I thought you needed me and wanted me."

Her meaning eluding him, he gazed at her in bewilderment. "What about us, Kat?" he casually repeated. "Of course I want you; I'd be a fool if I didn't! I just told you I'll come to see you as often as I can. But right now, my schedule's unpredictable. Don't fret, love; I'll fit you in," he teased.

Fit me in! she mutely exploded. "I'm not a business matter! I don't want an occasional visit! After what happened between us, I thought you would take me with you. I have to locate Jake Hammond; I can't do it here," she angrily informed him. "Did this mean nothing to you?"

"Of course this meant something to me! Why would you think it didn't? But I can't take you with me! I've told you before, there's no room in my kind of life for commitments. I promise to come here as often as possible; what more can I do? If you think Skagway is rough and uncivilized, it's nothing compared to the Yukon Territory. Men suffer and die in there. I'll try to locate your father. But you'll have to remain here with Harriet. That's the best deal I can offer," he remarked unwisely, again alluding to her as a business matter.

Dread washed over her as she prayed she was misunderstanding him. She was observing him intently, absorbing his tormenting words and their dire indications. Evidently he was viewing this intimate episode in a much different light. "Are you suggesting I stay as your . . . mistress?" she voiced her fears aloud in a tremulous tone. "You don't want to marry me? You don't . . . ," she stammered.

"Marry you?" he echoed in disbelief. "Where would you get a crazy idea like that?" he snarled, as if the very thought attacked him savagely. Hell's bells, he wished he could! It was impossible.

She paled at the frigid tone in his voice and the brittleness in his eyes. "But we just made . . . love," she quietly argued, as if that fact changed anything. "I need your help. Let me go with you."

"Is that why you submitted to me? You hoped I would feel obligated to marry you afterwards? If that's why you did, Kat, then you made a grave mistake. I told you bluntly that marriage wasn't for me, and I bloody well meant it!" he snapped, cursing the fact he would be forced to hurt her. He realized he was handling her and this situation wrong, but he was trapped, just as she was.

"You said I was your woman! You begged me not to leave you! All lies to disarm me?" she accused, his sharp words cutting into her soul.

Studying her explosive reaction and defiant expression, reality slapped him on the face: she actually believed he should marry her. Even if he did want her, marriage, a home, children, responsibilities, commitments, and truth . . . They weren't for Landis Jurrell anytime soon . . . It tormented him to realize he wanted her and needed her, but couldn't have her except on her terms, impossible terms at present.

His mind was spinning. Was she desperately lonely and afraid? Did she view him as a protector, a solution to her many problems? He hadn't tricked her. How could he stall her, but keep her?

He calmly explained his views once again, "I did say you were my woman, Kat. But a woman and a wife are worlds apart. In all honesty, I do want you. I find you the most stimulating and refreshing woman I've met. As for deluding you—there, we don't see eye to eye. From the first moment we met, I haven't given you any reason to expect love or marriage. In fact, I made my feelings on those subjects very clear. Perhaps you were teasing and playing games the other night, but I wasn't! I was deadly serious. I told you there was no place in my life for them, at least no time soon. I didn't force you to make love to me; you wanted me just as much as I wanted you. If you want to call it rape or seduction, feel free to do so. But you know that isn't true. I can't take you with me, and I can't marry you now. If you want me, great; if not without marriage, fine," he stated more harshly and indifferently than intended, riled by the thought of losing her because of his refusal to marry her.

They were each so involved in their argument, neither noticed that off in the distance, three shrill blasts announced a ship's arrival.

During this lengthy explanation, Kathy had time to comprehend her mistakes. Fury, disillusionment, shame, and agony stormed her ravaged heart. Yet, her pride and resilient nature took over in this devastating situation. No matter what he claimed, he had cruelly used her and deceived her! She would never forgive him for this pain which knifed her heart, this humiliation which stormed her mind, and this wanton hunger which viciously chewed at her traitorous body! But let him witness her defeat? Not on her life!

"Evidently we're at cross angles," she stated. "When I asked for you to take me along, I meant to search for my father, not remain with you. Once we find him, I'll either go with him or return home. You did say you hired out as a guide; how much do you charge?" she asked, her voice strangely calm, her expression obscure. "Just to clear the air, Landis, I was also serious the other night. Marriage sounds bad enough, but to a man I would rarely see? That doesn't appeal to me. As for an intimate relationship between us, it wouldn't work; we're too different. I'm not foolish enough to call it rape or seduction. So are you for hire or not?"

"Nope! I'm already hired out to several explorers who'll be mapping the upper Yukon area, then to a group of trappers looking for new hunting grounds," he claimed to halt any further discussion of that ridiculous idea. Had she merely been using him, setting him up?

"You must know this area very well. Why can't I come along, at least to Dawson? You can earn twice the money with one job. I won't pursue you or be any trouble. I must find Jake Hammond. Tell me about the Mounties," she abruptly pressed, ignorant of these formidable men who might aid her.

Why was she so anxious to tag along with a stranger? he wondered. Was she trying to spy on him, or use him to find Hammond? She was far too inquisitive and enchanting. What better secret agent could there be than a bewitching woman? Who would suspect this creature? After his meeting with Bill at the Mounty station, he should. Suspicious and cynical by nature and training, Landis wondered how far this mercurial female would go to disarm him into complying with her wishes, or orders. Where was Jake Hammond? Sergeant Thomas had quickly responded to that name; he was anxious to find Hammond! What better way to deviously contact Jake than to put out feelers for a missing father! Damn, he was a blind fool! He had allowed this female to get to him! "Yep, I know this area better than any other man. But I'm not for hire by you," he stated crisply.

"I see," Kathy murmured thoughtfully. "I guess that means you'll be leaving soon and won't be back for a long time?" she speculated.

"I don't know. What difference does it make to you?"

She smiled enticingly. "I was just recalling your previous offer. Don't you think it a bit selfish to keep a mistress sitting around Skagway for such a lengthy spell? It would seem to me that a man would want his woman with him. You know, to keep him warm, to entertain him, to take care of him?" she taunted him with an angelic smile.

What a cunning feline she was! He needed to find Hammond. First, he had to find a way to keep Kathy here, where he could watch her and where she would be safe. With luck, his feelers would entice Hammond to Skagway. Besides, he wanted Kathryn Hammond, and she wanted him. Before he could come up with some crafty reply, she asked, "Are there other guides like you around here?"

"Some. Why?" he cautiously inquired, eyes and ears alert.

"If you're too busy or too stubborn to help me, I'll find another guide and hire him. My . . . business is vital."

"You can't travel in deserted country with a stranger!"

"Whyever not? You and I are strangers, and I was willing to hire you." She realized that news didn't sit well with him.

Provoked, he growled, "After what just happened between us, you can hardly call us strangers!" He couldn't allow her to leave.

"You mean this?" she parried, waving her hand over the bed. "As I said, a foolish impulse, a moment of distraction and vulnerability. But become your mistress? No, Landis. Besides, I have some pressing business. I doubt I'll be around next time. Have you forgotten I never planned to remain in Skagway any longer than absolutely necessary?" she reminded him, boldly pushing a straying lock of sable hair from his handsome face.

Possibly he wanted her, but selfishly without strings.

"But you said you wouldn't leave me, that I was every-thing you wanted!" he irrationally exploded, furious at her supposed deception. "Were you lying or teasing?" Damn this traitorous vixen!

"We both said many things in a moment of reckless passion. I didn't realize what I was saying. What dif-ference does it make? You've bluntly informed me of the only interest you have in me. Since you travel to Dawson so frequently, I see no urgent need for me. If memory serves me correctly, you're the one who'd be absent all the time. The only way I'll become your woman is to go with you. Relax, love; I did say woman, not wife," she rebuked him when his eyes gleamed with amusement. No matter, she was only taunting him!

"Then you'll be returning to Seattle soon?" he ventured, fiercely trying to control his ire and intrigue. How to gain more time . . .

"Don't be silly. I've already related my plans to you; I'm going to Dawson just as soon as I find an appropriate guide. Any suggestions?"

"You can't be serious, Kathy! I've already told you how dangerous and rugged it is out there. Hell, you're a woman!"

"More dangerous than staying in Skagway?" she scoffed. "With you and Marc here, I should be perfectly safe!"

"Damnit, you can't go!" he snarled in rising fury. Whatever her motives, it was too dangerous.

"I can, and I will!" she defiantly confronted him. "You don't own me. You have nothing to say about what I do or where I go!"

He captured her face between his hands and forced her to look at him. Their stormy and defiant gazes met and battled. He challenged, "As you put it moments ago, what about us? I need time, Kat."

"There is no us. Under the circumstances, let's forget we even met, assuredly forget this afternoon. I need help, and you're refusing it. All you care about is yourself."

There was a loud and persistent knocking on the cabin door. Kathy flinched in surprise, then forced herself to appear sedate and poised. "Company, Mr. Jurrell. If you don't mind, would you please dress before answering the door. I know your reputation means little to you, but I'll be staying here a while longer."

He glared at her, nettled by her behavior. He got up, shouting, "Keep your shirt on! I'm coming!" He hastily pulled on his clothes and ran his fingers through his touseled hair. He headed for the door. She huddled against the wall to conceal herself. Landis opened the door just enough to see who was there. "What can I do for you, Moore?" He stepped outside and pulled the door shut.

Kathy jumped up and glanced around. Sighting a water pail and basin, she hurriedly washed off, mentally denying the implication of the blood on the cloth. She quickly retrieved her clothes and dressed. She lifted a brush and worked on her tangled hair, preparing to flee this tormenting place at the first available moment. How was it possible to endure so much heartache and sacrifice in eighteen short years? Why had she been singled out by Fate to be attacked by these destructive forces? Here she was stranded in a godforsaken land trying to accept her mother's untimely death, looking for a father who had abandoned her, being assaulted by a savage brute, and having her heart torn out by a traitorous lover. Had she blindly and wantonly given herself to a man she had known for only a few days? What powerful magic did he possess? Anger and spite filled her; Jake Hammond and Landis Jurrell owed her, and she would find some way to collect those debts!

Landis returned in a foul mood. He paced the floor for a short time, as if utterly oblivious to the sapphire eyes which were tracing his every move. Suddenly sensing her presence, he whirled and looked at her. "What are you staring at?" he snapped irritably.

He was clearly unnerved by something Moore had told him! Where were his tenderness and charm? "Nothing, Landis; absolutely nothing," she replied in a frosty, bitter tone. She headed to the door.

Just as she was about to open it, he called out, his voice strained and muffled, "I'll be leaving at first light tomorrow. If you change your mind, I'll be back in a few weeks. I've asked Moore to keep Slavin away from you. Goodbye, Kathy . . ."

She turned and looked at him. He had his broad back to her. She wondered what he was feeling and thinking. She opened her mouth to speak, but couldn't. What was left to say?

She left without looking back, though she heard the cabin door open. Yet, he didn't come after her or utter a word. She could feel his burning gaze on her back. She lifted her head proudly and continued her solitary walk toward the supply tent. She didn't get far before two men approached her, two who had sailed on the *Victoria*.

One man halted at her right side and the other blocked her path. Her nostrils detected the heavy odor of whiskey. "How's about we have a little talk?" the large man slurred, grinning lewdly at her.

"Excuse me," she stated firmly, trying to pass them. The second man caught her arm and prevented her departure. "Don't go getting prissy on us. We just want to talk."

"Let go of me," Kathy demanded, her heart racing in panic. She was suddenly aware of the crowded beach, packed with men who had just arrived or men who had been stranded here.

"Let's go sit a spell and have a wee nip," the first man coaxed.

"No, thank you." She tried to handle this matter calmly. "Mr. Moore will be looking for me. I have chores to do."

"Aw, come on, gurly. We're lonely," the second man added, the first one taking hold of her other arm.

Kathy feared they were about to drag her off in spite of her objections. Each hour she realized how dangerous Skagway was alone. She shuddered, wishing she had the gun Harriet had given her.

"You men aren't pestering my wife, are you?" Landis's voice boomed from behind her, as he reached for her and pulled her to him.

"Wife?" one man echoed, both staring at the towering man.

"That's right. The name's Landis Jurrell, and I don't like men harassing my wife," he warned, knowing most men in these parts were aware of that name and the physical power behind it.

Landis's ruse worked. Grumbling, they staggered off. He glanced down at the trembling Kathy. The ship in the canal had supplied the answer to his problems. "Let's talk, Kat," he said.

She met his gaze, then thanked him. She wanted to shout it wasn't necessary to come to her rescue, but it was. It was clear she couldn't take care of herself against such odds, gun or no gun. "I'd best return to Moore's area and stay there," she stated resentfully.

"You see that ship?" he asked, pointing to it. She nodded. "The captain has the authority to perform marriages. I want you to stay here where it's safe and I can see you again. You need protection. I think you just witnessed you can have it with my name."

Kathy stared at him. "You think I'll be safe if we pretend we're married?" she asked, his meaning unclear. "You'll loan me your name if I'll play your wife?"

"I'm offering you a compromise, Kat, a marriage of convenience. If you'll stay in Skagway while I search for your father, I'll give you my name as protection. No one has to know the truth. After things are settled, we can have it dissolved." That should convince her!

"Marry you? But you just said . . ."

"I know what I said," he interrupted her. "You're in enough danger without heading inland. The only way I can protect you is to keep you here and by giving you my name. Are you interested?"

"Don't you think that's a heavy sacrifice?" she sneered. His offer didn't include love or permanence! His name in exchange for what?

"After what happened today, I owe you that much, Kat. I didn't mean to mislead you, but evidently I did. I'm not saying I don't want you or have strong feelings for you. This is the worse possible moment for me to think about a woman or marriage. But it seems the best solution for both of us. If you prefer, it can be a marriage in name only. I wouldn't go to such lengths to gain a beautiful mistress. I honestly want to help you, and this seems the only way." As far as anyone would know, the marriage would be legal. There wouldn't be any need to dissolve it later; it wouldn't be valid, for Landis Jurrell didn't exist, but Kathy didn't know that . . . A false

112

marriage would help both of them . . .

"Are you serious? A wife in name only? I don't trust you, Landis. Why are you really doing this? You don't care about me."

"You're wrong, Kat, and I'm deadly serious. You need my name. Look around us. How safe would you be if I walked off?"

In spite of everything, Kathy knew he was accurate. This idea was crazy. He didn't love her or want to marry her, but he would. Maybe he cared more than suited him . . . Was it a guilty conscience? She annoyed him when she asked for time to make her decision.

"I'm leaving at first light, remember? I won't be back for nearly a month. Think you can survive that long without me?"

"You or your name?" she quipped sassily, nettled.

"Both. This isn't the time for pride, Kat."

"Maybe I don't want to marry you, for any reason. I'm going to find Jake Hammond, with or without your help."

"I told you, woman, I'll look for him wherever I go! Marry me, Kat, right now."

Before Landis left, he felt he needed to settle this crazy situation. How could he keep his mind on his business if he was fretting over her? He was going to demand the truth about why she was in Alaska, even though he couldn't offer the same to her. He had been a bloody fool to swing by here again this soon, but Slavin demanded a close eye. Evidently Kathy hadn't known he was still around.

Landis waited for her answer. Kathy was plagued by confusion and fear. Wild as it sounded, it was an excellent solution. His name held power and protection. Damnit, he did owe her! She met his steady gaze and nodded. "In name only," she coldly added.

Landis frowned, nodding agreement to her condition. Shortly, she was standing with a ship captain, exchanging vows with this quicksilver man. He hadn't even allowed her time to tell Harriet! The ceremony was fast and cold. The captain was rushed and distracted; for correct name-spelling he asked Landis to enter the information in his log-book. The captain was mildly surprised when Landis asked for two copies of their marriage certificate, but hastily complied. Landis signed one, handing both to her for signatures. After signing them, one was rolled and given to her; the other one was signed, folded, and stuffed into his pocket. As Landis spoke with the captain, she gazed at the ribbon-bound license and the gold band on her finger. She was surprised he had given her his mother's wedding ring which he carried in his pocket on a gold chain. Now, all she had to do was make certain this marriage was never consumated! Unless . . . but that was a golden dream.

Ashore, Landis led her to the cabin, under her protest. "For looks only, Kat. We just got married, it'll look strange not to be alone. Don't worry, I won't touch you! Stay here while I get us some supper and deliver our good news. One look at you, and they'll know it's a joke." With those nasty remarks, he left her alone.

Landis went to the supper tent to see Harriet. Before he told his news, he probed for some answers which plagued him. He revealed Kathy's battle with Marc, saying she was resting in Dray's cabin.

Harriet was worried about Kathy. What Kathy needed was someone to love her and protect her. "I had hoped . . ." She halted.

Mystified, he pressed, "You had hoped what, Mrs. Pullen? Go ahead and say what's on your mind," he coaxed. "Evidently it has to do with Kathy. I'm trying to help her and protect her."

"I misunderstood your friendship; that's all," she told him. "It was a natural mistake considering the way you acted toward her," she quickly explained. "She's so naive and trusting."

Kathy's previous words came flooding back to him like a dam breaking loose and waves crashing into his head. He softly demanded, "You mean Kathy feels more than friendship for me, more than gratitude for my help with Slavin? She thinks I'm romantically interested in her?"

"It isn't my place to answer for her," Harriet wisely stated.

"Perhaps Kathy had some girlish notions about me or us; but more than that, I seriously doubt it," he guilefully fenced.

Harriet studied him closely. Now she understood; he didn't want to see it. "She might act childish and naive, but she's very much a young woman. I only hope you won't lead her on and hurt her. You're older and experienced. It's only natural for an impressionable, young girl to find you charming." Distressed, Harriet chatted too openly.

"Hurt her? Lead her on? Did she say I had?" he asked.

"She didn't say anything about you. I'm afraid she can't handle another crisis or loss right now," she candidly informed him. If this manly creature was only playing games with Kathy, they were cruel ones!

"Will you answer one question for me, Mrs. Pullen?"

"If I can," she replied, puzzled and guarded.

"Did Kathy really come here to look for a missing father? Do you know her well enough to answer truthfully?"

Harriet gaped at him. "I know Kathy very well!" she

angrily retorted. "Why would you doubt her claim? Yes, Mr. Jurrell; she most certainly did! I might add, at my suggestion and insistence because she has no other family. I also knew her mother. I was with Kathy before, during, and following Dory's death. It was Kathy's mother who told me about Jake Hammond and her wish for Kathy to locate him. Naturally Kathy is resentful and hesitant, with just cause. She didn't know what to do after her mother's death. I talked her into coming here with me to look for him," she said in honesty.

Landis became pensive and moody. Clearly something was eating at him. He didn't seem to care for this news! He anxiously paced back and forth in deep, silent thought.

Landis halted in his tracks and turned to Harriet. "Why doesn't Kathy know what her own father looks like? Why did he desert them? Why did he come to Alaska?" he quizzed. "To help her, I need more facts," he alleged.

"She was only two when he took off. Dory told Kathy, as well as me, there were no pictures of him. As to why he left them, Dory wouldn't or couldn't explain. Frankly, I think Dory knew more than she related; I even believe she had more to do with Jake's departure than Kathy could even suspect. Since Dory's dead and Kathy's alone, Jake is the only one alive who knows the truth. If Kathy's to ever have peace of mind, she has to find him and resolve her bitterness. If you have no honorable intentions toward Kathy, don't lay any more troubles in that child's lap. Stay away from her, please," she implored, sensing his mistrust and his powerful pull on her young friend.

"If by honorable intentions, you mean love and marriage, Mrs. Pullen; I can assure you that problem doesn't exist. Kathy's very beautiful and vulnerable;

she's in constant danger here, from more than Marc Slavin. I think I've solved the problem of her safety until she can locate her father. She's going to remain here while I search for him. Moore's promised to watch over her."

Before he could finish his explanation, Harriet injected skeptically, "Safe? How can she be safe with men like Slavin running loose? She's one female surrounded by thousands of men. It's bad enough to be a woman here, but a beautiful one?"

"After the beating I gave Slavin, he can't show his face for ages. She'll have you, Moore, and his men to watch over her. Besides, I gave her my name this afternoon as protection. I'm not boasting, Mrs. Pullen, but few men dare to tangle with me."

"What do you mean, 'gave her your name'?" she asked curiously.

"After that fight with Slavin, I carried her to the ship in the canal and married her. Once word gets around she's Kathryn Jurrell, she'll be safe. I'll be leaving at first light. I'll check in every few weeks. With luck, I'll find Jake soon and she can return home."

Harriet's mouth had fallen open at that shocking news. "You two got married?" She couldn't believe her ears!

"It was the only solution to her problem," he stated.

Harriet observed him and listened. She astutely read between the lines of his speech. He married Kathy, then came over here to interrogate her best friend about her? He surely didn't appear a love-smitten bridegroom! He made their union sound like a deal of some kind! Something odd was going on. Had he tricked her during a moment of terror and confusion? To her, Jurrell didn't seem the marrying kind. "Is Kathy all right?"

117

"She's fine, Mrs. Pullen. We'll be staying in Dray's cabin tonight. I thought I'd take some supper over there. Naturally we need to talk and get acquainted. You can see her tomorrow after I leave. She's still unsettled about this afternoon. She needs privacy and rest."

Considering they were married, there was nothing Harriet could say. But this wasn't like her Kathy! She prepared two bowls of stew, placing them on plates with baked bread. "Coffee?" she inquired.

"No need. I'll borrow some wine from Dray's stock. Thanks, Mrs. Pullen. See you in the morning." He strolled out with their meal.

Outside, Landis paused to give Moore a similar explanation, who was as surprised as Harriet. Yet, he agreed it was the best solution for all concerned, aware it wasn't a regular marriage. Moore promised to protect Kathy until Landis's return.

Kathy tried to keep her eyes off of her new husband as he served their meal and poured two glasses of wine, but she was too aware of him and their privacy. When he was seated, he held up his glass and murmured, "To my golden torment, Kathryn Jurrell."

Kathy ignored his playful taunt. "If you find any clue about my father, you'll let me know immediately?"

"Absolutely, Mrs. Jurrell," he agreed, grinning roguishly.

"Stop calling me that," she scolded his mocking manner.

"You best get used to it; that is the reason for our little ruse."

"Why did you really marry me, Landis?" she asked seriously.

"You know why, Kat," he replied, eyes locking on her face. "But I'm not quite certain why you agreed."

"You know why," she echoed his words.

"Do I?" he challenged, smiling provocatively.

"Yes, for your name," she alleged, dismayed by his mockery.

"And no other reason?" he nonchalantly continued.

"Revenge!" she snapped to shock him.

He chuckled merrily. "Can you afford it's price?"

"Does it have one?" she debated saucily.

"Always, love, always," he huskily murmured.

The meal passed in stony silence. Kathy retired to the other room, to toss restlessly on Dray's bed until fatigue claimed her. Landis quietly entered the room, to stand over her and study her. For the first time since this drama began, he couldn't decide if he had made a terrible mistake or the wisest decision in his life. It all depended on Kathy and Jake. He went to his bedroll and finally fell asleep.

Five

When Kathy awoke, she found herself alone. Realizing how late it was, she hurriedly straightened the cabin and headed to the eating tent. Landis wasn't in sight. Kathy wondered how to explain this weird situation to Harriet. How had she taken the astonishing news? "Sorry I'm so late. What can I do to help, Harriet?" Kathy asked from behind the busy woman. What had she gotten herself into?

Harried turned and smiled. "You look chipper this morning," she said, waiting for Kathy to open the confusing subject.

"What smells so good?" she asked, coming forward to the stove, stalling noticably.

"Apple pies again. The men seem to love them, so I thought I would cook more tonight," she replied, continuing with her task at hand.

"You can hardly blame them. I bet they haven't had dessert since they've been here. Plus, your cooking is the best I've tasted, including my mother's. Did Mr. Moore say anything about my absence last night and this morning?" she gingerly began.

"He understood," Harriet replied. "I can't believe you're married," she blurted out, unable to contain her curiosity.

"That makes two of us," Kathy responded in a tone which Harriet found perplexing. "Where's Landis?"

Harriet warily glanced at her. "He left after breakfast."

"Left?" she echoed incredulously. "But . . ." She stammered, then declared uneasily, "Oh, yes, he said he was leaving at first light. In the excitement, I forgot. Any coffee left?" she changed the topic.

"Kathy, do you want to talk about it?" Harriet invited.

"No. Yes. I'm still confused, Harriet. We're not really married; we didn't . . . sleep together last night," she rashly confessed.

"But you are married to him, Kathy," Harriet reasoned.

"Just until he locates my father," she vowed nervously.

"What if Landis isn't satisfied with a pretense?" she asked.

Kathy blushed, then said, "He has no choice. In name only was his idea," she carelessly divulged. "I should be grateful to him, but he's so infuriating and arrogant. It sounded logical yesterday."

When Harriet felt compelled to reveal her conversation with Landis, Kathy was stunned. "Why would he question you about me?"

"I don't know, dear. Perhaps he's curious about his new wife."

"But I'm not his wife," she argued anxiously.

Harriet smiled encouragingly, dropping the rankling subject. They could discuss it again later, when Kathy was calmer.

As Kathy sipped her coffee, she realized she hadn't learned anything about Landis Jurrell. He might never show up again! She didn't know where he was, how long he'd be away, how he earned his money, where he lived, nothing! At least playing the happy bride would guard her privacy and survival. If only he could locate her father soon. But what would Landis expect for his assistance? When the time came, could she walk away from him? She was impatient in less than a day! She couldn't sit idle. But, what else could she do? She felt helpless, trapped. When she voiced her frustration, Harriet suggested she ask Moore's men to help her.

"That wouldn't help me any. They only work nearby. If my father was still in this area or had spent any time here, they would know about him. Since they don't, he's somewhere inland or gone. In such case, what good are those lumberjacks' help? If Landis can't find him, I'll decide what to do about leaving or staying."

"You might consider staying?" she exclaimed, that news stunning her. Did Landis Jurrell have anything to do with her new plans? She had no right to ask or to interfere, much as she wanted to give Kathy some motherly advice. Until she asked, it was improper to offer.

Later, the men came pouring into the supper tent like water rushing over a cascade. Their off-color jokes ceased the moment they entered the tent. Their friendliness and good humor were impossible to ignore. As Kathy served their meal, they chatted with her, congratulating her marriage and telling amusing stories about the prospectors and the local Indians. It was difficult to remain somber when surrounded by such gaiety and courtesy. When supper was over, the two women were surprised by the tokens of appreciation left on the tables at several places: small golden nuggets.

Finding them as she cleared the tables, Kathy squealed in delight, "Look, Harriet! Gold!" She collected the

twelve pieces of shiny rock and handed them to Harriet.
"You take them. With these added to your purse, it won't
be long before you can build a proper cabin for your
children. Besides," she mirthfully remarked, "I bet those
apple pies inspired such generosity. I've never seen such
excitement and glowing faces. If I were you, I would buy
some supplies from Moore and bake some to sell to the
other men around here. There's no telling what they
would pay for such a treat."

Harriet's eyes lightened with enthusiasm and deep
thought. "You're right, Kathy. I'll do it! I'll ask Moore if
it's all right first."

"How could be possibly say no? If he does, you could
threaten to go into business for yourself. That should
change his mind instantly. Wait a minute!" she exclaimed.
"Why not save everything they pay you until you have
enough to build a cabin, then cook food to sell? You could
easily earn enough to send for your children within a few
months. I'll help you get started. I'll put up the money for
the cabin. By the time I'm ready to leave, you'll have
enough to repay me."

"I couldn't let you do that, Kathy," she argued softly,
yet a dreamy look came to her eyes as she pondered this
incredible plan.

"Why not?" Kathy inquired with a brilliant smile. "If
the money is invested in a log cabin, it can't be stolen.
Besides, a cabin would allow us some safety and privacy.
it's the perfect solution for both of us. I'm going to do it!"
she announced as if the whole matter was settled right
then and there. "I'm going to hire Moore in the
morning."

Harriet speculated on these optimistic plans. Kathy
was right; it was an excellent compromise. "It's a wild
scheme, but I love it! Count me in," she hastily agreed

123

before she could change her mind.

When Harriet tried to divide the gold nuggets, Kathy refused to accept any. "Save them for buying goods for our new home. If we make a list of the items most urgently needed, we could order them when the next ship arrives. By the time the cabin's ready and the supplies arrive, we'll have enough money. If not, I'll cover the expenses."

"I can't let you squander your savings, Kathy. It isn't fair to take advantage of you. Are you forgetting you covered my passage?"

"Don't be silly, Harriet. I have just as much to gain with these investments as you do." Harriet couldn't disagree with that logic. "Later, I'll have the money for ship passage by selling you our cabin. It's perfect: your children arrive and I depart . . ."

"Oh, Kathy, I can hardly wait. Once we have the cabin, it'll make this place seem more like home. But I hope you'll stay on with us. I've become quite fond of you." She didn't ask, what about Landis?

The two females were so full of suspense and hopes that they could hardly settle down to get to sleep that night. They talked and planned far into the chilly night. By necessity, Kathy prevented any conversation about Landis Jurrell. She acted as if she had put him completely out of her mind, which she had not.

After breakfast, Kathy asked Moore to linger. Suspecting she wanted to discuss Landis or his hasty departure, he did with undisguised reluctance. They sat at the front table as Harriet left them alone.

"Mr. Moore, you seem annoyed with me. Because I neglected my duties? I don't expect to be paid for any days I don't perform my tasks. Harriet did both chores so she should also receive my day's pay."

"Is this what you wanted to discuss with me?" he speculated.

"No. I want to hire you to build me and Harriet a cabin. If you can't, then who do I see about such a job?"

Landis hadn't mentioned building a home; he had a cabin near Dawson. Moore wondered why a man would leave his new bride in a place like this, rather than take her home with him. "Wood and labor are terribly expensive here," he politely commented on her farfetched suggestion in an indulgent manner, noting she had excluded Landis.

She looked him straight in the eye and stated matter-of-factly, "There are men starving out there on the beach. Surely some of them could be hired to build my cabin for a reasonable rate. As for the lumber and supplies, I'll pay whatever amount you say is fair. You strike me as an honest, dependable man."

To quickly end the conversation, he sighed and informed her, "A cabin from start to finish would cost you . . ." He became silent to assess the amount of work and materials required. Just to humor the girl, he declared, "A sturdy cabin would cost you about five hundred dollars." He fully expected her to start weeping in disappointment or to cry out in shock.

Instead, Kathy tacitly mulled over that large amount and his patronizing attitude. "It couldn't possibly be done for . . . say three or four hundred dollars?" she debated. She needed money to carry on her search, cash for furnishings, and money for food and winter fuel. She waited while he refigured his blunt declaration. Did he hope she would quit and leave? Perhaps he didn't need or couldn't afford two cooks.

"I suppose it could be done for . . . say three-fifty at rock bottom. Do you realize how long it will take you and

Mrs. Pullen to earn that kind of money? By then, cabins will be costing six hundred to build," he announced, trying to awaken her from her dreaming.

He was astounded when she withdrew a velvet purse from her dress pocket and counted out three hundred and fifty dollars. She calmly met his disbelieving gaze and stated, "Begin our cabin as soon as possible. We would like to move in before winter. I can manage only fifty more dollars. If that isn't enough, can you take the rest from my future earnings? I promise to remain here and work hard until the debt's paid. I won't be unreliable again. Is it a deal?"

"Landis didn't say anything about a cabin. Did he give you this money to hire me?" he asked before thinking. Odd, since Landis had been in a big rush to leave the morning after their hasty marriage! A cabin bespoke a permanent stay. Why two homes?

His boldness shocked Kathy. "This money is mine. He left early; we didn't have time to discuss it. Does that affect your decision?"

"I have to admit this cash and your suggestion caught me by surprise," he meekly explained, even more puzzled. "Are you sure you want to build a cabin here?"

"Yes. I would appreciate it if you don't tell Harriet how much it costs. Then, I can sell her my half for what she can afford."

Moore studied her intently. She surely was a mystery! This situation with Landis didn't make any sense. He wondered if her change of heart had anything to do with Landis's black mood before leaving. He shrugged and agreed to serious consideration of her terms. He picked up the money and shoved it into his pocket, saying he would let her know something definite by tonight. After all, his cooks needed a place to live comfortably, privately, and safely.

She smiled indulgently and commented, "That's fine with me, sir. I appreciate all you've done for me and Harriet."

He looked back at the defiant face of Kathy Jurrell and asked, "Do you still plan to work for me?" From that fat purse, she obviously didn't need to labor this hard, and she had a wealthy husband!

"Unless you prefer not to keep me, I'll be staying here while Landis searches for my father."

"Landis is looking for your father? Why didn't you go with him?" he innocently questioned.

"He said it was too dangerous and rugged where he was going."

"What if your father can't be located? What then?"

"I don't know. I wish there was something I could do."

"There's a Mounty outpost along the White Pass about twelve miles over the boundary, called Log Cabin. Landis will probably start there." The trail between here and there was mighty treacherous.

"I'll have some news for you tonight. See you later, Mrs. Jurrell."

Following supper, Moore informed Kathy of his favorable decision concerning her cabin. He said he had hired four men to cut the lumber and five men to do the construction. He stated a completion date of only three weeks. Kathy and Harriet were ecstatic. Kathy and Moore shook hands and the deal was settled.

Within a few days, a new cabin was underway near the edge of the dense line of spruce trees. Moore had staked out that particular spot because of the protection the trees offered against winter winds and drifting snows. Each morning the two women watched the men performing their varying labors. Each night in the supply tent, they chatted happily. Once the lumberjacks learned of their plans, golden tokens appeared more frequently on the wooden tables.

Moore also agreed to allow Harriet to buy supplies from him to bake pies and cakes to sell. When the next ship came, she promised to order her own supplies and replace his. Surprisingly, the men paid outrageous amounts for the sweets. Harriet's little purse steadily fattened. The men, learning of her sewing skills, hired her to repair old clothes and to alter new winter garments to fit. Kathy wondered where Harriet found the time and energy to accomplish so much.

As for Kathy, she spent her days and evenings either helping Harriet or watching the steady progress of her cabin. The hard work had a favorable effect on her character and body. She became more self-assured and resilient; her body grew sleek and hard. She learned about Alaska and life itself from the amicable, earthy men each night as they related tales and information which she would one day find useful. Kathy shoved fears of Marc from her mind. She couldn't ignore Landis, for his reality was forced on her each day with questions and remarks. Yet, she learned to play her marital role exceedingly well. How she wished he would return, at least with word about Jake.

Slowly a new pattern settled in on Moore's little group; they appeared a family unit. After supper, the men would help the two women clear away the dishes, then sit around the tables. Once the chores were completed, they would often sing songs or play games. Within those first three weeks, the men had become so fond of the two women that they watched over them like mother and sister. The entire settlement quickly discovered these two women were not to be accosted in any form or fashion. In such a kindred arrangement, the women relaxed and bloomed, knowing they had nothing to fear anymore, inevitably adapting to this new way of life.

During that third week, the cabin was finished. The *Wind Rover* anchored with their supplies and furnishings, plus a sturdy lock for their door. Straw and ticking were brought ashore to make their beds. Their stove was carefully unloaded and delivered. The last of their supplies and goods landed in Griff's boat under his watchful eye.

When everything was in its place, the women halted in the center of the cabin to gaze around. Joyous tears clouded Kathy's eyes as they touched on heartwarming gifts from their friends. The cabin was a square of eighteen by eighteen feet. There were three shuttered windows for light and ventilation. Moore had constructed a small wooden opening in the bathcloset to simplify the emptying of water from the tub.

Kathy walked over to the front left corner; she trailed her fingers over the workmanship of the L-shaped cabinets. It would be easy and enjoyable to cook in this efficient area. A square eating table with four sturdy chairs sat nearby, a generous gift handmade by Mike and Griff. A black wood stove completed this kitchen section, a deep box for logs and kindling beside it.

Danny and Fred had skillfully fashioned an elbow angled seat in the left corner; Kathy grinned at its similarity to a church pew. However, with feather cushions, it would be most serviceable. Moore had surprised them with two smaller tables with decorative carvings.

Nathaniel Webb, a carpenter before getting gold-fever, had designed and constructed an oblong wooden frame as their double bed, attaching it to the front corner wall. With most furniture built-in or gifts, the women had little to purchase. Moore had walled off an eight-by-nine-foot area on the right corner wall. He had cunningly divided it into three varying sized enclosures: a clothes closet, a storage room, and a private bathing closet—each with its own door.

The bathing closet was Kathy's delight. Mike had placed several horizontal wooden poles in one corner for drying washed garments and bath linens. A stark white chamber pot trimmed in red sat behind the door. Griff had constructed a long shelf on which to place articles for grooming. Dray had kindly gifted them with a precious mirror to hang over the shelf, a marvelously large tub which sat in the back corner, and four oil-lamps with pink and blue designs.

Kathy looked over at Harriet and laughed cheerfully. "It's perfect. We have everything we need," she happily declared.

Mike playfully injected, "Except your husband."

Kathy smiled and agreed, knowing she should. "He'll be surprised when he comes home. I can't wait to see his expression," she murmured, her real meaning lost to each of them. She missed him; she wanted to understand him; she wanted him here with her.

They thanked the men for their unselfish labors and gifts, much of which had been done at night after a hard day's work on the timberline. The men were overwhelmed by their gratitude and affection as the women complimented them on their talented workmanship and generosity.

"Do you realize how much money you've saved us with all these furnishings?" Kathy thanked them profusely. "I really feel we should at least pay for the wood and supplies used."

"No way," Moore declined for them. "We enjoyed doing something useful." The others hastily agreed. Moore suggested they leave so the women could settle in.

Once more Harriet and Kathy surveyed the entire cabin, laughing and joking together. There was a warm fire in the stove; the storeroom was filled; their clothes were unpacked; and the bed was made. They finally sat down at the table to converse over coffee on this thrilling first day in their wonderful cabin of tightly hewn logs which gave off the scent of spruce. At last, Skagway was home . . .

"Kathy, what about Landis?" Harriet asked worriedly.

"I don't know when he'll return. He could at least send word," she said peevishly. "You know something crazy? I miss him."

"Perhaps that's his plan; absence makes the heart grow fonder."

"I doubt it," Kathy murmured, referring to him, not her.

"What if he brings Jake with him?" Harriet speculated.

"I'll just have to wait and see . . ."

At dawn the next morning, Moore came to inform Kathy his lead cutter was heading for Log Cabin with some reports. Having earned Moore's admiration and respect during these past weeks and having played her marital role convincingly, he was allowing her to tag along. He hinted about a possible meeting with Landis, at least gaining some news about him and her father. Elated, Kathy rushed to her home and dressed in appropriate clothing. The round trip would take two days. She met the genial Mike Henry at the edge of camp. He was loaded with a heavy backpack which included camping

131

gear. They began the long trek over steep hills and slopes, dotted with fragrant spruces and pines and powdered scantily with snow, which hinted at the impending winter. She had wanted to avoid winter, but that was before Landis Jurrell and her many hinderances. Suspense filled her. What if they did encounter Landis or learned something about her father?

The trek required countless hours of demanding, body-racking work. A well-travelled path at least offered some help with this arduous journey. Mike was very kind and tolerant, knowing Kathy's physical condition and stamina did not match his own. She grinned ruefully each time she breathlessly pleaded for a few minutes to catch her wind and to wet her dry throat. Just when she thought she could walk no further and was about to tell Mike to go on without her, he shouted, "There's the lake ahead, Mrs. Jurrell; we'll rent a boat to cross 'er. Just twelve more miles to Log Cabin. You can rest a spell now."

"I don't see how you've had so much patience, Mike. Thanks. This trip is most important to me," she said.

"Moore told me why he suggested you tag along. I only hope these men can help you. Since you and Mrs. Pullen came to camp, things have been so nice. If there's anything I can do to help you, just yell." His bright eyes glittered merrily. "It's such a long, hard walk over here. Course, if Landis is around, it'll be worth it. If it was winter, we coulda used a dogsled. There's snow then and the lake's frozen solid. Sure makes for easier and quicker travelling."

"Don't worry about me, Mike. I'll be just fine." She waited patiently as he made arrangements for their boat, then settled back in the sturdy craft while Mike used his powerful muscles to get them to the other side. He turned the boat over to another man until their return trip the next morning. Within minutes, his pack was in place and they were on the last leg of this exciting trek.

It was nearing dusk when they finally arrived at Log Cabin. They headed toward the Mounty Headquarters. Once inside the oblong, wooden building, Kathy apprehensively sat waiting for Mike to complete his business first. Later, Sergeant Thomas looked up and stated, "You're next, miss. What can I do for you?"

Kathy observed the way his keen eyes seemed to drill into her. "I'm searching for my father, sir," she began, then went on to explain her problem and her disappointment in being unable to find any trace of Jake Hammond. Thomas asked personal questions which she felt compelled to answer if he was to help her. Yet, she deeply resented the curious way he studied her and the indifferent and imperious tone of his voice. The interrogation insinuated Landis hadn't been here to discuss her problem—which struck Kathy as very odd.

Her mind was acutely analyzing his strange behavior. He almost seemed to resent her. But how was that possible? They were strangers. Why was he continually probing her for more information about her father, or rather demanding she tell him things she did not know? He sounded as if he mistrusted her.

When she could no longer tolerate his pressure and inexcusable conduct, she asked, "May I ask you a question, sir?" She hastily continued before he replied in either way, "If you've never heard of Jake Hammond, why are you asking so many questions about him? I've told you all I know. You're the authority. Find him for me, at least some word about his fate. This not knowing is sheer misery. If my father is . . . dead, then I would like to know. Landis Jurrell is searching for him, but we could use your help," she stated, witnessing the sergeant's inexplicable reaction to that news.

"Landis Jurrell is searching for him?" When she nodded, he scowled and oddly commented, "I doubt Landis can assist you."

She sighed heavily. Her mind was rapidly pondering this nerve-racking episode. Obviously this man didn't know they were married. She should tell him before he made embarrassing statements. Yet she hesitated, then probed, "Exactly who is Landis Jurrell and what does he do around here?" causing the man's brow to lift quizzically and his beady eyes to narrow and frost.

In a sullen tone, he stated, "I don't discuss Landis or any other friend with strangers to these parts. What's your interest in him?"

Cautioning herself to disarming guile, she cheerfully answered, "We met in Skagway where I cook for Moore's lumberjacks. Landis and I were married several weeks ago. Landis left to look for my father; I was hoping to catch him here. I guess he went another route." As with her father, Landis Jurrell was a haunting mystery which she needed to understand. She sensed Thomas's uncertainty and dishonesty.

"Married?" he echoed as if stunned. He recovered his poise and stated, "Sorry, Mrs. Jurrell, but I can't help you. I haven't seen him for ages. Don't expect to see him anytime soon either. He stays up north. If I do, I'll tell him you're looking for him."

She almost shrieked no, but realized how foolish that would sound. Besides, she didn't owe Landis Jurrell an explanation. If she was going to search for a missing person, why not begin here? After all, Landis had been gone for weeks! She wished she knew why the sergeant had nearly choked on her new name. Thus ended her unsatisfactory first visit into the Canadian frontier.

On the way to the area where they would camp, Mike and Kathy leisurely strolled along. Kathy glanced at him and suddenly blurted out, "Mike, when I mentioned my father's name, the sergeant looked and acted very strange. I don't like it," she murmured suspiciously. "Something's wrong. I don't trust him . . ."

As he began to unpack their supplies and bedrolls, he replied to her curious statements, "I think you're imagining things, Miss Kathy. The Mounties wouldn't be up to some illegal mischief. I think he was just startled to meet Landis's wife. I do hope you find your father. But if you don't, you have nothing to worry about. You have Landis. And when he's away, me and the other men won't let anything happen to you."

She smiled gratefully. "Thanks, Mike. Everyone in Moore's camp has made me and Harriet feel so safe and welcome."

As they joined forces to prepare their supper, Mike asked, "Why didn't you ask the sergeant to give Landis a message? He stopped in there a while back, and he's suppose to return in a day or so. But don't fret, he'll probably head for Skagway afterwards. I'm sure he's anxious to get home," he innocently commented, unaware of the blatant lies told by the sergeant.

Shocked and angered, Kathy observed him closely. "Are you telling me that Landis went to Log Cabin recently and he's suppose to return there soon?" she asked as calmly as she could manage.

"Yep. At least that's what Moore told me. Anyway, that other Mounty was talking about Landis's two visits. He said Landis told them about you and Mrs. Pullen's cooking. I bet they were envy green," he stated with a chuckle, missing the effect of his words on her.

135

Kathy reasoned on these disturbing facts. Those haunting feelings of trickery washed over her again. Sergeant Bill Thomas had actually gone livid and flustered at news of their marriage. Why lie to her?

As she lay in her bedroll staring up at the full moon and listening to Mike's gentle snoring, the memory of that fateful afternoon in Drayton's cabin came to visit her. Thoughts of that fiery union caused her traitorous body to quiver with longing. Gradually a bittersweet reality settled in: she wanted him desperately, but she couldn't trust him or his friends.

Drayton Cardone . . . He was different from Landis, but they were good friends. He seemed kind and honest, genuinely delighted by her marriage to Landis. In the past few weeks since Dray's return, they had become friends. They had played checkers many nights. He was a well-educated and well-travelled man. Often she sat listening to him relate his countless adventures and tales of daring and suspense, which sometimes included Landis. They had discussed plays which they had seen and places they had visited. Dray's friendship had relieved many lonely hours while she waited for Landis and news of her father. With connections to suppliers in Seattle, he did most of the ordering for everyone in the area. She drifted off to sleep thinking of Landis.

Mike aroused her just as the first streaks of dawn etched the horizon. "I hate to wake you, but we haveta get up and going if we're gonna make home before night." She was up and moving quickly, helping him with a light breakfast and with rolling the sleeping bags into a neat bundle. Once more their laborious walk was under way.

It was almost dark when they wearily trudged into the settlement. Kathy went straight to her cabin to freshen up before heading to the supper tent to help Harriet. She quickly removed her heavy pants, black boots, and parka. After putting on a lovely red dress, she brushed her hair and placed a red silk ribbon in it. There was a knock at the door. When she answered it, Harriet hurried inside.

Harriet was so glad to see her safely returned she hugged her fiercely. "I was so worried about you, Kathy. Did you learn anything?"

"Not enough, but more than I wanted to," she replied mysteriously, then related her intriguing visit to Log Cabin.

Harriet looked disturbed by her news. "I think I would be careful around your husband, Kathy. Evidently there's more to him than meets the eye. What do you think it means?"

"I don't know, Harriet, but I fully intend to find out."

To distract Kathy, Harriet informed her, "We have company tonight. A man by the name of Jack London arrived yesterday morning after you left. From the colorful tales I overheard, he takes big chances on those Yukon rapids. Sounds like he lives as if there's no tomorrow. A most pleasant and genial lad."

"Who did you say?" Kathy asked, becoming alert.

"Jack London. He lives near Stewart, above White-horse. He pilots boats up the Yukon River. The men say he's the best at running those dangerous rapids. He certainly has the size and manner to prove it."

"Describe him," she coaxed. "I might know him."

"He's around twenty, blond hair, very tall. Kind of serious, but friendly. An adventurer through and through. They said he came looking for gold, but gave up his search. Hasn't been here long."

Amazement flooded Kathy's face. "It surely sounds to be Jack. Maybe he can help me, since Landis obviously

137

won't. The sooner I can get this matter settled, the sooner I can get on with my life."

"You know Jack London?" Harriet inquired.

"He's like my brother. We've known each other for years. How can I tell him, Harriet?" she wailed abruptly, distressed.

"Tell him what, Kathy?" she entreated confusedly.

"About mother. Jack's been madly in love with her for years."

"London and Dory?" she ventured incredulously.

"I know, he's practically my age. You knew mother; she looked young; she was beautiful and carefree. Jack wanted to marry her. He wrote her all the time. Until the first of the year . . . At least she told me he quit writing. I thought he'd gone to sea. He'll be devastated. Poor Jack. He was so sweet to both of us."

Harriet left her to fret alone. Kathy quickly finished dressing, eager to check out this new event. She hurried over to the supper tent. As she walked in, a masculine voice sang out, "Kathy? Saints alive, what are you doing here?"

"Jack!" she squealed in delight. "Looking for you."

"Looking for me?" he asked, bewildered.

"I need help, Jack," she vowed, dreading her coming words.

"What's wrong, little sister?" he fretted, wondering what Kathy was doing in Alaska. His heart leaped; was Dory with her?

"Family business, you might say. I need to talk to you privately, Jack. But it'll have to wait until I'm finished here."

"You and I have some catching up to do. You're the last person I expected to see here. Lordy, how you've changed!" His eyes roamed her features. "Is Dory with

138

you?" he helplessly asked.

She inwardly grimaced. "No. I never dreamed I would see a place like this. It's just like those paintings we saw in San Francisco. At first it was awful. Now that my big brother's here, I feel better." She thought it best to have their family reunion and crushing talk in private. "I'll talk with you after supper. I work for Mr. Moore and I'd best get busy. I'll explain everything later."

She smiled, then spoke to several friends as she weaved her way through the jovial group near the front. She nearly froze in mid-step as she saw Landis waiting near the stove, his gaze locked on her. She almost forgot everything and was about to race into his arms. His stance and expression prevented it; he was glaring at her with unsuppressed anger furrowing his brow and squinting his stormy eyes. Surely it couldn't be jealousy on his face? Quickly recovering her poise and wits, she headed his way. She smiled and spoke politely to him before starting her work. After Log Cabin, she found their pretense difficult, something which clearly did not sit well with him. He was unaccustomed to being ignored or embarrassed in public. He fumed in tightly leashed fury; his smoldering eyes warned her to tread lightly. Mistrustful of him, she resisted his previous orders for romantic behavior.

He whispered, "Aren't you forgetting we're married? Is this any kind of greeting for a returning husband? You're playing with fire."

"Surely you don't expect me to fall all over you with hugs and kisses in public? Stop acting like a spoiled child, or you'll make everyone suspicious," she quietly scolded. "I have work to do."

Before Landis could react, Drayton came over to them. "I'm glad to see you two back safely. I told Landis Mike would take good care of you. You two want to visit me after supper?"

Kathy sighed in fatigue, partly for Landis's benefit. "I'm sorry, but I can't, Dray. I'm really exhausted."

Kathy hoped to avoid Landis tonight with her excuse. Without even glancing at him, she could feel the heat from his glare. She almost smiled in spiteful pleasure, but controlled herself. Let him stew for a while like I did, she mentally plotted.

"I understand. You're a lucky devil, Landis. I'll see you both tomorrow." Dray walked off to give them some privacy, cognizant of Landis's foul mood. Would he ever understand this unpredictable friend?

"We'll talk later, Landis; I must get busy," Kathy excused herself and headed to see what needed to be done, needing some thinking distance. The only person at the back of the long tent was Harriet, who was diligently working on the completion of supper. Twinges of guilt chewed at Kathy. She had agreed to do half of the work, but was not carrying out her part of the bargain. The only thing which made her feel better was her insistence that Harriet keep all of the gold nuggets which the men occasionally left for them.

Landis came over to Kathy. In a deceptively mellow voice, he whispered, "Seems you've made quite a few conquests while I was gone. I also hear you have your own cabin now. Been a busy four weeks, hasn't it?" All guilt and remorse had instantly fled his angry mind while witnessing her behavior with Jack. He hadn't expected to find her so carefree and independent. He dreaded her new courage and strength. She had been easier to manage before. Maybe she had forgotten she belonged to him; perhaps he should remind her!

Harriet sensed the mounting jealousy and fury in

Landis and cunningly asked Kathy to fetch some firewood to permit them privacy, knowing Landis would go after her. The other men were still standing around the entrance, laughing and talking, waiting for supper which was half an hour away. Having given his character a great deal of thought, Harriet inwardly winced as her foolish friend unknowingly challenged this valiant figure.

Kathy left to perform her chore, as if Landis hadn't even spoken. Yet, she was reflecting on her complex relationship with him.

He halted her task at the woodpile. "I was talking to you, Kathy," he snapped angrily, gritting the words out between clenched teeth, low enough to prevent being overheard. These past weeks of separation and denial had given him plenty of time to think and to worry. He had not expected this chilly reception! So much for an apology! So much for extracting her from trouble's mouth.

She scoffed, "Then save your energy, Jurrell. I was stupid to marry you for any reason. I want out. I don't need your devious help anymore." Just to test his reaction, she nonchalantly said, "Oh, yes, Sergeant Thomas said to tell you he's expecting to see you very soon." From the corner of her hooded eyes, she observed him intently.

Before he could conceal it, a look of astonishment claimed his face. "Why would he tell you that?" he demanded.

"I think he said something about not settling an issue on your recent visit. How would I know? We were discussing my father, the one you were supposedly looking for these past weeks. Sergeant Thomas's words revealed he didn't know him or anything about him, but I

141

think he does. I thought your Mounties were noted for honesty and assistance. He even pretended to be shocked at the news of our blissful wedlock."

"I'm sure he was stunned; I didn't tell him the good news. Since our little union won't last long, I was trying to contain it here. Your imagination is running away, Kat. Mounties never lie. They might color or conceal the facts sometimes, but never lie without cause. Did Bill Thomas give you any other messages for me?" he asked, his voice strained and his eyes impenetrable. Why had she visited Log Cabin? Worse, why had Bill played dumb! He shouldn't have travelled the Chilkat Pass, since Log Cabin was on the White. At least he would have been given some warning of her actions.

"When did you last see Bill?" she fenced with him, pretending to calm down and chat casually. "You've been gone an awfully long time."

"Why?" he warily insisted, tense and alert. "Afraid I had abandoned you? Did you miss me?" he huskily entreated.

"I'll tell you after you answer me," she parried, smiling provocatively at him. For some curious reason, she calmly rolled up the sleeves on his flannel shirt, disarming him with her mellow mood and enticing attention, her touch and nearness enflaming him.

"I took some reports over for Moore that day after we . . . got married," he wisely changed his statement, sounding as if he had been counting time by that particular day. "Why?" he insisted.

"When will you be going back to Log Cabin?" she asked.

"Why this sudden interest in me and my travels?" he asked, keen senses alive. To trick her into blurting out clues, he teased seductively, "You planning on hotly pursuing me into the wilds? Might be dangerous to get caught alone out there with the likes of me."

Dropping her pretense, Kathy snipped, "Why did Thomas act as if he didn't know who I was, since you two discussed me? He said he hadn't seen you in months and wouldn't be seeing you soon. Methinks he can't be trusted," she stated flippantly. "As for you, Jurrell, I don't trust you either."

"You're contradicting yourself, Kat. Did Bill say he wanted to see me, or he hadn't seen me?" he refuted her baffling statements. How could she know they had discussed her in great detail? What had Bill said to her? Something had her angry and edgy. Then again, he should have told Bill about this drastic change in their tactics . . .

"I must be exhausted, Landis. I can't recall clearly what he did say, except he didn't want to talk about you. He seemed quite annoyed and distressed when I mentioned us. Actually, he became quite defensive and brusque when I asked where to locate you. I definitely didn't like him at all." She returned to her work.

"What are you up to, Kat? Why did you sneak off to Log Cabin? Why did you want to find me? After the last time we saw each other, I presumed you didn't want to see me until I located Jake Hammond."

Without even glancing his way, she murmured, "I don't. I realized you're not even trying to help me. I guess I'll have to do it myself."

"And how do you plan to accomplish that wild scheme?" he sarcastically sneered. "As to your charges, I've been working on your problem for weeks, for all the thanks I get."

"Then why didn't you ask this Thomas about him?"

"Haven't you stopped to consider that might endanger

his life? It's clear he's using another name, if he's around these parts. That means, my golden Kat, he might have reason to steer clear of Mounties. I wanted to see what I could learn on my own before I involved them. Understand? If your father's in trouble or danger, the Mounties will be awfully interested in you, and in your husband."

To wipe the triumphant grin off his sensual lips, she smiled sweetly and remarked, "Then don't keep me in the dark all the time."

He chuckled and murmured, "I'd like to keep you in the dark most of the time. How long have you known London?" he demanded.

"That's none of your business," she asserted indignantly.

"When my wife greets another man more warmly than me, it damn well is my business," he snarled. "Only we know it's a farce."

Kathy started to provoke him with lies, but changed her mind. She was too weary to match wits tonight. "Jack and I are old friends. I haven't seen him in ages until moments ago."

"Just friends, Kat?" he pressed, his tone softening.

"Like brother and sister, Landis. No, more like father and daughter. He sees me as a child. He was . . ." She didn't finish.

"He was what?" Landis insisted gently.

What did it matter? "He was in love with my mother for years. He has no romantic interest in me, nor I him. He doesn't even know she's dead. God, how I dread to tell him. He's so sensitive, Landis. It'll break his heart." Tears sparkled in her eyes as she weakened.

Landis felt she was being honest with him. He pulled her into his comforting embrace. "You want me to tell him, Kat?" he offered.

"I wish you could, but I must. Thanks anyway, Landis." She snuggled into his arms, needing him and this brief sharing of tenderness.

When she heard Harriet call out "Supper's ready," she withdrew and smiled sadly at him. "I'd better go," she said, wanting to stay.

"Why don't you turn in, Kat? You're drained."

"I will as soon as we're finished with supper."

"Can we talk tomorrow? Please," he cautiously added.

"Yes, I think we should," she unexpectedly agreed.

"I missed you, Kat," he stated tenderly, caressing her cheek.

Kathy was afraid to confess her loneliness, already too vulnerable and susceptible where he was concerned. She smiled and took his hand. "Let's go eat," she suggested defensively, leading him inside.

Landis smiled secretly. He would never release her. He envisioned the words in the ship-log and on the license in his possession: Kathryn Leigh Hammond; Clinton Jurrell Marlowe; September 10, 1897.

Six

By the time supper and chores were completed, Kathy was fatigued and frustrated. Her trip to Log Cabin had depleted her physical energy; her baffling confrontation with Landis and her unexpected reunion with Jack had taken tolls on her emotional stamina. She explained her exhaustion to Jack and asked to meet him mid-morning the next day. While Landis was speaking with Moore, Jack walked her to her cabin.

"It's good to see you again, Kathy. But what are you doing here? How did you get tied to Landis Jurrell? Does your mother know where you are?" he fired his questions at her.

Her voice hoarse, Kathy told Jack nearly everything. "I'm sorry, Jack. I didn't want to hurt you, but you have a right to know the truth. It's over, Jack; she's gone. You're young; you'll find another love one day, someone who'll love you in return." For once, she felt like the adult and Jack the child.

Jack hadn't spoken since she began; he just stared at her in disbelief. In his anguish, her problems didn't register. "I guess I don't need to risk my life anymore to get rich to win her," he stated bitterly. "She can't be dead, Kathy," he fought the tormenting reality.

"Please don't do this to yourself, Jack. She's gone forever. Face it; she loved my father, not you. All the money in the world wouldn't have won her," she gently reasoned.

"You're wrong, Kathy; she didn't love Jake, never did. She just wouldn't give up his money and social status. I doubt you ever really knew or understood Dory. I accepted her as she was; Jake never did."

Kathy felt his words came from grief and didn't debate them. To pull his thoughts from her mother and his pain, she asked, "Will you help me find my father, Jack? He's in Alaska somewhere."

He gazed down at her. "What about your husband?"

Kathy lowered her head. She couldn't confess the truth. "Two can locate him faster. This is a big territory. Please," she begged him.

"Are you afraid of Landis?" he asked, sensing some emotion he couldn't comprehend. "How could you marry a total stranger?"

"Why should I be afraid of my husband?" she teased.

He eyed her intensely, but dropped his suspicions for now. "This territory's frightening and deadly, but I'll take care of you, little sister. Be nice to have family with me. A man gets mighty lonesome out there. It's cold and harsh; one wrong step, and you've ended it all. But I promise you'll be safe with me," he declared with self-confidence and a sly grin, assuming she meant to go with him.

"There's no one I would feel safer with than you, dear Jack. This means so much to me. We'll talk after breakfast." Kathy decided it would be best to clarify matters with a fresh mind and body, so she didn't correct his mistaken impression. She said good-night.

Jack remained there for a short time, staring at the

wooden door, cursing the terrible fate which had thrown them together again. As for himself, he was an adventurer and a wanderer by nature. But Kathryn Hammond . . . she was a different story all together. It was good to see a face from home, even under these conditions. She was still like an innocent child. She needed someone to take care of her, someone she could trust. Since she was Dory's child and his friend, that made him the likely candidate. Clearly things weren't right with Landis. Kathy and Landis, what an unlikely pair! Besides, Landis had Michelle in Dawson. Why was he toying with a naive child like Kathy? It didn't take much to figure out why he kept her in Skagway—and in the dark!

Jack couldn't allow anyone or anything to harm his eternally lost love's child, including a man of Landis's wealth and power. This crazy situation demanded some study and investigation . . .

Landis watched this curious exchange from the shadows, too far to hear their words. Kathy had vowed friendship, but it didn't appear that way from where he was standing. If she was too tired to spare her husband a few minutes, she was too tired to spare an old friend a lengthy chat! What would his friends think about her curious actions? He was sorely tempted to walk right up to her door and pound on it until she had to answer it and speak with him, but his pride prevented such an action. She was like tempting gold which plagued and enticed men to risk anything to attain it. In a way, she was just as valuable and elusive, and she could be just as costly and dangerous.

When he returned to Drayton's cabin, Landis spent the first few hours in his bedroll tossing and turning, unable to put Kathy out of his mind. Truth was, if only he could trust her to be what she appeared or claimed.

Yet, he was leery of this golden dream-come-true, this tempting female who asked too many suspicious questions.

Bill hadn't fooled Kathy with his claim of ignorance! She was surviving too easily to be the vulnerable female she claimed she was—only in his presence! Unable to assess her, he pushed thoughts of her aside to speculate on more pressing matters. On his visit to Log Cabin, Thomas had made himself crystal clear . . . perilously clear. . . .

As he tossed on his bedroll, his last conversation with Thomas returned. Bill's last words haunted and alarmed him: "You've got to do it, Clint. There's no other way. Find Jake Hammond and bring him in at all costs. If the girl's his accomplice, you know what has to be done. Do whatever necessary to unmask them. You know what's at stake."

Hellfire! That's all he needed; two devious women and two dangerous men to work on! At least they weren't in the same area. Kathy had to remain here! How else could he find a way to keep her after this mess ended? Now, he had London's interference to handle . . .

That next day didn't improve Landis's black mood in the least; in fact, it made it worse. He silently watched as other people took up every moment of Kathy's time and attention. She had carefully, no doubt intentionally, avoided him completely. She was never alone! Even when she served his breakfast and lunch, she behaved as if he were merely an acquaintance. But with others present, she was all smiles, as agreed. Evidently London had told her something which fueled her mistrust and anger. Suspecting she might be trying to pique him, he also pretended to ignore her. Yet, he discovered his eyes and thoughts on her too frequently to be comfortable.

His loins ached. Damn, he wished he didn't know what it was like to possess her! He'd been an idiot to get tangled up with that golden Kat! Somehow he had to master this obsession for her and get on with his now repulsive work.

He watched her cabin like a hawk after London had gone inside after breakfast. His envy and fury mounted with each hour that passed. What could they be saying and doing? he fretted anxiously. He paced Drayton's cabin until he thought he would explode with the tension straining at his taut body. Hellfire! she was his wife, his woman. How dare she treat him like this? She would spoil everything! His woman? That was the point; she wasn't his woman! He had created a tantalizing treasure which he couldn't enjoy or possess.

That afternoon wasn't any better for him. Kathy spent most of it with Harriet, again in her cabin. Kathy had found him irresistible in the beginning, but she had changed. How would she feel if she learned who and what he was? He had foolishly and carelessly destroyed that initial bond between them, one he needed to regain.

When Harriet finally left, Kathy departed with her to head to the supper tent to help with the evening meal. It seemed forever before that evening came to a close, for all the good it did him. Kathy was laughing and conversing with Jack and Dray. The three of them left the tent to get some fresh air. Nettled beyond reasonable control, he followed and joined them. She appeared apprehensive and cautious.

"Kathy, let's take a walk," Landis suggested genially, eyes dancing with playful mischief. How could she refuse? "I'd like some time alone with my bride before I leave again."

She smiled, seeing through him. "All right," she

readily agreed, realizing they had been acting odd for a newlywed couple. But then again, there was no way they could have any real privacy with Dray in Landis's cabin and Harriet in her own.

Taking advantage of this successful ploy, he took her hand and walked off. Soon, he slipped his arm around her shoulder and pulled her closer to him. They strolled silently toward the treeline. Near it, he halted and looked down at her. "We can't fool anyone the way we're avoiding each other, Kat. We'd better put some effort in this charade, or it's worthless to you. Am I that offensive?"

She looked up at him, moonlight revealing her features. "What do you expect? You marry me, then disappear without a word. You claim to be searching for my father, but I discover evidence which brands you a liar. You're treating me like a fool."

Landis stiffened at her insult. "A liar?" he repeated coldly.

"You were on a survey in the North County. You even had Thomas cover for you. When I discover your deception, you try to bluff your way out of it. Yes, dear husband, all lies."

"That isn't true, Kat. Everywhere I travelled, I asked about Jake. I swear it. I don't know why Bill lied to you, but I plan to ask him. I told you I was leaving that next morning; I didn't sneak out. I also told you I was leading a mapping survey. Didn't I?" he pressed.

Damn, he was cunning! Yet, she couldn't disprove his claims. "If I've misjudged you, I'm sorry," she stated unconvincingly. "But you must admit, it's difficult to play the blushing bride without a happy groom around. You haven't made any attempt to see me today. If anyone's messing up our act, it's you."

"You were exhausted last night. And you've been busy all day. What was I supposed to do, barge in and demand your time and attention?"

"Why not? You did moments ago. It isn't safe for me to go traipsing after you around camp. I told you I wouldn't pursue you or be any trouble. You ordered me to stay here and wait for you. When you finally show up, you make no attempt to explain or see me."

"If you're so good at obedience, why did you leave camp yesterday? You promised to remain here. Checking up on me?"

"No. It wasn't my idea. Moore suggested . . . never mind," she decided, knowing what her explanation would reveal. She pulled free and headed for the protective company of Jack and Dray.

Landis was quickly in pursuit. Before he could halt her, she was too close to them. What did she mean, it wasn't her idea?

"Ship coming in!" the outcry cut into the silent group.

Jack shouted, "Who would sail into the canal this late at night?"

"Whoever he is, he's a bloody fool!" Landis snarled, his tension revealed by his frigid tone, the reason for it obscure to all but Kathy.

"Well, he can't unload until morning," Jack commented.

"Speaking of dawn," Kathy snatched at this opportune moment to leave them. "I had better turn in; it's late and I'm tired. Good-night," she murmured softly, then left hurriedly. Landis scowled.

Dray teased, "Maybe you should carry your bride home with you to get some time alone." He didn't offer the use of his cabin since Landis hadn't revealed a desire to be alone with his new wife, which was the same reason Harriet hadn't generously offered the privacy of her cabin. Both knew why the marriage had taken place, but both also felt it could easily become real. "Too many males around for a beautiful lady alone, even married," he playfully chided his friend, then left to check out the commotion on the beach.

Jack grinned and agreed. But Landis simply questioned the blond giant, "How long have you known Kathy?" He frowned slightly.

Jack shrugged, resisting memories which included his beloved Dory. To conceal his anguish and to extract Landis's feelings, he said, "Not long enough. We met in San Francisco years ago. We spent some nice times together. She's a lovely and exciting lady."

Landis unwillingly nipped at his bait, "A married one."

"Happily?" he brazenly challenged. "I've never seen Kathy so jittery and sad. Why did she marry you, Jurrell?" he demanded.

"Why does any woman marry a man?" Landis fenced skillfully.

"If you two are in love, I'm a snowman. I'd bet my last grain of gold-dust you have some hold on her, one I plan to break, old friend."

Landis clenched his jaw and straightened. "Keep your nose out of my life, London. Kat married me willingly. She's been through some hard times lately; leave her be. I'll take care of my wife."

"From the Yukon? Look around you, Jurrell. This ain't no place for Kathy. Some marriage, you don't even live together, much less in the same area. If you're really looking for Jake, why not take her along? I know Kathy, Jurrell; something's wrong."

"Don't be a fool, Jack. We both know she's safer here. I can promise you, if Jake's around, I'll find him. As to our living arrangement, it's none of your business. But I'll say this much, Kat's a special woman. We married quickly, and she needs time. If there's one thing I know, Kat loves me and wants me."

That smug declaration astonished Jack. "What about you, Jurrell? Why did you marry her?" Jack boldly pressed.

Landis chuckled. "Would I marry any female I didn't want?" he responded.

Jack sneered, "I doubt you do anything without a reason. In your case, Jurrell, desire doesn't supply it. Do you love her?"

"Do you?" Landis sidestepped.

Jack knew this man wouldn't reveal anything to him. Kathy was in over her head. His course was plotted. "Yes, as a sister."

That told Landis a great deal, yet not enough to ease his worries. From his experience with her, nothing had taken place between them. A mischievous grin replaced his scowl as he reflected on a delightful scheme. A draw, the two men parted company.

Landis's chance came sooner than expected. Two men had arrived on the ship, men who needed to go to Fort Selkirk on mutual business with Dray at dawn. Fortune smiling on Landis, Jack was hired as trail guide. Luck riding high, Landis hoped Kathy was unaware of these events. She headed to Drayton's cabin in response to Jack's message. She was intrigued. If they were too busy for breakfast, why did they want to see her? Was Landis still around?

When Landis answered the door, her heart fluttered. He stepped aside and waved her in, smiling. She strolled past him, then turned and asked, "Where's Jack? He asked me to come over."

He replied in a husky tone, "He isn't here at the moment."

"Then I'll come back later." She flashed him a nervous smile. She wanted to ask when he was leaving, but didn't. She was wary of this intimidating solitude. She kept recalling his sarcastic words about their marriage not lasting long. She didn't know what to believe anymore.

He offered an irresistible temptation, "Would you like to view some pictures of the Yukon Territory to see why I insist you remain here? Then, I'll tell you how I've spent these last few weeks."

"Yes, I would," she replied, surprising him with a genuine smile.

He went to his backpack and withdrew several packets of pictures and sketches. He came over and handed them to her. She sat down and began to study the forbidding land which the pictures revealed in bold black and stark white. She glanced up at him and asked incredulously, "Are these for real, Landis? Some of these cliffs look like sheer drop-offs miles deep. Can you walk a trail this narrow?"

"Some of those trails are worse, Kat. In places, the path is slick and steep. If you lose your footing, you can slide downhill for twenty to thirty feet, if you're lucky. You can freeze within hours. As for the rivers, if you fall in, you can freeze in minutes. Even if you're pulled out, your wet clothes freeze. I've seen men lose hands, fingers, toes, and feet. It isn't a pretty sight. Have you ever seen a man crazed by starvation or cold? His mind snaps and he kills for survival. Plus, there're wolves who trace your path until you're too weak to go on or until you get careless. A ravenous pack can strip the carcass of a two-hundred pound moose in half an hour. Evil men prey on the weak, just like the wolves. I wouldn't want to see you injured, Kat, especially not killed. Don't leave Skagway again."

Startled by his unexpected plea, her head jerked up. She met his gaze, etched with concern and tenderness. She glanced back at the pictures as she deliberated the dangers and rewards. "I must, Landis; I have no choice if you can't help me."

"Damnit, Kat! I told you I'd find him. Just give me time, please," he entreated, his voice carrying notes of earnestness and fear.

Fear? she debated silently. Landis Jurrell didn't know the meaning of that word! He was so self-assured, arrogant, and strong-willed. How she would love to steal some of those qualities. "Why are you suddenly so concerned about me and my safety?" she asked, tormented by the tenderness in his eyes and voice.

"I've always been concerned about you, Kat; you're just too proud and stubborn to see it! Why do you think I married you!" he stormed impatiently at her.

"How can I see what doesn't exist?" she shot back.

Stunned, he fiercely disputed, "Then open your eyes, woman! Do you know what it cost to loan you my name? The last thing I need about now is a wife to worry over and cling to my shirt-tail!"

"Your sacrifice overwhelms me! I didn't hold a gun on you!"

"In a way, Kat, you did. I had to protect you. If you had waited for me, I would have married you one day. Do you think I can forget what happened between us? I want you, woman!"

Kathy stared at him, befuddled. Always passion, but no love mentioned! "Are you referring to our episode of blissful ecstasy?" she said sarcastically.

"For me, it was," he exploded in anger, wanting to shake some sense into her lovely head. "If I hadn't protected you, some other man would have. Until I decide why you churn my guts, I'm not about to lose you to another man. Blast it, woman, I've missed you!"

"Stop deceiving me, Landis. Our interlude meant nothing but physical release to you. You wanted a mistress, nothing more."

"You're wrong. To prove it, I'll go back to Log Cabin and question Thomas. If he knows anything, I'll force him to tell me." He regretted his promise the moment he uttered it; he couldn't allow her a hold over him.

"What does that have to do with what happened between us?" she reasoned, eyes blazing with unconcealed fury.

"How else can I prove I can be trusted? We shared something special, Kat. Something you're obviously afraid to admit, or wish to forget! Which is it?" he demanded, the muscle in his jaw quivering in loosely leashed anger. His eyes magnetically compelled her gaze to his. The force of their power brought forth the truth.

"I honestly don't know," she unexpectedly confessed. "I only know I want more from you than you can give. What do you want from me? It was your idea to marry! Why do you torment me like this?" she shouted, pushed beyond self-control.

"I want you, Kathy," he stated simply, eyes soft and alluring.

"But not enough, Landis. Not enough to make any commitment to me. You expect me to sit here waiting for you to show up every month or two to share a day in your bed as payment for your name! I need more than that, Landis. Just leave me alone. If you do have any honest feelings for me, then you'll want what's best for me; and that isn't a humiliating position as your legal whore. I was better off without you. It isn't enough," she whispered sadly, but honestly.

"If you loved me, Kat, nothing would matter except our being together whenever we can. You're my wife," he stated, feeling guilty.

Love? "You're a fool, Landis Jurrell! What about my happiness? What about my future? Should I simply waste away waiting for you? You're selfish and arrogant! It's useless; can't you see that?" she painfully argued against something she dearly wanted. Her voice and expression betrayed her as memories of their shared passion lingered in her mind.

"I know for certain I want you as I've never wanted and needed any other person. I can't lose you, Kat," he hoarsely admitted, his eyes fusing to a smoldering ebony. After all, she was mostly right.

"You can't lose what you don't possess," she wretchedly corrected him. "Perhaps you do want me, maybe even care for me; but I need more than simple affection and an occasional visit to your bed. How can you even ask me to live that way?"

"Right now, that's all I can give, Kat. My life's too complicated and dangerous to accept full responsibility. But things will change. Until then, Kat, I do need you."

"That's my point, Landis. We're strangers. For all I know, you could have another female tucked away somewhere. That would explain your lengthy trips into territories unknown without me. You're my husband; but I don't know where you go, or what you do, or where you live, or how to reach you, or when I'll see you again. Each time I ask you a simple question, you become cool or evasive, as if I've offended or attacked or angered you. We can't even communicate or trust each other." She sighed wearily.

"My business is secret, Kat. If I could tell you about it, I would. If I could take you with me, I'd do it in a blink of an eye. But I can't. It's too dangerous. Must I bear my soul to you to deserve your love and trust?" he flared.

"See what I mean! Why are you so defensive? You act as if you're some criminal with a black past to conceal. You don't have to tell me everything, but you refuse to tell me anything! Love is honest and open. You expect me to accept you on blind faith."

Wariness entered him. Was she trying to force him to reveal himself with deceitful promises of submission and love? There was no way he could expose himself, not right now. Some matters vital to Canada had to be settled first. He couldn't have her without the truth, but he couldn't reveal that critical information—even to win Kathy.

He pulled her to him and said, "I need you, Kat; love me."

His meaning clear, she shook her head. "We can't."

"Why not? You're my wife," he reminded her.

"Not really. If we make love, this marriage will be legal."

"Who'll know besides us? If you want out later, I won't hold you."

If, she mentally echoed. "What will people think if we're alone? Besides, Jack and Dray should return soon."

"Why should it look odd for a newlywed couple to be alone? I forgot to tell you, Jack and Dray left for the Yukon at dawn."

"He couldn't have. He sent me . . ." She halted as he shook his head, grinning. "You?" He nodded, then smiled tenderly.

"They'll be gone for days. We're all alone, Kat."

159

"A cunningly planned seduction, Landis? You calling in my debt? Please, just leave me alone. I can't take anymore of your lies and tricks." Tears glistened on her thick lashes.

She turned to leave. Landis whispered softly, "No matter what you think, Kat, I do love you and want you," he confessed in a brief moment of weakness and dread.

She halted her retreat to turn and gaze at him. "What did you say?" she asked, her heart drumming wildly.

It had been a rash declaration, one he couldn't repeat. "You heard me, Kat. Are you leaving or staying?" he probed softly.

"What about our deal? In name only?" she asked fearfully.

"Is that all you wanted from me, Kat? My name?"

She met his penetrating gaze and earnestly replied, "I don't care who or what you are. I wanted you to love me enough to . . ."

"To marry you? I did, Kat, even though it was impossible. Because you weren't willing to wait for me. I don't give a damn about our bargain. If you can't be alone with me, I won't be back while you're here. I want you as my wife, truly my wife someday, Kat."

"Someday, Landis? Is that months? A year? Several years? Ten years?" she questioned his elusive promise.

"I don't know, Kat," he admitted honestly.

"What if you change your mind? What if I find my father?"

"First, I won't change my mind. Second, if we do find him, how would that change anything between us?" he hinted in dread. What would he do if she loved him enough to confess she was an American spy?

"If you do love me and want me, why can't I go with you? I wouldn't interfere in your work. I wouldn't even question you about it," she promised. If Jack felt it was safe enough to travel inland, it was surely safe enough with her powerful husband.

He swayed her logic when he said, "I couldn't bear it if you got killed or hurt, Kat. How could I concentrate on my work if I'm worrying over you? Please don't ask me to endanger your life."

He came forward and pulled her into his possessive embrace. "God, how I want you, Kat. When I'm away, all I do is think about seeing you again. When I saw you with Jack, I nearly went crazy."

"Why? I told you we're only friends. I explained about mother and Jack. He didn't give me time to break it to him gently. He besieged me with questions the other night. I was so tired I don't know how I got through it. I should have let you handle it for me."

He captured her face between his hands and covered it with kisses. His mouth greedily devoured her sweet lips and explored the passion he discovered there. Smoldering coals quickly ignited into a raging fire which consumed them. She clung to him, almost savagely returning his kisses. Her hands moved up and down his back, savoring the feeling of his hard muscles conditioned by the arduous existence he led. These weeks of loneliness and denial were forgotten in the heat of their need, as were all problems between them. For a time, nothing mattered except this bittersweet yearning to join their bodies and souls.

"Will you stay, Kat?" he entreated, his tongue teasing her ear.

"How could I possibly leave?" she replied, clinging to him.

He eagerly undressed her, then removed his clothes. As his hands moved over her nude body, the fires of passion flamed higher and brighter. Her body was alive with tension and desire. He lifted her and carried her to his bedroll, not Dray's cozy bed. He gently deposited her and lay down beside her. His hands roamed her body as expertly as he roamed the surrounding territory. Enslaved by a heady and uncontrollable desire for him, she could not stop molten lava which flowed through her body. She wanted him with an intensity which surprised both of them.

He entered her carefully and began to move slowly, savoring this moment he had anticipated and had feared to never experience again. "I love you so much it frightens me, Landis."

He looked into her limpid eyes. She had said it all. "I know, love. I can't give you up, Kat. Wait for me until I work things out."

She gazed into his passion-darkened eyes. She smiled happily. "I will. No matter how long it takes," she dreamily promised, ignorant of what the future held.

He smiled just before his mouth claimed hers, very gently to explore and taste the sweetness there. Quivers of desire filled her. Under his patient and fiery assault, all doubts crumbled and vanished. Her whole world seemed to reel and disappear. She experienced those same fierce demands and hungers she had known that first time.

He nibbled at her ear, warm breath calling to her. She trembled in great need. Her arms encircled his back and pulled him closer to her. She abandoned her mind and body to her rising passion, coming to him in willing surrender, entreating the pleasures which awaited her.

As he gradually began to move within her, the feeling was overpowering and tormenting. An intense hunger and ache chewed at her entire body. She clung to him, silently begging for release from this urgent need. Yet, his loving torment continued. He teased her lips and taut breasts with soft and demanding kisses. His hands travelled her body with intoxicating, irresistible caresses. He whispered words of encouragement and temptation into her ears. She moaned in yearning and pressed closer against him. Her whole being was aflame for him.

Landis's pace soon quickened as the fires of passion burned out of control. He guided her to rapture's peak. When he finally carried her over that blissful summit, she cried out his name over and over between kisses. At last, she understood the depth of love and height of passion. She realized what she had instinctively sensed that first moment she had gazed up into his twinkling eyes—this was the man who held her fate and heart within his hands. Now, he was hers . . .

They made love for hours, storing emotions and memories to see them through the days ahead when they would be separated by his work. There was a craving within them which demanded to be sated. He would take her tenderly and leisurely, then suddenly with a savage intensity which almost frightened her. Eventually, they lay exhausted and contented within each other's arms.

Mid-afternoon, Kathy abruptly sat up and shrieked, "What time is it? I've got to get dressed and leave. Don't you see, Landis? If we had a real marriage and our own cabin, we wouldn't have to worry about anyone or anything."

"Please, Kathy, don't make this any harder for us. It can't be arranged right now."

"Why not? We love each other. It could always be like this," she coaxed, unable to comprehend his reluctance.

"Trust me just a while longer. You'll understand everything later; I promise. Not now, love. I'm sorry, but

163

it has to be this way."

"You mean I should just accept what you say simply because you say it?" Kathy lashed out.

"I've already told you, Kat; we can't share a life right now, not for any reason," he declared.

She stared at him in stunned disbelief. "Even after what we just shared here together?"

"Listen to me, Kat!" he angrily stormed at her, distressed. "We can't be here together, but if it makes you trust me more, I could take you to a safe place until I can get things straightened out. I wouldn't abandon you like Jake did," he vowed tersely.

"You mean take me somewhere and dump me. No thank you! You won't have any problems to straighten out. How could I be so blind and stupid!" She jumped up and began to yank on her discarded clothing. "Stay out of my life and sight! I won't be taken in again!"

"Wait a minute, Kathy! I didn't mean it like that."

"You didn't mean anything! That's the problem with you, Landis; you're a liar and a user. Damn you! I hate you! Don't come near me again! I won't fall for any more tricks. Rest assured, Landis; you won't have to worry about me. If you come near me, I'll kill you!" she screamed at him, driven beyond control by his seeming betrayal.

"I won't let you leave like this, Kat. You're wrong about many things." He reached for her, but she avoided his grasp.

"The only thing wrong here is you, anything and everything to do with you!" she stressed. By then, she was dressed and hastily brushing her hair. He reached for her again, but she twisted away. She pulled the small derringer from her dress pocket and levelled it on him. Her eyes were like chips of blue ice as she stated, "I said to

leave me alone. The next time you press me, I'll use it!"
She held the gun so tightly that he didn't see the safety
catch was on.

He locked his wide gaze on the deadly weapon. From
the way she held it, she knew how to use it. From her
expression, she definitely would if he pushed her too far!
There was no need to press.

Ashamed of her wantonness and infuriated by his
obvious pretense, she smugly announced, "Perhaps we'll
see each other soon. Jack and I will be heading inland.
You're no help to me; I'll just have to seek the information I need from some other source. Give Thomas my
best when you see him. See if he wants a report of my
trip, too."

Landis watched her. Kathy never realized that she was
giving Landis the impression he expected: that she was
an American spy—and that she suspected his true
identity . . .

"Goodbye, Landis Jurrell," she stressed his name sarcastically.

Entrapped by their game, he warned, "If I were you,
Mrs. Jurrell, I would watch my tongue and steps carefully. You're not leaving Skagway with another man.
Like it or not, you're mine," he thundered, tempted to
reveal just how legally she was bound to him.

Feeling a heady sense of power since he was so clearly
piqued, she taunted him, "We each have our assign-
ments, so let's be helpful by avoiding each other." She
saucily coaxed, "You handle your . . . business, and I'll
take care of mine." She had to escape this scene. She
began to back out as a skilled professional at this sort of
thing, his numerous slips falling to register in her distraught brain. She gingerly unlocked the cabin door
without taking her eyes from him, expecting him to

pounce on her and halt her retreat. He was such a disarming bully!

Landis glared at his defiant wife, thinking, if your business conflicts with mine, love, I'll see to it that you fail miserably . . . "If I come across your father, should I give him a message?"

Assuming he was only pointing out her need for him, she shook her head and inexplicably lied, "Don't bother; my father's dead." If he thought for one moment she would let him see how deeply she was hurting, he was sadly mistaken! She would continue this nonsensical game to the bitter end! She could be just as poised and cold as he was!

Watching her retreat from a crack in the doorway, Landis's eyes mirrored his anguish and confusion. Jake wasn't dead; but if she wasn't a Hammond, then she wasn't Kat Marlowe. He had overlooked that angle. "No one betrays Clinton Marlowe. My golden Kat, you've a great deal to learn about treachery and passion. . . ."

Seven

Something nagged at Kathy's mind: Landis had appeared to believe her wild rantings. Landis had offered only his name as protection, nothing more. Reflecting on her rash words and actions, she shouldn't have been surprised by his responses. She had been childish and demanding. As with her, he needed time to adjust to this drastic change. Even with a mock marriage, she was his wife. Before she drove him away, she must search her own heart and mind. For her own emotional survival, she needed to take another long and hard look at the mysterious and smug Landis Jurrell . . .

Positively, she wasn't going to pull any information or a commitment from that guarded creature. She wondered what his connection was to Sergeant Thomas. What did Bill know that she should? Perhaps Jake's disappearance wasn't intentional or an accident . . . She must find the truth!

Kathy did a great deal of thinking and planning, as did Landis. By supper, the undercurrents between them were obvious. Evidently it was a marital tiff, so the lumbermen amusedly ignored their battle of wills, joking with Kathy and Landis as usual. Most assumed the newlyweds didn't have enough privacy or were suffering from too many lengthy separations.

Kathy served their meal with speed and skill: things learned during these past weeks. She felt comfortable and safe here in Moore's camp with her friends and her private cabin. But after her visit to Log Cabin and her new confrontation with Landis, she was more determined to get on with her search, impatient for the truth and a resolution to her emotional turmoil.

Landis was in an unpredictable mood—if he was ever predictable. It was apparent he was trying to act calm and collected, but tiny traces of annoyance reached her. During the meal, he caught her eye and grinned, then asked, "How about some coffee, love?"

Several men at his table glanced at him, then resumed their conversations. Moore relaxed, deciding his foul mood had nothing to do with Kathy. Perhaps Kathy was miffed with Landis for refusing to take her into the interior, or perhaps dismayed her husband was leaving again soon. Landis had rocked between moody and mellow ever since that first day of her arrival. Something was eating at his friend, something besides worry over his wife's safety. Kathy was a good kid, a hard worker; Moore and his men liked having her around.

Kathy walked over and filled Landis's cup. She even leaned over and handed him the sugar. "Anything else, dear?" she sweetly asked.

"I'm going to miss this good food and service when I leave."

"You wouldn't if you take me with you," she coyly murmured, hoping to inspire playful nagging from his friends.

Mike and Danny chuckled. Landis glanced at them, then turned to send Kathy a loving reproof, but she was gone. He silently fumed as he sipped the hot liquid and mentally disciplined Kathryn.

"You sure are in a sour mood tonight, Landis," Mike concluded, observing the stormy-eyed man sitting across the narrow table.

"I got things on my mind," Landis gritted out.

"Such as leaving the little woman behind so soon?" Mike teased.

"Partly. Anyone seen Slavin around since I nearly killed him?" Landis sullenly asked his friend.

"Nope, but I heard he headed up Dawson way. Could be to find Doc Farley. You did some heavy damage. We're keeping a close eye on Kathy for you," Mike assured the apprehensive Landis.

"Anyone else harass her?" Landis asked gingerly.

"Not that I've seen or heard. She stays close to Moore's area or her cabin. Who would dare go near the wife of Landis Jurrell?"

"Not to mention tangling with twenty big brothers," he jested.

"More than that, there's also Drayton and Jack."

"I'm lucky to have such good friends," Landis stated genially.

"You're right," he casually concurred, chuckling merrily.

"With winter settling in, those tenderfeet and sourdoughs will be bored and rowdy. I'd appreciate it if you'd keep a closer eye on her."

Mike suppressed his amused chuckles. "Why don't you hang your snowshoes here this winter?"

"I've committed myself to several jobs. When those blizzards fly in, there's no telling how rarely I'll get down this far. She's safer here than alone in my cabin. Course she's a wee bit upset about my leaving her alone so much. She'd be delighted if she knew the Yukon in winter," he mirthfully and guilefully chatted to halt any curiosity.

"Can't blame her, Landis. You ain't had much time together."

"She'll get sick of me later. I've promised her the whole summer." Mike, Danny, and Landis shared their laughter.

To change the subject, Mike inquired, "How's that charting going for the railroad? Those fellows from England making any progress?"

Landis went over his last talk with Hawkins the engineer. "The mapping's finished; the decision's theirs. Mighty expensive plans. It'll take around two years to complete over the route Heney planned. The locals won't like this news. From the troubles inland, they don't take kindly to having their land overrun with prospectors and trappers."

"It'll open up the interior. I'd sure like to see some help with transporting that lumber," Danny hastily remarked. "You think there'll be real trouble when the railroad starts construction?"

"Without a doubt," Landis ventured. "Those Eskimos and Indians don't need more outsiders trampling over their lands and taking their resources. You can't blame 'em. Progress always leads hostilities and troubles in her path, greedy men willing to do anything to prosper."

"I'm sure ole Soapy'll love to have all those workmen visit his saloons," Mike knowingly asserted, grinning guiltily.

Randolph "Soapy" Smith—there wasn't a man in the Yukon who didn't know about him and his devious exploits. Soapy was a feared and powerful villain. Suspecting his gambling tables were illegally run, men still flooded to them to be cleaned out of their earnings. If the trappers would mark their furs as the Mounties suggested, without a doubt, they could be traced to Soapy and his henchmen. Those who had crossed Smith had scars to prove their run-ins with his legendary iron knuckles—if they lived to display them. He was ruthless, cunning, and untouchable. Although the Mounties wanted him behind bars, Soapy stayed one step ahead of them, always covering his tracks. If Soapy didn't supply three urgent needs in this wilderness of countless men—women, whiskey, and gambling—someone would kill him. As a heartless pimp, he peddled women's flesh as easily as he breathed. Once entrapped in Soapy's lair, there was no safety or escape.

"They'll enjoy Soapy's offerings only if the Mounties don't catch him in one of his phony deals first," Landis ventured smugly. "That last crew I guided inland dropped some heavy facts. The Mounties are still having jurisdiction problems with the American Government. About eighty percent of the people in there are from the States. I doubt the locals and Mounties hold to them claiming land as well as gold and furs. If we're lucky, the Mounties will prevent another confrontation with America like that battle of fishing rights." The men nodded agreement.

"How does Smith get away with so much?" Mike quizzed. "You'd think the Mounties would close him up. I'm surprised he didn't get killed for those soap tricks he pulled. Can you believe a man would actually sell soap wrapped in a one-dollar-bill for five dollars? I'll never understand how he earned his name with that trick without getting himself killed. Amazes me how many fools come along every day. Those gals in his saloons are terrified of him. I heard he never lets one leave once she goes to work for him. I know for sure them gambling wheels are rigged. I nearly lost my shirt one night!" he explained, recalling that episode.

171

"Knowing and proving it are two different things, Mike. But the Mounties will nail him one day," Landis vowed confidently.

"Did they ever learn who killed those two Mounties? Two in the last three weeks, wasn't it?" Danny questioned.

Landis stiffened, then coldly replied, "Not yet, but Soapy's hand was probably in there somewhere. From what Bill told me, someone lured them into traps. They'll catch he . . . him. Did you and Kat have any trouble on your trip to Log Cabin? One of those Mounties was killed near there, the same day," Landis casually stated, furtively watching Mike's reaction.

Mike didn't want to reveal Kathy's problems there, so he said, "Nope," but failed to deceive the alert Landis.

"Was that the only time you took her there?" he fished again.

"Yep. Why?" Mike asked, sensing some point to these queries.

"That other Mounty was killed a few weeks earlier, near the same location. I don't think it's wise for Kat to be in that area again. Have you seen any strangers hanging around here?" he made one last try.

"None. But you don't have to worry; she was safe with me."

Mike looked up and politely suggested, "We best clear out and let the ladies clean up. It's getting late."

The men stood up and took their plates and cups to Harriet, all except Landis. As Kathy passed his table, he handed them to her and grinned. "Good food and service again tonight, Mrs. Jurrell."

Baffled by his mellow mood, her gaze was wary, as was her tone when she came back with, "I'm glad you noticed,

Mr. Jurrell."

"Oh, I notice a lot of things, Kat, maybe too much," he announced mysteriously, then swaggered out.

Kathy burned her gaze into his retreating back. Jack tugged on her arm and asked, "Any problem with him, Kathy?"

She turned and smiled at Jack. "No. But what are you doing here? I thought you left with Dray."

"I did, but I only went as far as the White Pass. We met up with Hard-Nose Pete and he took my place. I still have some supplies to pick up and deliver to Stewart. I'll be leaving day after tomorrow."

"You will be back soon?" she asked apprehensively.

"You bet. Make sure you pack warm clothes, girl."

"For what?" she asked, bewildered.

"For our search, little sister," he reminded her.

"I don't know what I would do if you weren't here, Jack. But I'm not sure if I should go along. I was hoping you would ask around."

"You look worried, Kathy. Is something bothering you? Did Landis say you couldn't go with me?"

The work completed, Kathy told Harriet she was going for a walk with Jack. As they strolled along in the chilly night air, Kathy related her visit and impressions about Log Cabin. Jack looked mildly surprised, but not skeptical. "I only know what I've heard and seen about the Mounties, Kathy. But it sounds awfully odd to me. If they do know something and they're not talking, there must be a reason. The sooner we trail your father, the better."

"If they lied, why? And I feel for certain Thomas did lie to me."

"But what could your father possibly have to do with the Canadian Government?" he reasoned aloud.

"I don't know. Do you think it's possible he crossed swords with them and they've done something to him?" she fearfully asked.

"If he broke the law, seems like they would tell you. If he met with an accident, why should that be a secret? Mighty strange . . ."

"Tell me about it! It's driving me mad with weird speculations. Why keep his fate a secret? Since there's no American law here, I'll have to solve this riddle myself."

"With my help," Jack merrily announced.

They sat down on two large rocks near the water's edge, the breeze playing havoc with Kathy's long tresses. She reached up to hold the curls from her face. "It's chilly tonight," she absently remarked.

"Chilly? This is mild compared to winter. No less than mid-fifties tonight. In a month, it'll drop near zero."

They began to reminisce on their days in San Francisco, unaware that Landis was observing them. When Kathy shuddered from the brisk night air, Jack picked up his light woolen shirt and tossed it around her shoulders, then sat down beside her. As Kathy began to respond to Jack's questions about her mother, their conversation was softly muted, suggesting loving feelings and words.

Landis watched from the shadows until he could contain his fury no longer. He casually strolled over to join them. In view of their quarrel earlier today, Kathy couldn't believe his boldness. He propped his booted foot on the rock deserted by Jack and gazed out over the moon-speckled water in the Lynn Canal.

"Lovely night, isn't it?" he nonchalantly murmured.

"It's cold," Kathy corrected him, then stood up. "It's late. I'll talk with you tomorrow, Jack. Goodnight."

"I'll walk you to your cabin, Kat," Landis suggested just to annoy her, taking her arm and leading her away.

"G'night, Jack."

To avoid an unpleasant scene, Kathy kept silent. At her door, Landis leaned over to kiss her. She turned away; he chuckled devilishly. "Is that any way for a wife to treat her husband?" he taunted roguishly.

"Why are you harassing me?" she asked seriously.

"I'm not, love, just trying to play my part convincingly."

To punish him, she responded, "Then by all means do it right." With that, she put her arms around his neck. Drawing his head down, she fused her lips to his, stealing his breath and reason. Before he could react, she stepped away and smiled. "Goodnight, dear husband."

"You're playing with fire again, woman," he warned huskily.

"Since you're my devoted and loving husband, you won't burn me, will you?" she challenged. "Maybe this isn't a bad deal after all."

"For once, I fully agree," he announced, seizing her and kissing her with fiery passion. When he released her, she merely stared at him. "Goodnight, Mrs. Jurrell. Pleasant dreams." He walked away.

She composed herself, then went inside, her body enflamed.

Jack studied Landis for a time after his return, then asked, "What's going on between you and Kathy? Are you mad because I've agreed to help her?" As her self-appointed guardian, Jack felt he had the right to protect her, even from her husband if necessary.

"You know why she shouldn't go inland," Landis replied.

"I don't understand this marriage, or your attitude," Jack boldly stated. Jack wondered if this man realized he knew about Michelle. It was hardly a secret up north those two were close. Jack wanted to ask if Landis had broken off his unlikely relationship with one of Soapy's girls, but wisely didn't probe that area. Maybe he should check it out. He had known Landis for months, and enjoyed wilderness treks with him, but felt he knew little about the man inside. Now that he was in Kathy's life, he wanted to know all he could learn.

"Are you going to take her along?" Landis demanded.

Clearly Landis was riled. "I don't know. She seems worried about displeasing you. Why can't you take her? She'd be safe with you. She's desperate to locate Jake Hammond."

Worried about displeasing me? Landis mentally echoed. "Did you ever meet her mother and father?" Landis inquired.

Jack grimaced before saying, "Her mother, yes. But her father's been gone since Kathy was a child. Why?"

"Just wondering what kind of man he is. Might help my search."

"No good, if you asked me."

Jack's voice and expression said it all, so Landis didn't press him. He asked, "What was Kathy like when she was younger?"

Jack eyed him, then replied, "Kathy spent most of her childhood in boarding schools and the summers with her mother. She hasn't changed much. She's bright, charming, and well-bred. Kathy's . . . Kathy. She's warm and honest. She's good company, witty. She grew into a beautiful and caring woman. Maybe I just feel old, but she's still a carefree child to me. I spent a lot of time with her and . . . her mother. I guess I feel responsible for her. What else you want to know about her?" Maybe he could help Landis understand and accept her.

"Did she ever do any kind of work back there?"

"No, they had plenty of money to live on, enough to travel a great deal. From the way I heard it, Jake Hammond was a very wealthy man. Kathy did play several recitals in San Francisco; she's a talented pianist. I thought she might play concerts later. You can imagine how shocked I was to find her here."

Jake Hammond must have been wealthy if they lived off his money since Kathy was a child. Kathy said there hadn't been any word from him since he left. That meant he hadn't been sending money or messages home . . . or did it?

"Don't you think it dangerous and impulsive to come this far to search for a father who deserted her, one she doesn't even recall?"

"Nope! Wouldn't you do the same in her place?" Jack wanted to deny she was impulsive, but her recent marriage prevented it.

"But I'm a man. I can take care of myself."

"Kathy needs to know the truth. Have you learned anything?"

"Not yet. I nosed around. If he's here, he's staying hidden."

Landis straightened up and gradually flexed his taut muscles. This talk wasn't going far, so he ended it. "See you tomorrow, Jack. You needn't worry about Kat; I promise to take good care of her. If you locate Jake Hammond first, will you send word to me?"

"I'll send word to Kathy; she'll tell you. See you around, Landis."

To avoid a verbal battle with Kathy the next morning, Landis struck out early, stopping later to eat a cold meal on the trail. His first stop would be Log Cabin; his second, Hudson Bay Company . . . The competition between them and the Alaska Commercial Company could shed some light on some nasty events taking place.

Nine days passed in Moore's camp. When Kathy was bored, she helped Harriet. Often fights broke out among the poor men stranded on the crowded beach. Two desperate thieves were taken prisoner by the Canadian Mounties in their splendid uniforms; it was ridiculous the Americans didn't have some form of law in these parts! Makeshift huts sprang up like gaunt guards against the approaching winter.

Other days were spent unloading goods brought to Moore from the ships which anchored in the Lynn Canal. With winter imminent, Moore was stocking up on supplies and gear, victuals and chattles as the men here called them. One ship, the *Carnivie*, was like a floating store. When it anchored, Moore took Harriet with him to select the items needed for his camp.

Dray also accompanied them to the supply ship. He planned to stock up on gear and supplies the "cheechok-hos"—newcomers—would need for spring panning and winter trapping: picks, shovels, ropes, snowshoes and glasses, blankets, staples, weapons and ammunition, crampons, packs, canvas, pans, utensils, steel traps, lanterns and oil, and canteens. He purchased some fishing supplies for the locals. His largest investments included two sleds and five wheelbarrows. If a miner used a sluice, he constructed that himself. Knowing most men came here woefully unprepared for winter or gold-mining, he bought heavy packs, flannel shirts, long-johns, and included a variety of sizes in nailed boots and woolen socks. A wealthy man, these goods were easily covered with furs and gold.

The cooking and service continued to please the men and their boss; the life pattern now seemed indelible. Certain men would cut wood for the fires and others would be assigned the duties of guarding Moore's area or unloading supplies. Three other cabins were under construction by men who believed they had struck it rich and planned to spend the winter in Skagway to challenge the Yukon again in the spring. This labor did have two favored effects on the small settlement: the population and stability of Skagway were growing, and some of the more unfortunate men were given ways to earn money for survival or for departure. Moore's company was also building Dray a larger structure to use for storage and as a trading post, to rival those inland.

Each day, the weather hinted more boldly of what was soon in store for the inhabitants of this harsh area. Heavier snows could be sighted on the peaks overlooking Skagway, and three light powderings of white flakes had touched their settlement lately. The days grew shorter and the winds brisker. Warmer fires became a necessity. The dogs, mostly huskies and malemuts, in the pens to the far end of the settlement, instinctively sensed winter and sleds would soon be a fact of their lives. Their barking and nipping became more noticable each day.

Kathy began to feel pangs of impatience and loneliness. If harsh weather arrived earlier than expected, her search could be postponed until spring. She didn't want that! She anxiously awaited the day when Landis or Jack would return. On occasion, she had walked around the entire camp with either Mike or Dray. She questioned them about the dogs, sleds, the Indians, the saloons, and anything else which caught her interest. It was a desperate attempt to fill her warring heart and mind.

During the next few days, some trappers arrived to sell off what few furs and hides they had taken during the summer months. They sold or traded them to Drayton for supplies for the winter, the big trapping season. Dray spent one afternoon showing Kathy the difference and quality in the furs he purchased. Kathy eagerly accepted any distraction from her cares, disappointed there was no word or visit from her errant and mysterious husband. Even fighting with him was better than never seeing him! Had he dismissed her from his sight and mind?

One ship arrived with letters from Harriet's children, causing her to weep with loneliness. Kathy tried to comfort her, telling her it wouldn't be much longer before she could send for them. "I should send for my horses, Kathy. There's money to be made transporting goods inland for Drayton and Mr. Moore. When I earn enough money, I can build a boarding house. Men could bring their families with them. We'd have a real town then. It's just taking so long."

"You mean take goods over the White Pass like those men?"

"I could do it. I've worked hard all my life, Kathy. Think of the money to be earned. I could sell pies over there, too."

It sounded like a wild scheme, but Harriet could pull it off if she wanted to. "I'll help if I can, Harriet," she generously offered.

"You're a dear girl, Kathy. You know who's coming today?" she suddenly changed the subject.

"Who?" Kathy uneasily responded, hoping for and against her reply being Landis Jurrell.

"That Soapy Smith everyone's talked about."

Kathy laughed at the look on Harriet's face. "He's quite a legend here. Might be interesting to meet him."

"Surely you don't mean that! He's dangerous and wicked," she warned, watching the spark of intrigue in

Kathy's sapphire eyes.

"How often does one get the opportunity to meet such a colorful character?" she teased, tugging Harriet's red curls.

"If I were you, I would stay clear of a man like that."

That afternoon while the stew was simmering, Kathy left the tent for a reviving walk. Her eyes widened in astonishment. A man came riding into Moore's area on a huge white stallion. Kathy observed the stranger from a short distance. He was wearing a white silk shirt, a black suit, a wide sombrero, and knee-high boots in shiny black. A diamond stickpin glittered on his ruffled shirt. His features were dark, partially concealed behind a black beard neatly trimmed to a devilish point. An undeniable air of arrogance and self-assurance emanated from him. She wondered if this could be the notorious Soapy Smith. He certainly made an unforgettable impression!

The man radiated prosperity. The way his eyes darted about, he seemed a man who was well aware of all that went on around him, a man in full command of his destiny and those around him. His expression was smug and insolent, reeking of power. Yet, there was a sinister aura about him. Kathy recalled the rumors about him. If so many people knew about his crimes, why didn't the Mounties arrest him? Was everyone here terrified of him? Or was he simply too cunning to avoid capture?

Kathy shrugged. If all those rumors were true, someone would have killed him by now. It simply wasn't logical.

As Kathy headed for the tent, Smith prodded his horse over to her, halting the massive animal in her path. Kathy came to an abrupt stop and glanced up at the audacious stranger. Shielding her eyes from the glare, she softly demanded, "What is the meaning of this, sir?"

"Do my eyes deceive me, or am I viewing the most exquisite creature alive?" he silkly murmured, twirling his midnight mustache with clean fingers that had neatly trimmed nails. "Randolph Smith at your service, ma'am," he added, removing his hat and bending forward in his saddle in a respectful manner.

Kathy flushed at his brazen manner and piercing gaze. "I beg your pardon?" she stated in surprise.

On closer inspection, he was a striking man. The coldness in his deep eyes had been replaced by a curious sparkle. He smiled and asked, "Whom do I have the pleasure of addressing?"

To prevent any further discussion, she stated crisply, "Mrs. Landis Jurrell, and I have no need of your services, Mr. Smith."

"Perhaps in the future," he hinted, eying her closely, his interest and pleasure vivid. "It isn't often we get such a lovely creature up this way. Needless to say, I'm well acquainted with your husband."

Kathy wisely remained silent and watchful, her intrigue captured by his mention of Landis, more so by his curious expression.

"But why is such a beautiful wife slaving in a place like this?" he asked, fully expecting to be answered. When Kathy inhaled sharply at that bold inquiry, Smith quickly changed the subject. "Have you located your father yet?" he answered distinctly. "I've heard your husband is seeking him for you."

"Not yet. But I'm sure Landis will locate him soon," she calmly announced. "If you'll excuse me, I have chores."

Before Kathy could hurry off, Smith offered, "If you wish, I can ask around for you. I have many contacts in this territory."

"I'm sure you do, Mr. Smith. If you do hear anything, I would appreciate your sending me word," she tried to terminate the conversation once more.

"Why not stop by my establishment after you join your husband? If I receive any news, I'll tell you then," he stated, his tone guarded and unreadable, sounding as if she were the reason for his visit.

"I'm waiting for Landis here," she informed him.

Smith glanced overhead and sighed. "I fear winter will alight before he succeeds. If you do come inland, I would consider it an honor to grant you my hospitality."

Kathy stiffened noticably. Smith quickly added, "I have rooms to rent over my saloons. It would be easier for you . . . and Landis to carry out your search from Dawson."

Smith appeared well informed on everything and everyone in the area. Was her imagination running wild, or did it sound as if Smith was trying to entice her and Landis to his saloon? That was absurd, so she dropped her suspicions—too quickly . . .

"I see you do not trust me. Ah, lass, such are the pitfalls of wild rumors. I could be of valuable assistance to you. This area is mighty expensive and dangerous in winter. But of course, with a wealthy and powerful husband, you would have no need of my offer."

Kathy uncontrollably reacted to that news, just as Smith hoped. His conclusions were accurate as usual; she knew little of Landis Jurrell! So much the better, for he knew more than enough . . .

Kathy wondered at Smith's meaning when he said, "If you ever find yourself in dire straights, Mrs. Jurrell, please call on me. I can offer you a job, protection in my territory, and help with your search."

"I beg your pardon?" Kathy stated as if insulted, confused.

"This is a hazardous territory, Mrs. Jurrell. Husbands often get killed. If you know cards, a faro or roulette dealer earns a great deal of money. Also, there are several theaters if you are versed in acting. Bored men pay hefty for their entertainment. I wouldn't offer a lady a job in my dancehall," he lazily clarified. "And it's plain to see you are a lady of good breeding. If you ever have need of earning money quickly, come to see me. I'm sure I can find a respectable position for a woman of such fine quality and intelligence."

"I'm happily married, Mr. Smith, and I'm certain no harm will come to Landis. Besides, I know nothing of card games, nor am I an actress. I do play the piano and sing, but never in establishments such as yours," she stated.

"Luck rides with me today!" he shouted in excitement. "You could earn a fortune singing and playing for entertainment. Most days, I take in six to eight thousand dollars. Do you realize how much there is to be made with your talents?" he speculated with enthusiasm.

"As I said, I'm not, and never will be, interested in such work. Good day, Mr. Smith."

"I'm a businessman, Mrs. Jurrell. I would be a fool to pass up such a golden opportunity. It would be profitable to both of us. At least give it some thought," he urged, smiling broadly.

"No, thank you. If you'll excuse me, I already have a job."

Kathy walked away, her skirts swaying with her movements. She entered the tent and was lost to Smith's sight, but not his roving mind. When his sidekick Zack joined him, Zack chuckled wickedly and remarked, "I know that look, Soapy, but she ain't like the other women. Forget her. She's Jurrell's woman, and we don't need more trouble with him."

"You're blind, my friend. Kathryn Jurrell will soon be ripe for the plucking; I'll see to it. That golden dream is worth a fortune, one I plan to collect. Time, Zack, that's all I need. Mrs. Jurrell?" he sneered skeptically, then threw back his head and laughed heartily.

"She don't look the loose type to me," Zack noted enviously.

"That isn't what I have in mind for Mrs. Kathryn Jurrell."

"I don't follow you . . ."

"No? But she will. If her father's alive, I'll make sure she never lays eyes on him. Once she gets inland, she won't leave."

"You can't hold her prisoner. You forgetting about Jurrell and the Mounties? They're real touchy since those other two went and got themselves killed," he murmured satanically, chuckling.

"There are ways of holding women captive without breaking any laws, my ignorant friend, many ways . . . And just as many paths of revenge. Twisted justice, Zack; Jurrell will dig his own grave."

Kathy didn't see Smith again until the next morning at breakfast when he ate in Moore's tent. He was very polite and cordial, but Kathy avoided him as much as possible. After the meal, Kathy and Harriet were clearing the tables. Smith had left six gold nuggets for them. When Harriet discovered them, she remarked, "You take 'em. I don't care to have that kind of money in

185

my pouch."

"You think he stole it?" Kathy teased her friend.

"No doubt he did, one way or another! You be careful, Kathy. I saw the way he kept watching you. He gives me the shivers."

Kathy halted her work to look at her. "He's probably just curious about me," she tried to dispel Harriet's uneasiness, which matched hers.

Harriet declared nervously, "I hope he leaves soon, or Landis hurries back." The older woman frowned at her innocent slip.

"Me, too," Kathy responded instantly, then grimaced.

"Do you, Kathy?" she asked in concern.

"Honestly?" she inquired, sounding weary and sad.

At Harriet's nod, Kathy said, "Yes and no. Is that honest enough?"

"You love him, don't you?"

"I suppose so," Kathy admitted, then wished she hadn't.

"Do you think you can work things out if he comes back?"

At wit's end and desperately needing advice, Kathy confided the truth behind their false marriage to her friend, but did not disclose the nature of their fiery relationship and her personal feelings.

A man returned to speak with Kathy, but halted as she began her engrossing confession. Neither female noticed the dark shadow which hovered ominously outside the doorway . . .

"He could change his mind," Harriet said.

"I doubt it. Besides, he's as much a mystery as my father. I don't have the energy or wits to solve two puzzles. All I need is the use of his name until I find Jake," she falsely alleged.

Harriet and Kathy briefly analyzed her trip to Log Cabin once more. Then Harriet asked, "Have you given any thought to methods?"

"Yes, Jack's going to help me." Kathy went on to explain Jack's suggestion and her reluctance to accept it.

"What about Landis?"

"I'm not certain he's really helping me. I can't trust him. Time will tell," Kathy murmured, suddenly dejected and frightened. She recently began one new life; soon another one would be glaring her in the face. Well, she couldn't dwell on that crisis yet. The women returned to their chores, the conversation halted.

A business meeting took place between Dray and Smith. When it was over, Dray sent for Kathy. When she entered his cabin, he looked at her strangely. Was it about Landis? "Is something wrong, Dray?"

"Smith told me he offered you a job in Dawson. Why?" he came right to the point.

She looked confused. "I have no intentions of working for Mr. Smith. Why would he mention it to you? It was probably a joke."

"Smith doesn't joke, Kathy. He's up to something. I'm worried about you. Do you really think it's wise to head inland with Jack?"

"How did you know about . . . Landis!" she concluded in annoyance. Dray was his close friend, but he had no right to reveal their secrets!

"I don't like Smith having his eye on you," he blurted out.

"I'm perfectly safe. Besides, I haven't made a decision to go inland. I'm waiting to see what Landis learns. Has there been any word about him from the trappers?"

187

"Not yet, but I keep questioning everyone who arrives. Don't fret; he'll be home soon. The Yukon's a big territory."

Kathy thought she would scream if one more person made that same comment. She smiled indulgently and left.

Dray wanted to question and advise her, but held his tongue. Maybe he should try to get word to Landis about Smith. He dropped that precaution; Smith was leaving, and Landis should return soon. Dray leaned back in his chair and mused on these incredulous occurrences. Kathy was a charming girl. It was obvious she was in love with Landis and wanted to be at his side. What Dray couldn't understand was Landis.

Why was Landis asking so many questions about his own wife? The first thing he did every time he returned was interrogate certain people about her and her actions. Oh, he did it furtively and skillfully, but Dray wasn't fooled. Jealousy? Worry? Insecurity?

Landis was furious about Kathy's plans with London. Dray didn't blame him, but neither did he understand his mysterious and moody friend. Landis kept on the move, mostly alone, which seemed to suit him. He showed up every so often to sell furs, furs Dray had accidentally discovered had been purchased from Eskimos! Other times he traded gold for supplies, gold he had supposedly panned from a claim he never worked. Tough and cautious, there wasn't a man or danger he feared. Maybe he was intrigued or fascinated by Kathy, enough so to tie her to him. But Landis seemed unwilling to change, to permit her company.

Dray fretted over his wild speculations and budding suspicions. Dray had gotten the impression Landis didn't trust Kathy. It must have something to do with his business, whatever that was; for certain, it wasn't trapping and panning! Or with her father, for Landis had an uncommon interest in Jake Hammond. Landis was trouble where foes were concerned. It was rash for anyone to pit himself against Jurrell.

After supper, Kathy was clearing the tables. The tent was deserted by everyone except Smith, Kathy, Harriet, and two of Smith's men. Burning with intrigue, Kathy determined to use her wits to discover any clue Smith held. Under the guise of idle curiosity, Kathy allowed Smith to begin a conversation with her. They talked about countless subjects, Kathy doing the questioning and Smith the answering. Having related her plan to a worried Harriet, her friend stayed in the tent. Smith knew she wanted information from him, and he patiently waited to ensnare her.

"I'm afraid your quest might be in vain. You've got to keep in mind, Mrs. Jurrell," Smith leaned forward and spoke amiably, "the lumberjacks see few people except other lumberjacks or friends. The Mounties are concerned only with lawbreakers. The men who come to Skagway are usually picking up supplies or gear, or they come to sell furs and gold. If you stay here, I doubt you'll glean any information. As to your husband's search, I'm doubtful anyone will confide in him. He has a way of making people nervous. Most people in these parts mind their own affairs; they don't like investigations."

"You sound as if you don't like my husband," she boldly said.

She was shocked by his next words. "I don't. We've had several run-ins. Jurrell's like a law unto himself; men don't tangle with him. He leads a dangerous life. A man like that earns lots of enemies. He isn't a threat to have at your back, day or night."

Kathy knew how she should react to his insulting words, and she did. "I don't care to hear such remarks about my husband, Mr. Smith. If you'll excuse me, I'll say goodnight."

Smith chuckled. "At least allow me to thank you, Mrs. Jurrell."

Puzzled, Kathy asked, "For what?"

"For taking Jurrell out of circulation. All my women are crazy about him. When he comes to my saloon, they fight over who's going to entertain him. Maybe there'll be some peace and quiet now." He eyed her intently to test her reactions to those statements.

Kathy knew he was playing some game with her, so she curtly declared, "I don't blame them. But I do hope you'll tell them he's married now. I wouldn't want your girls embarrassed." Kathy realized Smith had said "comes," not came. "Goodnight, sir."

He grinned and stated, "Pleasant dreams, Mrs. Jurrell."

Once inside the cabin, Kathy threw her cape on the bed and paced the floor. Harriet looked at her. "Something troubling you?"

"I'm just tired. Goodnight." She was quickly changed and in bed. Harriet accurately felt it was to avoid a discussion about Landis.

Smith went to the tent his men had put up for him. Considering recent events, perhaps Kathy was the perfect diversion. He sighed dramatically, but such a beautiful and innocent scapegoat . . . When his plan was finished, he called Zack inside to relate it. "You know what to do after breakfast. Timing is everything, Zack. Don't fail me," he cautioned, handing Zack his newest scheme . . .

Eight

As Kathy began to clean the cabin the next morning, a knock sounded loudly on the door. She went to answer it, finding a stranger standing there holding a letter. "Landis Jurrell hired me to bring this letter to Mrs. Jurrell. I was told she lives here," he said.

"I'm Mrs. Jurrell." Kathy reached out to accept it, thanking him. She closed the door and hurriedly opened it. Anticipation raced through her. She quickly scanned the contents, greatly surprised by the words there. Slowly and carefully she read it again:

Kathy,

If Mike hasn't left for Log Cabin, come with him. I'll meet you with Jack. News about your father. Bill's going to help us. Problems up here. I'll be at Log Cabin till morning. Can't come to Skagway. Unless you've changed your mind, it appears you won't need to borrow my name much longer. . . .

Landis

Kathy jumped up to pace around. Should she go meet him? How could she refuse? If Mike hadn't left already, time for action was short. The last sentence ripped at her heart. How could she lose him? Changed her mind? Could that mean . . .

Kathy rushed over to Moore's tent, catching him just as he was leaving. She anxiously revealed her news. Moore informed her Mike had been gone for two hours. Her expression mirrored her tension and dejection. At the height of her dilemma, Smith joined them.

"I was leaving, so I stopped to say goodbye. It was a real pleasure to meet you, Mrs. Jurrell. I couldn't help but overhear your troubles. I'd be honored to deliver you to Log Cabin; it's on my way."

"No thank you, Mr. Smith," she politely refused.

"Come now, you'll miss your news and your husband. Ask Moore if it's safe to travel with me," he challenged, knowing Moore wouldn't speak against him to his face. When Kathy didn't respond, Smith insisted, "Tell her, Moore. What possible reason prevents her trip?"

Backed into a corner, Moore replied, "Don't see why you can't tag along to meet Landis. Traveling by horse, you could overtake Mike." Moore didn't want Smith's vengeance turned loose on him and his men. Besides, Landis was waiting for her. Smith had cunningly figured out this plot.

Should she tag along? There was no indication in Landis's message as to when to expect him if she didn't go. She had no choice.

"You don't have to go," Moore hinted.

"I thought you wanted to join Landis and find your father," Smith refreshed her two desires. "Whatever. Goodbye," he said.

Kathy panicked. There was no time for lengthy deliberation. "I suppose you're right. I'll be ready in ten minutes."

Smith smiled politely and said he would be waiting. Kathy hurriedly changed into pants, boots, and a parka. She wrote Harriet a note explaining her hasty departure, leaving Landis's note with it. She stuffed some clothes into a pack and quickly joined Smith outside. As he took the burden from her, she called Griff over.

"Griff, will you watch the cabin until Harriet returns? I'm going to Log Cabin to meet Landis," she rapidly announced her plans.

Griff glanced at Smith, then nodded. "Ye be careful, Missy. I'll hold ye responsible for her safety, Soapy."

"She'll have my protection. You needn't worry. She'll join up with her husband at Log Cabin," he genially attempted to ease Griff's disquiet, and to further disarm Kathy.

With that, Kathy was helped to mount one of Smith's horses. They rode off toward the trail to the White Pass. The moment Harriet returned from the supply ship, Griff rushed forward to relate the news.

"She wouldn't!" Harriet squealed, paling.

"She was going to join Landis," he added.

"Maybe she left a note," Harriet stated wishfully. She went to the cabin and discovered, not one, but two.

Moore knew Harriet would be distressed, so he stopped by to explain, "She was anxious to find her father and see Landis. She'll be fine. They should arrive by dusk."

Harriet shook the note in his face. "Read it," she almost shouted. Moore did, but failed to grasp her point. "He always calls her Kat. And he knows Mike leaves at dawn," she expressed her fears.

Moore debated, "Look what it says. Who else knows

such things?"

"Someone does. That note isn't from Landis Jurrell."

Moore scowled, then said, "Even if it's a trick, Smith will guard her. Once she gets to Log Cabin, she'll find help there."

"What about that insidious Smith?" Harriet speculated in dread.

"We all know she's with him. He won't harm her. Once she's with Sergeant Thomas, she'll discover the truth. She's smart."

After Moore left Harriet to fret over Kathy's departure, he decided to send a man over to make certain she reached Log Cabin all right. If Landis got waylaid, she'd be stranded.

This trip by horse was much swifter and easier than walking. Smith's group arrived at the lake and rowed across while two men swam the horses over. They made their destination by mid-afternoon. The trail to this point had been narrow, causing them to ride single file, denying any conversation. It widened before the clearing for Log Cabin.

Smith slowed his mount to permit Kathy to catch up with him. Just as they entered the clearing, Kathy's gaze caught sight of a towering physique she would recognize anywhere. Her heart leaped with joy and suspense. Leaning negligently against a porch post and deep in conversation with a Mounty, Kathy saw Landis before he saw her.

Smith hadn't expected Jurrell to really be there and quickly altered his devious plan. He glanced at Kathy, aware Landis's ego would suffer at seeing this exquisite creature travelling with him. What man wouldn't find her compelling? Too bad he needed her for other reasons, critical ones. He couldn't afford a slip-up now; if the Mounties wanted a "golden dream," he would supply one. Who better than a stranger who made them wary? Kathy had stepped into Smith's trap when she unknowingly revealed the Mounties' suspicions . . .

Smith laughed and quipped, "See, safe and sound as promised."

Ecstatic, she cheerfully said, "Thank you, Mr. Smith."

Smith chuckled, not at Kathy's words, but at the expression on Jurrell's face: total shock, then fury, branded Landis's face at the sight before him. So, Jurrell was really interested in his little wife. So much the better for Smith's plans . . . and Jurrell had it coming! If it could be proven the Mounties couldn't handle this territory filled with Americans, perhaps Canada would sell it, as Russia had Alaska. All it required was courage, money, time, and daring to destroy the telegraph's plans, to devastate the impending railroad's progress, to harass the men who worked for Hudson Bay Company, to secretly rile up the locals, and to prove the famous Mounties were powerless. That is, stop all progress until America could take over and make him territorial governor. It wouldn't take much plotting from Smith; America and Britain had been disputing over Canada for years.

Besides, Smith already had several American corporate interests on his side, just waiting until he gave the word to move in and take over the resources here. If his partners in America could settle the unrest over the Federal control over the railroads and he could hinder the Close Brothers of London's plans, the new railroad could belong to them! He had been shrewd to stir up the Eskimos and Yukon Indians against the invading trappers and goldminers, not to mention the fishing industries' intrusion. It would be impossible for a handful of Mounties to handle so much unrest over such a vast area. And if Jurrell could be distracted by the blond beauty, he would have that much less time to devote to observing Smith.

They rode forward and dismounted, Smith helping Kathy down. He grinned at Kathy before stating, "My pleasant duty's over. You men, rest and water the horses. Until our next meeting, farewell, my lovely lady," he said to vex his foe, tipping his hat to Kathy.

Kathy smiled timidly at the glaring Landis, then wondered at his glacial reception. Smith walked past the seething man without speaking and entered the station. When Landis didn't approach her or speak, Kathy walked away from the hitching post, heading toward the treeline. Not having been on horseback for a long time, she flexed her back muscles and gently massaged those taut ones near her waist. She halted some distance from the Mounty Headquarters and leaned against a tall pine, inhaling the fresh air, closing her eyes, waiting.

Kathy could sense Landis's approach. She had put some distance and privacy between her and the others with the hopes he would follow her and explain his outrageous conduct. So much for playing his role.

"What the hell are you doing here with Smith?" he exploded in a tight voice. Surely she wasn't working with him? he thought.

Kathy's eyes flew open. "I beg your pardon?"

"I asked what you're doing out here alone with Smith and his men!" he gritted out between tightly clenched teeth.

How dare he speak to her this way! "I heard you the first time, Mr. Jurrell. Mike was already gone. I had no choice but to travel with him," she told him angrily, her eyes flashing blue fire at him.

"Do you know who he is, Kathy?" he demanded.

"Of course," she murmured in a rankled tone.

"Then, do you know what he is?" he snarled, his body taut with fury and frustration. "I should strangle you."

Nettled by his stormy attack, she sarcastically said, "I suppose he's a man. But alas, science wasn't my best subject."

"You're asking for it, woman! He's the biggest criminal in these parts. What are you doing here with him?" he asked warily, piqued by her nonchalance and daring.

"Asking for what, Mr. Jurrell?" she stormed back at him.

"You're asking for trouble. I can't believe Moore and Harriet would let you leave camp with that . . . snake! You should be spanked."

"Well, they did," she said to taunt him.

"Are you out of your mind? You're my wife. You can't go traipsing around with other men!" he berated her.

"Stop being so hateful. I told you, he was the only one coming this way. Where's Jack? What news do you have for me? Spit it out and we can complete our business. I didn't come here to battle with you."

"You're doing this to hunt for your father?" he asked incredulously. "Why the hell did you come here?"

Kathy stared at him. "Because of the note, you devil! If I had known you would act like this, I wouldn't have come!"

Landis assumed she was referring to a message from Jack, but why head to meet him in Smith's company? "How did you get mixed up with Smith?"

"He's been in Skagway for days. He offered to help me."

"I guarantee Smith won't help you anywhere, but into the beds of his saloon. Once he gets his slimy hands on you . . ."

She reached up to slap him, but he seized her wrist in a painless grip. "You filthy-minded bore! I'm not going to Dawson. He was bringing me here. How dare you suggest such a thing! I'm not a tramp!"

"I never thought you were," he snapped back.

"Well that's how it sounded! Now release me this instant."

"You want to find your father this badly, Kat?" he asked, his tone and mood suddenly mellow. Perhaps even contrite?

"That's why I'm in this godforsaken land. I hate it here. There's too much suffering and sacrifice. I want to get on with my life. I need to find him," she stated in a voice laced with frustration and sadness.

"If it's that important to you, then get your things; you're coming with me," he impulsively stated.

"Coming with you? Where?" she asked in astonishment.

"I don't know. Wherever Jake Hammond is. We'll look until we either find him or we're certain he isn't here."

"But you said you wouldn't take me inland," she argued.

"You can't expect me to leave my wife in the clutches of that vulture. If you're this set on going inland, then I'll take you. If I don't beat some sense into you first," he fiercely declared.

"Why this sudden change of mind? You afraid I might find him before you and Thomas? Why did you ask me to come if you're going to treat me like this? You don't have to attack me for one mistake."

"What are you talking about? You've got one wild imagination, Kat. I haven't discovered anything. Maybe I did treat you badly, but that's no reason to get tangled up with Smith. Are you trying to spite me or make me jealous? What if I hadn't been around today?"

"You arrogant fool! I'm not trying to make you jealous or spite you. I have more important things on my mind!"

"Listen to me, Kat; Smith is dangerous. If you don't believe me, ask anyone in this entire territory. One of Bill's men can take you back to Skagway. If you don't want to come along with me, then wait for Jack. When I saw him yesterday, he was packing to head down."

"You're not making any sense, Landis," she stated in exasperation. "If you don't have any news, why did you send that letter? You practically demanded I come here today. Now you claim you have no news of my father. And you didn't have to remind me I was only borrowing your name. If it upsets you this much, then take it back. I know you said to come with Mike, but he was gone. I tried to ignore Smith's offer, but Moore convinced me it was all right."

His ploy to unmask her worked, but not as he expected. Something was amiss. "You're the one speaking in riddles, Kat. I haven't the vaguest idea what you're talking about, or doing here. Would you start from the beginning and explain this to me?"

Kathy was utterly bewildered, but she complied. Landis gave that information some keen study. It wasn't possible. "I didn't sent any letter, Kat. I swear it," he vowed, observing her warily. Who could possibly know such details about their marriage besides the two of them?

"You must have," she insisted, her thoughts matching his.

"I just got here this morning, and I was heading for Skagway tomorrow—to try and talk you out of going inland with Jack when he arrived," he added. After Kathy

199

repeated the note word for word, Landis pointed out the same two errors Harriet had astutely noticed.

Kathy paled, reaching for the sturdy tree to steady herself. For the time being, she believed him. "But if you didn't, then who did? Why? Only a few people know our marriage is a sham."

Kathy and Landis stared at each other. Kathy actually looked distressed and alarmed. "Evidently someone knows too much about us, Kat. The question is, why lure you here?" Landis spoke first.

"But I haven't talked with anyone except Harriet and Jack. You're the only other person who knows the truth," she vowed fearfully.

"I'm certain Dray suspects it. After all, he doesn't know we've ... spent time together. If Moore had doubts at first, he's convinced now we're madly in love and happily wed. That makes only five people, Kat, five without motives for this deception. What could it possibly accomplish?"

"Nothing, except earning your fury and verbal abuse!" she declared, recalling his earlier harshness. "How was I to know the letter wasn't from you? Jack wouldn't have sent it and signed your name." Suddenly she brightened with a wild conclusion. "You don't think Moore or Dray would pull this to get us together, do you? Moore did persuade me to come. And Dray's resolved to see us happy."

"I'm willing to bet Smith was towering over Moore when he agreed. It galls me for men to be so scared of Smith. Moore was crazy to let you leave camp. I'll have a word or two for him. As for Dray, he minds his own business. No, Kat, I'm sure they didn't set it up."

Kathy's apprehension and puzzlement were convincing to Landis. "What did you and Smith talk about?

Surely you didn't drop such hints to him?" he speculated worriedly, witnessing her astonishment.

"Don't be absurd." Kathy willingly related her conversations with Smith, including Smith's comments about her husband. When Landis grinned, she asked, "What happened between you two?"

Landis shrugged noncommittally and said, "I'm about the only man around here who stands up to him. He's afraid I might give others the gumption to resist him. As to his girls, that kind of female doesn't appeal to me," he stated smugly, pleased by the tone of her voice when she had mentioned that lie. "Besides, one infuriating vixen is enough to handle, especially when she's the most beautiful one around."

Kathy flushed at his stirring words and expression. "I'm infuriating?" she teased.

"Infuriating, frustrating, willful, and ravishing," he declared.

"So are you, Mr. Jurrell. You're the most arrogant, insufferable, exasperating man I've met. You keep me in a constant state of confusion and tension. I never know what mood will greet me next," she informed the chuckling Landis.

"At least we don't bore each other," he ventured playfully.

"How can we? We're hardly around each other," she chided.

Landis smiled mischievously and hinted, "Is that why you pulled this little ruse, to join me? Don't tell me you're missing me?"

Kathy's smile faded. "Surely you don't think I planned this?"

"I was teasing. Let's see if Bill can help solve this puzzle," he said, watching her. They walked to the structure and entered. Landis poured Kathy some coffee and invited her to sit.

As Smith was heading for the door, Landis remarked, "I hear you offered my wife a job in Dawson, Soapy. Forget it; she has enough to occupy her time and energy." Landis looked at Kathy and smiled. Kathy inhaled sharply and appeared ready to protest his personal implication. Instead, she forced a smile and allowed her baffling husband to control this situation. Yet, she pondered his motive.

"You forget I have a theater there. I hoped to persuade Mrs. Jurrell to bring some culture to this uncivilized land. She sings and plays the piano. It would be most lucrative for both of us. Too, it's the best location to carry out her search," Smith alleged craftily.

"Whatever the reason, Soapy, Kat doesn't belong near a place like that. She tells me you escorted her because of some phony letter from me. You wouldn't know anything about that message, would you?" he asked, his voice and expression mocking. Landis absorbed Soapy's knowledge of his wife. He looked at Kathy, then at Smith. "Somebody's playing a trick on us. I didn't send Kat a letter."

Bill quickly stated, "If someone sent you a note, someone's trying to lure you out of Skagway. Do you have any enemies here, or someone who might want to meet you secretly?" he hinted, unsure of what help Landis wanted.

"No one knows me outside Skagway. I don't think anyone would have reason to harm me," she softly protested, disconcerted.

"What about your father or that Slavin fellow from the ship?" Landis conjectured without warning to make certain her reaction was spontaneous and credible, as he watched Smith for any clue to a possible association with that foe. "He's still around and bent on spite."

Kathy gasped and stared at him. Why would he mention Marc? "But he hasn't been seen since your fight," she exclaimed.

"If he's after revenge, Kat, he could be luring you inland. We know the message didn't come from me. You'll stay here tonight, then Sergeant Thomas can have one of his men take you home in the morning. I think I'll check out this mystery before I join you."

Kathy looked up at him, holding her silence. Smith excused himself. Kathy patiently waited for her husband to explain; he didn't. His mention of Marc disquieted her; there was no way Marc could know the things written in that note. Also impossible was his hint at her father. This episode was getting stranger by the minute . . .

Thomas asked for a description of the man who had delivered the note. Landis and Bill exchanged looks when Kathy accurately described one of Smith's henchmen. Bill said he would check around to see what he could learn, but didn't enlighten Kathy to the man's identity. Distracted, Kathy ignored their reactions.

Smith stepped to the door to remind Kathy of her belongings. He glared at Landis, his mood tinged with fury at Landis for suspecting his scheme. That was another strike against Jurrell! Once more, he bid Kathy farewell and smiled.

"I'll fetch your things, Kat. You stay out of the chill," Landis ordered. Kat was safer if Smith felt theirs was not a love match.

The look which passed between the two men warned Kathy of their hatred for each other. She remained inside while Landis went for her pack. After Smith and his men rode off, Kathy sighed in relief and thanked both men for their assistance. "I shouldn't have come with him," she confessed, to diminish Landis's irritation with her.

"You handled yourself exceptionally well, Mrs. Jurrell," Bill complimented her. "It's not wise to make an enemy."

"An enemy? Of Smith? How?" she inquired.

"You shouldn't be so trusting, Mrs. Jurrell. In this territory, there are plenty of men who would take advantage of you. Anyone who defies Smith's wishes becomes his enemy," Bill warned.

"Perhaps I was impulsive," she confessed, not daring to focus an accusing look at Landis. "But I was tricked."

"Landis and I have spoken at some length about your problem. It seems I gave you the wrong impression when you came to visit me. I don't know if Jake Hammond is around here; but if he is, I can assure you we'll also attempt to locate him," Bill informed her—but didn't tell her why he was so anxious to locate the elusive Jake.

Kathy blushed and sent Landis a scolding look. Bill chuckled. "Landis told me you didn't believe me, but I don't blame you. I had lots on my mind that morning and you were quite a shock to me. Landis said you were exceptionally beautiful and utterly charming, but I didn't believe him until I saw you myself. It's easy to see why he hog-tied you."

Kathy flushed once more, wanting to ask what else Landis had said about her. "I'm sorry if I misjudged you, sir. You must admit you did act very odd."

"I've had two Mounties killed lately while investigating some mysterious happenings. Suddenly a beautiful stranger walks in looking for some mysterious man. You must also admit I had reason to be wary."

Kathy's tension slowly fled. She smiled at the now genial Bill. Evidently she had been wrong about him.

Landis sat down. The cozy setting and Landis's mellow mood unsettled her. What now? she mused.

Both men laughed. "I'll have one of my men see you home in the morning. If you'll excuse me, I have something to check on."

"Thank you, sir. I really do appreciate your kindness and help." Kathy watched Bill amble out of his office, leaving them alone. She looked over at Landis. He was sprawled in his chair, watching her intently. She couldn't comprehend why he hadn't told Bill she wasn't returning to Skagway. Perhaps they would discuss their plans later. "Why did you mention Marc? Is he still here?" she asked.

"I'm sorry about that, Kat. But he hasn't left yet. I came across him near Whitehorse," he told her, a slight tic twitching in his jawline. There was a brittleness to his eyes which alarmed her.

"Did you two fight again?" she anxiously pressed.

"Forget about him. I don't think he'll cause us any more trouble," he evaded her query, his teeth clenched in reflection.

"You don't have to worry about me anymore, Landis. I can take care of myself," she declared, knowing something violent had taken place between them. "I carry my gun, and I do possess a powerful name," she cheerfully reminded him.

Landis's skeptical look challenged her statements. "I seem to recall those facts, Mrs. Jurrell," he taunted devilishly.

She grinned, but kept silent. "I'll take you home in the morning. I was serious, Kat; I don't want you leaving Moore's camp again."

"But what about my going inland with you," she reminded him.

"I didn't mean it, Kat. I was just trying to get you away from Smith. You frightened me when I thought you were that desperate."

"But . . ." she started to protest.

"No buts, woman. I can move around faster and safer with you safe at home," he stated with chilling finality.

"One of Sergeant Thomas's men can see me back to Skagway. I wouldn't want to disturb your busy schedule," she shot back.

"Whatever you say," he coolly agreed, then ceased their conversation as Bill returned.

"I'll have some supper sent in, then you can use my cabin tonight," Bill stated matter-of-factly.

"I really couldn't put you out like that, sir."

"It's the only place with privacy, Mrs. Jurrell. The other men bunk in a larger cabin together when they're here. I can sleep with them or in my office for one night."

"That's very kind of you, sir." Kathy couldn't help but wonder where Landis would sleep tonight, considering they were married.

Supper was eaten in pleasant leisure. Most of the talking was between Kathy and Bill. He related colorful tales of his Mounties and the Yukon Territory. Kathy strained to ignore Landis, but he watched her like a hawk. When the meal was over, Bill questioned Kathy about her father once more to make certain he had all the pertinent facts.

Kathy was aware of how closely Landis was hanging on her every word. Yet, he never asked a single question. Kathy offered to clear the table and wash the dishes, but Bill refused. He asked Landis to show Kathy to his cabin. Kathy was hesitant, but was forced to accept to avoid a silly scene. Her body was quivering with suspense.

Kathy recalled their last encounter. He was always harping on no commitments, but he had declared love for her. Why were his secrecy and freedom so imperative? One moment he vowed "in name only"; the next, how much he wanted to keep her. They had made passionate love, then quarreled bitterly. He had tricked her before with a note; had he done it again, to gain a short privacy?

Landis opened the cabin door and placed her pack inside. He turned to leave. "If you need anything, let me know."

"I'm fine, thank you. Goodnight, Landis."

As he was closing the door, he halted and looked back at her. "Kat . . ." he began, then stopped.

"Yes?" she asked expectantly.

He sighed heavily, then shook his head. "Never mind." He closed the door and took a long walk in the head-clearing night air.

Kathy bolted the door and leaned against it. She would never understand that mercurial creature. Damn him for always being there to help her! Damn him for allowing her to fall in love with him! Damn him for attracting and repelling her like some powerful, cruel magnet! Why did she have such trouble recalling what a rogue he was at times like this when he was compelling and beguiling? Would this destructive love and desire for him always be present?

It wasn't yet nine o'clock, but there was nothing to do except go to bed. Not expecting to have need of a nightgown on the trail, she hadn't packed one. There was a cheery blaze burning in Bill's fireplace. She wandered around the masculine and homey cabin, then began to undress. Bill's quarters were warm and secure; so she decided to sleep in her chemise and bloomers. She pulled down the covers to find clean sheets. Suddenly she realized Bill must have ordered one of his men to tidy up, to change the linens, and to build a fire while they were having supper. Preparing a bridal chamber, she scoffed sadly.

Bill Thomas . . . have I pegged you wrong? Or is this another way to disarm me? And you, Landis Jurrell, why are you suddenly so displeased with me? How will it look if you sleep elsewhere?

Kathy suddenly bolted upright in the bed. When Landis had alluded to men changing their names, he had looked and sounded strange. Was he hiding out? If so, why make friends with Mounties? She flashed over their two nonsensical arguments.

She had said her father was dead. He couldn't have believed her outburst; for he was searching for Jake, wasn't he? If Landis was in trouble, naturally he would be suspicious of her after all she'd said. That would explain his reluctance to get involved with any woman, particularly marry one. Naturally he couldn't marry a woman using a phony name or risk telling her the truth about him. Marry her with a phony name? But that would mean their marriage wasn't valid. No, he wouldn't risk more trouble by illegally marrying her.

He obviously didn't want anyone getting too close to him. Could it be possible his feelings for her were real, that he only wanted to protect her from trouble? She recalled how her constant questions had provoked him. He had asked her to trust him, to wait for him to work out something. What? A pardon? Proof of his innocence in some crime? Proof they were no longer searching for him?

Landis had displayed a violent streak during his fight with Marc. It was possible his temper had gotten him into trouble. He wasn't a man to accept punishment, especially if he felt his crime justified. Surely she was clutching at straws; maybe she only wanted to find some reason for his past actions and moods. What would she do if she did learn he was a criminal on the run? What would she do if that was the only reason he couldn't make a commitment to her? Had he endangered himself just to protect her?

Kathy got up and walked to the fireplace. She sat on the bearskin before it and held out her chilly hands to the heat. Was he afraid to love? Was he afraid of being hurt, of losing his freedom? How could he make passionate and consuming love to her if she meant nothing to him? What about all the things he had said to her? Why was he so protective if he didn't care? Why was he jealous of other men?

In light of such thoughts, it was foolish to pressure him with questions and demands. If she gave him the chance to get to know her, he might open up to her. Could she risk more pain? Landis was unique, the only man to stir her heart to love and her body to passion. If there was a slim chance of winning him, wasn't it worth the time and effort? What if she did accept him as he was and blindly trust him?

Give it a try, Kathy, her heart pleaded. It's crazy, Kathy, her mind quickly argued; he'll only hurt you. Her heart hastily debated, can you hurt more than you're hurting now? Would it be such a loss if you had him for even a short time? Her mind was silent.

There was a strange thudding at the door. Kathy jumped and looked that way. She hurried over to it, calling out, "Is someone there?"

"It's Landis, Kat. I have some wood for the fireplace."

Kathy's heart raced wildly. "Hurry, this wood's heavy!"

"I'm not dressed," she stated foolishly through the locked door.

"Put a blanket around you. I won't peek," he teased.

She could hear his playful laughter through the closed door. Still, she didn't move or speak as she pondered what to do.

"Do you want someone else to bring it in? It gets cold during the night; you'll need it later. My arms are breaking, Kat."

"All right. Just a minute," she agreed. She hurried to the bed and picked up an extra blanket lying across the foot. She threw it around her shoulders and snuggled into its folds. She unlocked the door and held it open for him. When he walked passed her, she unconsciously bolted the door. Or was it a wishful action?

"Can you lend a hand? I don't want to just drop it on Bill's floor."

She went to him and began to take one log at a time and stack it near the hearth. When his arms were empty, he leaned forward and brushed the dust from his flannel shirt. He grinned at her. "That should keep you warm tonight. You need anything else?" As he spoke, he replaced the blanket which had unknowingly slipped from one shoulder during her task, his fingers trailing lightly over her silky flesh.

Kathy trembled and inhaled at the contact. She tightened her grip on the protective blanket. Landis's hand reached up to caress her suddenly flushed cheek. "You're so very beautiful, Kat. It riles me every time I think of how you effect me. You're trouble, woman. If I had any sense at all, I would stay away from you and those bewitching eyes." Something was troubling him deeply.

As his hand dropped to his side, Kathy murmured

shakily, "Why don't you? We don't exactly have a normal marriage."

He lowered his head and sighed quietly. "I'm sorry, Kat; I never meant to hurt you. You were just so vulnerable and irresistible. I couldn't help myself. Maybe I did take advantage of you. I should say I'm sorry about what happened between us down there, but I'm not. I've never met a woman like you before. God, you came along at the worst possible moment in my life. Frankly, I don't know how to deal with that fact," he admitted with a rueful grin.

Her next words stunned him. "I'm partly to blame, Landis. Things just happened too quickly between us. I can't hold you responsible because I misread your intentions and feelings. I screamed a lot of crazy things at you because I didn't want you to see how much you had hurt me. I wanted to at least have some pride left. I don't even recall half the things I did say; I was just blurting out the first thing that came to my mind. If I promise to never pressure you or question you, can we be . . . friends again? I hate this hostility between us."

"I hope I'm hearing you right, Kat. You are saying you'll forgive me?" he tested his understanding.

She smiled cheerfully. "Under the circumstances, it would be best for both of us. After all, you do seem to be the one around when I'm in trouble. We are married, but I shouldn't have made all those demands on you; you don't owe me any explanations or promises."

Landis's expression was guarded and fathomless. His midnight eyes concealed whatever he was feeling. He gazed at her for a long time. "Would you mind telling me why you've changed your mind about me since our last meeting?" he asked. "I was positive you hated me."

Kathy faced the fire and gazed unseeingly into the bright flames. She should have expected his skepticism about her sudden aboutface, but somehow it bothered her. She should have moved toward him slowly. She should have known it would panic him. Was he afraid she might insist on staying married? She had never been good at playing emotional or coy games. "It's difficult to explain. I'm not even sure I understand it myself. But I got the impression you were sincere. I started thinking about us and realized the mistakes I've made. I gave you plenty of reasons to be wary and resentful. I suppose it did appear I was trying to guilefully entrap you, but I honestly didn't mean to act that way. I thought you and I . . . had something special. When I realized you didn't feel the same way, I wanted to hurt you back. That was childish and spiteful. I don't feel that way any more. If you want to be friends, I'm willing. If you don't, I think it's best if we end our relationship as soon as possible."

"We did have something special, Kat," he murmured huskily behind her. "I should have realized you aren't the kind of woman who could accept what I offered. But I do care about you, Kat, more than anyone else. I have things going on in my life right now which I can't explain. I'm not in a position to make any promises or commitments. That doesn't mean I don't want to; I just can't. When you indicated all or nothing, it had to be nothing. Then, I realized I would lose you forever. I want you, Kat, and I need you . . . whether I have the right to say such things or not. When I asked you to wait for me, I meant it. Someday, I will be able to make those promises and commitments. If we wish, we can have a real marriage."

She turned and looked up into his moody eyes. "I don't understand, Landis. First, you say it's a mock marriage. Then, you say . . ." She halted. "I'm sorry. I said I wouldn't do that again."

When she lowered her head and started to turn back to the fire, he caught her shoulders and halted her. "Please don't, Landis," she whispered sadly. "Right now, we both have other things to do. Maybe someday we can . . . we can test these feelings for each other. Until then, it isn't safe or wise. I want to believe you, but I'm afraid to."

"You don't trust me, do you?" he inquired, lifting her chin to compel her gaze to his. Evidently she was just as wary of him as he was of her. Could he blame her?

"That would be silly since you've already proven you have my best interests at heart. I really don't know what to think or feel."

"Why, Kat?" he gingerly probed.

"I thought love would be easy and natural. But it isn't like that. It hurts, Landis. I don't know what to do or say around you. Whatever it is, it's usually wrong. There seems to be too much anger and pain and secrets between us. It shouldn't be like that."

Her eyes were so clear and honest that they tugged unmercifully at his heart. "Do you love me, Kat, really love me?" he challenged.

She lowered her lashes to conceal what was vividly written there. She wanted him to convince her she wasn't mistaken, so she cautiously began, "I thought what I felt was love, but I'm not so sure anymore. Perhaps I only found you irresistibly attractive. Maybe I was just terrified by Marc Slavin and this awful place. Maybe I turned to you for protection and comfort. I was vulnerable, frightened, and susceptible when you came along. Suddenly you were there with your strong arms and courage to protect me. You were handsome and virile, so masterful and charming. Wasn't it natural for me to yield to my dashing, chivalrous knight? Is that what love is?"

"Why do you question how you feel? You didn't make love to me out of gratitude. And you're certainly not a woman to be swayed by a man's good looks and physical appeal. Why are you fighting it?"

"Because it hurts so much!" she protested. "I don't know you, Landis. How can I love a total stranger? What does that make me, a woman who falls into bed with a stranger, even if we are married?" she implored him to explain.

He smiled. "I'm not really a stranger, love. You've been closer to me than anyone else. Does it matter so much that I can't confide in you just yet? I love you, Kathryn Jurrell, and I need you. Isn't that the most important thing?"

Kathy pulled free of his grasp and walked away from him. She needed distance to think clearly. "May I ask only one question, Landis?"

He tensed, but nodded.

"Once you're in a position to tell me about yourself, will there be any other reason to keep us apart?"

"I'm not sure I follow you," he stated in haziness.

"I want to make certain I don't misunderstand you again. Are you saying you'll make a commitment to me after you settle whatever you're keeping secret now? Or do you mean you only want me for as long as I need your help and name? All I need to know, is it possible for us to have a future together one day? Do you love me in that way, to want to share yourself and your life with me?"

"I can't say what the future will hold, Kat, but I do know I want you in mine," he responded cautiously.

"As what? A wife always waiting for you to come around on occasion? As a convenience?"

"No, Kat, as my love," he replied.

"Is there a difference, Landis?" she probed.

"Yes, Kat, there's a big difference. You'll have to trust me completely. There'll be times when we'll be separated for weeks, maybe months. I'll do and say things you won't understand. Most of the time I'm gone, you won't know where I am or when I'll be back. I won't be able to explain, Kat; I can't."

"I see . . . are you in trouble, Landis? Are you hiding out here? Landis Jurrell is your name, isn't it?" When she saw his mixed reactions to her questions, she quickly vowed, "I don't care who you are or what you've done. I only want to help you, to understand you. I wish you could love me enough to trust me, Landis."

"Don't you see, Kat? You can't unintentionally drop any clues about me if you don't know them. I will tell you this much, woman; I'm not in any trouble with the law and I'm not hiding. When the time's right, I'll tell you everything you want to know."

"Is what you're doing this important?"

"More than you can imagine."

"Is Landis Jurrell your real name?" she asked once more.

He grinned. "Does it matter?" he parried noncommitally.

"In light of our relationship, it makes a big difference."

"In all honesty, Kat, you are very legally and definitely married to me. Needless to say, we don't have grounds for its dissolvement. Looks like you're stuck with me," he stated warmly, cunningly telling the truth.

She relaxed noticably. "You're not American, are you?"

"Nope. I'm Canadian. I come from the McKenzie Territory. I'm thirty-one and I've never been married. I've trapped furs, transported supplies, panned for gold,

215

hired out as a guide, and done just about everything else I could find. My parents were killed when I was twelve. Since then, I've been on my own. I learned to look out for myself when I was still a child. Maybe that's my problem, I grew up too fast and too hard. I've never needed anyone or anything. When I was nineteen, I met a man who changed my life and thinking. I've been working mostly for him ever since. I can't tell you his name or what I do for him. Things were going smoothly until I went to Skagway not long ago and met one Kathryn Hammond. Since then, she's turned my life inside out. What should I do about her?'' he teased.

Kathy laughed at his entreating expression. "What do you want to do about her? It seems to me she's an awful lot of trouble, and she's much too demanding. She's spoiled. She's willful. Most of all, she's very foolish. I'm not sure she's worth your time and trouble."

"What if I disagree? She can be a little she-wolf at times, but she's mighty soft and warm. You think she's willing to trust a fellow like me and wait for him?"

"I don't know. Why don't you ask her?"

"I'm afraid she'll turn me down flat."

"I doubt you have an ounce of fear in your entire body, Mr. Jurrell. Where is that masterful air of yours? Why not just sweep her off her feet? Don't ask her, just tell her."

Landis strolled over to her, gripping her gently by the shoulders. "Woman, you're all mine. I'm warning you now, you better be patient and loyal. And you'd better stay out of trouble. Is that clear?" He kissed her pervasively, pulling her tightly against his body.

That first kiss fused into another one as he held her possessively. Kathy's hands eased around his waist and up his broad back. He was so hard and strong, yet he could be so gentle and tender—and the bold contrast was arresting. She returned his kisses with rising passion. His lips trailed over her face and throat. She sighed in contentment and with longing. Unsure of this new arrangement between them, he leaned back and asked, "Do you want me to go now?"

Kathy was nearly breathless from his stirring kisses. "What will the other men think if you leave me alone here?" she jested.

"You're right, woman; we do have assigned roles to play. Our time together will be short. But if this was my last day on earth, I'd want to spend it with you. There's no way I can leave you tonight."

Landis's lips covered hers once more. Her arms went up around his neck, the blanket falling lightly around her feet. His agile hands removed her chemise and his shirt, the touching of their bodies sending fires through them. He gently ravished her mouth as he lifted her in his arms and carried her to the bed. He lay her down, then doused the lantern by the bed. Landis slipped out of his pants and boots, stretched out beside her, then rolled toward her and kissed her soundly.

When his mouth left hers to tease at her breasts, Kathy shuddered with desire. Her fingers went into his sable hair, relishing its softness. How could she deny this was what she wanted more than anything in the world, including finding her father? Their lips fused once more as Landis eased her undergarments off, leaving nothing between them.

As he deftly plundered her mouth, his hand sought out another place to increase her passion. Kathy's whole body was aflame for his. When the kisses and caresses became blissful torment, she coaxed, "I need you, Landis. Love me. Please love me."

"I do, Kat. I will, love." He eased within her receptive body and pressed tightly against her.

She moaned at the sweet sensation of interlocked bodies. Slowly he entered and withdrew from her, time and time again, her passion matching his. Warm and erratic respiration entered her ear as he nibbled at the lobe. He spread kisses over her satiny shoulders. Her hands mindlessly roamed over his powerful shoulders and back, claiming each inch of rippling flesh.

"God, how I've missed you, love. It's been too long," he huskily vowed, fearing he couldn't restrain himself.

Kathy's mouth hungrily accepted his kisses and her body arched to meet his drives. "Love me . . . love me," she pleaded in the throes of heightened ecstasy. She cried out against his mouth as the potent release came, signaling Landis that he no longer should hold back.

His rhythmic strokes increased in speed and purpose. Soon, he was shuddering with the force of his own release. "I'll never let you go, Kat, never," he promised her. No matter what he had to untangle to protect and to hold her, he would.

He rolled to his side, carrying her with him, refusing to release her for even one moment. His breathing slowly returned to normal; still, he held her tightly against him. For a long time, neither spoke. It seemed a time for silence and closeness. Kathy nestled her head near his throat, her left hand wandered through the furry mat upon his chest. He rested his chin against her silky hair, stroking it with one hand, the other moving up and down her arm. She closed her eyes and savored this long antici-pated moment. It was as if they had finally found each other, as if they were at peace with themselves and the whole world. It felt so good and so right to be together here like this. What better commitment than his love?

"You make it difficult for me to think about anything but you, Kat," he finally spoke first.

"Is that so bad?" she happily asked. "All I've thought about for weeks is you."

"You mean after the urge to kill me passed?" he joked lightly.

She laughed. "Landis Jurrell isn't easy to ignore or forget."

"I hope it's impossible. Things will work out, Kat; you'll see."

"They already have, Landis." She turned her head to look up at him, his face dark against the glow of the fire. "No matter who or what you are, Landis Jurrell, I love you with all my heart. I would wait for you until the end of forever if I had to. I only need to know you love and need me, too."

"You, my golden dream, are all I love and need. One day, I'll prove it to you."

"You already have, my love."

"Trust me, Kat; I promise you won't be sorry."

"I know, Landis, and I do."

She pressed her lips to his. His embrace tightened. Within minutes, they were making love again. It was slow and provocative, each teasing the other with kisses and caresses. When their passion could not be bridled, they rode wildly and freely to sweet pastures of serenity.

Kathy snuggled into his arms and was promptly asleep. Landis propped up on his elbow and gazed down at her. Was his good fortune real? Could this woman trust him and accept him without question? Could he do the same with her? Please don't be deceiving me, Kat, he thought. I wouldn't want to hurt you . . . He lay down and closed his eyes, sleep nearly impossible. Perhaps he had overreacted to her defensive outburst. How could this child-woman be a sinister threat?

Maybe she was right; maybe this was happening too quickly. She was getting to him. Trouble was, he couldn't relax or relent until that letter to America about Jake Hammond came in . . .

Kathy yawned and stretched as lovely memories of the night before filled her first waking thoughts, rolling to her side to greet her husband, her fiery lover. But his side of the bed was cold and empty. Kathy sat up and looked around, warm air touching her nude body. Landis wasn't in the cabin, but a bright fire was going. There was a note on his pillow; she seized it and read it. She smiled as she viewed the handwriting, which didn't match the puzzling note's in Skagway. She suddenly questioned why she hadn't realized that point before, as this was her second note from him. Perhaps her excitement had prevented it.

Kat,

Thought it best to let you sleep late. Come to Bill's office when you're awake, then I'll take you back to Skagway.

Kathy was slightly miffed by the absence of affection in his note. How she wished she could have awakened to him beside her, then made passionate love before their impending separation. She supposed she should be grateful for what little time they could share. But how long could they continue this way, resigned to stealing a few hours together? She missed him already and they were still together in a way. Hearing men's voices, she peeked outside to hopefully catch a first glance of Landis.

She was surprised to see it was mid-morning. She had slept awfully late, delaying their return to Skagway. He could be so considerate when he wanted to be and she resented another separation.

Eager to see him, she bathed off with the water and towel so thoughtfully laid out for her. She hugged herself and laughed softly, dreaming of the long hike to Skagway with her love. She hastily dressed, sorry she didn't appear more feminine for Landis. He loved her as she loved him. How foolish she had been! At last, things were right between them. Now, to seek her love . . .

But the morning hadn't gone as smoothly and happily for Landis. An early riser, he had slipped out at dawn and headed for the cook-house, stretching out before the fire and sipping the coffee he had just made. When three other Mounties entered, Landis made some discoveries which stunned him.

Late last night, Trace Blitch had returned to Log Cabin from headquarters to the East. Since Landis had turned in for the night with his wife, he wasn't disturbed. No one teased him this morning, but their sly grins spoke loudly. Being a self-contained loner, this situation with Kat caused him to feel vulnerable, too human. Obsessive love was a weakness, and Landis Jurrell bitterly resisted that image.

Trace Blitch entered the room, sending Landis a roguish grin. When the sturdy Mounty handed him a letter from America, he chuckled and teased, "I knew you were eager for this letter from Washington, but seems I couldn't find you last night. When do I get to meet the angel who shackled Mr. Wanderlust himself?"

Landis flashed him a reproving grin, then reached for the letter. He was briefly tempted to cast it into the fire without reading it. Instead, he stood up and pulled on his

221

parka to avoid the early morning chill. He walked out and headed for the edge of the woods. He leaned against a towering spruce tree and ripped open the envelope from George Preston, a friend who had previously worked with him on several international problems, who was presently assigned in Washington.

Almost reluctant to learn the contents, Landis began slowly, smiling at George's flair for wit. To make certain he wasn't missing a single fact, Landis read the letter two more times, each time with rising vexation. Things didn't add up to his liking.

Recalling how Kathy had easily drawn him into her golden trap once more, rage gnawed at his gut. He balled his fist and slammed it into the immovable tree, bruising his knuckles. He cursed his fury and stupidity, rubbing the bleeding hand. What to do with this information? For sure, let her know she didn't have him fooled one bit, at least pretend she hadn't!

Landis stalked to the office and stormed inside, slamming the door behind him. Bill glanced up from his desk, the genial grin quickly replaced by a baffled scowl. "What's up, Clint?"

Landis halted abruptly and pensively stared at his fellow officer, one whose rank matched his, for the time being. He was on loan to Bill in Bill's territory, but he didn't like working in the dark. Bill had been tight-lipped since Landis's marriage. Professional rivalry? Fear of an accidental leak? Landis didn't volunteer any information. That little witch would pay dearly if the letter was true. Betrayal and anguish gnawed at him. Again, he feared she wasn't Kathryn Hammond. "Nothing," he growled moodily, nursing his injured hand and his wrath.

Bill looked at the wound. "What happened to your hand?"

"Dropped a log on it," he lied. He went to a side table and began to wash away the blood. He pulled a cloth from a medicine box and went to stand before Bill's desk. Before he could pull any speculations from Bill about Jake, the door opened and Kathy came in, smiling at both men.

Bill returned the genial smile, but Landis sent her a black frown. She came forward, instantly noting his injury. "What happened, Landis? Let me help," she offered, reaching to take the cloth to bind the wound. His reaction surprised both Kathy and Bill.

Landis pulled away, muttering, "I've had plenty of practice, Mrs. Jurrell. We need to talk," he coolly informed her.

Kathy fused a lovely scarlet and kept silent. What had gotten into him? Why was he so sullen and terse this bright morning?

Without delay, Landis took her arm and led her to Bill's cabin. "Are you angry with me for some reason, Landis?"

"Should I be, Kat?" he sarcastically replied.

Bewilderment washed over her face and settled in her eyes of sapphire. She mutely watched him wind the cloth around his hand and tie it with his teeth. He looked up, his gaze impenetrable and cold. "Why did you really come here, Kat?" he demanded icily.

"You know why, because of that mysterious letter. Exactly what are you asking me?" she inquired, sensing that wasn't his point.

"Don't you agree it's rather curious for a young woman to come to a dangerous place like this looking for a father who was killed in Texas years ago," he enlightened her. "Seems to me a woman who knows so many high officials in the American government could find some assistance and protection from them. Why do you need a simple Canadian's help? Tell me, are you truly Kathryn Leigh Hammond?"

Kathy's face drained of color at his nasty tone and the implication behind his words. Landis grinned maliciously as if he had unmasked some vile criminal.

"What? How do you know such things?" she asked, struggling to get the question out, her heart racing wildly.

"I have ways, helpful friends in high places, too."

"You've been checking on me?" she inquired in disbelief. "Why?"

"Why, indeed?" he sneered. "Seems you forgot to tell me quite a few things about yourself, my tawny-haired bride."

"You know far more about me than I know about you," she scoffed, then added, "much more." She stared at him. "How dare you invade my privacy in such a despicable manner. All you had to do was *ask* me, ask me anything. You had no right to investigate me."

"Didn't I? After all, you are my wife. Since you seemed so intent on worming your way into my life and confidence, I wanted to know if you were worth keeping. Now, I want to know why. Would you care to enlighten me?" he snarled.

"Well you're vastly mistaken! I had no intention of ever seeing or speaking to you again until last . . . yesterday. This marriage means nothing to you. You've been playing games with me ever since my arrival. Think what you will; I couldn't care less," she shot at him, the dire scene tormenting her and destroying her recent happiness. He was serious! How could he do and ask such things if he loved her?

"Well, it wasn't a total loss; we did share a pleasant honeymoon," he cracked, enjoying the look of humiliation and anger on her face. "If you know what's good for you, wife, you'll hightail it to Skagway. This time, stay there until I give you permission to leave," he commanded, making a grave error.

"You don't own me; you can't order me around!" she shouted.

"I do, and I can," he vowed. He held his breath as he ruthlessly attempted to seek one plaguing truth, "Our marriage is ironclad, Kat; I'll never release you. As long as you live, you're mine."

Kathy paled and trembled, gaping at him. "You're mad!"

"No, Kat Jurrell; I'm deadly serious," he stated.

When she vowed to end their charade, he chuckled mockingly, not the least concerned or convinced.

"See you around," he sneered, heading for the door to leave.

"I hope not!" she avowed at his retreating back.

Landis chuckled wickedly, then came back to hand her the letter he had withdrawn from his shirt pocket. "Might be fascinating reading," he hinted. He seized her and almost savagely ravished her mouth, then left. He picked up his gear on the front porch and disappeared into the woods, heading for Whitehorse.

Kathy read the letter in amazement, as she rubbed her tingling lips. Last night had been a cruel charade. No doubt he had sent that letter to lure her here for revenge. What was her crime against him? Why doubt her? Did he think her to be some . . . some what? As Landis did, she had to read the letter a few times:

Salutations my friend Landis,

Re: September 9 letter, I have investigated the matter as thoroughly as possible considering the length of time since Jake

Hammond's departure from Washington in '81.

Jake Hammond was owner of a highly profitable shipping firm near here. From what I could learn, he had connections with many American government officials (mostly in the offices of Sec. of State, Interior, Attorney-General, Sec. of War, and Navy). He was known to socialize with several Presidents.

Seems he left Washington on business in '81 and never returned. There were some hints of a marital dispute, but couldn't locate anyone who knew the truth of it. He was reported killed in Texas about five years ago.

As to the daughter you mentioned, she's traveling with her mother at present. Don't know where or why. I did learn Lamont in the War Dept. is keeping an eye and ear on both women. She's eighteen and said to be most beautiful. Both women continued their friendships with previously mentioned families. Mighty important connections if you asked me. The mother hasn't remarried to date. I did learn the daughter was seen often with Garrick Dillon.

Dillon was quite a character in these parts. He worked for the Attorney-General's office until he was caught stealing information and selling it to other countries. Poor fellow was shot for spying. As you know, Americans don't deal nicely with traitors.

Appears Miss Hammond was in great social demand. She was often seen in the company of young men working in "sensitive" government positions, if you catch my drift. Might be coincidental.

Sorry I can't send more facts. Will continue quest. Hope you find these helpful.

Your friend,
George Preston

Kathy began to laugh and cry at the same time as she deliberated the implications in that letter. She had vowed last night he could trust her; but if he was in trouble, it wouldn't appear that way. "You bloody fool! It's all lies," she whispered softly. "I despised Garrick Dillon. I only saw him on occasion when my mother insisted he be the one to escort me to a dinner or the theater. As to friends in 'sensitive' areas, they were friends of my parents; I didn't select them. Contrary to your insinuations, my love, I did ask everyone I knew to help me find my father. His death was just a legal device to settle his estate. Papa's partner suggested it. Papa hadn't been seen or heard from '81. It seemed logical to assume he was dead, but I never accepted it. The only way we could touch his holdings and settle matters was to have him declared dead. Garrick arranged it with the help of the Attorney-General's office. It was only a ruse, like our marriage."

Landis clearly didn't trust her; his mind was set on seeing her as some threat to him. This letter only gave him an excuse to return to his carefree ways. What would happen when he learned the truth? He never explained himself; why should she? If she was supposed to trust him, then he should trust her. Last night's dream of a real marriage was now a frightening nightmare. Somehow she had to find her father and settle both painful battles.

Bill and Kathy ate breakfast before she left. Later, one of his men escorted Kathy back to Skagway, as Mike had gone on to Whitehorse yesterday. When she entered Moore's camp with the splendidly dressed Mounty, Harriet and Griff went to meet her.

"Kathy! I've been worried sick about you. What happened?"

"The note was a trick; it wasn't from Landis. I spent the night at Log Cabin and Sergeant Thomas sent me home," she briefly explained her adventure, excluding the agonizing details. After thanking the observant Trace Blitch, she instantly asked if Jack had arrived during her absence as Landis had informed her. Trace lingered in hearing range.

Harriet told her Jack had arrived yesterday, then quickly left by the Chilkat Pass to intercept them. "He was frantic when he discovered you'd left with Smith. He knew the letter wasn't from him."

"Will nothing go right for me here?" she wailed, stomping her foot in annoyance. "I've got to find him, Harriet."

"Don't fret. According to Jack, Landis should arrive today."

"I saw Landis at Log Cabin. He isn't coming here. I meant Jack; time's running out." Determination filled Kathy's voice and eyes. She would find her father and prove Landis's suspicions false and absurd! "I must find Jack; he's taking me inland."

"You can't leave here, Kathy; it's too dangerous."

"I have no choice; Landis is too busy to help me."

Griff inserted, "Moore's got two Eskimos taking supplies to Whitehorse tomorrow. He might let you go with them."

"I'll convince him; you'll see," she vowed confidently, smiling at the laughing Griff and sourfaced Harriet. As if the decision was a foregone conclusion, she rushed to her cabin to pack for her latest journey.

As she packed, Harriet informed Kathy of some daring plans of her own. She had sent for the horses she had left behind in Seattle. She was building another cabin, a larger one. She fully intended to transport goods over that pass and establish a hotel here. Kathy felt Harriet could accomplish anything she set her mind to doing.

"If you plan to head inland, why are you fighting my decision?"

"I'm used to hardships and labor; you aren't, Kathy dear."

"I'm learning fast, Harriet, or hadn't you noticed?"

Their gazes fused in understanding. They burst into merry laughter, wisely waiting until later for a deeper talk.

Nine

Kathy could hardly believe how easy it had been to persuade Moore to let her go to Whitehorse with the two hired Eskimos. Perhaps he relented because of her desperate lie, claiming she was meeting Jack and Landis. Her daring ploy had worked, for she was on the steep trail which inched its way to that wild interior. Moore had almost reneged when it had begun to snow. Fortunately they had left Skagway before the flurry grew into winter's first full-fledged storm.

Not that it hadn't snowed sparse amounts before this day, but it had always been light and had melted quickly. Today, however the winds were exceptionally chilly and the flakes were falling more rapidly and heavily than before. The two Eskimos seemed unconcerned, so Kathy decided this was a natural occurrence.

This journey had begun with a sense of familiarity for her. They had trudged up the canyon over trails beaten down by overloaded pack horses and countless feet of prospectors. Kathy tensed each time they passed near precipitous cliffs, then sighed in relief when the danger was past. The Eskimos would nudge each other and chuckle at her white face, offering only words of encouragement, but no help, as gentle Mike had done.

It was apparent to Kathy they didn't care to have a sluggish, frightened female along. She knew she was slowing down their pace, but she did the best she could. She was quick to follow orders and resolved never to complain. Even when she was so weary and breathless she feared she couldn't move another step, she forced herself to do so.

Kathy was delighted the two men didn't even hesitate for a moment as they passed near Log Cabin. By the time they had reached White Pass—the boundary line between Canada and Alaska—they had ascended over two thousand feet. Following those rugged and treacherous miles, the countryside suddenly gave way to smaller foothills and inspiring scenery. The descent was swifter and required less energy and skill to master. By the end of that arduous day, no relief was in sight.

The two men didn't halt in any tiny settlements. The walking trek steadily progressed, Kathy allowed her mind to empty of all except her efforts and the impressive countryside. She had never seen any place so rugged and formidable. Despite the sights and sounds, the endless trek became a grating monotony. Several times they spooked animals. Once, she feared a large caribou would actually charge them. He snorted loudly and pawed the ground a few times in warning, then arrogantly trotted off at a slow pace. They saw a few foxes and other furry creatures which hurried off too quickly to be recognized.

They braved on to the edge of Lake Bennett and the end of the White Pass trail. The men calmly set to making camp for the night. After consuming a meal of cold biscuits with dried meat and steaming coffee, the men rigged a brush shelter to shield Kathy from the still falling snow. Kathy was grateful for this unexpected show of kindness.

The older man grinned at her as she shuddered from cold. "Woman need *mukluk* to keep feet warm. Like so," he indicated, holding out his moosehide boots with fur lining. "You do good on trail. Umiakia surprised. You *tillicum?*" he asked eagerly.

"What's a.... *tillicum?*" she inquired hesitantly.

Umiakia laughed heartily and gently nudged his younger son. "Friend. You be friend of Umiakia and Aishihik?"

Kathy smiled warmly and nodded. "Friends," she hastily agreed. "I'll try to keep up, Umiakia, but it is difficult. Not because I'm a woman, but because I'm not used to this territory," she added, laughing.

"You do good, *tillicum* Kathy. We see Whitehorse soon."

The two cups of hot coffee failed miserably to warm Kathy. She snuggled into her sleeping bag with its sparse offer of comfort and heat. "*Tillicum* Kathy take off parka. Warmer in poke."

Reluctant, she obeyed him. He knew this precarious land better than she did. Sure enough, within minutes she was warmer and more comfortable.

"Work good, yes?" he asked, leaning over her face.

She grinned and replied, "Much better, Umiakia."

Kathy observed the old man for a time. The parka he had put on at nightfall was made of sealskin, lined with mink felt, and trimmed at the neck with thick coyote fur. He had covered his head with a hat of rabbit fur. Such wisdom and friendliness were etched on his sienna-colored face. His mustache and beard were a sparse and wiry mixture of silvery white and dull brown. As if refusing to warmly cover his lower face, his beard looked more like unshaven stubble. His lips were so thin his

232

mouth appeared as a wide slash above his chin. His dark eyes were hooded and slanted, giving him an oriental mien. Numerous creases near his keen eyes radiated like ribs in a fan. To Kathy, he seemed rather small to be so resilient and agile. She concluded she admired and liked this unpretentious and confident man. She felt perfectly safe with him and his timidly remote son, who rarely glanced at her or spoke to her.

In spite of the wind and cold, the exhausted Kathy was soon asleep. Yet, it hardly seemed her eyes had closed when the genial man was prodding her to wake up. "We go fast. Storm coming soon."

Kathy was chilled to the bone before she could slip into her parka. She quivered; her teeth chattered. "Is it always this cold here?"

"This not cold, *tillicum* Kathy. This warm next to winter," he cheerfully delivered his depressing news.

There was a great deal of commotion in this particular spot. Tenderfeet made or purchased boats for the trip across the treacherous Lake Bennett. Sawed lumber was stacked haphazardly, some for sale and some waiting to be taken to Skagway. Here, more cabins dotted the landscape than in Skagway, as did more snow. The tents were also larger and thicker. Curls of smoke indicated most of them had some type of heat—which she craved.

Remains of broken boats lay rotting along the lake's edge. As both men loaded their canoes, Kathy observed the reflections of snow-capped mountains on the blue water. Sighting jagged rocks which severed the surface, Kathy prayed these men were excellent boatmen. Several acquaintances stopped to chat briefly with the two men, but Kathy paid little attention to them or their muffled conversations.

It seemed that hours passed in soul-shaking terror as

Umiakia struggled against the turbulent lake, Kathy hanging on to the sides of the small boat. She dared not open her mouth to speak, fearing she'd be sick. There were other boats braving this agitated span of water; she prayed the men would control them and keep their distance. The idea the craft could overturn and send them into glacial water alarmed her. She sat very still to avoid any perilous tilting and remained silent to avoid distracting the grinning Umiakia, who appeared to be enjoying this awesome challenge with nature.

The churning flow of water crashed against and around the rocks which invaded its domain. A violent whirlpool was pointed out to her, one which both men skillfully avoided. The little boats seemed to take on a daring of their own, whirling with or against the raging waters which pulled at them. They were taken down a stretch where steep slopes loomed on both sides, imprisoning them in the swirling powers of liquid nature.

Umiakia called out to her over the roar of the water, "Hold tight, *tillicum* Kathy. Shoot come. No fear, I be good man."

Almost instantly the craft was forcefully seized by the seething rapids and dashed this way and that. She uncontrollably screamed in terror. The din of water and wind ripped savagely at Kathy's ears. Her face was ashen; she had no time to think of getting cold or wet. The craft went up and down, spraying water in its urge to leave this demanding area. Now she understood why Umiakia had covered her with this water resistent oil-cloth!

As water splashed over the sides of the boat, her gloves and shoes were soaked, numbing both hands and feet. As if the impossible couldn't happen, it did. The speed of the descending chute increased and the fury of the water mounted. When Kathy felt she couldn't take this intimidating glacial water and fear any longer, Umiakia was working with skill and power to head the boat into the bank at Whitehorse.

"Over, *tillicum* Kathy. We rest; get dry."

Too frightened to move, she sat as if in shock. Umiakia beached his sturdy boat. "Come, must dry to stop chill," he urged the fear-frozen girl.

"I'm . . . coming," she stammered between chattering teeth. She made the rocky trip to the other end of the boat and stepped out, never in her life so happy to touch solid ground, snow and all!

The Eskimos were greeted by men awaiting the supplies. Without wasting any time, the boats were unloaded and stored for their return trip. Kathy was taken to an oblong building where rooms could be rented by those who could afford such luxuries. Umiakia made the arrangements for her, paying the man with the money she had previously given to him. He had warned of the dangers of allowing anyone to learn she had money.

"You dry; rest. Umiakia send food, water. Fire take chill. Find Jack; he come, *tillicum* Kathy."

"You are most kind, Umiakia. How can I ever thank you?" she whispered, her throat dry and scratchy.

He grinned and left. Kathy entered the room and looked around. The furniture consisted of a narrow bed, a small table with a lantern, and one chair. The windows were covered with sheets of cloth nailed to the wall. She sighed in dejection. At least the place looked clean. A knock came to the door. Kathy answered it; a large woman was standing there.

Without waiting to be invited in, she pushed past

Kathy and headed for a rock fireplace. Shortly, she had an inviting blaze going there. She lit the lantern on the table, casting a dim glow in the depressing room. Without speaking a single word, she left.

The woman returned, carrying a tin tub. She placed it by the fireplace and lumbered out, to return with one bucket of steaming water and one of cold. "That's all the time and water I kin spare. Don't git many ladies o'er here. If it don't do the job, ye'll have to fetch some more yourself," she announced, her speech and manner crude. "Silly to bathe when it's freezing. Body oil keeps ye warm and fights the bite of snow. I'll fetch your victuals when they're ready." She left in a huff, wheezing.

Kathy had observed this seemingly reluctant service. Why should the woman complain; she was paying for this "luxury"! She locked the door and stripped off her damp clothes. Lifting the bucket of hot water, she poured it in the tub, plagued by thoughts of Landis once doing these similar chores for her. She added cold water and sat in the tub. She bathed as quickly as possible, the tub small, the water scant, and the room still cold.

She dried off and put on fresh, warm clothes. She placed the chair near the fire and hung her wet garments there. She was utterly fatigued and wanted nothing more than to throw herself across the bed and go to sleep, but she didn't. Her mind was plagued by Landis and Jake.

By now, Kathy recognized the insistent knock of the serving woman, Mrs. Kelsey. Kathy opened the door to permit her to remove the water and tub, casting a curious look in her direction. The woman returned with her meal: thumb biscuits, hot coffee, and venison stew.

Kathy smiled and stated, "Thank you, Mrs. Kelsey. It looks delicious, and I'm starved. You've been most kind and helpful. I'm sorry to be such a bother for you; I know you must have endless chores. This is my first trip here, so I didn't know what to expect. I'm here to join my father and husband," she added to dispel the woman's resentment of her presence.

Oddly, the roughly dressed woman smiled at her. "You best watch yourself around these parts, ma'am. Ain't no place for ladies." She walked to the door and left without another word, the door closing softly this time behind her oversized rear.

Kathy shrugged and locked the door. Evidently these people didn't take to strangers. Laying the clothes on the floor, she pulled the chair to the rickety table. The food did look appealing. She ravenously consumed her first hot meal since leaving Skagway. She smiled as she lifted the coffee pot to refill her cup. No doubt Mrs. Kelsey wasn't so hostile after all.

Afterwards, she replaced the chair and wet garments before the fire. There was nothing to do but wait for either Jack or Umiakia to come. But neither came. Only Mrs. Kelsey showed her severely lined face once more to deliver an armload of wood and, thank goodness, an extra blanket! Kathy smiled and thanked her. The woman nodded.

Wind whistled around the building; the air grew chillier in the little room. It was too late for anyone to come calling tonight. She peeked out. The snow was falling rapidly, moonlight playing over the white covering, as did the winds. She went to the bed and removed her parka, then slipped into a heavy flannel gown and eased between the cold covers, snuggling beneath them, quivering. How she wished Landis was here to . . .

Stop it, Kathy, she warned herself. Finally she relaxed and warmed enough to fall into exhausted slumber.

237

Dawn had hardly shown her face when someone knocked on her door. She pulled the blanket around her shoulders and went to it, annoyingly recalling another such time. "Who is it?" she called out.

"Umiakia," the reply came. "We go Dawson take supplies. Jack in Stewart. You come?" he inquired.

"You mean Jack isn't here?" she asked in panic.

"No here. No come. I take to Stewart."

Kathy certainly didn't want to sit around this horrible room and she had no way of returning to Skagway. She fumed as she realized Landis was right about coming inland. There was no decision. "I'll be ready to leave shortly." She would prove her mettle!

This new journey began in relative silence. The majority of the Yukon River was easily travelled. Occasionally they would approach rapids, but few had the awesome force of those first ones. The flow of the water was swift, allowing them to make the ruins of old Fort Selkirk in half a day. Umiakia related how previously hostile Indians had destroyed it. A small settlement called Selkirk had replaced it.

After a short and uncomfortable night in the open, they continued their trek. Kathy noticed a stark change in the scenery. Small boom towns lined the river's banks and large river steamers were making their last runs before the river froze. Kathy was sorely tempted to catch one of those larger boats, but felt too safe with her new friends to risk meeting another Marc Slavin. Tremors washed over her; Landis had said Marc was in this area. She shoved aside ominous fears and doubts. They floated past one winding bend after another. The White River joined the Yukon, adding her swirling dark water to the clear emerald Yukon.

Soon, the water was muddy and obscure again. Kathy

prayed unseen perils were not lurking beneath the impenetrable surface, waiting to seize unsuspecting crafts. By late afternoon, the swift currents had urged them into Stewart. As they docked near the settlement, Umiakia suggested, "I see Jack here. You wait. No safe alone. Bad men. Pretty woman. Jack no here; you no stay. Wait in Dawson," he stated matter-of-factly.

Kathy spoke to the quiet son of her friend, or at least tried to carry on a conversation with a man who knew less English than his father. Eventually they fell into silence, each observing their surroundings. As if instinctively feeling eyes on her back, Kathy turned and looked towards a group of men. She didn't like the way they were ogling her. She focused her attention on her silent companion.

One brazen prospector strolled over and asked, "You heading to Dawson to work for Soapy?"

His implication was clear. She haughtily snapped, "No! I'm going to meet my husband; he's a Mounty." That should discourage him!

As if she had struck the fear of God into him, he hastily apologized and walked off to join his friends. They chatted for a few moments, looking at her every so often before they ambled off.

Kathy saw Umiakia hurrying toward them. From the look on his face, she knew what he was going to say. "Jack gone Klondike. Take men. You come Dawson. Be safe. Leave word you there. He come soon. Umiakia take supplies; earn money for winter."

Kathy raged at her fate. By now, she should be accustomed to having her plans go awry. She was utterly bewildered. Why would Jack desert her, forget about her? Men, she scoffed mutely.

In her vexation, she mused, no doubt Soapy will be

delighted to offer his hospitality! She shuddered as she recalled that insidious creature who reeked of evil, who had spoken so maliciously of Landis. Kathy instinctively knew she must avoid all contact with him, if possible. A nervous titter escaped her lips as she realized Jack and Landis had enticed her into the domain of the very man both demanded she avoid.

Umiakia took her strange laughter as fatigue and agreement. He hopped into his boat and pushed it away from the bank. The seemingly endless journey was underway again.

Dusk approached early this time of year; the men headed for shore two hours downriver. "See Dawson next sun," the older man informed her.

The boats were left loaded this time. Only the supplies needed for camping were taken out. They found a place near a thick line of trees beside a sloping hill to offer some protection from the night winds. Kathy trudged in the deepening snow and lay her burden down. Having need of some privacy, she motioned she was going for a walk, her face glowing most noticably. For some reason, she picked up her pack and headed over the hill into the concealing trees. She hadn't walked far when she realized she was carrying the heavy pack. She laughed and sat it beside a tree, then walked a little further. When she was assured of privacy, she relieved herself. Just as she was about to head back, following her swiftly vanishing tracks in the snow, several shots rent the silence. She halted and froze, sensing danger. She remained motionless, not knowing what to do. She was wise enough to know the Eskimos had rifles, but that was pistol fire!

Time seemed to stand still as she wavered in doubt. Summoning her courage, she cautiously headed toward their camp. She retrieved her pack. When she gingerly entered the clearing near the river, she halted and gaped at the sight which greeted her horrified senses: the two Eskimos were lying face down in the snow and the boats were gone! The landscape was a vison of white; snow falling as a steady rain. The flakes varied in size, from minute to large. The changeable currents of wind seized them, hurling them down one minute and then every which way the next, covering objects on all sides. She was afraid to seek the truth, but knew she must.

She dropped her pack and went to Umiakia, rolling him over. She suppressed a scream as she stared at the flow of blood from his forehead and the gaping hole there. Her gaze flew to the crimson-stained snow, as more white powder sought to cover it. She shook him and called his name: nothing, he was dead. She slowly went to check on Aishihik, fearing his lethal fate. He, too, was dead.

Kathy pushed herself from her kneeling position and glanced around. Everything was gone. The snowstorm threatened to continue and she was utterly alone. She was surrounded by evil and death. She slipped her hand into her pocket and lightly fingered the little gun which Harriet had given to her, suddenly elated to have it.

Panic washed over her. Where was she? What could she do about her friends? She had no food or protection from the weather or foes. She brushed tears from her cheeks, fearing they would freeze into ice. The winds tugged at her furry hood, more than the cold air chilling her soul. She couldn't stay here alone. There was only one course of action: she had to head along the riverbank toward Dawson. Someone might find her and help her. She instantly recalled the gaping men at Stewart. She was defenseless and vulnerable. How she wished she were in Skagway in her warm, safe cabin. Landis's warnings returned to haunt and to mock her.

Ignoring her fatigue, she lifted the pack and headed toward the riverbank. She couldn't keep death company. In less than two hours it would be dark. Thoughts of wolves played havoc with her lagging courage. She walked as quickly as she could, the soft snow pulling at her feet and slowing her pace as she helplessly sank into it like quicksand. Puffs of white smoke went before her as she breathed heavily. Despondency flooded her; she knew she couldn't survive out here alone. She looked skyward, icy flakes falling into her face and extracting her body heat, leaving drops of water behind. She had an eerie feeling of being utterly alone in this deathly silent world. Yet, there was a wild and fierce beauty to her surroundings. Moist clouds had come to sit on the taller treetops and ridges, hovering as some oppressive force. Was Jake Hammond or Landis Jurrell worth this peril, this terror?

A shout caused her to whirl around. She froze momentarily. Had they come back to kill and rob her? Had they realized there was another person in the party? Perhaps a witness to be silenced?

Through the haze, her frantic eyes detected one man approaching her. He was tall; yet, the dim light and his hooded mackinaw concealed his identity. She turned and fled from him, dropping her pack in her desperate attempt to avoid this unknown peril. She didn't get far before she tripped and fell into the snow. She struggled to regain her footing.

Kathy was seized and yanked to her feet. She fought wildly until he shouted above the wind, "Kat! What the hell are you doing up here!"

She instantly halted her struggles and looked up into the furious face of her husband. "Landis! Thank God," she shouted, clinging to him.

For a time, he held her protectively. Her arms went around his waist and she fiercely embraced him, weeping. "Stop that crying, woman, or you'll have a face of icicles," he warned, attempting to calm her hysterics and ignore her disturbing embrace. "I told you it was dangerous in here, but you wouldn't listen! Now look what you've gotten into!" he thundered, trying to calm her down.

She looked up at him. "How did you find me?"

"You found me," he parried. "What happened back there?"

"We stopped to camp. Umiakia and his son were setting things up while I left to . . . I heard pistol shots. I knew something was wrong. When I finally returned to camp, they were dead and the boats were gone. I just started walking toward Dawson. You scared the life out of me; I thought you were one of them." She shuddered violently. "What are you doing here?"

"You didn't see who did it?" he asked.

"No. What should I do?" she implored, eyes misty.

"How should I know?" he snapped tersely, then reminded himself of the truth Harriet had revealed about his letter from America. "Where were you heading? I told you to remain at home." He didn't tell her he had been tracking her since he discovered her infuriating departure. Presently, he was too riled to reveal he had gone to Skagway after cooling off to demand an explanation. Damn, she was a time-consuming, rankling female! He had been a fool to think marriage would keep her put and out of trouble!

"When you ordered me home, Jack had just left. I was trying to catch up. Moore said I could go to Whitehorse. Jack wasn't there, so the Eskimos took me on to Stewart.

JANELLE TAYLOR

But we discovered he's somewhere in the Klondike. Umiakia wouldn't leave me behind. He left a message for Jack to say I'd be in Dawson. Everything's going wrong," she wailed miserably.

"You've only yourself to blame, Kat. We all warned you about the Yukon," he scolded her. "I saw Jack and talked with him. I told him you weren't coming inland. That's why he didn't wait around."

"I suppose you're delighted to be proven right! I could have been killed for all you care! I'll pay whatever you charge if you'll take me on to Dawson to wait for Jack," she said angrily.

"I'm not heading for Dawson. I'm on my way home; I have a cabin on the Klondike. If you want to tag along, fine. If not, Dawson's that way, about a half a day by boat and two by foot," he informed her, pointing in the direction they had been heading earlier.

"Go to Dawson alone? You must be insane!" she screamed at him. "If you would help me, I wouldn't need Jack."

"Suit yourself. Just don't offer a tasty meal to any wolves," he joked lightly on her predicament. He turned and headed south to pick up his backpack, leaving Kathy standing there.

"Where are you going?" she shouted at him, stunned.

"Home, wife," he laughingly called over his shoulder. He continued to lengthen the distance between them, the snow gradually enveloping him, hoping his ploy would work.

Kathy didn't know what to do. How could she risk spending time alone with him? He was much too disarming and mistrustful. Damn him! Why did he always seem to show up at the most opportune time for taking advantage of her? As the shadows closed in on

244

him, panic shot through her. She was tired and hungry. She was afraid. Damn him for always being there when she needed him! And damn him for knowing it and using it!

"Landis! Wait!" she cried out in alarm. Would he actually abandon her in her peril? Was he that angry and spiteful? The bully!

She ran toward where he had disappeared. She squinted into the swirling grayness, finally locating him. He was leaning over his pack, doing something. She raced over to him and shouted down at him, "You brute! You wouldn't dare leave me here alone! I'm your wife!"

He looked up at her and grinned, white teeth flashing in the vanishing light. "Wouldn't I, Mrs. Jurrell? You disobeyed me; you allowed me to believe the misleading facts in that letter," he announced. "Troublemakers should pay for their mistakes."

She gaped at him. "What makes you think they were lies?" she challenged. How dare he treat her this way!

"A wind whispered in my ear," he replied, chuckling.

"You mean Harriet," she deduced, their words hitting home. "You've been to Skagway? Why?" she probed inquisitively.

"Why not? You coming?" he asked.

"You've made up your mind about me. I'm not going to waste energy trying to change it. You're an obstinate, cynical snoot!"

"You already have," he murmured humorously.

"Pray tell, how so?" she sneered, eyeing him warily.

"Any fool who would go to the lengths you have to find a missing father must really have one, Kathryn Hammond Jurrell," he concluded.

"Maybe I was plotting another way to have you rescue me so I can spy on you or entrap you," she snapped in frustration.

"If you really wanted me, you would be putting in more time and effort," he remarked, actually sounding rankled that she wasn't!

"Why should I? I already have you," she alleged to nettle him. "As you vowed at our last . . . battle, I plan to hold you captive."

"I could be persuaded to hang around willingly," he murmured, eyes sparkling with a flurry of thoughts and feelings.

"How very generous of you, dear husband," she skeptically purred. "I doubt you would have listened, so why go after me?"

"I care about you, Kat. It was a shock to receive that letter after our last night together. I thought you meant every word. When I got that letter the next morning, I was furious. You read it. What was I supposed to think in light of your statements at Skagway?" he reasoned irritably.

"You got the letter after we . . ." she halted thoughtfully.

"I wasn't playing games. I was just about convinced I was wrong."

"Why did you have that man check on me?" she asked.

"Because of things you said those two times in Skagway. And I was trying to gain facts about your father from a friend in Washington to help you. I'm a wary man by nature, Kat. My business calls for secrecy. I had trouble believing you were for real. Most of the time, I hoped you weren't!" he said suddenly, winking at her. "Hungry?" he asked to change the topic, hoping she didn't recall the date on Preston's letter.

"Starved. My soul for some hot coffee," she said.

"It's a deal," he replied.

"I didn't mean that literally," she attempted to disarm him.

"Doesn't matter. I prefer your heart in exchange for sharing my food and bedroll," he quipped in return, chuckling devilishly.

"Share your bedroll?" she parried mirthfully. "Is there a charge for saving my life again? At this rate, I'll be eternally indebted to you."

"It gets mighty cold at nights. I didn't see one with your pack."

"That doesn't mean I have to share yours," she taunted.

"Suit yourself, Kat. When you're cold enough lying there in the snow, you'll gladly share body heat. Right now, mine's at boiling level."

"I doubt body heat is all you have in mind to share." Kathy chided herself for her reckless abandonment of breeding and caution, but Landis made her respond to him in such a wild way!

"Tonight, it is," he responded. "By midnight, it'll be freezing. I don't mind something soft and warm next to me."

He headed to the woods. "Where are you going?" she inquired anxiously.

"To fetch some wood for a fire," he replied.

Kathy stood there feeling foolish. Landis piled some small branches in the area he had been clearing in the snow. He worked until smoke was curling up, but couldn't get a decent fire going. "I guess that means no coffee," he muttered unconcerned. He pulled some biscuits and dried meat from his pouch. "You hungry enough to eat anything?" he asked.

She sighed and accepted the proffered food. She slowly consumed it, standing. He unrolled the sleeping bag and placed it on branches to keep it off the cold earth. The snow had ceased to fall. Kathy sat on her pack, watching him closely. He slipped into the bag, clothes and all. "Night, Kat."

He snuggled into the bag and closed his eyes. Kathy sat immobile. She was shaking from cold. "You're a fiend, Landis Jurrell," she finally stated, afraid to trust herself inside that cozy nest.

"How so, Mrs. Jurrell? Surely you don't expect me to sleep on the snow? I'm willing to share with my lovely and defiant wife. If you weren't so damn obstinate, you would be snuggled in here with me. You planning to sit there chattering all night?"

"All right, you win," she acquiesced.

"That's more like it. Take off your parka and boots. Roll them up tight." He slipped out of the sleeping bag and did the same.

"I'll freeze!" she argued.

"No, you won't. It's warmer that way."

She did as told, then eased inside. He squirmed down into the confining bag. "Snuggle up to me," he suggested.

"I will not," she nervously refused, dreading his contact.

"Then get out and let me put my coat on. It's either share body heat or no go," he demanded sullenly.

"All right!" she conceded, unwilling to leave his side and warmth.

She nestled into his arms and he straightened the bag, pulling it up over their heads. "We'll smother," she muttered.

"Not with the end open," he chuckled. His arms closed around her. "Relax, Kat," he murmured.

His warm feet rested against her icy ones, her arms

were trapped between them. Her head fit into the crook of his neck. The full length of their bodies touched. Kathy lay there wondering what he was thinking and feeling. He leaned back and whispered, "I'm not going to attack you. Go to sleep, Kat. It's been a rough day for both of us. For a while there, I thought those men had taken you and . . . We've got a long walk tomorrow. Sleep, woman." His fears drained away.

She lifted her head and looked over at him, their faces close enough to feel the warm breath of the other. "Were you really worried about me? Were you coming after me?" she inquired.

"Would you believe me if I said yes?"

"I don't understand you at all, Landis. You blow so hot and cold that I don't know what to feel or think," she openly confessed.

"I think I made a complete fool of myself at Log Cabin," he acknowledged readily. "I'm sorry, Kat. I know I seem to be saying that an awful lot, but I can't seem to help myself. You have a way of pushing me beyond my control. Why did you stay silent?"

"I should have denied your charges, but I didn't think it would make any difference. I didn't know you had just received that letter. Why did you marry me if you're so mistrustful? Why did you have me investigated?"

"I can't explain, Kat. It has to do with my work. You just acted too suspicious to suit me. Those facts were distressing."

"You always use your work as an excuse for everything. I'm sorry, Landis, but I can't accept that. Help me find my father and I'll prove I'm honest. We can't keep tearing at each other."

"What if he isn't here, Kat? What if you never locate him?"

"He must be! He isn't dead, Landis; he can't be! I have to find him and talk to him. Please help me," she pleaded earnestly.

"I'll do what I can, Kat," he finally agreed, knowing that was the only way to settle more than one vexing problem.

"You will?" she pressed for reassurance. "You mean it this time?" Their eyes fused in longing, each mutely praying for a miracle.

"Yes," he vowed, reaching out to caress her cheek.

She spread kisses over his face. He chuckled. "You best stop that, woman. It's too cold to get undressed. But if you keep that up, we'll have to," he warned, his senses alive and his body aroused.

She snuggled into his powerful arms and sighed happily. "Go to sleep, Kat. We'll talk in the morning. You're safe with your trusty guide."

"Good night, Landis," she whispered softly, closing her eyes and pressing close to his warm and inviting body.

"Be still, woman. I'm not made of stone," he jested.

"I'm glad you're not, but I was beginning to think you were."

"The best thing for both of us is to go to sleep, Kat. We've got a long walk ahead. I don't like the looks of the sky tonight; we're in for some foul weather soon."

"What about Jack?" she asked.

"If he's in the Klondike, we'll be seeing him in a few days. He'll be delighted you're with me," he jested with a deep chuckle. "You'll be safe and warm; I promise."

She laughed. "Will I, Mister Jurrell?"

"Most of the time," he lightly parried, drawing her closer to him.

"What more could a helpless victim ask for?" she

replied, resting her face against his drumming heart.

"What more indeed?" Golden dreams tormented his mind and body.

It wasn't long before both were sound asleep beneath the moon, warmly entrenched in each other's arms and the tempting sleeping bag. A lone wolf howled in the far distance. Kathy never heard it. But Landis did, his keen senses alert even in light slumber.

Ten

Kathy snuggled deeper into the sleeping bag and nestled against the warm object to avoid the chill which nipped at her face. "You planning to sleep all morning, Princess?" a mellow voice whispered into her ear.

A smile made gentle creases near her closed eyes and mouth. She opened her eyes and gazed into ones of laughing ebony. "Good morning, Mr. Jurrell, you tyrant," she teased, lovingly caressing his firm jawline.

"I suggest we make haste, Mrs. Jurrell, before I take advantage of this delightful situation and we get caught in an early blizzard."

She peeked over the sleeping bag and studied the leaden sky. "You really think it's going to be that bad?" she worriedly inquired, looking at him.

"I've been in these parts since birth; I know the signs by now. Up, woman. I'd rather be in my cabin before it strikes."

"Me, too," she hastily agreed.

He chuckled merrily. "Good," he lazily commented, passing his forefinger over her lips. "What a torment you are, my golden dream."

She quivered. "We definitely better make haste if you're going to look at me like that," he warned

252

mirthfully, his eyes softening and glowing with a response she recognized: tender—but dangerous—passion.

"How far to your cabin?" she asked instead, thoughts of being alone playing havoc with her concentration. "You never told me you have a cabin here."

"We should get there before nightfall, barring any trouble. Hopefully Ben will have supper ready and waiting."

"Ben?" she echoed. "Who's Ben?"

"Weathers, an American. He's been living with me for the past two years. He prospects and traps. Nice fellow; you'll like him."

"We won't be alone in your cabin?" she hinted, traces of disappointment ringing in her voice. She wondered what people thought about their marriage, when he had a cabin here and she had one there.

He laughed merrily. "It's according to how long I can convince you to remain there. Ben comes and goes every few weeks. He's a loner like me. We get along nicely. We have adjoining claims."

"Won't he object to you bringing a strange woman home?" She observed him closely. Why hadn't he mentioned his friend and cabin before?

"Ben Weathers is an easy-going fellow. Besides, it's my cabin, and you are my wife." His eyes glittered with amusement.

"But he does share it with you," she argued.

"I told you, he's only there about two weeks out of every month."

"I don't think I should stay there with him present, Landis. He might get the wrong idea," she mildly protested, fretting over the permanence and honesty of their union. Why all these secrets?

"Worried about your reputation?" he teased in amusement.

"Someone has to," she stated in irritation. "After all, you did make it perfectly clear to me this isn't a regular marriage!"

He caressed her cheek and calmly advised, "Don't worry about it, love. Some day we'll make it very regular."

She wanted to ask when, but couldn't. Needing reassurance, she reasoned, "But how can we gain an annulment if we openly live together? You said no one should know but us. What about this Ben?"

"It's obvious you're in love with me and can't resist my charms, so why would we need to destroy this intriguing marriage?"

"You're a rake, Landis Jurrell! Are you sure you want to remain bound to me, or any female? Stifling chains?"

Lusty laughter filled the still air. "You're incredible woman. I would be a blind fool to throw away a golden treasure. Do I look like a dull-eyed simpleton? Fact is, I'm starting to enjoy this set-up."

"That isn't the issue, and you know it. Why do you call me Kat; you make me sound like some wild, uncontrollable critter!"

"Wild, no. But most assuredly uncontrollable. Why are you getting so riled up?" he asked in bewilderment.

Unnerved, she snapped, "I don't know!"

He suddenly sent forth peals of taunting laughter. "What's so funny?" she demanded, pelting his chest with her fists.

"You, Kat. You're as blasted frustrated as I am."

"What do you mean, frustrated?" she naively demanded.

He began to nibble at her lips and ears. She quivered.

"Stop it, Landis," she weakly argued. "You said we couldn't . . ."

He leaned back and informed her, "That's what I mean by frustration. We're both heated up and we can't cool off here."

She glared at him, then suddenly smiled. "As I said, Landis Jurrell; you are a rake. Let's go before I freeze."

Landis offered Kathy some dried jerky from his pack, then told her they couldn't have any hot coffee. She sighed regretfully, accepting the dark brown stick. "This is awful. How do you stand it?"

"It's very nourishing, my golden torment. Chew on it while we're traveling. Those snow clouds are moving in fast."

He gathered his possessions and placed them on his back. As he reached for hers, she declined, not wishing to be more trouble than necessary. "A backpack gets mighty heavy after a while," he noted.

"When and if it does, I'll give it to you. If I can't take care of myself, then I shouldn't be here." She was delighted and relieved when he didn't mock her.

"Suit yourself. Just let me know when and if you need help. I don't want your stubbornness to slow us down. I'm anxious to get home. Blizzards are deadly, Kat."

Kathy apprehensively glanced at the sky, then shivered with cold. This was going to be a very demanding day, and she was determined she wouldn't be a weakling.

"Ready?" he asked in suppressed amusement.

"Lead on, my dashing guide," she responded.

At her choice of words, he grinned mischievously and charged, "You certainly have a dangerous way of getting what you want, woman. Looks like I'm your guide whether I want to be or not."

"You could always leave me stranded here in these icy

wilds," she parried. "But then who would share their body heat with you along this glacial journey?"

"This is the first time I've enjoyed such a luxury. I wouldn't want it to become habit-forming."

"Would that be so terrible?" she speculated, pretending to adjust her pack but watching him from beneath lowered lashes.

"Most assuredly. I go places where no woman should go, sometimes no man. You'd be a deadly distraction in some situations."

"I would not!" she objected, defiantly sticking out her chin.

"I can just see you now, screaming and clinging to me while a pack of starving wolves are tearing after us. I wouldn't be able to get off a single shot. I'd be so worried about your survival that I'd endanger both of ours. Not to mention having to fight off dozens of love-starved prospectors," he teased her.

Kathy had gone white at his first statements. "You mean wolves actually stalk people and eat them?" she asked horrified.

"It's been known to happen. If the winter's harsh and food scarce, they'll kill and eat anything. But it's too early for them to be so desperate. But, if they catch sight of such a delectable piece of meat, they might battle me to get it," he irresistibly added.

"You're just teasing me, Landis Jurrell! That's mean to scare me like that," she admonished him.

"Let me warn you; I don't want any arguments or defiance. When I give an order, you jump. Is that clear?" he demanded gravely.

"I'll obey, Master. You don't have to get so nasty."

"Yes, I do, Kat. You've got a willful streak a mile long. I don't want any backtalk. You're not in civilization anymore. This place has perils you can't even imagine. If you hesitated for one minute to obey me, you could get us both killed."

"Just what are you trying to say, Landis?" she asked, confused.

"If I say halt, you stop dead in your tracks. If I say run like the wind, you do it. If I say shut your lovely chattering, hush up immediately. Even if the order sounds silly, do it anyway."

Kathy stared at him. His mood and look were strange, serious. "Whatever you say, Landis," she agreed, without understanding why.

They began to head northward. Within a hundred yards, he halted abruptly and shouted back at her, "Be still and quiet!"

Instead, Kathy hurried forward to join him and anxiously asked, "What's wrong?" She glanced around, sighting no danger.

He whirled around and glared into her expectant, unturned face. "You are, Mrs. Jurrell!" he snarled.

"Me?" she debated. "What did I do now?"

"What orders did I give you back there?" he demanded tersely.

She repeated them. Her bewildered expression told him she didn't catch his drift. "Did you obey me just now?" he challenged. "I said be still and quiet. Were you?"

"But I thought something was wrong," she tried to excuse herself.

"If something had been wrong, we could be in trouble right now. What if I had seen those men lurking ahead? When I speak, woman, you obey," he thundered, his voice echoing around them.

"You don't have to get so huffy, Mr. Jurrell! I understand completely. I'm not dense!" she yelled back at him, hurt and angry.

"I'm trying to make sure you reach my cabin, woman. If you don't react to my commands, you might not."

"You wouldn't leave me out here?"

"That isn't what I meant. You don't seem to grasp the dangers around here, Kat. When you're in my territory and under my guard, you'll do as told. I'm not going to see you hurt or killed."

"You've made your point. Do you have to keep belaboring it?"

"Not if you really get it. Let's go," he snapped imperially.

Landis walked away. Kathy watched his retreat for a minute before following after him. They walked for nearly one hour before he whirled to his left, drawing his gun and shouting at her, "Hit the ground, Kat!"

Without the slightest hesitation, she fell flat into the snow and rested her face on her crossed arms. She was still and mute. He smiled, replacing his weapon. He strolled to her and stood looking down at her. "Let's go, Kat; you did fine that time."

She lifted her head and glanced around. Her line of vision included his black boots and arrogant stance. She pushed herself to a sitting position and looked around. His words sank in. Nettled, she glared up at him. "Another test, Mr. Jurrell?" she snippily asked.

"Next time, it won't be. I can trust you to react quickly."

He leaned over and pulled her to her feet, then began to brush the snow from her clothing. "I can do that myself!" she snapped in rising annoyance, feeling his behavior unjust. "I hope you're satisfied this time," she sneered at the domineering rogue.

"Yep. Sorry you're upset. That first time you defied my orders. I had to make certain it wouldn't happen again," he relented slightly.

"You've already explained how vital it is for me to obey you. I said I would. In case you haven't noticed before, Mr. Jurrell, I'm a fast learner," she informed him coolly, her implications clear.

"You certainly are, Mrs. Jurrell. I won't have need to test your intelligence and obedience further, so calm down. You'll need all that energy and spirit today."

"You sound just like a Mounty issuing orders," she protested his bossy attitude and unnecessary harshness.

"Do I?" he murmured, drilling his gaze into hers.

"That, or worse. I'll obey, Sergeant," she vowed, mockingly saluting him. He frowned and turned away from her.

He told her to follow him, which she sullenly did. A light snow began to fall, steadily increasing its intent to heavily add another white cover on the ground. Soon, a blanket of fluffy snow covered the crunchy white one as far as the eye could see, gradually pulling at each step taken. Kathy was huffing from her exertions, white mist clouding from her nose and mouth each time she exhaled. She thought she would actually freeze solid if she didn't get warm soon. Her nose and cheeks felt numb. Her lips felt odd, moving distortedly each time she opened them. Her teeth chattered noisily. Her gloved hands were comfortable, but her thumbs ached with cold. The glacial air plagued her lungs as she fought to breathe without drawing in more of that icy air than necessary.

Kathy's legs were exhausted and her back ached. They had trudged in silence, but for the muffled sound of footsteps in the snow and the winds playing in the trees. It had been several hours since their disagreement; neither had spoken and Landis hadn't even glanced back at her. The trees were covered with snow, their limbs hanging low from the weight of the white intruder upon them. Each time the wind blew briskly, the leaden limbs would seem to shudder in relief and divest themselves of their burdens.

Every so often, Kathy would brush the mounting snow from her hood and shoulders. She didn't know if it would melt and soak her or if it would freeze and weight her down. For certain, the pack on her slender shoulders weighed enough without Mother Nature adding her load!

Surrounded by tall trees and falling snow, the approaching white-capped peaks were concealed. Kathy was amazed by the sudden contrasts in this awesome frontier. It was almost an abrupt contradiction of land-scape—from towering and magnificent mountains, to perilous gorges, to raging rivers with deadly rapids, to splendid glaciers, to yawning canyons, to forested cliffs and gently sloping hillsides.

A careless person could tumble into an abyss or fall off a precipitous cliff. He could be cast from his boat into those churning waters and dashed against jagged rocks or pulled into a powerful whirlpool. This land lent itself to a stark reality of the wildness and power of nature, to selfish tragedy and hardships. How much worse could a place be? Why would anyone in his right mind wish to live here? Merely surviving another day was a fierce challenge. Was that it? Did these men savor the danger and adventure here? This life was definitely not for Kathryn Leigh Hammond! But Kathryn Jurrell?

As Kathy observed Landis's broad back and masterful movements, she realized he wasn't having any difficulties at all. But why should he; he was accustomed to the rigid demands of this arduous area. He walked as easily as if he was taking a leisurely stroll on solid ground. The way his strong arms swung at his sides, he obviously wasn't cold or weary. What an unusual and splendid creature he was! In spite of her resolve, Kathy knew she couldn't keep up this pace without some rest . . .

She had been praying for the last two miles that he would halt and offer her some rest. When it appeared he wasn't going to reveal any consideration, she knew she must.

"Landis, wait up, please," she raggedly called out.

He halted and turned around. "I need to stop for a while," she reluctantly informed him.

He wasn't breathing hard! How she envied his stamina. "We aren't making good time, Kat, and the weather's getting worse. I've been walking slowly for you to keep up. Do you really need to stop?"

"Please let me rest just a minute," she pleaded. "My back and calves are aching, not to mention my ankles."

He scanned her weary face and slumped shoulders. He was pushing her hard, but it was necessary. "Sit on your pack for a little while," he tenderly relented.

A radiant smile flickered over her face. "Thanks," she murmured and dropped on the bundle, sighing heavily. Landis handed her some jerky, which she began to chew, frowning at its taste and texture.

"Tell me something, Kat; what will you do when you find your father?" he asked from seemingly nowhere, looking off into the trees.

"I honestly don't know, Landis. I suppose it depends on how he reacts to seeing me again. I find it hard to believe he even cares about me. I've never heard from him. If he learns I'm here searching for him, he might resent my intrusion. He might even avoid me altogether. Who knows, maybe I won't find him." She sighed dejectedly, then coughed to clear the lump which had formed in her throat.

Landis was deeply moved by the anguish and uncertainty written in her sad eyes and on her somber face. "If he's here, we'll locate him; I promise you that, love. If not, you have me." He squatted before her to gently massage her calves and thighs.

She smiled at him. She warmed to that tender streak which was showing again. "What if he doesn't wish to be found? What if he doesn't want to have anything to do with me? He might not even like me if we do meet. Maybe he feels like you do," she unwittingly accused.

"And how do I feel, Kat?" he asked for clarification, halting his movements, his gaze locking with hers.

"You like being alone and carefree. You don't want to be saddled with responsibilities," she reiterated his previous statements.

"I think it's a wee bit late for both of us to feel that way, Kat. Jake did get married and have a child. Whether he wants them or not, he has responsibilities to you," he asserted confidently.

"What if he decided he made a terrible mistake, one he feels he's corrected by abandoning me? He doesn't even know my mother's dead. For all I know, he could care less that's she's dead and I'm alone," she reasoned, bitterness lacing her words. "Maybe he feels he doesn't owe me anything. He left us plenty of money and surely he knows I'm of age now. I used to think that maybe he fell in love with someone and ran off with her. After all this time, it wouldn't seem impossible for him to have another woman. As you told me before, a man doesn't have to marry the woman he loves."

"I'm not like other men, Kat; you can't compare me to them or to your father. How do you know your mother didn't drive him away?"

Kathy was suffused with anger. "How can you say something like that? You didn't even know my mother. She was beautiful and charming. She was witty and intelligent. She came from a very good family. She loved him. She waited around for his return until she died. My father's cruel and selfish. I hope I don't find him!" she exploded.

"Then why don't you leave this wilderness and go home?" he reasoned in a curious tone, waiting tensely for her reply.

"I don't have a home, except the cabin. Mother sold the house in Washington before we started looking for Papa. I don't have any kin either. Just where do you suggest I go, and do what? Are you eager to be rid of me, Mr. Jurrell?"

"Look at yourself, Kat. You don't belong in a rough place like this," he chided, tugging at her defiant chin.

"Where do I belong now, Landis?" she asked sadly.

"Someday with me, Kat," he gave a reply she didn't wish to hear.

"I wish I knew you, Landis. First, you ask me to play around. Then, you suddenly marry me. Now, you practically demand I leave Alaska and the Yukon. What do you want from me?"

"Right now, I don't have the right to ask anything, Kat." He pulled her to her feet and turned her around. Slipping his hands under her clothes, he briefly worked on sore muscles near her waist.

"Will you ever?" she pressed for a clearer answer, turning.

After a lengthy silence, he looked her straight in the

eye and stated, "Several times you've accused me of misleading you and taking advantage of you in moments of distress; I won't do that again, if I can prevent it. I can't make you any promises until I can keep them. I can tell you one thing; if I were Jake Hammond, I could never have deserted my wife and child. We better get going," he quickly added, vexed at having revealed such sensitive feelings.

"You're afraid to reach out to me, aren't you? You're afraid I'll threaten that freedom and privacy you love so dearly. Every time you start to relax around me and share a part of yourself with me, it makes you stiff with panic. You don't have to worry, Landis; I'm not going to entrap you. If any bond ever develops between us, it will have to come from you first. I won't pressure you or use feminine wiles on you. But you owe me more than future promises. If you keep pushing me away every single time, one day I might not be there when and if you change your mind," she gently warned.

They stared at each other. "Are you threatening me, Kat?" he demanded, his tone laced with an emotion she couldn't read.

"No, Landis, just giving you fair warning."

"It isn't necessary. I know what I have to gain or lose." He turned when she didn't respond. He loaded his pack and placed it over his shoulders. "You ready for me to carry that pack now?"

"I'm doing just fine. You needn't trouble yourself."

"Fine. Let's go." Once more the depressingly endless silence and torturous walking began.

Landis fell into deep and moody reflection. There were countless hardships and perils in this vast, bitter land. Suffering and strife were intimate companions to many of these men, sometimes including himself. Every day he challenged danger and fate to control his own destiny, one threatened by more than a few enemies and forces. Most of the men who came here were fools to believe Alaska and the Yukon were generously offering their golden dreams without costly prices.

Like Kathy, he had an elusive search of his own to carry out. Conquering this frozen earth would probably be easier than what he had to master. In his day, he'd found lots of gold. But Kathy was a special treasure, like a nugget of rare worth. He called her face to mind: eyes of richest and clearest sapphire, complexion like creamy white pearls, hair as golden as the treasure most men sought here.

But the timing was all wrong. All of his life, adventure had been his first love, danger and excitement ruling most of his days. As he'd told Kathy once before, love was like gold, charming dreamers, taking away their freedom and clear wits. Yet, on every turn, there she was at his side again, accepting his unspoken challenge to prove him wrong, to tame his strong will, to remove his tightly controlled loneliness. Harriet had been right; Kathy was changing. She wasn't that starry-eyed, innocent, vulnerable girl he'd met that first day. She was strong, resourceful, and resilient now. Was he mostly responsible for her changes, to blame for others?

She'd become very much a woman since coming here, molded in some ways by the hardships and despairs she'd encountered. From their first meeting, he'd been open and honest about his feelings. Even knowing such things, she had daringly offered her heart and body to him. But each time he was compelled to slow down things between them, he was hurting her without meaning to do so. Sometimes he could read the defeat and bitterness in her lovely eyes, though she fiercely tried to hide them. Surely she loved him and wanted him?

Was he being a fool? What if he did push too hard once too often? What if she used up her store of dreams and tears, of patience and sharing? You are my golden torment, Kat, he thought. I want you, and I can't relent just yet. Two others have died trying to carry out this job. I can't risk involving you or allowing you to be hurt more. I've got to locate Jake Hammond, and get you back to Skagway where you'll be safe until this situation is settled.

Still, he couldn't help but wonder what he would do and say if the moment for choosing between her and his duty was forced on him. He was too accustomed to having his way, to having his total freedom. If she decided to leave this territory, would he stop her? Could he? Did he have the right to make such a decision? You're wrong about me, Kat, he said to himself. My heart's not as frozen as this glacial territory. Would my life ever be the same if I lost you?

She had said she wouldn't entrap him or charm him; yet, that was exactly what she was doing. He was trapped between her and his duty. Besides, he couldn't forget Rodgers's last message before his death, warning of a deadly dream with eyes like sea-water and hair of golden silk. What made matters worse for him was Telford's last message that he was going to meet a "golden dream" for information. Both mounties had vanished, to later turn up dead, after two similar clues. It sure would make matters simpler if both men hadn't been killed after Kathy's mysterious arrival, while she was in the same area. Why had she asked if Landis Jurrell was his real name? Why had she mockingly called him sergeant? Then, there were those two strange letters.

Landis scoffed at his suspicions. How could this gentle creature be involved in something like international intrigue? What was the matter with him? Where were those keen wits and instincts which he so often depended on for solving such problems? He knew; Kathryn Hammond Marlowe was playing havoc with his concentration! Jake Hammond was the answer to his dilemma; once found, the truth about her would be clear. That is, if Jake was actually her father . . .

As if he could mentally force the information from her head, he turned to drill his eyes into her. He stopped. Panic seized him. She wasn't behind him, nor in sight! Landis dropped his pack and raced back around the last curve in the trail, breathing heavily in his alarm. Then, he saw her. She had dropped to her knees about two hundred yards back. So deep in his mental study, he wouldn't have heard her call out to him. If he hadn't come to awareness, she could have been left far behind. Fury aimed at both of them surged through his body.

He hurried back to her and stormed as coldly as the weather, "What are you doing? I was almost a mile ahead of you before I realized you weren't behind me! We'll freeze when that blizzard sets in!"

She looked up into his frigid expression, her face pale and cold. "We've been walking for hours, Landis. I had to rest a few minutes. I was going to catch up. I'm not used to this climate and to walking forever! I'm tired, and I'm hungry and thirsty. My hands and legs are numb. I can't go any further. I can't," she whispered raggedly, lowering her head in exhaustion, too weary to feel ashamed of her weakness.

He dropped to one knee and seized her shoulders, shaking her. "Listen to me, woman; if you want to die, then sit here on your tail while you freeze. I'm going home where it's warm and cozy, where there's hot food, a bath and a bed. I'm tired, and cold, and hungry, too. So stop your whining and get to walking."

"I'm not made of endless energy and strength like you are, Mr. Jurrell. I'm human, in case you haven't noticed! I can't move!" she protested weakly.

"You'll stand up and start walking this minute or I'll drag you the rest of the way," he ominously threatened. "We'll be there in a couple of hours if we get going. We've only got two hours of light left. In case you haven't noticed," he snarled, "that blizzard is stalking us like a grizzly! Look behind you!" he ordered.

Landis knew he had to force Kathy to move out. If she was so tired that she was refusing to take another step, he would have to make certain she did! Anger and pride normally gave a person extra energy; he had to work on those emotions.

"Do you recall how many times I warned you about coming inland? But you had to do it! If you can't cut it here, why did you stupidly come in? Only a fool would lie down and die out here! I've seen men so eager to live they crawled on their bellies the last few miles to help! You really talked big back there. But when the going gets tough, you lay down and cry like a baby. Do you want me to die, Kat?" he tried another approach, the first one seeming to fail.

"Don't be ridiculous," she muttered feebly, eyes tearful.

"I can't leave you here alone. If you don't get off your lovely ass, then I'll have to remain here with you. When that blizzard strikes, we'll both be dead. Frankly I'm not in a dying mood tonight. Either get up or I'm going to tie a rope around you and drag you with me."

Kathy began to weep. Landis quickly brushed at her

tears, shouting, "Stop that or your eyes will freeze shut! Take my hand," he offered, standing up and extending it to her. "Let's go home, Kat."

She looked at it, then closed her eyes briefly as she summoned the will and strength to take it. He was right; they had to get home before nightfall or the storm hit, whichever was first. From the way it was snowing, it would be a close race. Home, what a lovely word.

She placed her hand in his and murmured doubtfully, "All right. I'm coming. I'm sorry, Landis."

He pulled her to her feet, then removed her pack. "You can't carry both, Landis," she faintly argued.

"I've carried twice as much weight ten times further than my cabin, and quicker," he stated smugly. "You want a lift, too?"

Kathy risked a glance to their rear. The landscape was obliterated by what appeared an ethereal wall of white. Limbs encased in white, only dark trunks of trees could be seen, their upper branches blending into the white backdrop. The snow was swirling wildly and dancing freely on the brisk winds. She had to stare hard to detect faint outlines. Even the staunch evergreens appeared a muted gray. As she gaped at this ominous visitor, she fearfully realized the obscure white wall was moving closer and closer to them.

He tossed her pack over his left shoulder, then slipped his right arm around her waist. "Hold on to me for a while," he suggested.

"I know I'm a pain, and I'm sorry. I didn't realize it was like this in here," she confessed softly. "I'm glad you found me."

"Now you know. When you get back to Skagway, how about staying there? I'll look for your father," he stated.

They began to retrace the steps of Landis's frantic race

back to her. Kathy leaned against his hard body for support, his arm remaining around her waist. What had he been thinking to bring her along? he thought. He should have taken her back to Stewart. Hours ago, she would have been warmed and fed. It was too late for regrets now. He secretly glanced down at her. She was staring ahead, a look of sheer determination on her face as she took agonizing step after step. His heart soared with love and pride.

She looked up at him to ask him a question which had been plaguing her mind all day to find him watching her intently. He hastily focused his gaze ahead of them. Were those lines of intense worry etching his handsome face? He was truly concerned about their survival? It felt so good to be snuggled in his arms. As they reached his discarded pack, she smiled at him and stated optimistically, "I can make it now. What about the two men back there?"

"Their bodies are frozen by now, so they'll be all right. When we get home, I'll send a message to Log Cabin. You didn't see any of the attackers?"

"No, I was too far away and hidden. I'm sorry. Do you think the Mounties will find out who did it?"

"Haven't you ever heard their slogan? They always get their man—or woman," he teased to lighten her mood.

As if shocked by that news, she inquired, "You mean you have female criminals? What could a woman do wrong here?"

"Don't they everywhere?" he jested, placing the pack on his shoulders. "There are crimes, then there are crimes."

She thought about that statement. "I suppose so," she concurred.

"Ready?" he hinted, winking at her.

"No, but let's go anyway," she teased in return.

The ~~last leg of their journey~~ was a nightmare for Kathy. It was a painful blur of forcing herself on and enduring the aches of her rebellious body. Landis moved as if by instinct, seeming to follow an inner compass in this area visibly altered by nature. Several times Landis had to take her hand and tug her forward when she began to unknowingly linger behind. She finally reached the point when she was even too fatigued to plead or to cry.

Within a mile of his cabin, she collapsed to her knees. He bent over her and encouraged, "We're almost there, Kat."

"You go on without me. I can't go any further, Landis. I . . ."

Before the last words could come forth, she went limp. He grabbed her to prevent her from falling face forward into the snow. He shook her and called her name; she was out cold. When he realized he couldn't arouse her, he was left with only one choice.

He lay her on the ground and walked off a short distance. He removed both packs and hid them beneath some overhanging branches, dislodging their coats of white. It was almost dark and he could barely see; yet, he knew this area well. He went back to Kathy and picked her up in his arms. He headed for his cabin, the white blanket at his feet so deep now that it threatened to trip him. He wished he had his snowshoes, but he hadn't packed them this trip. He would retrieve the packs in the morning. Right now, he had to get her inside and warm.

After a while, his own energy was draining. This kind of walking was difficult alone, but carrying someone else . . . He shifted her light weight and gently tossed her over his shoulder, making his task easier on him. Finally, the cabin loomed just ahead.

He inhaled in irritation; the cabin was dark. That meant Ben wouldn't have a cozy fire and hot meal ready. He reached the door and unlocked it, stumbling inside in the darkness. He headed for his bed and placed Kathy there. He pulled off her boots, testing her icy toes. He drew off her furry gloves and kissed the palm of each cold hand. He struggled to remove her parka, pants, and flannel shirt without awakening her. She needed rest and sleep more than food.

When she was undressed, he placed her under the covers. He grinned as she snuggled into a tight ball to get warm, not once opening her eyes. He pulled the covers over her and tucked her in. He closed the cabin door, after kicking out the snow which had tumbled inside. Then Landis went to build a fire to melt away nature's icy fingers. Once he had a nice blaze nipping at the wood, he looked for a note from Ben. He always let Landis know where he was and how long he would be gone.

Landis scanned the words on the page and smiled broadly, eying the bundle in his bed. Ben had left early this morning, to be gone for two weeks. Landis cautioned himself not to whistle merrily as he prepared some coffee, then hot biscuits. What better way to ferret out the truth from Kathy than to have her in his control?

"One day I'll repay you for this timely favor, my friend," he murmured, then laughed softly.

Eleven

Kathy snuggled into the softness of the bed, sighing and stretching languidly. She felt deliciously warmed and relaxed. After yesterday's torturous journey . . . yesterday? Flashes of her hazardous ordeal swept through her gradually awakening mind: the glacial weather, the endless cold and physical demands, the misery, the doubt of survival, and Landis's continuous pressure and harsh words. She recalled her collapse in the freezing snow near dark. Was she dead?

She trembled and her eyes fluttered, fearing to test this dire thought. "Cold, love?" a vibrantly rich voice inquired.

Her sapphire eyes flew open and she looked into ones as dark as midnight itself. Her gaze scanned his handsome, bold features. His ebony hair was slightly mussed, as if he had just returned from the windy outdoors. Her eyes eased down his chest, noting the furry mat which was peeking from beneath a heavy shirt and fur-lined jerkin in deep brown. His large hands rested on hips encased in black pants.

Landis enjoyed her scrutiny, one which caused a tightening in his loins. He smiled, eyes and mouth softening. He ran fingers through his hair, watching her. "Hungry?" he asked, sitting down.

"I'm not dead?" she exclaimed.

"You did sorely tempt fate, but I don't give up my property so easily," he laughed.

Kathy sat up, the covers falling to her lap. She moved her shaky hands up and down her arms to test for feeling. She glanced at her unfamiliar surroundings. "Where are we?" she inquired.

"My cabin. Breakfast is about ready if you care to join me."

"How did we get here? I remember passing out on the trail."

"I carried you. I might add, someone as light as you is heavy under those conditions," he laughingly informed her, tugging on a straying curl.

"Why?" she asked. "You said if I couldn't make it you'd leave me behind," she refreshed his previous threat.

He threw back his head and laughed heartily. "That was just to give you spunk. You know I wouldn't leave you out there," he tenderly scolded her. "You best put some clothes on before I forget about food. You must be starved; you missed supper. You were so exhausted I couldn't awaken you."

She looked down to see she was undressed, then gasped and pulled the covers to her neck. "Is your friend here? What did he say about my unexpected arrival?"

"Ben's gone for two weeks," he stated, caressing her flushed cheek.

"You mean we're alone here?" she squeaked, suddenly unsure of herself and this heady situation, observing his sensual grin.

"Yep. You get dressed and I'll finish breakfast," he suggested, not making a romantic advance, to her surprise and disappointment. After all, she was in his bed and alone in his cabin. He was awfully spirited—yet restrained—this morning.

"Are you still mad with me about yesterday?" she asked.

"Only for venturing in here. Maybe now you'll believe me when I tell you this isn't a safe place for you. I should get you to Skagway as soon as possible," he added, which baffled and disappointed her. "I believe you've had a menacing taste of my territory."

"You're mighty eager to get rid of me all of a sudden, Mr. Jurrell. What happened to your invitation to stay with you?" she scoffed.

"I assumed you'd be demanding to leave after my over-bearing treatment yesterday. To survive, I had to keep pushing you, even threatening you. I think you can see that now. As to staying here, you'll have to remain at least two weeks, or find someone else to take you back. Think you can endure my offensive company that long?" he hinted with a sly grin.

"The loner gets lonely? You want me to stay until Ben returns?"

He chuckled, his eyes dancing with mischief. "I can think of better reasons to enjoy your company for two weeks. If I simply wished a female's company, there are plenty in less than a day's reach."

She tensed in annoyance, her smile vanishing. She pertly stated, "No doubt they quarrel over who's going to entertain you when you reach Dawson."

"No doubt," he playfully fenced. "But that sounds more like words coming from Soapy's mouth than this lovely one," he charged, running his finger over her lips. "I'm not a priest, Kat, but I don't hanker to spend time with cheap women. I'm a man, but I do have a fetching wife."

She travelled his arresting features and virile physique. She grinned and remarked brazenly, "Yes, Mr. Jurrell, you are a man, very much so. Do you go to Dawson often?" she probed helplessly, looking down at her hands.

He smiled and playfully accused, "Why, you jealous?"

"Why should I be? After all, you are my husband. But I was referring to going there for other reasons," she lied noticably. "If you're going to search for my father, that seems the best place to start."

"I'll take you there in a few days, if you wish. Of course, you'll probably want to stay once you see it. It's the only civilization around."

She laughed saucily and asked, "You want to keep me to yourself for a while? Afraid I might trade you for another protector?"

"If there's one thing this territory has, it's plenty of available men. But I think you'll be better off with me. I do have a prior claim."

"For fear of enlarging that swollen head of yours, I won't agree. You have a nice home here," she noted, vividly changing the subject.

"I like it, and it does the job. Coffee?" he suggested, heading for the stove in the adjoining room.

"Marvelous," she replied, getting out of bed. "Where are my clothes?"

"I was tempted to hide them. But being the gentleman I am, I dried them by the fire instead. Over here," he pointed to where her clothes were warming by the open fire.

She retrieved them. Landis eased up behind her, allowing his strong arms to encircle her waist. "They might not be warm enough to put on yet."

She felt them. "It appears they are. Thanks."

Still, she didn't make any attempt to free herself and dress. Instead, she leaned back against his hard body, placing her hands over his. "You saved my life, Landis. How will I ever repay you?"

"Give me a moment; I'll think of something."

"I'm sure you will." Her body quivered as much as her voice.

"I'm not a strong man when it comes to rejecting golden dreams."

She turned in his embrace and looked up into his enticing expression. "Then why do you?" she boldly challenged.

Their eyes met and fused silently. His hands unlocked and wandered up into her silky tresses, then roamed over her shoulders and down her arms. He abruptly pulled her arms loose, then backed away a few steps. Bewilderment flooded her eyes. "Maybe this golden dream is too costly. I'll finish breakfast," he stated again, his frame taut and his mood odd.

"Self-preservation again, Mr. Jurrell?" she humorously teased. "Aren't you forgetting some dreams are free for the taking?"

"Nothing comes free, Kat," he parried. "Everything, including love and passion, has its price and responsibilities."

"You could be wrong, you know. Maybe the price isn't so terrible after all. Besides, you've already made a hefty down payment."

"I'm not sure I should accept your challenge."

"You're an adventurer, Landis. You live for danger and challenges. Afraid you'll lose this one? Or just afraid to find out?" she taunted, knowing there was only one way to get to him, one way to prove to him he was wrong and too cautious. Once these two weeks were gone, she had to know one way or the other if Landis's heart could be won. She loved him and wanted him desperately; she must bravely take this chance, as she felt it would be her last one. Once he realized what it could be like between them, some of his barriers would be broken down. She had to prove love was worth the risk; that she was worth possessing for a lifetime.

He eyed her skeptically. "You're a brazen hussy," he jested, hoping for one last stab at self-defense from her heady appeal.

"It isn't my fault; you made me that way," she lightly parried his attempt to change her mind. "Just give me two weeks," she coaxed.

"If you fail, you'll hate me," he warned. He had offered a mock marriage, then tricked her. He had forced the secret about her father from Bill Thomas. She needn't worry; he would locate Jake, but not for her. Afterwards, she would despise him, for it would cost her her father once more . . .

"Will I?" she fired back, smiling seductively.

"Defeat has a way of inspiring such emotions, love."

"What if I win?" she unflinchingly speculated.

They stared at one another. "What if I say no?" Landis asked.

"I'll leave today for Dawson," she vowed seriously.

"I see . . ." he murmured thoughtfully. "Even if I say yes, you still can't win, Kat. The timing's all wrong. Two weeks or two months couldn't make a difference right now. I would be lying if I allowed you to believe it would. I need more time, time you refuse me."

"I'm not demanding a commitment, Landis. I want to learn if there is a chance for us. To date, we've been at each other's throats every time we meet. Isn't it about time for a truce? Is that too much to ask?"

"You're fooling yourself, Kat; you want far more."

"And you don't?" she asked apprehensively.

"I can't afford to fall into this golden trap."

"Why do you always refer to me as a trap?"

"That's what you are, woman, a golden trap to lure me into your clutches," he teased. "Even if you prove whatever it is you're trying to, I can't yield. We'll be back to battling again."

"Can't? Or don't want to?" she scoffed.

"Can't, for certain," he confessed.

"I promise you won't be sorry. Afterwards, I won't make any demands on you or your precious time. I want you to learn that sharing love and yourself aren't so terrible. Just this once, give us some time and effort."

"It's the sharing I can't do at present. I've already told you I can't reveal my business or personal life, not even to my wife."

"I don't give a damn about your secrets! Only you. I won't ask a single question. If I say anything that annoys you, just tell me and I'll hush."

"Mighty tempting terms, woman. I just wonder if you can keep them."

"Try me. The minute I fail to keep my end of the bargain, you can kick me out. What have you got to lose?" she anxiously bargained.

"What if you become habit-forming?" he jested.

"That's your problem," she stated with a silvery laugh.

"That's been my problem ever since I met you."

She laughed and approached him, moving her hands provocatively up and down his firm chest. "Is it such a despicable one?"

"You're asking for trouble, Kat; you know that, don't you?"

"Perhaps," she acknowledged seductively, easing up

on her tiptoes to kiss him. "But you certainly make a stirring bundle of it."

He savored the sweetness of her mouth and touch, then leaned back and stared into her liquid eyes. "Two weeks, then you'll go back to Skagway to wait for me there?" he prompted.

Wait for him there? Why not here, or go with him? She smiled, feeling a heady sense of victory already. "I promise."

"Then you're on," he quickly accepted her challenge, covering her receptive mouth with a stirring kiss. "You realize breakfast will have to wait? I'm starved for more than food right now."

"So am I," she huskily concurred.

He slipped the straps from her shoulder, then unfastened the ties on her camisole. Kathy shamelessly allowed him to fully undress her, then himself. He lifted her in his arms and returned to the bed. He lay her there and joined her, stretching out beside her, where he reached for the covers and drew them over their nude bodies.

"You're so beautiful, Kat. Every time I look at you I want you. I must be the biggest fool around, but I'm going to rashly surrender."

She smiled as she offered her lips and body to him. Nothing mattered now, except having him. His lips tenderly ravished hers and he revelled in this new-found treasure. His hand slipped down soft skin to cup a firm breast and gently fondled it. It left to explore the full length of her body for as far as it could travel. His hand moved slowly over her chest, arms, and down her flat stomach. He deftly visited every curve and mound which came to his seeking fingers. Her flesh was so silky and yet sleekly firm. It was warm and pliant beneath his eager touch.

The enflaming expedition continued down her shapely hips and over slender thighs, to return by the inland trail to find a peak as yet unexplored. He lingered, testing and mapping his claim. His mouth slipped to her breasts to excite her beyond control, his warm tongue climbing each summit, to leisurely circle it and retreat to form another heady assault. His mouth and hands roved freely and wildly, stimulating her to a boldness of her own.

Kathy's trembling fingers wandered into his soft black hair. She drew him closer to her aching body. Her hand slid down his neck and played over the rippling muscles which flexed with his movements. His body was splendid, like a work of art. The flesh was hard, yet vital and smooth. She stroked his brawny shoulders and powerful arms, finding a small scar here and there.

Her exploratory trek took her over his supple buttocks and slim hips. Such power and passion could be felt within him. She moaned as her own passion heightened. His mouth came back to hers, nibbling at her lips and pressing kisses over her closed eyes. He whispered arousing words into her ears, teasing at the lobes so his warm respiration thrilled her. Her hand touched something, a hard object, which drew a groan from his lips . . .

Her hand closed around Landis's manhood, relishing the warmth and feel of it. He moved slightly, easing it back and forth within her gentle grasp. How intoxicatingly wanton and wonderful she felt. He eased between her thighs and guided himself into that warm, moist canal. Kathy arched to meet the entry which her body demanded to possess. He began moving provocatively, tantalizing her with the ecstasy of their contact. She gave herself over to this compelling dream-come-true.

His kisses became seductively savage, almost desperate in his attempt to give free rein to her passions as he tightly restrained his own. The blissful tension increased until she could stand no more. She cried out and clung to him as passion claimed its prize. He dismissed his control, to simultaneously travel the far reaches of pleasure with her.

Kathy mentally catalogued the stirring words he helplessly whispered into her ear as passion thundered through his body, "Kat, my love, my treasure more precious than gold, more wanted than freedom."

She tightened her embrace and rode the wild and carefree waves with him. His mouth claimed hers in a tender and lingering kiss as his drumming heart and ragged respiration slowed to normal. He rolled over, pulling her atop him, unwilling to release her. She curled against his body, both relaxed and satisfied. She dropped light kisses upon his shoulder as she fingered the furry covering on his chest. She listened to his thudding heart and smiled happily, sensing that even her inexperience in love had not failed to please him.

"Are you sorry you yielded, my intrepid guide?" she murmured contentedly. "I'm not such a terrible wife."

"You're a wily vixen who's cast her magic spell over me." His hand stroked her hair, then moved down to pull her more tightly against him. "I'm a possessive and demanding guide, Kat. Think you can tolerate me?"

"Completely, my love, completely."

"Hungry?" he asked after a while.

"Not anymore," she gaily remarked.

"I meant for food," he chuckled, enjoying her new spirit.

"Ravenous," she replied.

"Think we can join forces and rustle up some chow?"

"I think I can manage alone. I must prove my value."

"You just did, and most enjoyably."

She cocked her head to meet his twinkling eyes. "As I said, some dreams are free. I'll take good care of you while I'm here, Mr. Jurrell. You might discover I'm nice to have around for many reasons. The last time you were in Moore's camp, you did rant about expecting good service for your pay. And you did just pay me a very high salary."

"Is that a fact, Mrs. Jurrell?" he crooned, smiling.

"Indeed it is. Naturally I'm not as skilled as the women you're accustomed to, but I will try hard not to disappoint you. With time and effort, and a lot of tutoring from my dashing guide, I think I can keep you from being bored or restless."

He feigned dismay. "If you get any better, I know I'm in trouble. As far as I can see, you're the only temptation around these parts."

"You flatter me, kind sir."

He laughed. "Show your husband what other talents you possess; work me up a sturdy breakfast."

"At your service, Mr. Jurrell," she said, kissing him.

He eyed her suspiciously when she began to snuggle against him and boldly roam his body. "The stove's over there," he huskily muttered.

"I know," she responded, but continued her enticing game.

"You trying to tell me something, woman?"

She glanced up and laughed. "Only that I love you and love being here," she fearlessly answered, then rolled off the bed to dress.

"Halt!" he commanded. "You've got a few things to learn, woman. You don't heat a man up, then toss cold water on him."

She looked at her hands, then innocently told him, "I don't have any cold water, love. I was just going to fix your breakfast, even if it is midday. I can't allow my husband to starve."

His smoldering gaze scanned her naked body, then fused with her amusing one. Before she could playfully avoid his grasp, he seized her hand and yanked her back into bed. He pinned her squirming body beneath his, then kissed her until she was breathless. Holding her imprisoned, he worked feverishly on each breast until she cried out for mercy. He placed his taunting face within inches of hers and reprimanded, "Tease me, will you?"

Between giggles and thrashings, she vowed, "I didn't."

"To promise a venture, then to stop in your tracks isn't safe around me, woman. I take promises and challenges seriously."

She eyed him mischievously and mockingly asked, "You mean I can't kiss you without making love?"

"Not the way you were touching me while doing it."

"Then, I won't touch you when I kiss you."

"That'll be a feat to witness!" he exclaimed merrily.

He watched her give that exclamation some thought. Her eyes were soft and alluring, her manner was inviting. "You know something, Kat? It's good to have you here," he rashly admitted.

Surprise crossed her face. "You really mean that?"

"Yep. Let's eat, woman. I'm starved and I'm one meal up on you."

"You rogue! You let me sleep while you were stuffing!"

"I tried to rouse you, but you just wanted to sleep. I'm

sorry I had to be so rough on you yesterday," he apologized again.

"Next time, you won't have to," she promised.

"If we get in the same predicament again, I most assuredly will be the same way. You owe me, woman, and I plan to keep you around to collect. If I have to be rude to force you to survive, then I will," he warned, his expression serious.

"You are possessive and demanding. Maybe I'm getting into more than I realized. Maybe I should give this deal more thought."

"Not on your life. A bargain's a bargain. You're here for the duration of your challenge, my golden torment."

"Golden torment? From the way you were enjoying yourself earlier, I'm anything but that," she corrected him.

"For the next two weeks. But what about after you leave?"

"I'm afraid you'll have to deal with that when the time comes. If I'm to be miserable and lonely, you should be too."

"You're spiteful, Kat. Why would you want me suffering like that?"

"Because you bring it on yourself. It doesn't have to be . . ." Hastily recalling her promise to him, she smiled and stated, "I can't cook breakfast here, my charming gold-digger."

He caught her slip and hesitation. "Need any help? I'm experienced."

"You're skilled in many areas, my love. Thanks, but I can manage. I've certainly had lots of practice since coming here."

"In cooking?" he devilishly hinted.

JANELLE TAYLOR

"In lots of areas, Mr. Jurrell. But you do seem to be my tutor most of the time. Whatever would I do without you?"

"Any regrets there?"

"None. At least not yet," she added, biting his shoulder.

"Ouch! You trying to punish me for something?"

"No, just branding my property. You see, Mr. Jurrell, I'm also possessive and demanding."

"I was afraid of that. What female isn't?"

"Do you mind? After all, it'll only be for two short weeks."

"Don't remind me," he murmured, kissing her soundly.

He rolled aside and waved his hand for permission to arise. She grinned and stood up. "Any water to freshen up with?"

"On the stove. I'm a mind-reader," he warned with a sly grin.

"I hope not," she threw over her shoulder. She bathed and dressed while he stretched out on the bed to allow her some privacy. Odd, she didn't feel embarrassed. But then again, the area where the beds were was partitioned off with walls of hewn logs.

As she pulled on her clothes, Kathy studied her new surroundings. The cabin was large and homey looking. It was composed of two small bedrooms and one large room used as the kitchen and living area. At the far end was a storage closet. The windows were covered with heavy curtains, displaying a pretty pattern in deep blue and bold yellow on a dark tan background. She was astonished to observe several plush chairs and one short sofa! There was a handmade table near the brown sofa and beside one of the royal blue chairs. A wooden desk was in one corner of the living area, but the roll-top was down and no doubt locked.

The room was neat and clean. Several pelts were secured to the walls here and there, but no pictures could be seen. There was a lantern on the top of the desk and one on either small table. Another oil lamp was suspended from the ceiling in the center of the circle of chairs and sofa. She noted a wooden bookcase near the side wall, containing many books which she would scan later. She would later learn the windows had barred shutters, both inside and out to combat the harshest weather.

She noted the bar across the door, along with a sturdy lock. Her exploratory gaze roamed the kitchen area. There was a square eating table with four chairs. A row of cabinets lined one wall, holding dishes and staples. There was another working table next to the stove for preparation of meals and for washing dishes. Secured to hooks above that table were cooking pans and another larger one for dishwashing. Beneath the table she could see a few barrels which probably contained flour and such. A door opened off this area into a storage shed used for a large supply of firewood and gear for trapping and gold-mining.

She closed the door and went to the stove. A glowing fire was burning there. She smelled the coffee and sighed appreciatively. Kathy reached for an apron, but suddenly found Landis tying it around her waist for her. She glanced over her shoulder and smiled. "Find everything you need, love?" he asked, observing she hadn't started the meal yet.

"You have a nice home, Landis. I bathed and dressed first. I haven't looked for things yet. Save me time, and point them out."

Her study would have to continue later. Evidently the

other room belonged to this Ben Weathers. No doubt it was much like Landis's: a large bed, one tall chest, one chair, one trunk at the foot of the bed, and a triangular closet built into one corner. Sufficient for a man alone, she decided. Oddly, there was a picture hanging on his bedroom wall, an oil painting which depicted a winter scene of this territory.

The cabin squared off, Landis's room opened into the eating area while Ben's opened into the living area: side by side with two doors, but only one closed. She wouldn't go in there unless given permission for cleaning. The cabin was well constructed, snug and cozy. She was standing near the fireplace, where rocks reached from floor to ceiling and spanned over seven feet from side to side.

"You like it?" he pressed anxiously.

"Yes. I must admit it's quite a surprise for a bachelor's quarters. I didn't realize loners fared so neatly or comfortably. I can see you do very well on your own. It has a warm and friendly atmosphere."

"I take it you won't mind your stay here after all?"

She glanced around and sighed. "I think it will be most pleasant, and enlightening," she surmised, winking at him. "Now, how about a guided tour of your kitchen before we starve?"

It didn't take long working together to have fragrant biscuits cooking in the black stove's oven, cured ham frying in an iron skillet, and gravy simmering in another smaller skillet. They sipped coffee as they worked, each enjoying this genial setting. It seemed as though they were alone in the world. Landis took dishes from the cabinet and Kathy placed them on the table. He passed her tin salt and pepper dispensers, then joked about not needing the sugar. She giggled and told him to set it out anyway.

"You're most talented in the kitchen, kind sir. You'll make someone a nice wife," she teased him when he stole a kiss from her neck.

"We do make a great team, don't we?" he murmured against her ear.

"I was going to say the same thing, but was afraid you might take it the wrong way. I do hope you won't pounce on every innocent word I say."

Landis nearly said, don't be afraid to say anything you wish, but held himself back. "Smelling good in here, woman," he stated instead.

She intuitively knew what had taken place within his mind. "Why not sit down while I finish everything?" she cheerfully invited, feeling very much at ease as he mellowed before her.

He sat down, but pulled her into his lap and nuzzled her ear.

"Stop that, Landis Jurrell; or I'll not be responsible for a burned meal."

"Relax, Kat; everything's cooking just fine." He kissed her pervasively, running his hands up and down her back and arms.

"If I relax, I might forget all about cooking. You do have a way of mesmerizing me when it suits your purpose."

"Do I indeed?" he asked.

"You're most disarming and persuasive. I should take lessons from you."

"I thought you were," he crooned softly, a roguish grin capturing his face and pulling at her madly racing heart.

"If it's games you want to play, then I'll join in," she threatened, greedily devouring his mouth as she relented to his entreating arms.

When he leaned back against the tall chair, her head rested upon his shoulder. Their eyes fused and locked, sending passionate messages to the other. "It isn't a game anymore, Kat; is it?"

"How is it possible to want you so much it frightens me? Being with you is blissful agony. It's good and bad. Desire is a splendid appetite when it can be fed, but pure agony when it's hungry."

He leaned over to nibble on her ear, whispering, "The biscuits are probably burning." He needed to halt this serious talk.

She raced to the oven, yanking open the door without the thick pad. She screamed and jerked away her hand. Landis came over and seized it, scanning the injured area. She laughed. "Now I'm burning, too."

His gaze met hers as he beguilingly taunted, "In more than your hand?"

"You! You're impossible." She retrieved the pad and removed the perfectly browned biscuits. "See, I'm a good cook after all."

He reached for a jar of salve and rubbed it on the small burn. Both recalling their first meeting, their gazes fused. Reading the other's thought, they shared laughter. She thanked him and served their first meal together.

They chatted on safe topics as they ate. As they sipped one last cup of coffee, Kathy propped her elbows on the table and entreated, "Landis, why is there so much hostility between the Americans and your people? I can understand their resentment of so many men pouring into this territory to take advantage of the gold strike, but there's more to it. There's been trouble between America and Canada before, hasn't there?"

He looked over at her expectant face. "You don't resent my being American, you you?" she inquired, looking serious.

"Of course not. It's no secret there've been problems between your country and mine since the war of 1776. We are still part of the British empire," he reminded her. "I guess old wounds are hard to heal when fresh ones are frequently added."

"How so?" she asked, her full attention upon him.

"Animosities cropped up long before your Civil War. But during that war, Canada allowed slaves and soldiers to seek sanctuary here, which angered the Americans. You know why Russia sold Alaska to your country, don't you?"

"Not really. I know it's been a big joke to Mr. Seward."

"The Old Bear was hoping to build the States up as a counter-power to Britain's. Your country feared annoying the Russians and losing their friendship and support, so they accepted the deal. From what I've heard, the Russians lined many a pocket to help that deal go through. Another point, it would make one less power at America's back."

"But why would America relent to such pressure and double-dealing?" Kathy inquired with an innocence which warmed his heart.

"Power struggles. Self-defense. One less threat too close. It's no secret America hopes to entice Canada into her fold. That would make for a mighty large and powerful continent. Have you ever heard of James Blaine?" When she nodded yes, he went on, "Blaine said back in '91 that he expected Canada to seek admission to the American union. Britain didn't care for such statements. Then, there was all that mess about fishing rights a few years ago."

"I don't recall hearing anything about that."

"You should have; our countries almost went to war over it."

291

She looked stunned. "To war over fishing rights?"

"There was a big clash about '85 and America terminated a fishing treaty, and began fishing anywhere she chose in our waters. Canada felt compelled to confiscate those American fishing vessels. They finally worked out that disagreement, but another one came up near here. It started with the seal fisheries around the Bering Sea, somewhere between '86 and '90. There were rumors British warships were patroling the area. War talk got mighty common then. They finally signed another treaty in '92; and your country came out the financial loser, which still rankles the Americans. Things are stirring up again off the Alaska coast. Hopefully cool heads will win out."

"Is that all?" she pressed.

"Nope. There's the dispute between the Hudson Bay Company which is Canadian and the American Alaska Commercial Company. They've got some sticky competition going. The Bay Company has been in these parts for ages. They don't have the monopoly anymore, so they're trying hard to hold their own. The competition doesn't see eye to eye with some of their restrictions and policies. They don't hold to taking pelts and furs during the breeding season. That could wipe out a whole species. But it's hard to convince the private trappers and rival companies this would hurt each of them. Greed, Kat; it's a nasty and dangerous business."

"Why doesn't the Canadian government make laws to prevent such destruction and troubles?"

"They have laws, Kat. It's just difficult to carry them out when the territory's overrun with people grasping for anything of value they can find, or steal. It doesn't help matters that some of your people are claiming Yukon Territory in the name of America. Seems like the

States would set up some authority in Skagway and handle their own criminals and troubles; the Mounties have enough of their own. When they do catch a lawbreaker, the first thing he yells is he's American. I don't think Washington realizes how bad things are. With many of their criminals hiding out here and getting rich, you'd think they'd send someone to check things over. About the only people they do send are explorers, men wanting to see if this area's worth their time and trouble. You can bet your boots the gold strike caused quite a stir in your congress. Preston told me they're talking about an Alaskan homestead act. If they can take our gold and furs, the least they can do is help police this vast territory," he stated bitterly.

"If this area's so rich in resources and so likely to make trouble, why doesn't my country send help? It's foolish to buy property, then ignore it."

"Maybe your country hopes the trouble will lead to another sale."

"Surely you don't mean that?" she asked, offended.

"Look at it this way, Kat; Canada is located far from British help. It was beautiful and peaceful here until this gold strike."

"Bill Thomas must really like you and trust you," she casually remarked.

"What do you mean?" he asked, wariness edging into his gut.

"How else would you learn so much?" she reasoned.

"I have those friends in 'high places' who drop clues. And I keep my eyes and ears open, and my mouth shut."

"Is that a hint I'm being too personal or nosy?"

"Why are you so interested in this territory?" he evaded her question.

"If I was going to give any consideration to living here

permanently, I needed to know what things are really like. I don't mean the colorful tales and promises, but the truth. I thought you would tell me. You don't think there'll be real trouble between Canada and America, do you? I wouldn't want to get trapped in the middle. You told me several times I didn't belong here, that I can't make it. Is that really how you feel? Are things that terrible here, or do I lack the stamina and guts to take it?"

"That's a loaded question, Kat. Either answer I give makes me a loser," he mischievously jested, grinning at her.

"I don't follow you."

"If I say yes, you'll get angry, or take my word and leave. If I say no, you might stay and get hurt. After yesterday, I'd be a fool to say you lack guts and willpower, but it revealed that you have a dangerous impulsiveness and innocence. If greedy men weren't involved with the policies and companies on both sides, there wouldn't be any trouble. Smith is one of those greedy men, Kat. He's an agitator. He degenerates character and inspires trouble which is to his profit. Whenever there's serious trouble, Smith's hand is sure to be somewhere in it. Smith and his American accomplices are doing everything they can to add the Yukon to Alaska. Smith has grandiose ideas of being the first territorial governor. But once the railroad and telegraph are in here, his power will diminish. He doesn't want that until America controls this area," he carelessly dropped hints he shouldn't know.

"Why don't the Mounties stop him?"

"He always manages to stay just above openly breaking the law. Witnesses have ways of vanishing permanently around here, not to mention two Mounties who were working undercover to unmask him."

"He's really that dangerous?" she asked in amazement.

"More so, Kat. That's why I was so angry to see you with him. Soapy doesn't fire people and they don't quit; they vanish mysteriously or have fatal accidents," he noted.

"That doesn't speak highly of your Mounties, Landis. It seems someone could catch him commiting at least one crime."

"That's because they work inside the law and he doesn't."

"Then hire some man without morals or principles to handle him. Surely there's one man unafraid to go up against him? I'm surprised one of his victims hasn't slain him!"

"Some have tried. If he isn't handled properly, his death will only bring about his successor. Bill says, when he's defeated, it must be done as an example," he carefully informed her, seeking a spot to change the topic.

"But his example is do anything you wish and get away with it! How can people respect the law and fear it when they see it profitably broken?"

He chuckled. "What's so funny?" she inquired.

"You, love. You're naive and innocent when it comes to such matters."

"Why don't you take him on? You aren't afraid of anything or anyone, or so Dray said," she carelessly dropped a hint.

"And what else did Dray tell you about me?" he probed.

"Nothing. Nobody seems to know anything about the mysterious Landis Jurrell. Since Smith is defaming your territory, why not stop him yourself? You sound as if you have great love for the Yukon."

"I'll let a qualified Mounty handle that problem. I have a much prettier one to work on." He grinned at her. "More coffee, love?"

"Subject closed, Mr. Jurrell," she said, deciding he was ready to drop this line of conversation. "Anything else before I clean up?"

"No thanks. Need any help?"

"I'll manage." Before she stood up, she bravely asked one last question, "Were we married under American or Canadian law?"

"Why?" he asked. "You plotting your desertion already?"

"I just wondered if one country's laws were valid in another country."

He laughed mirthfully. "We were wed under English sea-law; binding anywhere, Mrs. Jurrell. That's why I chose the ship," he teased.

She smiled, then began to collect the dishes and place them in the pan. She lifted the water kettle and poured hot water over them. As she wiped the table, he stood up and flexed his muscles.

"I think I'll set out some traps while you finish. I should be back late this afternoon. Make yourself at home."

She beamed and nodded. He went into the adjoining room and gathered several traps, draping them over his broad shoulders. He attached snowshoes to his boots and picked up his gun. Landis headed for the door, then called back, "Lock the door and don't open it to anyone except me. No one, Kat, understand?" he stated sternly.

She walked over to him, drying her hands on a cloth. "Be careful, Landis," she beseeched him, aware of the perils in this land.

"I will. Just keep this door locked. Ben won't be back for weeks, so don't fall for anyone saying he's Ben. The cabin is impenetrable. Stay inside. There's wood in the back."

"Don't worry. I proved I can obey orders, sir."

"Yes, you did." He kissed her passionately and left.

Kathy locked the door as instructed, then returned to complete her chore. When everything was cleaned and returned to its place, she began to wander around the cabin. Landis had said for her to make herself at home. Home for two weeks, unless she changed his mind.

Kathy tried out each chair and the small sofa, finding each comfortable and soft. She caressed the pelts, noting their beauty and quality. She wondered why Landis had mounted them rather than sold them. She curiously checked the desk, smiling when she discovered it was indeed locked. How she longed to learn about her love. She peeked into Ben's room, but did not enter it. As expected, it was similar to the one now shared with Landis.

She strolled into Landis's bedroom. She ran her hands up and down the clothes hanging in his closet, his manly odor still clinging to several items. She absently wondered why he had sealed up the back corner, since it cut off useful space. Removing her clothes from the bag which had been placed on his bed, she shook them and hung them beside his, laughing at the pleasurable feeling which washed over her at this simple domestic task.

She made the bed and straightened the room, folding his clothes and putting them away in the appropriate drawers in his chest. When she opened the trunk at the foot of the bed, she saw linens and extra blankets. Although he had been on his own since twelve, the lack of personal items surprised her. Evidently men didn't keep souvenirs as women did. She picked up her pack to store it in the supply room.

When Kathy went to the storage room to place the

pack there, she nosed around for a time, observing how well stocked he was. Several weapons rested on a wooden rack with countless boxes of ammunition beneath it. Landis obviously liked to be well prepared. When her eye caught sight of a large tin tub, she nearly shouted with glee.

Landis would be gone for hours; this was a perfect time to wash her hair and take a bath. She hurried into the kitchen and grabbed several pots to heat water. But to her dismay, there was only one large bucket of water. She laughed aloud as she realized she was surrounded by snow. Landis had warned her to stay inside and keep the door locked. She hesitated, then decided a tiny indiscretion couldn't harm anyone.

She carried the pots to the door, hesitating once more before unlocking it. She peeked around the wooden door, seeing nothing but trees and snow, and halted to admire the peaceful silence of her ivory surroundings. The winds and snows had ceased, leaving behind a tranquil stillness. The ground appeared to be heavily dusted with white powder. The limbs on the trees looked snuggly, encased in woolly garments which warmly clothed their naked branches. Fallen snow piled against the door and nestled into the grooves of the log cabin. The sky was intensely blue and clear. As she scanned the deep snow and sloping drifts, she hoped Landis would be careful of hidden perils: holes, rocks, and fallen limbs.

Kathy hastily filled the pots with snow and locked the door. She placed them on the stove and impatiently waited. She was delighted she had packed a cake of lavender soap. When the steam began to rise, she filled the tub half way. She knelt beside it and washed her hair, rinsing it with another bucket to her side. She stepped into the tub and sat down. It didn't matter she was cramped. She leisurely bathed, relishing the refreshing task.

Afterwards, she sat before the fire to dry her hair, brushing it to increase its natural sheen. When it was dry, she brushed it once more, loving its silky feel and clean smell. Not wishing to upset this cozy setting, she hurried to get rid of the evidence of her defiance. She carried bucket after bucket of water to the door and flung it outside, covered in one of Landis's flannel shirts. As she tossed out the last one, a hand seized her wrist, imprisoning it in an iron grip. She screamed and jerked on it, pulling free for some strange reason. She stepped back and attempted to slam the door and lock it, terrified by her attack and state of undress. The intruder wouldn't permit her to close the door, placing his boot in the crack.

"Get out of here!" she demanded. "Landis Jurrell will kill you for this! Get out!" she screamed once more.

"Why should I, my naughty wife?" came a voice she recognized.

She flung open the door and gaped at him. "You scared the life out of me! Don't you dare do that again!" she shouted at him, hands on hips, face white, legs spread, and breathing ragged.

His amused gaze lazily roved the fetching sight before him. Her hands were concealed by the length of his shirt sleeves, but the tail didn't conceal those shapely legs and bare feet. No doubt that was all she was wearing! She smelled like flowers, and golden wheatish hair floated around her shoulders. Her misdeed was evident, all freshly scrubbed and shiny locks . . .

"You going to stand there freezing or will you move so I can come inside?" he taunted wickedly, his passion barely restrained.

Infuriated by his game, she stepped aside and offered, "By all means, come inside, Mr. Jurrell. It is your cabin."

Once he swaggered past her, she closed the door and locked it. She stormed past him and replaced the tub and bucket. When she returned to find him grinning broadly, she snapped, "What's so amusing?"

"Oh, I was just enjoying the sight. You really shouldn't lean over in a skimpy get-up like that. Might give a fellow ideas."

His implication clear, she fused crimson. "You're a crude beast, Jurrell! I'll fix dinner after I dress." She headed for his bedroom in a huff.

She jerked open his closet door and withdrew a shirt and pair of pants. She headed for his chest and removed some bloomers and a snug-fitting chemise. She whirled to find him leaning negligently against the doorframe, grinning at her. "What are you gaping at?" she asked, teeth clenched.

"My disobedient wife. I see you made yourself at home during my absence," he lazily remarked.

"You did say I could!" she responded pertly.

"I did at that, didn't I?" he murmured seductively. "You know you're beautiful when you're angry. My shirt becomes you, my wild ice maiden." Ebony eyes leisurely travelled ivory flesh and tawny hair.

"Is that why you constantly try to enflame my temper?"

"No. I do it because you have a willful streak which refuses to be tamed. I told you not to go outside or open that door for any reason."

"I wanted to take a bath! I didn't see any harm in that."

"You could have waited for my return. What if that hadn't been me outside just now?" he scolded her.

"But it was!" she heatedly protested. "Was it a terrible crime?"

"Do you know how many crazed men live here, men who'd love to get hands on a woman like you? Didn't you learn anything from your run-ins with Slavin and those killers? Being brutally raped isn't a pretty sight," he warned, his tightly leashed temper now showing. "If that hadn't been me, you would be in big trouble right now. I think I'd better teach you how to shoot and leave a pistol with you when I'm gone. But don't you ever open that door again, especially not dressed like that!" he thundered.

"You don't own me, Jurrell, and I can take care of myself!"

"If I hadn't released your hand earlier, I could have been inside and you would have been helpless to prevent any intention I had! How many times must I warn you this is wild country? Have you forgotten those men on the trail? You could have been killed!"

"And you'd be delightfully rid of me?" she sneered irrationally.

He surged forward and grabbed her. "Damnit, woman! What will it take for you to obey me? Get packed! I'm taking you home in the morning. If you get hurt, it won't be because of me! I'd never forgive myself."

With that statement, he stalked out, heading for the kitchen. He yanked open a cabinet and withdrew a bottle of brandy. He poured two fingers and tossed it down. Kathy knew she was wrong, but why was admitting it so difficult? Why was she being so hateful?

She came up behind him as he slowly sipped a second glass. "I'm sorry, Landis. You're right. I won't disobey you again."

"Just make sure you mean it this time," he cautioned

301

without turning, his body stiff with pent-up fury.

Kathy dressed and prepared supper, serving it to a still moody Landis. She had no way of knowing he had dropped the traps outside and headed for Dawson only to discover some disturbing facts. After the meal was eaten and the dishes cleared away, she slowly walked into the living area and sat down in the chair opposite the sofa where he was reclining. His eyes were closed, his head resting against the sofa back. Yet, he didn't appear relaxed at all. His body was taut; his jaw was clenched tightly; his face was etched in lines of angry resolve.

Something was eating at him, more than her error. Oh, Landis, if only you would talk to me, she thought. If only I could know what troubles you so deeply.

He looked at her, his expression unreadable. She lowered her thick lashes, wishing she hadn't destroyed their joyous truce. "I really am sorry. I promise not to do anything like that again. Do you want me to pack?"

He knew he should say yes, but he didn't. He shook his head and motioned for her to come sit beside him. She did so without question or hesitation. Landis pulled her close to him, resting his chin on her silky head as it nestled against his chest. They sat without speaking for a long time. Only soft breathing prevented total silence.

"It's late, Kat. We'd best turn in," he suggested, his voice strained, reflecting fatigue.

She arose, waiting for him to extinguish the lanterns. He took her hand and led her to the bedroom. She started to put on her gown, but he captured it and tossed it to the floor. "I want you," he said.

"I want you, too," she replied sincerely. She slipped off her garments and eased into the bed. He did the same.

As she curled against him, Landis muttered, "I'm worried about you, Kat. I hate to think what might have

302

happened to you if that hadn't been me. You don't seem to understand the way it is around here."

"I didn't mean to upset you, love. I always seem to say and do the wrong things with you. I shouldn't have opened the door. Thank God it was you. I'm just not used to living under fear and danger."

He smiled into the darkness. "Just don't do it again; promise?"

"I promise. Did you have any luck today?"

"Luck?" he echoed, his tone guarded and distant.

"With the traps, silly," she playfully clarified.

"I put 'em outside. I don't need to check them until tomorrow. Most varmits come out at night to take your bait," he stated carefully, craftily telling the truth, but cunningly misleading her.

Kathy sensed something in his inflection, but didn't press. She snuggled against him and closed her eyes. He lay on his back, one hand tucked under his head. He was distant and pensive. Kathy fretted over this behavior. He had said he wanted her; yet, he made no move to take her. He was ensnared in a world which didn't include her. Was it boredom, or that instinctive demand for self-preservation?

She moved her hand across the breadth of his chest, to return near his heart to toy with the curling black mat. She pressed her body closer to his, boldly laying one shapely limb over his leg, to rest between his well-muscled thighs. She turned her head to deliver warm and stirring kisses to his shoulder as she caressed the fuzzy hardness of his upper torso.

When he remained motionless and silent, Kathy took his lack of response as disinterest and lingering anger. Her body ached at his cold denial. She moved away and turned toward the wall. Landis lifted his head and studied her action, her outline dim in the glowing shadows from the firelight filtering through his open door. Her snuffle informed him of her silent weeping.

He cleared his mind of all matters except her and this raging need to consume her. "Why did you stop?" he tenderly chided. "I was enjoying it. I don't get a chance to relax in such a stimulating way."

"You didn't seem to be enjoying it. Your mind wasn't here with me. Are you bored with me already? Are you sorry you brought me here?" she painfully inquired, her voice tight with emotion.

"You couldn't be more wrong, Kat. I didn't realize you felt so daring or at ease. Lose your newfound courage so quickly?" he teased, stroking her slender back. "You have a devastating effect on a man. I was afraid if I moved or spoke, you might stop. I was just lying here thinking how great it was to come home to you and be greeted in such a heady manner."

"You certainly didn't appear to enjoy it," she charged again. "You're rigid and remote and edgy."

He seized her hand and placed it around his throbbing manhood. "Is that boredom?" he challenged, laughing softly as she attempted to pull her hand free. He caught her shoulder and pushed her down beside him, leaning forward to warm the icy peaks on her chest. They responded instantly to his moist, fiery tongue. His hand released hers to wander over her body. His mouth skillfully plundered hers as he murmured, "If you've turned coward, then I'll take the lead."

His kisses were tantalizing as they sent her soaring high where breathing was difficult and her senses swirled madly. His fingers lightly trailed over her chest, cupping each breast and thumbing each peak into eager readiness. The titillating journey continued down her stomach, feeling the sudden tightening there, roving over her nicely rounded hips, ending its stimulating trek in a golden forest which welcomed his invasion. His hand explored deftly and carefully, teasing her to quivering delight.

Her hand had remained on that intoxicating staff of pleasure, relishing its warmth and satiny texture. Slowly her fingers started a journey of their own. They lightly traced its full length, from crisply forested base to sensitive tip. How could anything be so torrid and silky, and yet so vital and hard?

Her heated response, her total surrender, and her enticing actions sorely strained his control. He moved above her, causing her hand to fall away from his aching manhood, but to instantly encircle his back. He tenderly drove into her, his movements deliberately provocative. She moaned against his lips, clinging to him. His mouth was demanding, his tongue teasing her lips before it fastened almost savagely to hers. Their bodies worked in unison for a mutual goal which quickly loomed in sight. They made love passionately, almost desperately and savagely.

Kathy's release came swiftly and easily, sending tingles over her slim frame. Joining her pursuit to heights previously unknown with other women, he plunged time and time again as his own release stunned him with its immense power. Bored and distant? There were no such things where Kat Marlowe was concerned!

The tranquil aftermath surrounded and encased them. He rested on his side, his face nestled to her fragrant hair. His leg was casually resting over hers, his arm holding her against his sated body. She sighed happily as he pressed a kiss to her forehead. She closed her eyes and relaxed into his embrace, deeply aware of the love and passion she would have been denied if she hadn't met this unique man, or if she hadn't found the courage to pursue her heart's desire.

When it seemed she was slumbering, Landis cautiously eased from her arms and the bed. He stood beside it for a long time, gazing down at her. He silently walked to his desk in the adjoining room and unlocked it with a key which he pulled from his pocket, on that same gold chain from which her wedding ring had come. He sat down and began to write on an ivory page. Every so often, he would look up and stare unseeingly at the wall before adding more words to that page.

Kathy watched him from the shadows of their room, musing over his action and intense mood. When he closed the desk and locked it, she quickly returned to the bed and pretended to be asleep. Landis quietly entered the room and checked on her, believing she was entrapped in the dark world of sleep. He walked to the chest and lay some papers there. He moved the picture aside, revealing a cut-out in the log behind it. He took out a package and put the new papers inside. After replacing them, he straightened the picture and re-adjusted the telltale string.

Satisfied, he came back to bed. As he settled himself, Kathy moaned and rolled into his arms. He embraced her and closed his eyes, with Kathy pondering his curious actions when sleep finally claimed her.

Twelve

Those next five days cast an intoxicating pattern over their lives. Many days and nights were consumed by fiery passion, while other times were absorbed by chores and conversations. Landis continued his daily task of trapping, or so Kathy believed. Fortunately for Landis, she never questioned why he didn't bring pelts home to be cured. He did bring home a slain deer, suspending it from a tree limb to carve and salt for the winter.

She donned her heavy parka to stand outside to watch his skilled hands at work. He chuckled when she thanked him for gutting and bleeding it before his return. Once the hunks of meat were cut to his liking, he salted all except one to cook for supper. Observing him, she was annoyed that he could very well survive alone. Was there nothing he couldn't do?

To her surprise, after he washed up, he actually prepared the roast himself. He covered the lean haunch with local herbs to make it tender and to bring out its best flavor. Once the meat was simmering, he dropped into a chair and called her over to him. Landis patted his lap, indicating for her to sit there.

She did so with undeniable eagerness. "You're quite handy to have around, Mr. Jurrell. Whatever shall I do when I return to Skagway and have to work so hard?

Worse, I'll be woefully out of condition after lazing around here for two weeks."

Genial laughter rumbled against her ear as she curled into his arms. "You can hardly call this out of shape, love," he murmured, affectionately patting her rump and stroking her slim and firm legs.

"You're prejudiced. You think I'm perfect," she coyly teased, looking up into his laughing face. She ran her fingers over his lean jawline which was stubbled since this morning's shave. She playfully slid her finger up the side of his face, over his proud forehead, down his nose, and along his sensuous lips. Admiring the entrancing planes of his handsome face, she halted to finger a thin white scar on his strong chin.

"How did you get this?" she asked inquisitively.

"In a fight, naturally," he easily replied, saying no more.

She seductively unbuttoned his shirt and sent her exploratory hand to finger another longer scar across his right shoulder blade. "And this one?" she probed, unperturbed by his guarded manner.

When he glanced down into her expectant face, it was only inches from his. "Aren't we curious Kat today?" he taunted her, then nibbled at her lips to distract her.

"It won't work, Jurrell. Either answer or say it's none of my business," she chided him.

"In a fight," he stated, still sensuously attacking her pouting lips.

"The same one?" she calmly continued her probe.

"Nope. Up here, there are lots of claim disputes as well as quarrels over trapping rights. I'm involved in both; I run into trouble here and there. This one," he began, touching the pencil-thin scar on his chin, "came from a man's ring when he slugged me. Seems he forgot where he laid his traps and tried to steal mine. This one came from a claim-jumper. He thought mine was yielding more gold than his. When I refused to move on or sell out, he tried to knife me in the back. I turned too quickly, and the blade skimmed over my shoulder. Any more questions, Mrs. Jurrell?" he stated, using that name as frequently as possible to impress it in his mind.

His eyes were sparkling with mischief. "Any more scars and scary tales?" she asked.

"You seem awfully intrigued by my body tonight. Think I should strip you and examine yours just as closely?" he threatened.

"In my opinion, you know every inch," she saucily retorted.

"That I do. Can't say as I found anything to worry over either. Too bad you don't have some flaws to subtract a little of your irresistible beauty and charms. For the past five days, you haven't given me anything to find fault with, just more golden trappings."

As Landis tickled her, a knock sounded on his cabin door. He clamped his hand over her mouth and hushed her. He whispered in her ear, "Go to the bedroom and close the door. Stay there."

"What's wrong?" she inquired.

"No questions right now. Just do like I said," he ordered tersely. "I don't want anyone to know you're here. I'll explain later."

She struggled to get up, finally accepting his assistance. He watched her until the door closed behind her, then went to answer the knock. He pulled his pistol from the holster hanging on a large peg, then concealed it beneath his overhanging shirt-tail. He pushed the bar over and unlocked the door, stepping aside in case of danger.

"We got problems, Cl . . . ," the Mounty began, but was hastily silenced by Landis's waving hand. Trace

Blitch glanced past him, seeing no one there. Intrigue filled his blue eyes.

Landis motioned him outside. They walked a few feet from the cabin. "What's going on, Trace?"

"Company?" Trace asked, flashing a curious look at the cabin.

"Yep," Landis stated, but didn't expound. "You want something?"

Trace allowed the private matter to pass. "You recall those men who came here months ago to explore the Yukon? Captain Ray, Lieutenant Wilds, and Richardson?"

When Landis nodded, he went on. "Seems they like what they see and plan to stay through next fall. You know what that means."

"They sent any reports back?" Landis asked thoughtfully.

"No. But Wilds carries around a packet of notes. The way he guards them, I'd sure like to get a peek at what's inside."

"Does Bill Thomas think the American government sent them here?"

"He suspects something's going on. Did Bill tell you General Funston nosed around in that same area? They appear mighty interested in those settlements claimed under American pre-emption. They've been asking lots of questions about our headquarters and the commissioner for this territory."

Landis walked off a few steps, hesitated, then came back to where Trace was waiting. He stuffed his hands into his pockets, the icy wind nipping at them. His broad shoulders were bent forward in a futile attempt to ward off the chill. "What's got Bill so worried? We've had explorers coming and going. I keep my eye open while I guide their expeditions. Haven't seen anything unusual.

Funston even spent a few days with me and Ben, mostly with Ben. He acted like he was on a holiday. He seemed quite taken with the countryside and resources, but he hasn't been back."

Trace looked him in the eye and speculated, "But Funston and the others didn't mention Jake Hammond's name. Bill thinks this Hammond is working undercover for the Americans. He suspects some of these expeditions by American Army officials have to do with passing information and reports back and forth, probably to this Hammond."

"Hammond's spying for the Americans?" Landis asked, that news most alarming. Is that what Bill was hinting at when he speculated Hammond was nosing around this area, for his government and not private interests? No wonder Bill had reacted so coldly and suspiciously to his marriage . . . Surely Bill didn't think Kat was involved, or that he might drop vital clues to her?

"Bill's been dong some checking on him. Seems Hammond has some connections to people in questionable areas. It's settled he came here a few years ago, but we don't know if he's still around. Some of those expeditions were phony, ways to contact Hammond. Bill thinks you should keep a sharp eye on his daughter," he said reluctantly.

"What do you mean?" Landis demanded, his tone wintry.

"I know you married her, Clint, but blinding emotions are deadly. Bill hopes her quest isn't a cover to sneak out some reports," he said gingerly, pondering how deeply his friend was involved with her.

"If she was in on this scheme, why wouldn't she use his code name? It sounds foolish to let us know he's here," Landis reasoned.

"Maybe she doesn't know what's going on. Or, maybe

she does. It's a perfect cover, Landis: daughter seeks missing father, then delivers papers home. Course, there's another possibility," he intimated carefully.

"Like what?" Landis snarled under his breath. "She isn't Miss Hammond; she's my wife," he foldly added. "She doesn't know who or what I am."

"There is a Kathryn Hammond, but is she the real one? Could be she's his accomplice. She has to locate him. A beautiful woman alone looking for her father . . . droves of men would be eager to help. Would make her job safer and swifter if she locked up with one, especially a powerful one in your position. You sure she isn't aware of your identity?"

"Does Bill think she's a phony?" Landis inquired sullenly.

"He's more inclined to see her as a pawn. I didn't spend much time with her, but she surely has the qualifications to be successful in whatever she wants to do. She caught you, didn't she?" Trace teased.

A black scowl flickered over Landis's face as he observed Trace's appreciative smile. "Who made the connection between Wilds and Hammond? Sounds crazy to jeopardize her mission by carelessly dropping his name, if she is on one," he harshly reasoned.

"Tent walls aren't impenetrable. McLorey was passing by, nosing around their camp, when he overheard the tail of a talk. One of the other men asked Wilds if he was going to look up Hammond while they were here. Wilds silenced him instantly and warned him never to mention that name around these parts again. Tim thought that strange and reported it to Bill. Bill started giving your wife's story another look. He's got one of our agents in Washington nosing around. Appears this Hammond was in tight with the War Department and the Interior Department. Fact is, he wasn't killed in Texas. We need some help on this case, my friend. Why don't you head back to Skagway and see what you can learn from the little woman. Doesn't sound like an unpleasant task to me. In fact, in your best interest."

Landis's frown vanquished his grin. "That won't be necessary. She's here with me."

Trace looked astonished. He stared at the cabin, then at Landis. "You mean she's here with you and Ben?"

"Just with me. Ben's upriver."

"I see," he muttered knowingly. "Business or pleasure?"

"Looks like both, doesn't it?" he coldly announced. "I think I'll mosey over to Wilds's camp tomorrow. I'd like to locate this Hammond myself. As you said, I have a personal interest in solving this case."

Trace brazenly advised, "It isn't wise to get personally involved in a case, Clint. Maybe I should handle this matter. Her story might check out after all." Trace wanted to ask why he married her, but didn't.

"Either way, I'll handle her," Landis vowed, his gut churning viciously at the idea of deceiving her in such a repulsive manner. Here he was trying to solve their differences, but more were blooming. "Do me a favor, Trace; whatever you discover, let me know before you report it to Bill. If Kat's in over her head, I'll need to work it out."

Neither man noticed as the door was eased open a crack, Kathy's curiosity overpowering. She couldn't see either man where they were standing, but she could make out their next words and recognized the voice of the Mounty who had escorted her from Log Cabin to Skagway.

"Bill got anyone investigating those rigged wheels at Soapy's?" Landis altered the topic, jesting, "You Mounties ought to stop him."

"He called in a man from McKenzie, one they won't recognize. He's dressed like a sourdough, using the story of looking for another claim around here. Hopefully we'll have some hard evidence soon."

"Did Bill learn anything about those two killings I reported the other day? I saw McLorey when I went to Dawson Tuesday. He said he'd give Bill the message. Kat claims she didn't see who did it."

"I didn't hear anything before I left headquarters, but I'll check for you. Did you talk with Carmack yesterday when you went over to Bonanza Creek? I really need any information you can glean for me."

"Didn't see him. Looks like they're getting settled in for the winter. Gonna be trouble there before long; some of those tenderfeet aren't ready for fall, much less winter," he scornfully sneered.

"Did you check out the Indians' dispute with Ladue's trappers?"

"I passed by two days ago. Ladue pulled his men out. Things are quiet for now. You Mounties expect me to do all your work for you?"

"Hawkins ready to go ahead with the railroad?"

"They plan to start clearing the route after the spring thaw, then work all year round. Can't say as I envy his crew."

"Won't be any trouble with the Chilkats, but there'll be plenty with those Tagish. Bill's planning to have a man assigned to peacekeeping along the way. We really appreciate your help."

"That sounds smart to me. If you see London, don't tell him Kat's here with me. I'd like to keep her around a while longer. My bones are cold. How about some coffee?" Landis offered.

"Thought you'd never ask," Trace teased, then chuckled.

"Tell Kat you're here to question her about the killings," Landis suggested. "I don't want her upset."

"Is there something between you two?" he fenced, laughing.

"She'll only be here for another week," he rashly blurted out.

"Seems to me like a cozy way to spend the winter."

"Got too much to do. She's going home next week."

"If you aren't careful, someone might take her off your hands."

"They can try, but it won't work. She's utterly smitten by me."

"What about when she leaves next week?"

"Come on. Let's get that coffee."

"We do need your help. You can get in and out of places we Mounties can't," he jested, grinning at his friend.

Kathy left the door and hurried into his bedroom. She sat down on his bed, her head spinning with the insinuations in their words. Then again, perhaps Landis didn't like being teased about her. That enormous pride of his was always getting between them. Too, he had lied to her. No, not exactly lied, just misled her. He hadn't been trapping. Was he simply trying to keep her presence here a secret, or was there more to it? She couldn't question him or demand an explanation if she didn't wish to be sent packing. But why keep her presence a secret; they were married! She was suddenly very curious about that secret compartment behind the picture, the one she hadn't dared to investigate even during his absences. Question was, why was he making secret ventures and then recording them? If it was simply a personal journal, why so covert? Landis was an exceptionally good friend to the Mounties, keeping them well-informed on happenings in this area. But why had he told Trace to lie to her? Was he worried about her safety?

The bedroom door opened and Landis came inside. Kathy glanced up at him, her expression devoid of the turmoil inside. "If you're awake, love," he began cheerfully, "Trace Blitch is here to ask you some questions about the shootings. Would you join us for coffee?"

His manner was foolishly formal. Kathy sent him a scolding look. She came forward and entered the other room behind Landis. "I would be delighted to entertain our first guest," she sweetly murmured, as Landis took three mugs and poured steaming coffee into them.

"How about we sit over here near the fire; I'm chilled through and through," he said.

Trace took a seat at the table as Landis passed around the coffee. Playing along with Landis's ruse, Kathy stated, "My husband says you wish to question me about the shootings. How did you learn about our attack? We haven't seen anyone to report them."

Landis quickly invented, "Trace said two miners found the bodies and took them to Stewart. When he investigated, he learned you had been with them. He came to ask me to assist his search for you. I filled him in outside."

Landis inwardly flinched at the skeptical look which glinted in her sapphire eyes. "How very convenient for you, Mr. Blitch. Now you won't have to freeze while searching for me. It's a good thing you stopped here first. No doubt my husband and friends would be alarmed to hear I was missing under such perilous circumstances."

Landis watched her intently. Her tone was deceptively polite and calm, but the underlying traces of sarcasm and coldness couldn't be ignored. No doubt just miffed at being ordered to stay in his room for so long. Or could it be distress over this particular conversation?

As they sipped the coffee, Kathy told Trace what happened on the trail. "I have my husband to thank for saving my life," she finished crisply. "We left word in Stewart for Jack to meet me in Dawson. If you see him, would you please tell him where I am? I wouldn't want him to worry."

"Most certainly, Miss . . . Mrs. Jurrell. I must admit you're safer here than in Dawson. Is there anything else you want to tell me?"

Kathy eyed him strangely. "Should there be?"

"Sometimes witnesses think of another clue later. If you do, send word to Log Cabin. We'd like to catch these culprits."

"Rest assured I will do anything to help you capture those killers, Mr. Blitch. But there's nothing else to tell. As I said, I heard the shots, but didn't see anything."

"What about along the way?" he probed. "Did you notice anyone watching you? Did anyone seem overly curious about your destination?"

She gave it some thought, then told him about the friends the two Eskimos conversed with at Lake Bennett and the incident with the lecherous prospector at Stewart. "Other than those two times, I don't recall anyone paying us much attention. Why?"

Trace chuckled and commented, "I'm positive you received a great deal more atention, Mrs. Jurrell. Beautiful women are rare in these parts. I was thinking about that mysterious letter you received."

She flushed lightly, then replied, "Thank you, sir. If anyone did look my way, I was too tired and scared to notice. If I had, my husband would be furious; he's very possessive."

"It's possible someone was following you to steal those supplies. It happens here too much. Or the letter culprit could be involved."

"Then why didn't they look for me and kill me?"

"They didn't need to waste the time. Leaving you

stranded in the wilds should have done the trick. Some men, even desperate ones, find it difficult to murder a woman outright. Whoever did it didn't count on Landis coming along to rescue you. You're lucky."

"Yes, I am," she concurred, failing to look at Landis.

The ensuing silence was severed when Landis invited Trace to eat supper with them and spend the night. "You Mounties sleep out in the cold too often. You can put your bedroll near the fire tonight."

"That's mighty kind of you. I hope you don't mind, Mrs. Jurrell."

"Certainly not. I'll prepare supper. I'll need your help, dear; I'm not acquainted with the meat you're cooking."

Landis looked over at her and smiled. "I'll be delighted to teach you, Mrs. Jurrell," he murmured.

Trace observed them. After the meal, Kathy washed dishes while Landis dried them and put them away. "Cards?" he suggested to Trace.

"Don't mind if we do," he agreed, relaxed and intrigued.

They sat at the table, playing poker. Kathy watched for a time, then they entreated her to play. She declined, saying she knew nothing of such games. When they eagerly offered to teach her, she smiled and refused.

"If you gentlemen don't mind, I think I'll retire and read a while. I'm sure you gentlemen would like to chat alone. Goodnight, Mr. Blitch. Landis." She selected a book of poetry from his shelf and entered their room, feeling uneasy with a guest in the cabin.

Landis hurried inside on the excuse of lighting the lantern. He grinned ruefully and shrugged his shoulders. She stared, then thanked him. She noted his quizzical expression, but turned her back to him. "Good night, Kat."

The door closed for privacy, the air was soon chilly.

She couldn't very well open it, so she shivered. She tossed the book aside and snuggled under the covers, yearning for Landis's body heat. No matter which way she turned, she couldn't get comfortable or warm. She tossed for hours, her fury rising against Landis and Trace.

The men played cards until midnight, then turned in. Trace reclined in his warm location, while Landis discovered Kat supposedly asleep. He kept thinking about the woman beside him, unable to sleep. She had been in a crazy mood tonight. But if she knew the truth, she wouldn't be in his bed.

At last, all three were sleeping fitfully. Trace was the first to awaken, grinning as he eyed the closed door. A worried scowl replaced his smile. Now he understood why Bill Thomas had been trying to withhold the truth from Landis until they could prove it; Landis actually loved her. Having witnessed Landis's temper, Trace dreaded the time Landis would have to betray Kathy.

To Trace's surprise, both were exceptionally cheerful and talkative. When breakfast was over, he almost hated to leave the pleasant atmosphere and warm cabin. Landis yanked on his parka and walked a short distance with him. They talked for a while, then parted company. Trace headed for Dawson, and Landis returned to his cabin.

As she made his bed, Landis came up behind her and seized her around the waist. "How'd you fare last night, love?"

Thinking it best to keep on a light note, she smiled and confessed, "I nearly froze. You were right about body heat. What about you?"

"The same, if not worse," he confessed.

"You best get used to it again, Jurrell; I'll be leaving soon," she reminded him, intentionally trying to

319

pique him.

"You could stay longer," he unexpectedly coaxed.

"And have you accusing me of taking advantage of you in a weak moment?" she teased, her laughter unnaturally high.

"You got a better offer?" he asked, slightly perturbed.

"I'm not for sale. Besides, you have work to do. Will you take me trapping with you today?" she abruptly asked.

"Trapping?" he echoed, his voice hollow.

"Why not? I'd like to see how it's done. It'd be nice to see the scenery with such an experienced guide. You're not trying to keep me a prisoner here, are you?" she jested, turning to face him.

"It might not be wise for anyone to learn you're here," he commented, his blank expression shielding his emotions.

"Afraid I might tarnish that carefree image of yours, Jurrell?"

"I was thinking of your safety while I'm out," he chided.

"You did marry me. Why keep your wife's presence a secret? Living together is common, isn't it?" she asked the startled man.

"I'm worried about you, Kat," he replied honestly.

"You underestimate your prowess, love. Think you'll miss me?"

"More than I care to admit. Why not stay a while longer?" he encouraged once more, wanting her at his side.

"I don't think your friend would like that set-up. It would be a little strained with you gone. I'll see you when you come to Skagway on business. Did I tell you Harriet is building her own cabin? That means I'll be all alone," she informed him.

His ebony eyes glittered. "You drive a hard bargain, woman."

"Do I?" she purred seductively, caressing his chest.

He caught her hands and warned, "If you keep that up, I'll be late." He instantly caught his error and tensed.

"Late? Do the animals have clocks?" she mocked.

"If you don't check the traps early, scavengers attack the catch. Torn pelts don't bring much money. I best clear out while I can."

Kathy determined to delay his trip. She smiled wantonly and murmured, "I missed you last night. Do you have to go so early? I thought we could . . ."

She grinned and fondled his chest. "Could what?" he inquired, a lazy smile making creases near his mouth and eyes.

She began to unbutton his shirt, placing kisses down his bare chest. When the shirt was undone, she snuggled against him, running her hands up his well-developed back. She eased up to kiss him, her lips eagerly tasting his. Her torrid mouth nibbled at his neck, causing him to shudder. Having prepared for this test of her appeal, she was out of her shirt and pressing her naked chest to his before he knew what was happening. The contact was staggering to his self-control.

She encircled his neck with her hands and pulled it down to fuse his lips with hers. She greedily devoured his mouth as she tempted him beyond reason. Her breasts burned into his chest, sending fires raging through his entire body. One hand slid down his chest, passed his drumming heart, over his taut stomach, to brazenly caress the bulge in his pants. The back of her hand moved up and down the evidence of her effect upon him, precariously swaying his resolve to leave.

When he hoarsely murmured against her lips, "Kat, I must go. Later, love," she shamelessly unfastened his britches and boldly grasped his throbbing manhood, her touch gentle and intoxicating.

Her provocative hand massaged the swollen flesh as she continued to ravish his mouth. "I need you, Landis. Please don't go," she pleaded.

"I must, love," he raggedly replied, feebly attempting to pull free from her blissful torment.

"No. Please stay. I'll help with the traps later," she wheedled, trying to undress him completely. What else could be more important?

He stated ruefully, "Later, love. I must go now. It's getting late and I won't be able to make my rounds." He had a critical meeting in Dawson. Why now? he demanded, his body a sheet of fire. If he lingered here much longer, he would never make Dawson and return before nightfall. He forced his unbridled passion to cool and to come under his rigid control. "I promise to make it up to you tonight," he vowed in a strained voice.

"I need you now," she whispered. "Why did you allow me to get this far if you had no intention of making love to me?"

"I'm sorry, Kat, there isn't time," he refused unwillingly.

"Then make the time. What else do we have around here?"

"I have things to do, Kat. Please don't make this any harder on us." He looked into her passion-glazed eyes, then tenderly caressed her cheek. Time, his mind echoed; it could be our enemy . . .

"Please," she whispered brazenly, entrapped by her own scheme. She was trembling from the force of fierce desire.

He closed his eyes and sighed heavily. He released her and turned away, fastening his britches and shirt. He stood tall and stiff, mastering the urge to make savage love to her. She watched his stalwart frame as her power over it diminished, then vanished under his tight leash. She walked out. She went to the fireplace, gazing into colorful flames as she buttoned her own shirt, tears easing down her cheeks. She had played her hand and lost. Shame filled her as she pondered her wanton behavior. She had actually begged him to possess her, body and soul. Now she knew he had things more important than her and this time together . . .

He watched her for a time, too aware of the mistake he was making. "I'll be back as soon as possible, Kat. I'm sorry."

"Don't trouble yourself on my account. Perhaps I should have left with Trace. You're clearly too busy for me," she coldly retorted. "If you pass Jack along the trail, would you ask him to escort me home? I do have a job at Moore's," she stated, her voice suddenly calm and cold.

He came over to her, cognizant of the passing time. "Jack doesn't usually pass through my trapping grounds, but I'll send word if I see anyone. I wish I could stay, Kat; I can't." He couldn't beg.

She whirled and glared at him. "If you say 'I can't' one more time, I'll claw your eyes out. You can do anything you wish. Once more I misread your meaning, Mr. Jurrell. It was my understanding the two week truce included both of us. Evidently I was mistaken. If your measly pelts are so damn important, by all means go and collect them," she shrieked at him, her eyes and tone saying far more.

"It isn't the . . ." He caught himself and halted. "You're wrong, Kat. I have to do this." There was almost a hint of novel pleading in his tone, one which baffled her.

She knew he wasn't referring to trapping, for that wasn't where he was going. "It won't be the first or the last time I'm wrong about something, Jurrell. I really thought you would give us a chance. But you have no intention of doing so. Do whatever it is you have to do!" she shot back at him. "I promise you, I'll never try to seduce you again."

"Kat," he entreated, reaching out for her.

She jerked away. "Don't you touch me, you selfish brute!"

The coldness in her eyes and voice alarmed him. If he left now, it would breed trouble between them. Wasn't satisfying her feelings just as important as the meeting he would be missing? In this present mood, she would leave the first chance she got. Still, he defensively blamed his final decision on his mission.

"You're right, Kat. Trapping isn't that important. I can't leave you like this. We've hurt each other enough as it is," he admitted. "I'll stay here with you."

Kathy was stunned by his decision. She stared at him in disbelief. "You'll stay home?" she inquired. When he smiled and nodded, she continued to gape at him. "But you said . . ."

He pulled her into his arms and silenced her protests with a searing kiss. When the heady kiss ended, she leaned back and looked up at him. "I don't understand you at all, Landis Jurrell."

"Sometimes I don't understand myself, so that makes us about even. I don't want to hurt you, Kat. If I leave, I could lose you. I can't risk that, now that I've discovered how important you are to me."

It was evidently more than she had realized if he was willing to stay home. Would he resent her for forcing his hand? The romantic mood was broken, anger and mistrust filled her. He would rebel against this feminine ploy to control him. She shrewdly backed down for the moment, her point proven to some extent, fearing his enormous pride.

"I'm sorry, Landis. I'm acting like a child. I suppose I'm just tired and edgy. I didn't get much sleep last night. It would be ridiculous to ruin your catch. I'll be all right."

He lifted her chin. Tears were misting her liquid blue eyes. "I'll stay if you want me to, Kat," he offered seriously.

"I know, Landis. I'll be fine. You go ahead. I'll take a nap and be in a better mood when you come home. I don't know what possessed me to behave like that. Women are silly creatures sometimes."

When he leaned forward to kiss her, she turned her face away. "Later, Jurrell, if you want to leave here today," she warned.

"Are you sure, Kat?" he asked once more, wavering in doubt.

"Go on; get out of here," she merrily commanded. "Just remember you owe me," she reminded him playfully.

He went to fetch his parka. He returned and smiled at her. "I'll be back as soon as possible." With that, he left.

Kathy waited only a minute before seizing her parka and heading outside. She went from tree to tree as she observed his direction. He didn't head into the forest; he headed for the trail to Dawson. As he disappeared from sight, she leaned against the tree and cried. Forcefully halting her tears, she retraced her steps and locked the cabin door.

She removed her parka and hung it in his closet. She headed for his desk. It was locked, as usual. She walked into the bedroom, to the picture. She moved it aside. The hole was empty. As she stared at the picture, the dangling string caught her eye. A trap! She quickly lifted the lower end of the picture and replaced the telltale string. It was clear he had taken the package with him. . . . She paced the floor for a long time, wondering what that furtive packet contained.

When Landis returned near nightfall, Kathy greeted him with a hot supper and a wary smile. It was after they had made love that he realized something wasn't right. Kathy outwardly appeared calm and cheerful, but he sensed things weren't the same between them. Her eyes were cloudy and fathomless; her mood was subtly cautious. She had made passionate love to him, but she hadn't yielded as before. A spark was missing somewhere. Even her laughter didn't ring with spontaneous music as before. Her smile seemed forced. Perhaps he shouldn't have left . . .

As he lay there in the darkness with her curled against him, Landis fretted over this noticable change. Had his rejection stung deeper than he had realized? Even his surrender hadn't eased the sting. She had bared her soul to him. His denial had been like a slap in her face. She had shamelessly pleaded for his touch. She had brazenly enticed him. Her pride was surely singed. He had promised to make it up to her, but had he? No, to so easily remove a knife in the heart was impossible. That damn meeting, he fumed. It hadn't been worth it, for Graystone hadn't even shown up! Was another Mounty dead?

Landis had been correct in his assessment. Those next few days, he became more and more aware of the distinct change in Kathy. She tried to appear content with him, but he would look up suddenly to find her staring at him. When he would question her look, she would smile faintly and state she was "just thinking." When he queried her line of thought, she would laugh and say, "Nothing important. Just silly girl thoughts." Landis was worried, for she seemed to be moving further and further out of his reach. Was she afraid to reach out to him again? She hadn't initiated any overtures since that fateful morning. She didn't refuse his advances; instead, she greedily accepted them as if there would be no tomorrow. But she was quieter these days, as if her mind was miles away. His attempts to draw her out only half succeeded.

One night when she sat down on the chair rather than coming to sit beside him on the sofa, he asked, "Kat, is something wrong?" Of late she had been avoiding him unless he verbally requested her nearness or sensuously swayed her.

She glanced up from the book whose pages she hadn't turned in an hour. "Wrong?" she repeated.

"Are you still angry about the other day?" he pointedly asked.

"Why should I be angry with you, Landis?" she innocently inquired, her gaze assuming that newly acquired impenetrable expression.

"You haven't been yourself since then. I know I upset you. I apologized. What more do you want?" he asked, frustrated.

"Why should I complain, Landis. You've been keeping your end of our bargain," she stated. "When do we head for Skagway?" she abruptly asked. "No doubt Moore's ready to replace me by now."

"Damn the bargain!" he exploded, coming to kneel before her. "Why are you punishing me, Kat?" he accused. "Tell me what's wrong."

"Is that what you think I'm doing?" she inquired sadly.

"You're damn right I do!" he thundered, startling her.

"I guess it's the lack of activity. I was very busy in Moore's camp. Now, all I do is sit around waiting for you to come home."

"I thought you'd get tired of seeing my face from morning to night. Is that all it is, boredom?" he softly asked.

"I haven't seen anyone for two weeks, Landis. There're only so many chores to do, the same ones daily. You're gone all day. I get lonely and restless. What about my father and our search?"

"Why didn't you tell me?" he questioned, concern vivid in his softened gaze, masking his belief she wasn't being honest with him.

"I said I wouldn't make any demands on you. I've tried very hard to keep that promise. The last time I . . ." She didn't finish.

"The last time you what, Kat?" he prompted, imprisoning her hand with his own.

"It isn't important, Landis," she said, freeing her hands. "Isn't it time to turn in?"

"The last time you what, Kat?" he demanded to have his answer.

"All right," she acquiesced. "The last time I tried to show you how much I needed you to stay here with me, you spurned me. I told you I wouldn't behave like that again. I don't dare ask you any questions; you get your back up every time I touch on some forbidden subject. I don't know what you expect from me, Landis. I feel like I'm walking on thin ice around you. As long as I comply to your rules and meet your terms, everything's fine. I didn't realize it would be so demanding to live on the edge like this, afraid to say the wrong thing, afraid to do the wrong thing. I've really tried, Landis, but you keep shutting me out. If I'm not on constant guard, I make the wrong move. That constant guard is fatiguing and taxing, Landis. I can't live like this."

"You want to know more about me, is that it?" he warily asked.

Tears slipped down her cheeks as she observed his suspicious look. "You still don't trust me, do you?" she sighed unhappily. "Why?"

"Is that what you want, a full confession to prove my feelings for you?" he challenged. "Haven't I shown you how much I need you?"

"Even if I made such a rash demand, you wouldn't comply. Do you realize you haven't brought home one single pelt in two weeks? It's obvious you haven't been trapping. I'm not asking you to tell me where you go every day; I'm only asking you not to lie to me anymore. Either keep silent or tell the truth. Is that so much to expect from your husband?"

He tensed. "You don't think I've been trapping?"

"I know you haven't," she declared confidently.

"I told you my business was secret, Kat. I can't confide in you."

She shoved him aside and jumped up. She whirled to confront him. "Damn you, I'm not asking you to tell me anything! Just don't lie to me. I'm not a possession without feelings. Stop being so defensive! I love you, Landis. I don't care who you are or what you do. Just stop deceiving me. If you'll lie about one thing, you'll lie about others. How can I trust you when you play me for a fool every day? All you have to say is, Kat, I'm going out for a while. I won't ask where or why. Forget it! It doesn't matter anymore. It's past time to leave here."

She turned to walk off. He was up and pursuing her. She struggled to break his hold on her. He pinned her against the wall. "Listen to me, Kat!" he stormed.

"No! I'm tired of your lies and pretenses. You only want me here so you can keep your eye on me. If you get a few added benefits, so much the better for your victory. I'm tired of playing your games. Take me home," she demanded painfully.

"All right! I lied to you!" he shouted back. "But I had no choice. I couldn't tell you where I was going or why; I still can't. I don't want you to leave, Kat," he added, his harsh tone mellowing.

"It isn't working. Can't you see that? You're as much alone in this cabin with me here as you were before I came. You don't need me; you don't need anyone. If I weren't cramping you, you wouldn't be sneaking off and then lying about it. You say trust you, then prove I can't."

"You're mistaken, Kat; I do need you. You're tearing my guts out. I can't even think clearly anymore. Every minute I'm gone, all I can think about is hurrying to finish so I can return to you. Damn you, woman, you're like some vicious disease eating at me!"

"It's the same with me. We're destructive to each other. You view me as an evil threat to be controlled or destroyed. I'm not your enemy, Landis; why can't you see that? I only want to love you, and you won't allow it. It's tearing me apart inside. Things can't be right between us until you resolve whatever is bothering you. I thought I could prove you were wrong about me, about us, by coming here. You won't give an inch, because you can't. And I've given too much. We've got to end this nightmare, or there's no hope for us."

"I can't let you go, Kat," he stubbornly refused.

"You can't stop me," she countered.

"There's got to be some way," he entreated.

"Tell me the truth."

"I can't," he murmured, dreading the repercussions of his refusal.

"I don't mean about you or your life. I mean about us."

"What do you mean?" he grasped.

"All I ask is that you don't lie. If something's a secret, say so. Don't say you're going trapping if you're not. Just say you'll be back later. No questions and no demands. Just the truth from now on."

"No questions?" he repeated.

"None," she promised, praying she could keep her vow.

"All right, Kat. I'm going to Lost Chance tomorrow. It's on the Klondike, downriver. I have to see a man about something. In two days, I have to go back to Dawson, then on to Eldorado. I'll be home each night. I can't say why." If she really was a spy, he prayed she wouldn't betray him.

Their gazes locked and searched the other; she smiled. "Was that so difficult? You will be careful?"

"My whereabouts were for your ears alone," he cautioned.

"Praytell who would I inform here alone?" she teased.

"The walls? They're reputed to have ears," he murmured, his tautness and tension fading rapidly.

She laughed, sounding for the first time in days honest and warm. "Not a single soul, Mr. Jurrell. I swear it on my name and honor."

His mouth came down on hers. When he dragged it away, she grinned and asked, "Would it be shameless to suggest we retire for the night?"

He chuckled, playfully cuffing her chin. "My thoughts exactly."

"The war isn't over yet, Jurrell; you've only won another battle."

"But victories add up," he sensually hinted, sweeping her into his arms and bearing her to his bed. After a searing hour of lovemaking, he looked into her serene face and whispered, "You're home, love."

Landis watched her sleep for a time. His tormented mind prayed, please be innocent, my love. Even all my power is useless if you're not who you say you are. Even so, if you truly love me, I'll find some way to help you and hold you . . .

Thirteen

While strolling outside the next morning for some invigorating air, Landis looked up to see Ben trudging along, snowshoes crunching on the frozen white surface. Landis genially greeted his partner, "Welcome home, Ben."

The older man flashed him a winning smile, his corn-flower blue eyes revealing admiration and confidence. His face remained bronze from a summer outside, the skin slightly weathered by nature's strong elements, but barely lined with age. His tall frame retained agility and strength. Even at forty-eight, he could best most men he confronted. Ben was steadfast, affable and easy-going. A staunch worker, he was resourceful and intelligent. As with Landis, Ben Weathers was self-contained, and fiercely protective of his emotions and his privacy.

With similar personalities, they had struck a friendship at their first meeting two years ago. Invited to stay with Landis until he could settle himself, Ben had never left. Not that he hadn't suggested it a few times, feeling he was taking advantage of his new friend's generosity, but Landis had always smiled amiably and said there was no hurry. They had discovered this arrangement benefited both of them: one man was present to see to the cabin and their adjoining claims: gold and trap-lines. Later, Ben had discovered another reason to stay, one also profitable to both of them.

From the way Ben handled himself around traps and pans, it was obvious he was experienced, an aid for Landis's cover. Arriving from the American Northwest, Ben had claimed to be weary of the laws which interfered with men there. He added he wanted to be free to roam a new wilderness, to challenge danger and fate for success and survival: things which kept men like him young and strong. Suspense, activity, and the fresh outdoors were like drugs to him. As with Landis, he savored pitting himself against perilous odds—and winning.

When Ben halted near Landis, he pushed back his parka hood, silvery streaks nearly invisible in the wavy blond hair which hung to his collar. "Trapped any decent furs while I been gone?" he teased.

"Afraid not. But I did catch something prettier and worth a lot more," came the mischievous retort.

Ben's brow lifted inquisitively, amused by the glow in Landis's dark eyes. "Prettier? That sounds like a woman," he concluded.

"Eyes as blue as a summer sky. Skin as fair as snow, hair like cornsilk, both as soft as mink," Landis said proudly.

"That unknown sparkle in your eyes tells me she isn't one of Soapy's new girls," Ben ascertained, then chuckled.

"Nope! She's one of the new cooks in Moore's camp. Came up the first of September from Seattle," Landis playfully added more clues.

"Have you gotten past her protective father? With a description like that, he probably has her guarded every moment."

"He can't. She's an orphan. Came with Mrs. Pullen to work," he casually stated, waiting to spring his astonishing news.

"Ah, yes; you mentioned the famed lady with red hair who has the lumberjacks eating out of her hands. Kind of strange you didn't tell me about her beautiful companion, especially if she can turn the head of one notorious rake named Landis Jurrell," he ventured, eyes twinkling. "That defensive streak working overtime?"

"Can you blame me? She has Moore's men acting like her big brothers. Not to mention half the men there were hotly pursuing her. Could be why I snatched her so quickly," he announced, chuckling.

"Snatched her?" Ben inquired, noting Landis's devilish mood.

"Luckily I was first to meet her. I charmed her and won her."

"You? I've never known you to take after a filly before. She must be something quite special."

"She's smart and brave; puts me to shame on both counts," he alleged. "Don't faint, Ben, but I married her," he dropped his stunning news.

"You married her?" Ben echoed, knowing it would change things.

"Yep," Landis stated. "You know me, Ben; love and marriage never tempted me before," he admitted.

"Until now?" Ben speculated.

"Marriage conjured up visions of chains. But one look at Kat, and it was a losing battle," he muttered, knowing the problems which were keeping them apart and the fiery passion which was drawing them together.

"When did this major event take place?" Ben asked.

"September tenth," Landis unwillingly admitted.

Ben studied his friend for a time. "Why the big secret? Where have you been keeping her?" he quizzed, thinking it weird he hadn't been told before.

Considering the time lapse and their long friendship, Landis felt compelled to explain the reason behind their hasty marriage for her protection. "She's staying here for a while," he divulged.

Ben glanced at their cabin. "She's here? I thought you said she was living in Skagway?" His gaze revealed his astonishment and bewilderment.

Landis briefly related how she had come to be here, forgetting to mention her search for her missing father.

"She staying for good?"

"Surely you don't mind her visit?" Landis said.

"Visit? I know she caught your eye too soon to please you, but it doesn't sound like you to take advantage of a young girl in trouble, Landis," the older man softly chided him, curiously piqued by the false marriage.

Landis eyed him; Ben was serious. "We've known each other since September. We are married. She's the one who wanted to stay here a few weeks," he defensively informed his disappointed friend.

"For a man who loves his privacy and freedom, do you think it was wise to let her? If she stayed, that means she loves you. How do you plan to deal with it when she has to leave?" Ben reasoned, keenly aware of Landis's character and feelings, until Landis met this particular woman. It would shock Landis if he learned how much Ben knew about him, including his real name and identity. Ben was puzzled and annoyed by this selfish ruse.

"I'll think about that when the time comes," he declared, vexed by the guilt Ben was making him feel.

"How long is she planning to 'visit'?" Ben probed.

"Until she wants to leave," Landis casually stated.

"What if she never wants to leave? What if she gets underfoot? You know how the other men will treat her if you drop her later," Ben made Landis face reality.

When Landis didn't reply, he softly guessed, "Do you love her?"

"Why else would I marry her? I also like having her around."

Ben assumed Landis was feeling guilty about his trick, but was too selfish to consider the effects on his phony bride. No doubt she was very beautiful, susceptible, and vulnerable. Naturally she was trusting and naive, else Landis wouldn't have such a hold on her. "I should warn you, Landis; if you treat a woman like a real wife, she'll start to believe she is one. So much for your little charade."

"Kat and I have an understanding, Ben. I'm not misleading her. She knows I can't settle down yet. A man like me can't change overnight. She accepts me like I am," he contended, too rankled by the hard time Ben was giving him.

But Ben knew why the timing was wrong for them. What Ben couldn't figure was why Landis was deceiving her; without a doubt, he hadn't unmasked himself. "For now," Ben burst his bubble. "She might demand more or walk out on you. Believe me; I know from experience. Years ago I met a lovely creature, eyes as green as grass, hair as black as fertile land, skin and teeth like rare pearls. We . . . lived together for a while. She wanted more than I could give her. She finally left me for another man, and I never saw her again. A female can demand a lot from you; can hurt you deeply."

Ben sighed regretfully as he recalled his painful past, a past which had cost him a precious little treasure with hair of gold and eyes of blue. But a marked man had no right to happiness, to reclaim a lost treasure. Besides, her hair was probably black now like her real father's . . . That golden childhood fuzzy had fooled him for two years.

"You're sorry you lost her?" Landis gleaned astutely.

"Yes," Ben murmured sadly.

"Why didn't you marry her?" Landis asked, intrigued.

"You won't come out of this without scars, my friend, not if you have any feelings for this girl. Look at me; I'm getting old, and I have no one. I rashly lost my little love. If you're smart, you won't throw away this chance and wind up like me," he replied vaguely.

Landis studied his friend. Ben had never revealed such intimate details about himself. Landis hadn't even considered such powerful emotions and conflicts within this vital man. There was more to Ben Weathers besides what was revealed on the surface. "I can't change right now. Kat will hang around until I do."

"If she doesn't?" Ben parried.

"I won't release her, Ben," he disclosed. "You want to meet her? See if I'm being the rake you think I am." He laughed merrily.

"Sure," he agreed, smiling at Landis, dropping the nasty discussion.

They entered the quiet cabin. "She's still asleep. I'll go tell her you're home. She's been most curious about you."

"Filled her head with tall tales no doubt," he quipped.

"Naturally." They joked easily. "The coffee's ready."

"I'll put my things away. I take it she isn't borrowing my room?"

Landis grinned roguishly. Ben headed to his room to store his belongings, giving Landis time to talk with his bride. Ben chuckled as he realized he hadn't even asked her name. Considering the vast distance between Skagway and the Klondike, it didn't seem unusual the sourdoughs he'd come into contact with lately hadn't mentioned the golden dream in his friend's bedroom, but it

JANELLE TAYLOR

did strike him odd that Landis hadn't previously mentioned a new wife.

Landis walked over to the bed and sat down. He gazed at Kathy, gently shaking her shoulder and calling her name. She began to stir, sighing peacefully. Her lids fluttered and opened. Sleepy cornflower blue eyes met smoldering ebony ones. She yawned and stretched, rubbing her eyes. She smiled, reaching up to caress his lean jaw. Landis's hand stroked her wavy blond hair with streaks of silver.

"Good morning, love," he murmured huskily. "Ben's home."

She sat up and stared at him. "He's here?"

"He's putting away his gear. He's dying to meet you." He grinned cheerfully. "I told you not to worry about Ben. He's already scolded me about being unfair to you."

"He did. Why?" she guardedly asked.

"Because he knows I'm trouble, and he's heard how beautiful and fragile you are," he jested.

"Was he upset to learn I'm staying here?" she fretted.

"Not at all. Thinks I'm a damn lucky man. So do I. I'll get breakfast started while you dress. He's a bit miffed I kept you a secret."

"All I have are pants and shirts. I'll look awful to meet him," she anxiously concluded, just like a woman, missing his last sentence.

He laughed and kissed her soundly. "You couldn't look awful in anything. Ben's friendly and easy-going, so don't worry. He isn't judgmental," he declared, unconvinced at present.

"I'll be ready soon," she whispered, tension gnawing at her. Had Landis confided in Ben? Did Ben consider her a mock bride living here?

When Kathy joined them, she saw a tall and robust man pouring coffee at the stove. She hesitated. Landis

338

went to her, his arm possessively encircling her slim waist. "Ben, this is Kathryn Leigh Hammond Jurrell," he announced, looking down into Kathy's timid expression. Kathy returned Landis's blazing, encouraging gaze and smiled.

Ben's coffee sloshed precariously as his body shook. He stiffened and paled. Ben slowly turned and gaped at the exquisite blond who was briefly aware only of Landis Jurrell. Cautioning himself, Ben came forward, hooded eyes shielding his thoughts. He smiled and nodded at Kathy. "You're right, Landis; she's absolutely breathtaking."

Kathy blushed, lowering her long lashes. She smiled and thanked Ben, glancing at him for the first time. "It's a pleasure to meet you, Mr. Weathers," she ventured politely, her manner and speech displaying her good breeding and gentle air as the stranger studied her.

Perceiving her uneasiness, Ben smiled warmly and coaxed, "Ben, please. Coffee?" he offered, trying to dispel her tension and his own crazy speculations as to her paternity. She was like a fragile flower: she didn't appear the type to live under Landis's terms. But, evidently she didn't really know who—and what—her husband was.

"Thank you, Ben. Landis has spoken of you most frequently."

"Has he now?" he genially responded, casting his friend a rueful look. "All bad, I suppose?" It couldn't be me, Ben mentally fretted.

"Not at all. It sounds as if you two are much alike," she remarked, her soft tone compelling.

"I'll take that as a compliment, seeing how you feel about him."

She blushed once more. Were her feelings that obvious, even to a stranger? Ben and Landis both laughed. Kathy sent Landis a reproving look, but Ben a radiant smile. "If you gentlemen will excuse me, I'll get breakfast ready. Are you hungry, Mr. We . . . Ben?"

He chuckled, dismissing the implausible ideas racing through his mind. "Starved, Mrs. Jurrell," he confessed, still observing her.

"Kathy, please," she happily corrected, liking him instantly.

"Kathy," he readily responded.

The two men sat down to chat while Kathy busied herself with their meal. Landis noticed the way Ben kept stealing glances at Kathy; evidently she was a total surprise to him, even after his warning. When the men's gazes met, Ben amusedly lifted his brows and pursed his lips, nodding his appreciation of Landis's taste. Ben's solemn look intrigued Landis, until he decided this cozy setting might be refreshing those painful memories which Ben had confided to him. Possibly Ben was perturbed with him after meeting such a charming lady. Maybe he shouldn't have joked about love.

Kathy served the men, then sat down. At first, they mutely devoured the food. Later, the two men discussed their trapping, then spoke of the area's troubles. Kathy listened with absorption watching both impressive men as they conversed easily. Landis had spoken truthfully; they were perfect companions.

Ben remarked, "Maybe I should become a writer, Landis. I've certainly gathered enough colorful tales of romance, adventure, and peril. Of course, people wouldn't believe they were for real if they saw my journal. But it'll be nice to read it when I'm old."

"Do you have a family somewhere?" Kathy asked.

"Not anymore," Ben answered, looking down at his plate.

Kathy wisely sensed she should avoid that unhappy

340

topic. Ben suddenly glanced up and grinned. "'Course Landis is like a brother to me."

"Where did you live before coming here?" Kathy felt safe to ask.

"Came up from Montana. I didn't think there could be any place colder. I learned I was wrong my first winter here. Landis tells me you're from Seattle. I hear it gets mighty cold there, too."

"We sailed from Seattle, but I'm from Washington," she stated.

"From Washington state or the American capital?" Ben asked, his gut knotting, praying the first would be her reply.

"The capital. My mother and I were travelling . . ." Kathy abruptly halted. She hadn't permitted that heart-rending and frightening time to plague her in weeks. "I'm sorry. Will you excuse me a minute?" she whispered, then hurried to Landis's room, closing the door softly.

Ben was dismayed. He looked at Landis and inquired with great concern, "Did I say something wrong? Surely she didn't run away from home? The Yukon's a long way from Washington."

Landis shook his head. "No, Ben. Kat's just upset by something she remembered, probably for the first time in weeks. She's had a difficult time recently, then this place wasn't what she expected."

"She mentioned her mother. Why did she leave home to come here alone? She doesn't appear the adventuress. Problems back there?"

"Her mother died unexpectedly in August. Kat was left alone in a strange city. She and her mother were friends with Harriet Pullen, the woman I told you about. Mrs. Pullen persuaded Kat to come here," he briefly expounded, too distracted to observe Ben's reactions.

Ben was staggered by this news, but fiercely concealed his anguish. "I'm sorry. Perhaps I should speak with her," he deliberated aloud, sharing this girl's pains and problems. "She's awfully young to be alone. What about kinfolk?" he probed.

"I think we should let her work it out alone. Maybe I shouldn't have brought her here. It'll only be worse for her when I send her back to Moore's. I think you can see why I was compelled to help her."

"Yes, but I can also see why you shouldn't have," Ben commented hesitantly, unsure of how Landis would take his unsolicited advice. "If you don't love her, Landis, you should end this quickly and mercifully. Sounds like she has enough worries. Send her home to America."

Landis halted himself before declaring his great love and need for Kathy. That would sound suspiciously contradictory. He was forced to credit his motives and actions to protection. "You sound just like Mrs. Pullen," Landis teased. "Kat's as safe here as in America alone."

"Evidently the woman has her best interests at heart; do you? She doesn't belong here, Landis, not with you or in the Yukon."

"I know, Ben. But how do I convince her without hurting her?"

"She's in love. Whatever you say or do, it's gonna hurt her deeply. You should give her a real marriage or release her. With her mother's death, I pity her. I also admire her and like her."

Landis met his piercing gaze. "You've got heavy instincts for a loner, Ben. But the decision to leave must come from her. If I force her to go, she'll hate me. I can't allow her to turn to another man to spite me," he stated.

"She won't leave as long as you give her reasons to stay."

"You mean I should entice her to leave by behaving badly?"

"If you're really concerned about her welfare, you will."

"She'll despise me, Ben," he muttered sadly.

"She will anyway if she starts to believe you're selfishly using her. At least make your real feelings known to her," Ben urged.

"I have," he vowed in exasperation.

"No way, my friend, not the way you treat her and look at her. You've got false promises written all over you. A girl in love has difficulty seeing reality. She doesn't think about the future until she wakes up one day and realizes it's passing her by while she's playing house."

"I've never been caught in a predicament like this before. I want her, Ben," he confessed, omitting the vital words: I love her.

"It's my guess she hasn't either. One day, you'll be sorry."

"If I can locate her father, maybe things will be all right for her."

"What do you mean?" Ben jumped on his friend's words, his acute interest undisguised. "I thought you said she was an orphan?" he wisely added.

"That's why Kat agreed to come here with Mrs. Pullen," Landis began, then gradually explained the whole story of Kathy's search for Jake Hammond and her many pitfalls along the way, including her battle with Marc Slavin and her mock marriage to Landis.

Ben listened intently, asking questions here and there, until the depressing tale was unfolded before him, all except Landis's true feelings for Kathy. For a man who needed privacy, Landis had gone out on a limb to simply protect her. So much depended on a love-match between them . . . Yet, Ben never exposed more than sincere curiosity and empathy.

"You're looking for this Jake Hammond for her?"

"I'm asking around to see if I can do any good," Landis stated.

"Why do you doubt it?" Ben probed casually.

"Kathy went to Log Cabin to see Bill. He did some checking around, but no news on Hammond. If he was ever here," Landis added, then jumped up to refill his cup, scolding himself for revealing too much to Ben. After all, Landis had to keep his suspicions about Jake Hammond a secret . . .

When he sat down, Ben was eying him with intense scrutiny. "Am I wrong, or do you have some sneaking suspicion she's lying?"

Landis stroked his black stubble. "Why would I doubt my wife's claim?" he debated.

"She's staying here for more than one reason; you want to keep an eye on her. For Sergeant Thomas or yourself?" Ben taunted.

"What would I have to do with Mounty affairs?" Landis retorted.

"They're your friends. If they needed help, you'd comply. But you don't quite trust her. I wonder how you'd feel if you located Jake Hammond and discovered she was being totally honest. I also wonder how she'd feel if she learned why she's really here with you now," he speculated gravely.

Landis grimaced, knowing he was saying too much. "Let's drop it, Ben. If you want to help us, ask around for this Hammond character."

Ben chuckled. "Me?" he said in amusement. "I make it a rule to mind my own business so others will mind theirs."

The conversation ended abruptly as Kathy opened the

door and returned, but didn't sit down. Her eyes were red and puffy, indicating a battle of tears and anguish. She set to clearing away the dishes.

Ben caught her hand and smiled up into her sad face. "I'm sorry if I called to mind unhappy memories, Kathy. Landis explained about your problems. Is there anything I can do or say?"

Landis watched this tender exchange, pleased with Ben's unexpected sympathy and insight. "You're very kind, Ben. I'll be leaving soon. Jack's coming to take me to Skagway."

"Jack?" he echoed, mutely adding, what about Landis?

"Jack London. He's an old friend of mine. He's going to take me home while Landis looks for my father."

Ben cast a curious glance at Landis. "Why don't you take her to Skagway or on your search? You know this territory better than most. It would give you plenty of time together, and alone."

"I offered, but she seems to prefer her friend Jack. She's afraid to trust herself alone in the wilds with me," he jested, to cover his strange refusal to accompany his own wife. "With us gone so much, Kat wouldn't be safe or happy here alone," he added.

At his odd lies, Kathy's face went scarlet and she inhaled sharply. Her reaction enlightened Ben, who pretended not to notice it. Landis shrugged and stood up, taking his dishes to the washpan. "You want to lay some traps today?" he asked Ben to ease the tension.

"If we want to make any money this winter, we'd best get at it," Ben said. "That was the best breakfast I've had in years, Kathy. Thanks. See you tonight," he stated lightly, then went to his room and closed the door.

Kathy looked at Landis. "Whyever did you say such things, Landis? If you'll recall, you're the one who refuses to take me along or keep me here. You embarrassed me. I think it's best if I leave, now that Ben's home I think we'll all be more comfortable."

"There's no reason to leave so soon or to be embarrassed, Kat."

"Isn't there!" she disputed softly. "When you talk about me and treat me like some . . . some cheap harlot rather than your wife, what is Ben supposed to think? Did you tell him it was only a mock marriage?"

"I didn't treat you any such way!" he argued.

"You did so," she vowed stubbornly. "You sounded as if you could hardly wait to have me gone."

"Kat, does it bother you this much what people think about us?" he demanded, his tone losing its harshness.

"Yes, I care what they say and think. What about my father, Landis? How will I explain my conduct to him? Either we have a real marriage or we don't. Do you want me to go or stay?" she pressed him.

Landis wanted to shout: you don't owe your father any explanations; he deserted you; and he lost his fatherly rights when he walked out and never looked back. Landis couldn't recklessly send such knifing statements home.

"Well?" she entreated, tears flowing down her cheeks.

"I love you, Kat. But you're setting yourself up for a painful awakening. You're not being realistic about your father. You've conjured up this glowing image of him. What if he's rotten? My God, Kat, he's already hurt you terribly."

"Please don't make this any harder on me, Landis. I must find him. Please help me," she begged, clinging to him.

"I promised you, if he's here and it's possible, I'll find him."

She hugged him. "I love you so much," she whispered against his chest.

"I know, Kat; I know," he murmured, unaware that his

346

friend had been listening to the entire passionate exchange.

Ben wondered if Landis was cruelly toying with or ruthlessly using this special girl. Was she Kathryn Leigh Hammond, his daughter? How? What about Dory's denial that he was the father? It didn't add up; this girl was his spitten image, not Morgan's! Landis couldn't be right in his suspicions, not unless Kathy had been sought out and sent here for a critical reason. If this innocent-eyed girl was not an American spy or his child, he dared not expose himself to her. Kathy's prior words and quivering voice returned to plague him.

Ben felt trapped. It could be a fateful coincidence or a poisonous snare. Did Landis suspect him? Had Landis discovered a method to unmask him? The girl's story was too pat to explain spying on Landis. Ben decided to watch them closely.

Ben waited a few minutes before he came out of his room as he sought to master his warring emotions and to reaffirm his belief he had never caused his friend or the Canadian Government any harm. That was the only way he could remain here, to safely glean his necessary information and to protect his friend. The reality of Landis's identity provoked Ben; Kathy was Jurrell's wife, not Clinton Marlowe's.

"You ready, Ben?" Landis asked, his eyes still on Kathy's face.

"I'll fetch the traps," Ben said, heading into the storage room. Ben resolved that nothing would harm either one, without just cause.

Kathy stood in the doorway, watching the men depart. She sighed heavily, then closed the door, certain this time her love was going trapping.

Fourteen

Those next few days proved incredibly serene for Kathy. She came to adore the genial Ben Weathers, listening intently while he wove colorful and amusing tales. She agreed to learn poker and whist. Each night they spent hours laughing, talking, and playing games. Ben made her feel right at home, totally at ease following that first awkward day. She cooked and cleaned while the men trapped. Noting the pelts they were bringing home to cure, she knew both men were working diligently. Landis didn't make anymore of those strange trips, as if he were reluctant to leave her side. She must be right, else why did he constantly hang on her every word?

Landis . . . that first night with Ben in the cabin had been strained. She had curled into Landis's arms and savored his kisses, but couldn't bring herself to make love. She had imagined Ben lying in bed in the next room, the quiet cabin lending itself to any noise. Landis had been slightly miffed by her reluctance, but had understood her hesitation and seemingly accepted it. That second night had begun much the same with Kathy reluctant to surrender to his heady assault on her senses. With patience and stimulating persuasion, she had inevitably lost her will to his masterful one.

When Ben appeared to behave no differently that next morning, Kathy's doubts and modesty gradually vanished. She was sure Ben could hear their softened whispers and happy laughter, but he never let on or made any comments. Why should he; they were married. But sometimes she would catch his keen eyes on them . . .

By the third day, their arrangement seemed natural, as if they were a family. She surrendered herself to this happy setting, blossoming with love and happiness. Landis also seemed perfectly comfortable, laughing freely and displaying open affection to her. After that night, she went to Landis with heated passion. She briefly denied her quest, one which would take her husband from her side at this critical period.

Unknown to Kathy, both men were playing vital and guarded roles. Landis was trying to decide Kathy's innocence and to get to know this girl/woman he had married, while Ben was trying to uncover the motives of both people. It appeared to Ben that Landis didn't know about Ben's real identity. Ben came to the conclusion Landis had emotionally entrapped himself while seeking Kathy as a protective cover for his missions and real name. Ben couldn't rationalize Landis's behavior, for he knew the marriage was invalid. Ben dreaded to imagine Kathy's humiliation and pain when that fact came to light. Yet, Ben loved Landis as a brother; still, Kathy was possibly his child, one totally different from her traitorous mother.

On the fourth day, Ben entered the cabin to find Landis chasing Kathy. She was giggling and darting around the furniture to avoid his grasp. Landis was grinning in playful mischief as he eagerly pursued her. Kathy shrieked in delight and raced to hide behind Ben, coaxing, "Help me, Ben."

Ben's arms stretched outwards, forming a guard between them. "Too bad, Landis; I've got her now. You'll have to battle both of us."

Ben and Kathy laughed gaily. Landis halted his approach to place his hands on his hips, standing with legs apart. His gaze and tone were mocking. "You two joining forces against me in my own cabin?"

"You asked for it, Jurrell," Kathy coyly announced.

"My brother and my wife! No wonder I stay home. Think I would trust you two conspirators alone?" he jested, making no move toward them.

"Why, Landis Jurrell, you crude rake," Ben sang out, chuckling. Ben vanquished his alarm, concluding there hadn't been any strange emphasis on Landis's taunting statements. Still, Landis was perceptive and cunning, and Kathy did look like him.

"Well if you're gonna steal my wife right under my nose, then I best turn in," he remarked. As he moved backwards, he tripped and fell over a chair. He crashed loudly to the floor, then remained still.

Kathy panicked, falling for his crafty deception. She raced around Ben and hurried to kneel beside her husband. "Landis! Are you all right? Speak to me!" she squealed in panic, paling and shaking.

Before she could react, Landis seized her and pinned her to the floor. "You're far too trusting, Mrs. Jurrell," he taunted, eyes gleaming with devilish victory.

"And you are too cunning and dangerous to be trusted," she retorted, laughing merrily. "Perhaps I wed too hastily and unwisely."

"You don't say?" he challenged, a beguiling grin focused on her.

"No, I don't say. I'm the luckiest woman in the world. Isn't that right, Ben?" she entreated, smiling up into her husband's eyes.

Concern flooded Ben, recalling an afternoon talk with Landis. Ben knew a sudden need to send Kathy home had to do with Landis's talk with the Mounty they had encountered. After watching them for days, Ben wasn't convinced of Landis's love and loyalty. It had to do with the way Landis furtively watched her and the way Landis seemed determined not to yield totally and presently to her callings of love. Jake Hammond had Landis tensed and worried. What was the cunning and relentless Landis after, to win Kathy or to use her to capture Jake, or perhaps both? If certain vital matters weren't pressing both men, Ben would expose himself. His confession would halt Landis's intense search and force a decision about his daughter. If Landis was using her, Ben would be here to comfort and protect her. Ben realized he loved his daughter deeply, but he had worked too hard and too long to destroy his mission this close to its climax. Supposedly wed to Jurrell, what could harm her in the next few weeks?

Possibly it was dawning on Landis—the undercover Mounty—that Kathy couldn't lead him to Jake. Defeat on any level didn't suit him, the real Sergeant Clinton Marlowe. What would Landis/Clint do and say when he discovered Jake Hammond had lived and worked with him as Ben Weathers for two years? Would Landis think he had been duped by both Ben/Jake and Kathy? When the truth came out, would their love be destroyed by the father she was seeking?

"You two gonna lie there carrying on like that all night? How about some cards and brandy?" Ben suggested, squatting down beside them, concealing his turbulent thoughts.

Landis groaned playfully, "You really know how to

spoil a fellow's fun."

Kathy giggled. "He didn't win fairly, did he, Ben?"

"Not in the least, Kathy. Next time we won't be fooled by his tricky mind," he declared sternly, meaning far more.

"Don't you two start in on me again," Landis wailed in humor.

"Somebody has to be on my side. Who better than Ben?"

Ben smiled. "Let's play some checkers."

When Landis was cuddled against her sated body later that night, Kathy realized that since Ben's return, Landis hadn't gotten up any night, after thinking her asleep, to make notes to conceal in his hiding place. Perhaps it was because he hadn't left the cabin on one of his mysterious trips. She knew he had taken the papers with him one day. Evidently they were business reports and he had turned them over to his unknown boss. Kathy frowned as she recalled checking the hole again to see if other papers had been placed there. It had been empty. She knew Landis would be furious if he caught her snooping, but she wanted to understand him and his work. She had been careful to re-adjust the picture and the tattletale string. She drifted off to sleep with questions about what those secret papers contained . . .

When Kathy stirred the next morning, Landis wasn't beside her. She got up and dressed. She found him eating breakfast with Ben. "Why didn't you two awaken me?" she mildly scolded them.

"You needed your sleep; you were mighty restless last night," Landis murmured, drawing a curious look from her.

"Did I keep you awake?" she apologetically asked, blushing.

"No. Something bothering you, Kat? Or just bored?" he inquired, his gaze unsettling her.

"No," she replied, her brow raised quizzically.

Someone knocked on the door. Landis went to answer it, almost as if he was expecting someone. It was the Mounty, Trace Blitch. They chatted a few minutes, then Trace left without coming in. Ben and Kathy had continued their conversation, unable to hear the men's muffled words.

Shortly after Landis closed the door, he said he had forgotten to tell Trace something. He grabbed his jacket and headed after the Mounty, his open parka flapping after him. "I'll be back," he called over his shoulder.

"More coffee, Ben?" Kathy asked, pouring herself another cup.

"Yes, thanks." Ben handed her the cup just as Landis opened the door and walked in, his parka now securely fastened . . . Ben grinned.

Landis told them he was going to change into warmer clothes before going out again, he had said it was exceptionally chilly and damp. He closed the bedroom door behind him. When he returned, he was dressed in snug-fitting black pants over longjohns and a creamy shirt in thick linen. A furry jerkin covered much of his shirt, it's missing sleeves evincing arms with their bulging muscles. He had pulled on knee-high boots in shiny black. Not ready to leave yet, the top few buttons on his shirt were still unfastened, allowing Kathy a glimpse of his brawny chest with crisply curling black hair.

"You going somewhere?" Ben asked.

"To Dawson," he freely announced, buttoning his shirt.

"Can I go?" Kathy excitedly requested. "I haven't been out of this cabin in weeks. I would love to see this infamous Dawson."

"Not this time. You remain hidden until the Mounties capture those men who attacked you. You can pack while I'm gone; I'll take you home when I return." Landis and Ben exchanged unreadable looks.

Kathy felt as if Landis had knocked the wind from her. "You're taking me back to Harriet's?" she asked, waiting for his reaction.

"I must, Kat," he pressed, drilling his gaze into Ben's. There was a curious interaction going on between them which Kathy couldn't grasp. "Aren't you going along, Ben?" she queried, focusing her attention on him.

"I'd rather be alone, if you don't mind, Ben," Landis quickly injected. "I'd appreciate you staying here to protect Kat until I come home. You two can get better acquainted," he casually suggested.

Kathy's gaze flew to Landis and froze on his blank face. "You're serious?" Kathy persisted, looking and sounding as if she had just received a death sentence for an unpardonable crime. She *was* home!

"Ben and I are getting busy, and I need time to search for your father. We can't leave you here alone while I'm traveling and he's trapping. You've been stuck here a month. I'm sure Harriet and the others miss you," he explained calmly. "I'll come to visit as soon as I can, or when I have some exciting news," he added to calm her.

Kathy watched him as if hypnotized. His meaning was all too clear. He was politely trying to send her on her way, out of his. She realized why he hadn't discussed this in private; he didn't want any fuss. "Leave when you get home?" she asked, her voice unsteady.

"I'll be gone for several days. Ben'll take care of you. I'd best get packed and going," he nonchalantly delivered this stunning news.

Landis entered the storage room to load his pack with supplies. He dropped it on the living-area floor as he retrieved his parka. When he was all bundled up, he placed the pack-board on his back and secured it around his waist. Kathy noted his thick sleeping bag, an extra blanket, a canteen, and a large pack which contained camping gear and staples. Besides his hunting knife and pistol, he slung a rifle over his shoulder and dropped two boxes of ammunition in his pocket.

"Are you expecting trouble, Landis?" she anxiously probed.

"Just a precaution, Kat. Ask Ben; this area is dangerous in winter. Men kill for food and shelter. Don't worry, I'll see you soon," he added again, sending his point home.

"I'll be packed and ready," she acquiesced, pride preventing her from demanding his motives or pleading to stay.

"See you later," Landis stated, then left without even kissing her goodbye.

He left quickly. Kathy watched his steady retreat until he vanished from sight. Still, she remained in the open door, staring at the spot where he had disappeared. Ben came over and pulled her away from the icy draft. "You'll freeze, Kathryn. Come over by the fire," he encouraged tenderly.

He led her over to it, but she remained stiff and silent. "I'm sorry, Kathy," he offered from behind her to ease her anguish.

She looked up into his contrite expression and asked, "Why?"

"Why am I sorry?" he asked, stalling.

"Why must I leave?" she sadly replied, tears welling in her eyes.

"Landis isn't used to having a woman around, especially a new wife. With you here, he's having trouble concentrating and working. I'm fond of you, Kathryn. You're a lady, and this wild land isn't the place for you. You belong in a safe, warm, busy home."

"But Skagway is awful, Ben. I like it better here with you and Landis. Why must I leave now? Landis and I are just getting to know each other, and things were going so well for all of us," she protested.

"I meant America. That's where a woman like you belongs. Maybe Jake will hear about you and come home," he encouraged.

"But what about Landis, Ben? I love him, and we're married."

Ben wavered indecisively; he also needed his child gone and safe so he could move around at will. He had earned Landis's trust, but the stormy affair between the lovers could sever it. He couldn't tell her they weren't wed without blowing his and Landis's covers. With Landis's cover marriage rapidly changing, his friend was running scared. Could Kathy forgive Landis for his traitorous ploy? From the way Landis acted and talked, he had no future plans to wed her. Again, Ben feared this set-up was to compel him out of hiding. Ben was vexed with Landis; he had to get his child away.

"You can't change him, Kathy, no matter how much you want to. You've shown Landis what you have to offer him. He can break your heart, Kathy. You best go back to America; you've no idea what your life can be like once you leave this cabin and Landis's protection. You're a good girl, Kathy; don't do this to yourself."

"You mean just give up on him? Just walk out and never look back?" she protested, gaping at him.

"Sometimes that's the only way to save yourself,

Kathy. Nothing is worse than to be trapped in a demanding love affair. You aren't his first love, Kathy; he loves something more. He's selfish where you're concerned. Start running and never look back until he's ready to settle down," he advised, his expression a mixture of anguish and bitterness. Even for his beloved career, it wasn't right for Landis to abuse this girl who was clearly in love with him! Ben had to prevent it.

"What if I'm sorry or mistaken?" she reasoned in agony.

"There are prices to pay when we make decisions that affect other lives. Sometimes we can't help hurting those we love. But when we're hurting too, we want to salve our own pains. Do you understand what it will be to have your vitality sapped, your reason for existing snuffed out like a candle? The longer you hang around dreaming, Kathy, the harder it will be to leave, the deeper the pains and scars. You're young and beautiful. You have your life before you. If Landis loves and needs you, he'll come after you. Maybe if you leave, it will open his eyes. If your loss doesn't affect him, you'll have your answer. Try it," he coaxed.

"You make it sound like some calculating game, Ben. It isn't! This is my happiness and love we're discussing. If I leave, how can I prove to him he needs me, that he can trust me?"

"Absence will teach him a lesson. He can deny his feelings with you here. Give him solitude to miss you, Kathy, time to sort out his feelings. His foolish mistrust should tell you something. Without trust and loyalty, there can be no love and happiness. He wants you to leave. Are you going to refuse?"

"I can't make any demands on him. He'll resent me if I do. Perhaps I should leave now; can you take me to

Skagway, Ben?"

Her sudden decision surprised him. "Me take you?" Ben asked.

"It would be easier that way. Do you mind?" she entreated.

Perhaps that was best for all of them, Ben concluded to himself. He nodded his head and smiled comfortingly. "I'll go fetch those extra traps we were repairing out back while you dress and pack. I'll need to set them and walk the traplines. Lock the door; I'll be gone several hours. Don't fret, Kathy, things will work out soon."

Ben left the exceptionally quiet cabin. Kathy knew what had to be done. Sighting steam rising from boiling water on the stove, she desired a bath before departing. She prepared things before packing. When all was ready, she discovered something which enticed bittersweet memories: a pot too heavy to lift. Evidently Ben had planned some washing today. She went to get Ben to help her, if he hadn't left yet. She unlocked the cabin door and started around the corner, her feet silent in the new-fallen snow. Torturous words froze her steps . . .

Beside a tree near the other corner, Jack London and Ben were arguing softly. Kathy flattened herself against the wall to listen. Fear and doubts danced through her head. Everyone she met acted weird; she needed some answers, answers no one seemed willing to supply. Perhaps it was past time for her to work on and solve her problems.

"Don't interfere, Jack," Kathy heard Ben say. "If Landis wants something badly, he'll go to any lengths to have it. We've all been friends a long time. Let them work out their problems when he returns from Dawson."

"Do you know why he went to Dawson?" Jack asked abruptly.

"On business, I suppose," Ben replied.

"Business, my ass, Ben. We both know where and how he's conducting his 'business' in Dawson. He married Kathy; he owes her." For Ben's help and understanding, Jack explained his past friendship with Kathy and her mother.

Ben turned away, needing to digest these clues. His shoulders were slumped, as if a heavy burden was resting there. "What is it, Ben? There's something you don't want to tell me?" Jack probed.

Ben sighed heavily. "Landis and I have been close friends for years, Jack. I wouldn't do anything to hurt him if I could prevent it. I know him well, his strengths and his flaws. You and I are friends, but he would never forgive me for helping you take Kathy from him. I've come to love that spunky girl; I wish I could help," he worried aloud.

"I swear I won't repeat anything you tell me, not even to Kathy. If you truly care about her, please tell me what you're hiding."

Ben made his decision. No matter the consequences, he must free his daughter from Landis's dangerous hold . . . or, force the truth on Landis.

"She's packing now; I'm returning her to Skagway while he's gone," he tried another approach, hoping to avoid the torturous truth.

"You mean, leave before he comes back? He'll be furious."

"You asked for the truth. If I tell it, you won't wish her to wait for his return. Are you ready?" he challenged in a strained tone.

Kathy flinched inwardly. What could be so terrible that she would spurn Landis? Horror filled her, but she prayed for Jack to say yes.

359

Ben added, "I've wondered why Landis doesn't want anyone to know she's here with him. They are wed, and he is searching for her father. Why not send out messages where she can be reached?"

"I don't follow, Ben," Jack declared.

Ben shook his head sadly. "He doesn't want a certain person to know he has a woman in his cabin, much less a wife. He probably figures he's pressed his luck long enough, and it's time to send her away."

"Trace knows she's here. Maybe others," Jack argued.

"Trace wouldn't tell a soul, and Kathy hasn't seen anyone else."

She closed her eyes tightly. Was she prepared for Ben's words?

"Tell me, Ben. Whatever it is, I must know to help her."

"The Dawson business has blond hair and blue eyes. Soapy's faro dealer. He's been there many times in the last few months, even since his marriage. From what I've heard, he stays in her room. He's heading there now. She's no match for Kathryn, but she and Landis have been seeing each other for over a year. Now I see why Landis kept his marriage a secret; it's a fake, Jack," he stated, sensing there was more to know from Jack.

Jack grimaced and revealed his own knowledge, "Her name's Michelle Darney, and he wants Kathy gone before Michelle gets wise?"

The color gradually faded from Kathy's face. Her ravaged heart screamed, you're lying! Landis wouldn't use me like that!

"Everybody knows about them. It's hardly a secret she's his private stock when he's in town. I prayed he had dropped Michelle."

Kathy's distraught mind questioned, how could they speak such malicious lies? Was she merely a pawn in everyone's personal schemes? Was no one to be trusted, even friends and a mysterious husband? Was she so blind she couldn't read the signs before her?

"Are you sure he went to see Michelle?" Jack persisted.

"Why would I lie? Go to Dawson; see where Landis is this very minute. For whatever reason, he's betraying her in the arms of another woman, just like . . . . If I didn't care deeply for Kathy, I would keep silent. Right or wrong, I love him as a brother. But Kathy's living in a dream world, and needs to wake up before it's too late. Maybe Landis is, too," he softened his accusations. "He seems to really care about Kathy."

"My God, Ben, everyone will be laughing at her. Just as I suspected, he's using her. Damnit, I think he's trying to get to Jake Hammond through the daughter!" Jack sneered in exasperation. "No doubt as a favor to his friend Bill Thomas. He really fooled me and Kathy. It makes perfect sense, his questions about her and her father. Why marry a woman you don't know, unless you want to watch her?"

Kathy's mouth fell open in shock.

"What do you know about her father?" Ben quizzed. Jack related everything he knew.

Ben knew he had said too much and might look suspicious. He backed off as Jack said, "The Mounties have a keen interest in Jake."

"That's only natural. She did ask for their help."

"My sweet and innocent Kathy," Jack muttered sadly. "Landis doesn't believe her claim; he isn't even sure she is the real Kathy Hammond, not from the questions he's asked me several times."

Ben speculated on Jack's words and his own clues. "Until this matter's settled, I think Kathy's safer in

Skagway," Ben concluded.

Jack pressed Ben for more information.

"I overheard a talk between Landis and Mounty McLorey in Dawson. I was standing behind a wood pile waiting for someone. They walked by, talking. I only caught a few words which didn't make sense then. After coming home, I was shocked to learn of the secret marriage and to find Kathy living here. When Landis told McLorey he would do anything to pull the information from that blond tart with innocent blue eyes, I didn't know who he was referring to. He told McLorey he would have the information within three weeks, maybe news about Jake. Since she can't supply it, there's no reason to keep her. In fact, I think Landis has come to the conclusion Kathy might be telling the truth. He might suspect someone is using her to get the information out." Ben didn't tell Jack how he came to possess such accurate facts, having known about Landis's hiding place for two years . . . Living in close proximity to that secret place, he was as well informed about Canada's secret matters as Marlowe and the Mounties. Plus, Ben had rationalized, a man in Clint's perilous job might need help or protection from a friend.

"Maybe Kathy isn't the only one who's misjudged him. I've never seen this side of him before. It disappoints me, Ben. Landis Jurrell is a lot of things, but I never knew he could stoop so low."

"Each man has his needs and principles, Jack. I've betrayed him by telling you these things. But I couldn't stand by and watch this travesty any longer. I thought Landis and I were alike, but I was wrong. When Landis finds out what we've done today, he'll probably want to kill us," he stated lightly, but Kathy sensed a worried tension in him.

Kathy recalled how Landis had beaten Marc. There was another side to him which she obviously didn't know. Soapy's words came to mind, "He isn't somebody to have at your back or to meet in the dark." Had Soapy been laughing at her ignorance? Had he suspected there was nothing between them? Was that why he had presumed she could be enticed to work for him? If what Ben said was true, Soapy had to know all about Landis and this Michelle. And Bill Thomas, was he behind her stay here in Landis's cabin? Who was Jake Hammond and why were they so intrigued by him? She had to know.

Evidently she hadn't been mistaken about Bill's first reaction to her and her father's name. Did that explain why Landis had her investigated? But why show her the letter? Wed her? Keep her? To deceive her? Was he really with another woman? Was everyone making a fool of her? What if that wedding at sea wasn't legal? It was clear; she must find Jake, and discover if Landis was betraying her.

She soundlessly went into the cabin, flinging herself into hasty preparations to leave with Jack, not Ben. There was no time for tears, regrets, or second thoughts. She had to find out where her father was—and who her husband was.

Ben knocked on the door later, calling out, "Kathy, I'm going to check the traps. I'll be back in a few hours. Jack's here."

Kathy unlocked the door. She didn't expose her plans to Ben; to prevent his protest, she would leave him a note. Ben smiled at her and left. Jack waited to speak privately with her.

Kathy was studying the cabin strangely. Here, she had loved wildly and freely; she had brazenly tasted the forbidden nectar of love's tender and savage passion. The

363

tempest in her soul was mounting as she accepted multiple treacheries as reality. A love wonderful and unique was not to be the end result of this traitorous interlude. She had kept her end of their bargain, as had he in a tormenting way: his protective name and more than two weeks here. Ben was right; she should walk away with her scanty pride intact. But such agony and bitterness filled her. Was Michelle the only barrier between them? No . . .

As Ben trudged along, his mind was troubled. He mentally vowed, one day, my lovely child, you will hear the truth from my lips and hopefully forgive me and your wicked mother. It took every ounce of willpower Ben possessed to keep from revealing it now. She had been told too many lies, now and in the past.

Kathy was dressed and packed, eager to end this nightmare. She focused impenetrable eyes on her friend Jack. "I want you to take me to search for my father, Jack," she asked.

"Kathy, I've been out of my mind with worry," Jack told her. "Landis told me you were back in Skagway, but Trace gave me your message from here. Kathy, what's going on?" he asked, witnessing her distress. "If he's harmed you, husband or not, I'll beat him."

"It isn't like that, Jack," she quickly attempted to calm his outrage. "He just isn't helping me. It's up to us to locate Jake."

Jack glanced around. "You want to go with me?"

"Yes. I tried to catch up with you, but we ran into trouble."

"I know. Moore told me about the two Eskimos being murdered. The killers won't be preying on anymore people, not after the Mounties finish with them! I'm glad you're safe and they're in custody."

364

"They've been captured?" she inquired, shocked.

"Didn't Landis tell you? About five days after they attacked you. They were taken while trying to sell the goods upriver. It was two desperadoes from America. Landis was in Dawson when they were brought in. I don't understand why he didn't tell you."

"Neither do I."

"Who is Michelle Darney?" she abruptly questioned.

Jack flinched. "Who?" he avoided instantly answering.

"Is she and Landis . . . You know what I'm trying to ask," she finished. "He's my husband; I have a right to know."

"They were seeing each other before your arrival, if that's what you want to know. But he's married to you now."

"Does he still see her every time he goes to Dawson?"

"Why?" Jack asked, wondering if he should answer or not.

"We're friends, Jack. Tell me the truth," she demanded.

"What did Landis say?" he fenced once more.

"Is he there with her now?" she pressed persistently.

He asked warily, "Why worry over a cheap whore?"

"Did he send you to get me?" she continued with her questions, ignoring his.

"No. I passed him at a distance; we didn't talk. Trace told me you were here. What's happening here, Kathy?" he tenderly insisted.

"Nothing, Jack. Ben was taking me to Skagway this morning. Now that you're here, he won't have to. Besides, that isn't where I want to go. I'm already packed. Let's go."

"But . . ."

She cut him off, "Let's leave before Ben comes back. I don't want to upset him. We'll talk later."

"Ben's out; what about locking the door?" Jack asked.

"He has a key. Let's get moving, my brotherly guide."

Jack secured Kathy's pack to her shoulders. "Ready?"

"More than you'll ever know," she teased to lighten the gloom.

Jack and Kathy headed off to the Northeast. Before they were out of sight, Ben came hurrying back to persuade Jack to take his place in taking Kathy back to Skagway. Her intentions were clear to Ben. He watched them until they vanished from his misty gaze. "You've already found me, Kathryn Leigh, but not when or where you expected. I pray Jack will keep you safe on your futile journey, then take you home where you belong. If only you knew the truth and how much it hurts to send you away. I love you, little one," he murmured to himself, having decided the devastating door to the past must remain closed forever.

Ben entered the cabin and went to Landis's room to read the note she had surely left for her husband. How very proud and resilient she was . . . An honest soul, she had told Landis where she was heading and why, to locate her father because he couldn't or wouldn't.

Fifteen

Jack had brought along an extra pair of snowshoes, making Kathy's task easier. It required over an hour of trudging in the awkward footgear before she got the hang of them. They were shaped like bear paws, with a slightly upturned toe and long tail. Made of seasoned white ash to avoid warping, they were cured to prevent sagging and tripping. The leather riggings bit uncomfortably into her feet even through her boots. Jack also delivered a wool shirt to retain her body heat, a gift from Harriet. At first, Kathy had balked at the belt and holster with a pistol and hunting knife which Jack insisted she wear under her parka. Jack was pleased to learn she actually knew how to load and fire a gun.

Kathy and Jack walked for two hours before halting to rest. Oddly, this trek didn't seem as strenuous as the one with Landis, once she adjusted to the clumsy snowshoes. Jack gave her tips on conserving energy and staying warm, things Landis hadn't shared. Perhaps, Kathy thought, to make her dependent on him, or to persuade her she was ill-prepared for this rough climate and terrain, or to control and weaken her spirit!

As they rested later, Jack gave her instructions and warnings. He handed her a pair of snowglasses and demanded she keep her eyes, tawny hair, face, and figure concealed from the men, who'd been without women for months, or even years. "We don't want any dangerous temptations."

When Kathy shrugged, he scowled and cautioned, "I'm serious, Kathy. Your voice could charm the devil himself. When men are bored and restless, they do crazy things. This area has a lawless atmosphere; makes men think they can do as they please. When a man's facing death every day, he holds little sacred. Let me do the talking. If there's any trouble, flaunt your husband's name; they'll think twice."

"I'll be very obedient, Jack," she vowed, seeing how grave and worried he was, ignoring his last suggestion.

"Let's get to it; we have miles to cover before nightfall."

They roamed settlements along the Klondike: Bonanza, Eldorado, and Lost Chance. The inhabitants were existing in countless ways in this deprived area: large and heavy canvas tents, to small and scanty ones, to roughly constructed lean-tos of branches, to four-foot high enclosures of logs without tops, to wooden shacks which tempted wind or fire to destroy them.

Kathy keenly observed this despicable way of life, scoffing at the riches which lured men here to vanquish them. From appearances, they were becoming poorer instead. Some men barely had proper clothing to ward off a mild chill, much less icy cold weather. Some begged for food or money like urchins on street corners. Jack warned her to ignore them, which she tried to do. But it was nearly impossible in some cases where the men were old and weak or still boys, all hopelessly dejected.

She witnessed two fights and several quarrels. She saw men huddled around meager fires, drinking whiskey to ease their mental and physical pains or tossing rocks to win a few flakes of gold-dust. In one campsite, two men were playing music while others danced jigs. The harmonica and fiddle blended into a soulful tune which wrenched her heart at their foolish, misguided plights. One generous and successful hunter was sharing his recent kill with some friends, the black eyes of the exquisite doe glazed in death.

Kathy's search led nowhere. No one had heard of Jake Hammond, not even from Landis Jurrell . . . Still, they continued. They inspired interest along their journey, but so far no trouble. As dusk was nearing, Jack made their last stop in Gold Bottom where he had a friend. Frank Hardy offered his hospitality. Being one of the successful prospectors, he enjoyed a large tent with a wood stove. He permitted them to bed down in his canvas home; but they refused to share his grub, insisting on using their own.

Kathy snuggled into her sleeping bag as she watched the two men share whiskey and a game of cards. She couldn't afford memories or deliberations to harass her. Later she would analyze what happened between her and Landis and why. It was too soon; the pain was too fresh.

Kathy's lids drooped. Each time her sleepy eyes touched on Jack, he was massaging his legs. Perhaps muscle cramps, she speculated. But during the day, she had noticed a pallor to his face which had gone ignored. He also ate gingerly, stopping to rub his gums. She wondered if he was becoming ill. She promised to ask him in the morning when privacy permitted. Gradually her eyes closed, not to open again until morning.

After a quick meal of coffee and biscuits, Kathy and Jack bid Hardy a farewell. For three days they covered the area between the Eldorado River and Dawson. Their progress was sluggish, and their gain was naught. They halted at Dominion, Sulphur, Little Blanche, Eureka, and Indian. Some nights they spent huddled beneath a tent of heavy branches; others, they enjoyed the warmth and generosity of Jack's friends. More days and nights blurred into an obvious defeat. Her spirits were sorely lagging.

Kathy tried to conceal her disappointments as time, strangers, and places flashed before her eyes. Jack suggested they bypass Dawson, since he had already checked there before. They rambled along the banks of Bear Creek, questioning the sourdoughs and tenderfeet. They followed the Yukon River northward toward Fortymile, the claims office, and Sheep Mountain. Here, they mostly confronted Indians and Eskimos, most unable to speak English.

They passed a miserable night with the leader of an Indian tribe, one which unnerved Kathy as the man kept watching her with sharp eyes. These people wore colorful or oddly formed nosepieces. Their clothing was of furs and sealskins. Their dwellings were nearly underground! The opening was framed with stout posts, and the earthly ceiling was covered with strips of bark and hunks of sod. In the very center of the ceiling was a hole cut out for the escape of smoke, the entrance of light, and the exchange of air. The fireplace in the middle of the floor did little to dispel the morbid gloom and biting chill. They ate from dishes made of birch bark. That night was long and demanding, allowing her little much-needed sleep or rest.

Kathy was delighted to leave early that next day. Returning from Fortymile, they halted at Chicken, Franklin, and other tiny clusters of tents and lean-tos whose names she couldn't recall. Two more nights were endured under the stars with Kathy shaking violently from the wind and snow. They skirted Dawson again, to walk seven miles southward to Fort Reliance. She had met Joe Ladue of the Alaska Commercial Company at their stop in Ogilvie. Joe had suggested they head to Reliance to question his trappers and traders, saying they travelled distances into the interior.

Joe's men couldn't tell her anything, but offered a warm place to sleep in their storage room. Jack was irritable and pale. He had eaten very little, his gums enflamed and his teeth loose. He rubbed ointment on his swollen, tender joints. Kathy was worried. He was stopping frequently to rest, as if his body was slowly weakening. It was time to alter her plans; they weren't getting anywhere. It was clear Landis wasn't asking around about her father, for Jake's name was unknown to those questioned.

Kathy demanded the truth about Jack's health. He moodily quipped, "Scurvy, Kat, a sailor's demon. I've been at sea many times. The cold and walking nags it a bit. Don't worry your pretty head; I'll be just fine."

"You're hurting badly, Jack. You need rest and some hot soup. You've hardly eaten in days. Why don't we head for Skagway? We've walked the entire Yukon River, as well as the Klondike and countless others. We've left word everywhere. If he's here, let him look for me!"

"You're just angry and exhausted, Kathy. If he's here, we'll find him," he stated with fierce determination.

"It's no use, Jack. Do you realize we missed Christmas? I'm freezing and miserable. I don't have the heart to search anymore. Maybe we can go to Dawson later. We can give it another go when it warms up and we're refreshed," she stated. He was proud; she wanted him to think it was her idea to terminate their fruitless journey.

"You really want to call it off?" he probed, rubbing his left leg.

"Yes. I want some hot food, a warm bed, and some friendly faces for a change." She dramatically sighed in fatigue and dejection.

"All right," he agreed. "I'll head to Stewart after I drop you. I'll keep my eyes and ears open. Which cabin should I take you to, Mrs. Jurrell?"

Kathy stared into space as she murmured, "Home, Skagway . . ."

Jack wanted to rent a boat, but the Yukon was mostly frozen. The trip was three torturous days over the Chilkat Pass. Some places were so steep and slippery she feared she'd plunge off the narrow path. Along the rocky cliffs, huge icicles were frozen to the rocks, some two feet long. The odd sight looked like the gaping mouth of an ice monster who was fiercely showing his razor teeth. When the sun was out, it dazzled the ice and white snow, causing her to squint until her head ached. They passed Dyea and headed for their destination.

After dusk, they wearily entered Skagway on the western side. Kathy knew it was long past suppertime in Moore's tent. How she craved a hot meal and warm fellowship! She had missed her friends, especially Harriet. She hastened, anticipating a cozy fire and hot coffee.

The cabin was dark, the door locked. No curl of smoke left her chimney. Kathy curiously glanced around, noting the vast changes since her departure over two months ago. Several new cabins had been completed and showed signs of occupancy. Dray's trading post and storage house were also finished. Countless new tents lined the edge of the forest. Dogs howled and barked in a distance where the pens were located.

"I wonder where Harriet is? It's awfully late to be out. Let's check the supper tent," she quickly suggested.

Two lanterns were still burning. Kathy pulled aside the flap and entered to find four men playing cards. Smiles and whoops of joy greeted her as Mike, Danny, Moore, and Dray jumped up to welcome her. Harriet rushed from the stove. They laughed and chatted, entreating details of her trek inland, asking about her husband.

"Wait just a minute," she murmured. "One at the time. I've missed you terribly. I've been freezing and starving for weeks. Jack and I are exhausted." As pre-planned with Jack, Kathy told them Landis was still searching for Jake while Jack brought her to wait in safety with her friends.

"No luck?" Moore asked wistfully.

"None, I'm afraid. We've tried every place between here and the end of the earth!"

"Don't get discouraged," Mike soothed her troubled brow.

"We've missed you and the good service," Moore injected into the flurry of conversation. "Is that generous husband sharing you again?"

"If my job's still open, it'll pass the hours away," she hinted. Moore quickly agreed, then the perceptive Harriet changed the subject.

"You missed Christmas and all the fun," Harriet informed her. "I've even moved into my new cabin. The boys are here, Kathy. I left my little girl in Seattle until warmer weather. The horses arrived too. I've been renting them out to earn more money."

"You've really been busy while I was gone. That's wonderful, Harriet. I'm so happy for you." My own lonely cabin, she mused sadly.

"There's been a lot of trouble while you were gone," Mike hinted.

"What kind of trouble?" Kathy pressed with interest.

"The usual for this time of year, stealing, fighting, and such. The Mounties are in and out every few days."

"The Mounties? But this is American territory," she reasoned.

"Yes, but they're the only form of law enforcement in these parts. They help us out when there's real trouble. They stay active this time of year chasing after criminals and rescuing people. My hat's off to the North-West Mounted Police. I've never seen any force more well trained or courageous. They've got their hands full with this heavy influx of prospectors, too many of 'em bad men," Mike sounded envious of those proud and daring men that Kathy mistrusted.

"I think we should overpower Mrs. Jurrell with questions tomorrow. They both look ready to collapse," Moore noted.

Jack was invited to sleep in Moore's cabin; he accepted. Griff walked Harriet to her new home, a short distance from Kathy's. Mike escorted Kathy to her cabin and built her a fire. She thanked him for his kindness. But she flew into bed, clothes and all, before the chill was chased away and was soon fast asleep.

That following morning, Moore convinced Jack to stay with him for a few days. A doctor had arrived during Kathy's absence, one with high expectations of earning armloads of gold with his much needed services and skills. He examined Jack under protest, to learn Jack's diagnosis was correct: scurvy. Both Harriet and Kathy hovered over him, forcing soup and lime juice into him. The doctor ordered bedrest, nourishing liquids, no tension, and applications of ointment on his throbbing joints. Jack rebelled at being treated like an invalid, but he lost the argument.

For Kathy, the day was consumed in joyous reunions with the lumberjacks and with keeping the stubborn Jack in bed. She savored the hot meals, lingering over them after everyone was finished. She helped Harriet clean up, then visited with Harriet's boys. That first full day home ended with Kathy feeling relieved and loved, but lonely.

That next day was similar. The lumberjacks left for the North Ridge timberline. Weather permitting, they cut trees to be hauled away later. During snow storms, they worked on their gear and tools: oiling, repairing, and sharpening. If all chores were done, some men earned extra money by building furniture for Dray to sell.

After supper, Kathy returned to her quiet cabin. She bathed and pulled on a nightgown. As she brushed her hair, she wondered how Landis had taken her actions. Worse, she fretted over her friends' reactions to her lie about travelling with her husband, for Harriet had informed her of Landis's visits during her absence. Knowing she was searching for Jake, why would he come here? Why was he so anxious to see her? He had deceived her too many times to be trusted. Was she doubting everyone now?

Dray had given her a bottle of red wine to share with Landis when he came home. Kathy sighed unhappily. She opened the wine and filled a glass. Noticing it was cracked, she sought another glass. Maybe the heady wine would help her relax and forget. A knock sounded on Kathy's door. She glanced in that direction, wondering who would come calling this late. Without unlocking the door, Kathy asked who was there. She was astonished when the steely voice said, "Landis, Kat. Open the door."

There was nothing to do but let him inside. Yet, she hesitated. Landis called out, "Open up, Kat; I'm freezing and we need to talk. I'll leave after we get something straight," he promised.

As Kathy opened the door and stepped aside, Landis stalked in and turned to focus his turbulent gaze on her. "Have a seat, Landis. Would you care for some wine; it's a gift to us from Dray."

Landis's darkened glare went past her to study the cabin, sighting the two glasses with wine. "So, you finally came home," the rage-taut man sneered contemptuously, eyes dark and stormy. "Who was my wife entertaining this late and half-dressed?" he demanded acidly.

Kathy's startled eyes flew to his face. She went white and rigid. Landis's eyes astutely took in her reaction. She glued her gaze to the intrepid creature, struggling to master her erratic respiration and racing heart. Her hands balled into tight fists, her chin quivered. "You'd better leave, Landis."

"I want to talk to you right now!" Landis demanded harshly, ignoring her shock and shaky request.

"Not tonight, Landis," she replied, unable to subdue the quavering in her voice. "Please go," she stated, opening the door.

Suddenly, Jack appeared and questioned, "What's wrong, Kathy?"

"Landis was just leaving," she murmured in a strained voice. "What are you doing out of bed? You know what the doctor said," she scolded Jack to prevent a nasty scene.

"That bed was eating me alive. I was taking a walk."

"You get back to bed instantly, or you'll spoil your progress."

Jack glanced at Landis, then back at Kathy. "You just arrive, Landis?" he casually asked.

"Yep," he replied tightly. "Kat and I need to talk privately."

"I said we'll talk tomorrow, Landis. You're obviously tired."

Landis was furious; Jack had never seen him so out of control. Landis slammed his palm against the door, the explosion of noise causing her to jump. "Now!" he fired at her like a rifle shot splitting the silence. "Either we talk in private, or right before your 'friend'," he ominously warned.

Jack witnessed this battle of wills and words. Kathy kept her lids lowered and her back to the door, her paleness deserting her face for a rosy glow. "I've been all over this territory looking for you. You're my wife, remember? We have a matter to settle tonight. I'm not leaving until you hand it over."

His mysterious words went over her head. "Couldn't we discuss this in the morning after you've rested and relaxed?"

"This is a private matter, dear wife, but I'll talk freely if you don't close the door," he threatened, his fury rising by the minute.

"I'm not going to talk to you or hear anything you have to say until you settle down," she bravely informed him.

"Landis, I think you'd better leave. This isn't the . . ." Jack began, but was tersely cut off by Landis.

"Stay out of this, Jack! It's between me and my wife; you've interfered enough. How dare you lead her all across that frozen hell!"

Kathy recognized that streak of dangerous fury which

emanated from her husband. She smiled at Jack and told him, "Landis is right, Jack. We should talk tonight. You get in bed and take care of yourself."

"You sure?" Jack pressed worriedly, scowling at Landis.

"Yes. Landis came this far on a freezing night, so I should listen. I did sneak off with you. After all, he is my husband," she stated laughingly to dispel Jack's concern. Jack frowned and left, but didn't go far, just in case Kathy needed help with that tempestuous husband.

When she closed the door and walked over to him, she said, "You had no right to embarrass me like that. What's wrong with you?"

"Where is it, Kat? Just hand it over and I'll be on my way," he demanded.

"Hand over what?" she echoed, staring up at him.

"You know what I'm talking about. I'm not taking any more crap from you. Just turn it over, and we'll call it even."

Kathy retreated a few steps in alarm. Landis followed to stand towering over her. "I haven't the vaguest idea what you're talking about!" she refuted, fear surging through her at the sight of his fury which he inexplicably unleashed on her.

"Don't play the innocent with me! Where is the packet you stole from my cabin? Do you still have it? Or did you give it to someone?" he fiercely demanded as she sank weakly into a chair.

"Packet?" she repeated in rising bewilderment. "You're accusing me of stealing something from you?" she exclaimed in outrage.

"You fled while I was gone and the packet vanished the same day. I'll do whatever necessary to get it," he coldly threatened, fists clenched at his sides. The look on his face astounded her: rage, resentment, and danger.

"I don't have any packet!" she argued. "Jack came by, so I left with him. You should be glad he saved you the time and trouble. I'm your wife; how dare you accuse me of being a common thief!"

"There's nothing common about you, Kat. You're a real pro. You really had me fooled. I was beginning to believe all that malarky about your troubles. You ensnare my interest and help; then, you marry me to entrap me," he sneered, his gaze contemptuously sweeping over her. "All the time you're making love to me, you're plotting to use me, to steal from me. You really had it all worked out, didn't you? This job required a lot from you, Kat. How you gonna ensnare your next victim, seeing as I'll never free you?" he went for the throat like some crazed wolf, tormented by her seeming betrayal. "You're as much my property as my horse and gun."

Kathy jumped up, knocking over her chair. She delivered a stunning slap to his taunting face. He seized her wrist and laughed in her face. "The truth bothers you, love?" he said cruelly.

"You wouldn't know the truth if it knocked you down and jumped on your chest! You're a beast, Jurrell!"

He put pressure on her wrist until she squealed with pain. She glared at him and gritted out, "Let me go, Landis, or I'll forget we're married!"

"Hand it over, then I'll gladly leave and forget everything," he snarled at Kathy. "Who hired you to spy on me and betray me?"

"I can't," she said hoarsely.

"That packet is critical. I'm not leaving here without it."

"I didn't steal anything," she cried, tears flowing down

her pale cheeks. "I swear it, Landis! It wasn't me!"

As they faced each other with rage, he accused, "You were spying on me all the time. Why?"

"I was not! If anyone deceived anyone, it was you! You practically demanded I leave. You were carrying on with that Michelle creature the whole time! What about our marriage and our bargain?"

His gaze widened. "Michelle? Is that what this is all about, revenge? Jealousy?" he ranted. Still, he couldn't say the truth: that Michelle was only his contact.

"You arrogant snake!" she shrieked, her anger at a dangerous level.

"At least she has loyalty. That's more than I can say for my own wife," he sneered uncontrollably.

Kathy fought to keep the welled tears from spilling forth. Never had she felt so tormented in her life. This was the man she had loved beyond her own life and will? She had married him and tried to make it work but now he was destroying everything. "You're so wrong about everything, Landis. If only you knew the truth. You're a bloody fool. Whatever existed, it's over."

Landis imprisoned her chin. "It isn't over until I have those reports. You're mine, Kat; I'll never free you. No divorce, no annulment, no escape. Whatever you are, you're Kathryn Jurrell."

All she had wanted was to find her father. Now, she was listening to her own husband, her love, calling her a liar and worse. She felt betrayed by both men, her life empty. She yanked free while his grip was loose. She walked away from him, leaning her forehead against the cabin door. It was over, everything: her quest, her marriage, her love, and her happiness.

Landis had a sinking feeling he had over-reacted, but couldn't relent or view matters rationally. He hadn't wanted her to leave, but knew she couldn't stay. Then Jack turned up babbling about Michelle. To make matters worse, Kathy had stolen his reports! Since they were in code, did she even comprehend the dynamite she was holding? She certainly had perilous ways of enticing him to come after her!

"Then you don't mind if I search your cabin," he challenged.

"I do mind. There's nothing here that belongs to you. Get out of my life and home. I hate you," she vowed in anguish.

"That's not what you told me at my cabin," he debated, leaning against the door, grinning roguishly at her. What if she was innocent or being forced to help somebody?

"I didn't know you then. I wanted to love you and share your life. I wanted to help you if you were in trouble or danger. Did you think I was asleep all those nights you left our bed after making love to me? Yes, I know about your hiding place. I peeked twice, both times the hole was empty. I've never read any of those pages I saw you writing on late at night. I have no idea who or what you are. I haven't even thought about it since Jack arrived and we left. If anything was there, Trace brought it that morning. Believe what you will, but I didn't take it." Agonizing tears dropped to her gown.

"Then prove it," he tenderly challenged.

"No. Is that why you were so eager to be rid of me, for Michelle? You were afraid she might find out you were duping me, too? Well, you can stop spying on me for your friend Bill; I don't know where Jake Hammond is. Jack and I looked everywhere; we couldn't find anyone who knew him, or anyone you'd questioned. Put that in your next report, Jurrell. This time, guard it with your life."

"Whatever you heard, Kat; I'm not in love with

Michelle. That file is critical to my business. I must have it back. Maybe I came down too hard on you. I'm sorry," he relented.

"Sorry?" she scoffed with a bitter laugh. "You have no conscience, Jurrell. It won't work. I've been given several glimpses at the real you. I despise who and what you are."

"If you didn't take it, then help me figure out who did?" he entreated, waiting to hear the reply to that desperate suggestion.

"How would I know? A man like you must have plenty of enemies. Why don't you ask Ben? He was there when I left."

"Ben was out trapping. He didn't see anyone."

"I didn't either. How could I? You kept me locked away like some wicked secret. Why don't you consider who would profit by the information in that packet? That should give you a clue."

Kathy inhaled raggedly, needing to end this draining talk. When she said he could search the entire cabin, he declined. "You're cunning, Landis. I'm sure you'll find the culprit. Just don't come asking my forgiveness when you discover the truth. Whether you release me or not, you'll never have more than a marriage in name only; I swear it."

"Would it make any difference if I told you that file can get me killed? Some secrets are deadly, Kat." He waited tensely. Silence. "Kat?" he hinted, tugging at her arm. "I'm a dead man if that file falls into the wrong hands. You'll be a widow. Is your freedom that costly?"

"That alone should tell you I wouldn't take it. You're my husband, and I loved you. I'm not going to defend myself to you. Our bargain was met, Landis; I kept my end. I guess you did, too, in your own way."

Landis knew he could talk and reason for days and not change her mind. If she didn't take it, he had work to do. Funny, he was beginning to believe her! "It isn't over, Kat. It won't be until that file is in my hands. Goodnight, my golden torment."

"No, Landis, goodbye. I'll be leaving on the first ship to arrive."

"I'll make certain you can't leave until that file is recovered."

"You can't stop me," she smugly vowed.

"Theft is a serious crime. I won't have to; the Mounties will," he lazily announced, then strolled out.

"What do you mean?" she demanded as he retreated. Silence.

Dressed in a nightgown, she couldn't pursue him. She locked the door, then raced to the window and unbolted the shutter. He was heading for Dray's, his fluid strides shouting his confidence. Could they arrest her for a crime she didn't commit? Could they hold her here against her will? The Mounties wielded great power and influence here. Would anyone come to her aid against them? Dread washed over her; he had her trapped like one of his helpless animals. In light of Landis's prowess and friendship, Bill would surely grant him any favor he asked, even imprisoning his own wife . . .

Sixteen

At breakfast, Kathy was subdued. The friendly lumber-jacks didn't comment on her lack of spontaneity, nor the cloudy glaze over her blue eyes. They assumed her somber state was due to lagging fatigue from her recent journey, to missing her husband, and to her vain search for her father.

As they cleared the tables and washed the dishes, Harriet remarked, "You look tired. Didn't you sleep well?" Kathy forced a smile, but its strain didn't fool Harriet. "Problems you didn't mention?" she deduced.

"Landis was here last night. He left before dawn," she sketchily offered.

"Did you two quarrel?" she inquired, concern etching her face. "You don't have to talk if you prefer. He came several times looking for you, almost acting as if you might be gone. Is he upset about Jack's help?"

"You know what happened after I went inland with Umiakia and Aishihik. I would have died if Landis hadn't come along. He took me to his cabin. I lived with him and Ben Weathers until Jack came for me. He's furious because of something that happened," she explained, not wanting to go into painful detail, but needing to talk with someone who would understand.

384

"Ben Weathers?" Harriet asked, letting the story unfold gradually.

Kathy smiled fondly as she spoke of Ben, telling of their times together. Harriet speculated, "Did something specific happen to anger him?"

"Yes," Kathy began. Her voice trembling, she related the tale.

Harriet gasped in shock, "Surely he can't think you took them!"

"He does, Harriet. I've got to learn who took them and get them back."

"Why? You aren't responsible," Harriet debated.

"He thinks I am. Until those files are back in his possession, he's going to arrange with the Mounties to keep me here under arrest."

"You can't mean it!" she gasped incredulously.

"He was serious, Harriet. He'll do anything for those files. He's refusing to release me from our marriage. What else can I do?"

"You're an American citizen. They can't falsely detain you. He was only bluffing. They wouldn't arrest Landis Jurrell's wife."

"He'll find a way to incriminate me. I've got to find those files."

"But how?"

Kathy paced a few minutes. "If I just knew what they said, I could reason out who had a motive for stealing them. The canal will be thawed by April. That gives me under two months to find them."

"You're leaving?" Harriet's face exhibited her surprise.

"Yes. I'm going back to Washington on the first ship. I don't belong here. Besides, Jake can't be located and I've lost Landis."

Harriet felt the reason for her departure had more to do with Landis than anything else, but she didn't say that.

"I need to see Jack. We'll speak later," Kathy ended the talk.

Harriet embraced her and encouraged, "Don't worry, Kathy. Your husband won't harm you; he's just overly upset."

Kathy bit her tongue to keep from shouting, he already has. But her eyes told the story for her. She slowly walked to Moore's, feeling like an innocent victim making her way to the hangman. She hesitated at the door before knocking. What could she say? Surely Jack had been stunned and disillusioned by Landis's behavior. Did she owe Jack an explanation and apology? Jack had loved her mother, just as futilely and blindly as she loved Landis. Surely Jack comprehended her anguish and rash mistakes. Jack appeared the only person she could trust, who would unselfishly help her.

Knowing Moore was gone, she knocked. Jack answered it, appearing astonished. He asked her inside, out of the cold. She shook her head, then asked him over to her cabin. Jack yanked on his parka and followed her. Kathy didn't care who witnessed this outrageous conduct or what gossip would be inspired by it. She invited Jack inside, then poured two cups of coffee. She motioned for him to join her at the table, then sat down wearily.

"Jack . . ." she began, then halted, not knowing where to start or what to say in her defense. Did she even have one? "I wish Mother were here; I need her and some advice," she cried in pain.

Jack caught her icy hands and stated hoarsely, "She's lost to us forever, Kathy. Dory would want me to take care of you. You don't have to say anything, Kathy. Landis should be horsewhipped for acting so badly."

The pressure too great to bear, she broke down and told Jack everything between sobs. The pieces of her life's puzzle fell into place, breaking Jack's heart. "Kathy, he's trouble. He's stubborn. When he wants something, he'll get it one way or another. I'm sorry he wanted you and hurt you."

"I want to . . . apologize for the scene you witnessed last night. I won't be seeing him anymore, if I can avoid it. I have no excuse for my behavior. I hope you don't think . . . so badly of me."

"You're in love with him. You trusted him. I understand. But Landis doesn't have any excuse for taking advantage of your innocence and love."

"I know I was a fool. But that doesn't change how I feel."

"You're still in love with him?" he gingerly asked.

"It hurts to be used like that. I really believe he . . ."

When she didn't finish, Jack did, "Loved you? I'm afraid Landis is a taker, Kathy. He found a way to get you. He lied to you."

"I know, Jack," she concurred, sounding very tired and despondent. "I need your help again," she informed him.

"Sure. Anything," he instantly agreed, puzzled anew.

"Can you venture any guess what might be in those files? Or who might want them so badly?" she queried unexpectedly, suddenly very calm.

He stared at her. "I don't understand what you're asking."

"The only way to clear my name and regain my freedom is to make sure they're found and returned," she solemnly concluded.

"I don't believe what I'm hearing, Kathryn Hammond! You want to help him, after what he did to you?" he debated.

"Don't you see, Jack; that's the only way to terminate

all ties? As long as I'm the only suspect, he has a hold over me."

Kathy related Landis's scheme to keep her in Skagway. "Can he pull it off?" she asked gravely, then exposed her plans to leave.

"I can't stay here. Can he do that?" she demanded persistently.

"Don't be fooled again, Kathy. The Mounties wouldn't treat you like that," he stated, but Kathy saw the look of alarm in his eyes.

"I've had my share of deceit, Jack. Please, don't you start with me, too. They can; and they will, won't they?"

Jack exhaled angrily. "Yes, Kathy. Landis can probably persuade them to help him. 'Course, that might just be his way of keeping you here until you both calm down and work out these problems between you."

"That's impossible now. Will you help me?" she asked again.

A curious light flooded Jack's eyes, one which hinted there was another suspect. "You know who and why?" she pounced on Jack's careless clue.

"Don't be a fool. You can't get tangled up with him. I could be wrong."

"Who?" Kathy forcefully demanded.

"Smith," Jack informed her. "Nobody has more to lose than Soapy Smith. Landis has been keeping an eye on him for Sergeant Thomas. He might have discovered some strong evidence and recorded it."

"Would Smith kill him?" she asked, recalling Landis's implication.

"Probably. First he would want to learn how much Landis knew about him and his operations. With two Mounties just killed, another murder would inspire a heavy investigation. Smith is wily."

"But if Smith has the file, he knows what Landis

was doing."

"Why risk another murder charge when he's holding the evidence in his hands?" Jack logically reasoned. "I'd bet my boots Smith has that file, or he knows where it is." Jack added, "There's some mighty suspicious dealings going on with some of those fur-trading companies in there. They would also be anxious to get their hands on an incriminating file."

Kathy decided, "The place to start is with Smith. Landis once told me Smith's hands were somewhere in all crimes here. Smith offered me a job, so I already have a logical reason to go there."

"You can't be serious! He knows you're married to Landis! He despises him. You'll get yourself killed fooling with Soapy!"

Jack was an adventurer. He lived for thrills and dangers, but had a blind spot where Kathy was concerned. "I know how to take care of myself. You saw me do it on the trail. I won't take any risks. I think it's a smart idea. You'll be around to watch after me."

"You can't go to work in a sleazy saloon!" Jack declared.

"I can, and I will," Kathy stated defiantly, chin stuck out in determination. "If Smith has that file, I'll find some way to steal it. And if you dare say one word to Landis about this, I'll never speak to you again, Jack. I swear it," she alleged, utterly serious.

"Kathy, it's dangerous and foolish," he argued.

"I'll get his damn file back and throw it in his smug face! Besides, I can't leave until it's recovered. Whenever you're well enough to travel, Jack, I want you to take me to Dawson. I'll pretend I'm taking the job to look for my father. I'll tell Soapy I broke up with Landis. Knowing my husband so well, that will sound logical. I'll say I'm only staying for a few weeks, then I'm leaving for America."

"Don't do this, Kathy," Jack pleaded.

"I must, Jack. I have no other choice."

They reasoned and argued. Kathy was obstinately set on carrying out this deadly farce. She faced Jack and demanded, "Whether you help me or not, give me your word of honor you won't tell a soul."

Jack was forced to say, "You win, Kathy. Just make sure you're careful. When do we leave?"

She promptly answered, "Today, as soon as I'm packed, if you're well enough to travel."

Jack acquiesced, "The sooner we get on that cold trail, the better chance we have of succeeding. I'll pull you out if you make one false move. I just pray old Soapy hasn't burned the file by now."

"Don't even think such a thing, Jack," she wailed.

Jack added one last caution, "Don't you think it strange Landis is always the one around to rescue you? To spy on you, first he had to get you alone with him. Clearly the marriage ruse failed him."

Kathy stared at him. "Surely you don't think he arranged that attack?" she protested, defending her mercurial husband.

"He appeared awfully desperate last night," Jack stated. "And what about that mysterious letter to lure you to Log Cabin and him?"

"You're talking about cold-blooded murder, Jack."

"You've seen his violent temper, Kathy. You don't feel he's capable of it? Stay clear of him, Kathy," he warned as he departed.

Jack went to Moore's cabin to get his possessions. This time, Kathy packed much differently. She folded lovely dresses and shoes. She added some ribbons and two wool shawls. "If I'm going to become an entertainer, I must dress the part," she teased, drawing laughter from the returning Jack.

She sent for Griff. When he arrived, she asked him to live in her cabin until she returned. "If it looks deserted, someone might be tempted to plunder it. Would you mind, Griff?"

He grinned at her faith in him and her need of his personal help. "I'll be glad to help ye, Mrs. Kathy."

"We'll join Landis in Stewart. I should be gone around six weeks. If I haven't located my father by then, I'll be back," she necessarily misled him. "Here's the key. Use anything you need."

Kathy told Harriet the same tale, then bid her and her boys farewell. Harriet fretted over another trip inland, but Kathy convinced her it was for the best. Kathy wisely didn't tell her friend what she would be doing there, to prevent her fears and worries.

They rented one of Harriet's horses to carry the extra weight, promising to send it back by one of Moore's men working inland near Lake Bennett. Checking her shrinking purse, Kathy concluded this job with Soapy would accomplish more than one need. Many had told her Landis was wealthy, but he hadn't shared any with his wife! Ship passage and her return trip from Seattle to Washington would be expensive.

"Why Washington?" Jack quizzed as they headed off.

"It seems like the logical place for a fresh beginning."

"Maybe I'll be ready to leave. We could enjoy each other's company on the voyage. I think I'll head back to San Francisco or perhaps New York. This cold ails me. Watch your step; it's icy along here," he warned.

Afterwards, they travelled in watchful silence, the perils countless and the trail narrow. Soon, Landis, she pondered before focusing her full attention on the demanding trek. Soon, it will be settled between us. I'll be gone forever from your land of golden torment . . .

Seventeen

For most of the journey along the bank of the predictable, now ice-matted Yukon River, Kathy was too preoccupied by her impending charade to think of the harsh weather and precarious conditions surrounding her. Her thoughts were of reaching Dawson and initiating her daring ploy. Many times she envisioned the shocked face of her self-assured, arrogant husband as she proudly and tauntingly slapped his precious file into his hands. Would he even admit he had been mistaken? No, he would probably believe the file had been in her possession the whole time! He would probably think she was feigning the dauntless heroine to impress him and to enchant him with her cunning and generosity! Kathy refused to consider the danger, should she be discovered. She didn't want Landis's enforced gratitude or fake respect, just his loyalty and love. To leave this tormenting territory, she had to sever all bonds to everyone.

Nearing their destination, a blizzard assaulted the land. Jack read the signs of nature, frantically striving for shelter. The snow was falling so heavily they could barely see; the winds so brisk, standing up was difficult, biting their flesh through their garments. The howling wind and freezing air tortured lungs and throat as they gasped to breathe, wheezing in near-futile attempts. A blue-white haze hung heavily in the air, obliterating the scenery.

Trees swayed precariously. Snow piled into lofty drifts. A thundering noise indicated a sturdy branch had brutally snapped from its host, several thuds echoing as it hit other obstacles on its deathly plunge to the frozen ground. The elements emitted eerie, mournful cries as the earth painfully relented to their attack. One thing was in their favor: the blizzard was to their backs, striking them at an angle as if to forcefully drive them on toward survival. Kathy had difficulty with her snow-shoes as nature weighed them down with an abundance of white misery. The horse neighed and held back, forcing Jack to yank and pull on his bridle and speak comforting words. His glittering eyes and nervous prancing displayed his terror, as if he instinctively smelled death.

Kathy's legs and feet were becoming numb and weary. Her body felt as if burdened by pounds of dirt. She actually feared they were going to die. She prayed in rising panic. Jack wasn't doing well either. He was weak and pale, his body steadily draining of all energy. His legs ached at the strain; yet, he knew the folly of halting. If only they could reach Hard-Nose Pete's cabin, less than a mile away . . .

Jack froze in his tracks, causing Kathy to topple against him. He shouted over the thunderous din, "We've got another half mile! Pete'll give us protection in his cabin! I'm going to unload the horse! He'll never make it with weight on his back! I'll fetch our things when the blizzard lets up!"

Kathy nodded in understanding, knowing to be heard would rip at her throbbing throat. She followed closely, having been warned they could lose sight of each other in three feet. She held the reins while he took off the bundles, hiding them behind a cluster of white-laden tree trunks. Afterwards, he was panting, agony written on his face.

"I'm sorry I got you into this!" she yelled over the wind.

He smiled, motioning her to follow. Within four hundred feet of the cabin, it couldn't be sighted through the fog and snow. The unforeseen happened. The horse whinned and reared, nearly yanking the reins from Jack's grip. Jack comprehended their imminent peril. A gusty wind caused icicles to tinkle like silver wind chimes, too cold for them to melt.

He instantly tied the reins to the nearest tree and whipped his rifle off his shoulder. He seized Kathy and slammed her against the trunk, positioning himself between her and what he knew was coming at them. He was tense and alert, straining to catch the next sound. He shouted to Kathy, "Get your gun, Kathy! Wolves! Hungry ones!"

She trembled, recalling Landis's words about their carnivorous appetites. "Damn! They can smell us, but we can't see them!" Jack thundered in alarm. The suspense was suddenly heavier than the snow.

Kathy seized her gun and cocked the hammer, her hand shaking. Had to be a pack, Jack mentally assessed, growls and snarls coming from several directions. Should he leave the horse as bait and make a run for it with Kathy? Trouble was, some might take it but others would pursue them. Backed against a tree offered their flank some protection.

"Will they attack?" she shouted, her eyes wide with terror.

"Yes! Don't waste bullets! Aim at their golden eyes!"

he instructed, not daring to waste any ammunition by carelessly firing warning shots into the air. When wolves smelled food and fear, they wouldn't give ground.

The leader of the pack charged first, darting forward to slash at the horse's hind leg. Jack shot at the furry gray blur moving with exceptional agility and speed. The horse danced madly in pain and fear. The attack was cunning and swift. A wolf viciously nipped at the animal's foreleg; another severed a tendon in a hindleg, causing the agonized creature to buckle, then remove his weight from it.

Kathy fired two ringing shots, while Jack managed to hit the flank of the other. With the smell of blood and victory came a frenzied attack by three more wolves. Kathy was close to the horse's head and saw one wild beast as he leaped at the animal's throat. The frightened horse reared to avoid those gnashing teeth, landing his hooves on the wolf's body. The wolf howled and momentarily retreated.

Jack was firing almost constantly now as two wolves charged from different directions, their primary interest still the horse. Kathy struggled to visually pierce the dense snow. Suddenly she realized what was lurking before her horrified vision. A lone wolf was standing motionless within three feet of her, seeming to devour her with its yellow eyes. He was powerfully built, all lean muscle, a thing of savage beauty. He was three and a half feet long. His thick, lush coat was a blending of gray and yellow with black patches. Kathy could detect the strength, vitality, and extraordinary cunning within him. He was master in this situation. He killed without mercy or feeling, his one instinct survival. Frozen in awe and heart-stopping terror, she almost sensed an evil intelligence in those keen eyes. Was he the leader, the one who controlled this calculated attack?

He stood there watching her, as if smugly challenging her to shoot him. Hypnotized, she couldn't raise the gun and pull the trigger. As if to flaunt his only interest in her, he passed his tongue over teeth like white razors. He stared a moment longer, then disappeared into the rain of white flakes. Kathy knew who was the superior one in this perilous situation: that predacious beast.

"Shoot!" Jack stormed, startling her from her mesmerized state.

She fired at any moving object, dreading the outcome of this battle. Jack painfully nudged her. "Don't waste bullets! Get 'em in sight first!" he hoarsely commanded, sensing her panic.

The horse sent forth a startling noise of anguish as one wolf slashed down his flank and bared inner flesh to the stinging elements and the wolves' greedy senses. The virgin white ground was spattered with crimson life. The snarls moved closer, increasing in volume and frequency. Kathy knew without Jack telling her; they were moving in for the kill. She shuddered in dread. This was no way to die! Where are you, Landis? she thought desperately. I love you.

"Cut him free!" Jack repeated his order.

"He'll run and they'll . . ."

"Damnit, Kathy! Free him or they'll take us down, too! If they chase him, we can make a run for Pete's! Do it!" he thundered.

Kathy pulled her knife from its sheath. Trembling, she could hardly saw through the near-frozen reins. The leather restraint gave way under her frantic attempts. The horse spurred into flight by his sudden freedom. He staggered a few feet in the soft snow with his debilitating injuries before the snarling pack was on him. They snapped at his throat, slashed at his legs, and ripped at his vulnerable underbelly. The roan thrashed wildly, trying to defend himself against impossible odds. A wolf leaped on his back as he sank into the snow; one perfectly placed gnash with those powerful jaws and sharp teeth ended the horse's agony as his spinal cord was severed.

As if of one mind, the wolves aggressively tore at the downed animal, ripping into warm flesh with fierce determination to taste their bloody victory. Kathy witnessed this violent, primitive slaughter. She was too petrified to be sick. She closed her eyes and swayed against the tree, wondering when those relentless beasts would come for them.

Jack pulled her to his hard body. He placed his finger to his lips for silence. He inched from the tree, compelling her with his remaining strength and will. He moved slowly to avoid catching the eye or ear of a feeding beast. Kathy blocked out the noise of their ravenous meal. She swallowed with difficulty, mere breathing a labor. Jack maneuvered her before him, sidling as he prodded her on while he kept his keen eyes to their rear.

Jack came to another abrupt halt, his action and grip stopping her movements. She turned to glance at him. He was rigid and alert. She tensed as she realized why; only the wind could be heard. The wolves were totally silent. Did that mean they were stalking them again? Couldn't they be content with the horse?

"Shoot me!" she screamed in terror. "Don't let them rip me apart!"

As he glimpsed blurs to his right and his left, the leader signaled the attack, racing at them full speed. Jack whirled and stuck his gun in her face. Just before pulling the trigger, shots rang out behind them. Yelps of pain could be distinguished above the wind as bullets struck their targets.

Jack whirled and fired point blank at the wolf leaping at them, sending his bullet into the wolf's chest and hurling his powerful body back into the snow. They were joined by two men, faces hidden by furry hoods and snow-glasses. Combining forces, the pack fled to their downed and safer prey.

With Kathy and one rescuer facing frontwards and Jack and the other man walking backwards, they made their way to Hard-Nose Pete's cabin—for it was Pete who had rescued them. Once inside with the door barred securely, Kathy collapsed to the floor to still her racing heart and to master her erratic respiration. *Alive and safe* kept ringing in her mind.

One of the men dropped to his knees before her, pushing back his hood and pulling off his snowglasses. He inhaled sharply at seeing her. "You all right, Mrs. Jurrell?" he asked in concern.

Kathy looked up into the face of Trace Blitch of the North-West Mounted Police. For once, it wasn't Landis to her rescue. She was relieved—and disappointed. Her mouth dry, she merely nodded, smiling her gratitude. God, how she was tempted to burst into tears! She craved Landis's comforting arms.

"Let's get those snowshoes and parka off and get you over to the fire. You're frozen clear through," Trace kindly offered.

She sat down on the bare floor while Trace unfastened the riggings on her snowshoes. He helped her to her feet, but she swayed precariously against him. He steadied her, then unfastened her parka. He attempted to remove it, but it wouldn't pass over the gun still tightly clutched in her rigid hand. "Give me the gun, Kathy," he firmly stated, pulling it from her relaxing grip. The parka came off and was tossed into a chair. He gingerly removed her snowglasses, viewing the stinging bites of ice and wind upon her beautiful face. Her breathing was still ragged as he prodded her over to the hearth. He brought her some coffee and told her to sit down on the bearskin spread before the fireplace. She obeyed automatically, clutching the cup to warm her hands. Trace observed her intently.

She remained stiff and silent, as if in shock. Trace coaxed the cup to her pale lips, encouraging her to sip the warm liquid. She did so without realizing she was obeying. He studied her for a few moments as Jack and Pete removed their gear and parkas. He went to his pack and pulled out a bottle of whiskey. He poured two fingers into a metal cup. He held it to her lips and commanded, "Drink this, Kathy."

She complied, instantly coughing as the fiery liquid spread flames down her throat. Tears filled her eyes and helplessly spilled down her wind-blistered cheeks. She winced at the smarting sensation. Trace immediately dried her eyes and face with great gentleness, then smeared some healing ointment there.

Between the stimulating coffee, strong whiskey, glowing fire, and the Mounty's aid, she began to relax. Kathy met Trace's lingering gaze and smiled. "Thank you, Mounty Blitch. Am I still alive?" she jested to dispel her remaining tension.

"Very much so," he responded, returning her grateful smile.

"How can we ever repay you? We were beyond hope. They killed Harriet's horse," she remarked breathlessly.

"Better to feed on him than you," he teased.

"I suppose so, but it was awful," she confessed with a shudder.

"Still cold?" he instantly inquired.

"Not anymore, thanks to you," she murmured appreciatively.

"I didn't charge those devils alone. Pete helped me. Mounties are famous for their timely rescues. But I've never experienced one with such beautiful results," he complimented her with a chuckle.

Kathy thanked Pete. He and Jack were warming themselves with some whiskey, chatting about their near-disaster. "Seems like you have three uninvited guests tonight, Pete," Trace stated, laughing mirthfully. "Appears old Landis owes us a heavy debt," he added.

"Good timing if you asked me. Plenty of victuals and firewood. Lots of lonely hours to ease. Don't mind seeing a pretty face neither," Pete rambled, toying with his scraggly beard.

"You get waylaid by the storm, too?" Jack asked Trace.

"Afraid so. I was in sight of Pete's when she cut loose. What are you two doing out in weather like this? Where's Landis?"

"We're going to Dawson. Kathy's gonna . . ."

Kathy coughed loudly to warn Jack to silence. Trace seized the unspoken message between them. Kathy stated, "We're taking one last look for my father. We plan to hang around a few weeks, then head home if nothing comes up. Landis should meet us there."

Trace let her half-lie pass unquestioned; her movements weren't any of his business. But Landis wouldn't be pleased. The men drifted back to conversing about the wolf attack and the unexpected blizzard. Kathy stared into the blazing fire, her mind somewhere else.

Later, when everyone was settled down and warmed, Kathy insisted on helping Pete prepare supper. That evening sped by; Kathy didn't offer any information, and

400

Trace didn't press her for any clues. The men drank a good deal of whiskey while they talked and played poker. Kathy sat before the fire, again entrapped by thoughts of Landis, her father, and her rescue by Trace. The hour grew late. Kathy was placed nearest the fire in her sleeping bag. Her pants and shirt were uncomfortable, but necessary. The men slipped into their bedrolls clad only in longjohns—naturally after warning her to turn her back.

By midnight, the glacial winds were still maliciously pulling at anything in their destructive path; the voracious wolves had finished their meal and darted away to seek a cozy place to sleep; the awesome blizzard continued to cast its raging fury on the defenseless land . . . and the four occupants of Pete's cabin were fast asleep.

Miles northeastward, two men sat at a square table eating in brooding silence. The older man pushed aside a straying lock of golden wheat tinged with silver and locked his sapphire gaze on his sullen companion. Ben finally asked, "Have you seen her since she left us?"

It was unnecessary to speak her name. Landis looked up, troubled lines creasing his brow. "I could care less if I ever lay eyes on that traitorous witch again! She could drop dead for all I care!" A curious tremor swept over him as the false words left his taut lips.

Ben sat up straight in his wooden chair, rankled by his friend's words and icy manner. "How can you be so cold-blooded and cynical, Landis? Kathryn's your wife. One day you're going to find out you've been wrong about her. When that day comes, which it will, you'll hate yourself for what you've done to her. She didn't steal your papers."

"Did you?" Landis sarcastically snarled, not really meaning his question, just attempting to halt this plaguing conversation.

"No, Landis; I swear I didn't steal your papers either. If you don't love her or want her, free her; but you do owe her an apology and some kindness. How would you really feel if she dropped dead?"

Landis stared off into empty space, refusing to answer. When he didn't, Ben probed, "What did they do with Michelle's body?"

"What was left of it after that fall was buried outside town."

"Did she fall, or was she pushed?" Ben pressed.

"We know it wasn't an accident, and it wasn't suicide either. Soapy will hang for it, along with other crimes," he swore ominously.

"They can't arrest him without proof," Ben noted.

"I'll get the Mounties their damn proof!" he thundered, striking the table so forcefully that coffee sloshed from their cups.

"Were you in love with her? Is that why you sent Kathryn away?"

"You're mighty curious tonight, friend," Landis remarked.

"I like Kathryn very much, Landis. She's had a rough time. I just hate seeing you add to her anguish with these wild charges and your violent temper. Is it so impossible to give her the benefit of doubt?"

"Utterly impossible, Ben. Mark my words, before Kathryn Jurrell leaves me and Alaska, she'll place those papers in my hands."

"Are you that confident? Or just pray you're right after what you've done and said to your wife? What happened in Skagway?"

Needing to talk with a close friend, Landis moodily exposed the events of their last meeting, adding past details which supposedly pointed Kathy guilty. Landis was tempted to reveal his Mounty identity to Ben and to plead for his assistance—but he couldn't.

The clues in those statements caused Ben to inwardly wince at what Landis must have put his daughter through—for by now, he was certain Kathy was his child. "You're stubborn, Landis, stubborn and mistaken. I've known her a short time, but I'd stake my life on her innocence. You blind fool, you don't even realize what you've lost."

"I tell you what, Ben; I'll wager you this claim that Kathryn Jurrell will be the one to return those papers," he vowed, gazing at Ben, whose expression vaguely reminded him of someone. But who?

"I accept your challenge," Ben calmly replied, surprising Landis.

"Maybe it'll be worth the loss if you're right," he freely admitted.

"I doubt it, Landis. By then, you'll have lost everything. Just like Dory, you'll force Kathy to seek solace in the arms of another man."

Landis studied the faraway look in Ben's eyes. Where had he heard that name before? "Dory?" he echoed. "Who's she?"

Ben stiffened at his careless slip. Ben parried, "The woman in Montana, the one I mentioned." Distracted, Ben didn't notice Landis's keen interest.

"Is she happy? Are you sorry about losing her?" Landis feigned normal curiosity and concern, his keen mind on full alert.

"I'd say she's at peace. As to regretting her decision, I'll never know. She chose another man over me; she had to live with that choice."

The bitterness and pain in Ben's voice compelled Landis to probe for more facts. Landis hadn't missed the past tense in Ben's words. As Ben drifted briefly in a haunting past world, Landis sent his perceptive mind on an exploration which covered the past two years. As if walking on thin ice over a pond, the barrier split and he fell into a river of answers and questions. If his wild speculations were accurate, Ben Weathers was actually . . . His heart drummed madly as he reasoned what that made Kathryn Hammond Jurrell. Had she sought out the very man who could unsuspectingly deliver her to her goal? If Ben knew Landis was Clinton Marlowe, Ben assumed they weren't wed. Had Ben told Kat? Both knew about the hiding place? Both had used and duped him? Was he blindly and rashly aiding their missions?

His dark eyes wandered over Ben's features. Why hadn't he noticed their striking resemblance? He had trusted Ben with his life! Kathy's recent search jarred his mind; if she knew the truth, why go to such lengths to continue her charade? Was it possible she was an innocent pawn, that she was ignorant of Ben's true identity? If the man who loved and had married Kathy could hold silent, why couldn't her father? Hell, maybe he was grasping at smoke! He cautioned himself to patience, to observe both people until he was certain of his facts.

"What was Dory like?" Landis inquired softly.

Ben responded from his daze, "She was impetuous, spoiled, willful. She craved riches and excitement. She was a sensual creature, wild and carefree. She liked taking chances. I fell in love with her the first moment I saw her. She was poised on a hillside, the wind playing through her clothes and hair. She had locks like silky raven's wings, just as black. Her eyes were like precious emeralds. The first time I gazed into them I was actually speechless. God, she was breathtaking. She was like an audacious child in a woman's body. Maybe that was the problem, she never grew up."

Ben's eyes glowed with tenderness during his reflections. Suddenly an icy glaze clouded them. "She was cruel and selfish. She wanted everything her gaze touched. She was too much like me. The things which attracted me to her in the beginning eventually drove me from her side. She made her bed with lies and deceits. I couldn't handle it, especially the men. That's why I eventually sacrificed everything and walked away." Coming to abrupt awareness of his words, he added, "That's why I couldn't keep her or stay in Montana. But Kathryn isn't like that. She's special, Landis."

"You were wrong about Dory; you could be just as wrong about Kat. She has you charmed, Ben. She's probably just like Dory." If Ben were being honest, Landis comprehended his anguish. Landis also realized why Ben would hold the truth from Kathy, if Ben believed this woman was his abandoned child.

Did Kathy think her marriage to Landis was false? Should he tell Ben it wasn't? Landis was more confused and mentally tortured than ever. He had to bide his time until he and Ben could confide in each other. After all, Jake Hammond was a cunning spy.

Ben shook his head. "The day hasn't dawned when you've faced your golden torment. If you think you're miserable now, wait a few months. You'll rue the day Kathryn Leigh was lost."

Eighteen

"I can't believe we're in Dawson," Kathy murmured to Jack.

Being cooped up with Trace Blitch and Hard-Nose Pete for several days had been quite an experience. She had cooked their meals and washed the dishes. The men had spent most of their time playing cards and rehashing olden days. When the weather had cleared sufficiently, the men had retrieved her and Jack's belongings. Pete had been the one to inform her that not even bones remained of Harriet's horse.

She liked both Trace and Pete. Trace had been the perfect gentleman, friendly and charming. He possessed an air of authority and revealed great pride in his work. He was good company to be confined with for the short days and lengthy nights. In light of Landis's threats, it would be wise to have a Mounty as a new friend.

Kathy turned her head this way and that as they walked down the muddy street toward Soapy's saloon. They had arrived mid-morning and taken two rooms at a boarding house of sorts. She had been amused and astonished by her first view of Dawson, heart of this wild territory, center for business and pleasure. Dawson was situated on flat-bottom land between two rivers, the

prosperous Klondike and the mighty Yukon. It was over-
crowded with thousands of gold-seekers, boisterous and
intimidating. The mud-packed streets were lined by
tottering wooden shacks, two-story clapboard buildings, rustic saloons, sturdy cabins, fancy gambling
houses, several theaters, and various businesses.

Even at noon, merrymaking filtered into the crowded
streets. There were endless rows of tents at both ends of
town. Frozen laundry popped and crackled in the wind.
Smoke from campfires and stoves darkened the sky
overhead, the dense clouds refusing to let it rise or
disperse. Each time a door opened, laughter and rowdy
talk pealed forth to beckon other lonely men inside. A
variety of music was heard, often clashing where buildings were close.

Dawson had some finer points: a semblance of a
church, two banks, one hotel, a newspaper office, a
photographer's studio, and four mercantile stores. But
one building stood out from all the others: the home of
Soapy Smith's saloon girls. Paradise House was built in
the center of activity, across the street from his saloon. It
was clean and sturdy, two stories high, painted white
with red trim. Numerous chimneys testified that there
were fires in every room. Kathy prayed she wouldn't be
required to live there while working for Smith, if he
hired her.

On the whole, Dawson appeared a town thrown up at
an urgent pace, one meant only to last as long as the gold
rush. Kathy had been disheartened to learn the exorbi-
tant prices charged for the scantiest of items or services.
Soapy had boasted of the excessive salary she would earn
but he had failed to relate the high cost of living. No
wonder his girls couldn't leave once arriving. Though
they made large amounts of money, it took all to survive.

No doubt females were lured here with promises of great riches, much like the dreamy-eyed gold-seekers. Once here, they were trapped into staying, unable to afford to leave. Maybe they didn't mind. After all, a job of that kind was probably the same anywhere.

Not everyone was destitute. Many had found enough gold to survive the winter and to pay for their pleasures. When spring arrived, they would return to the goldfields or their claims to begin this vicious circle anew. What a cruel joke! Some men had struck it rich; others were getting rich off of thousands of hopeless dreams and dull days. Bored and lonely, men lazed around in the saloons until their gold-dust was gone or the day ended. Such an empty and tragic way to live, Kathy thought.

To other's misfortunes, their rooms had come available yesterday when two poor fools were tossed out from lack of money. Kathy couldn't complain; the adjoining rooms were scrubbed, aired, and made ready for them. With so many people needing work to buy food, it was easy to find someone to bring in wood, to fetch water for baths, to do laundry, and to run errands. This hotel served hot meals twice a day. She almost felt guilty consuming such delectable food while others starved nearby.

After setting in, Kathy had treated herself to a steamy bath with scented soap. She had stayed in the water until chilly. She donned her best wool dress, a becoming and proper style, and put on her finest shoes for her meeting with Randolph Smith. She had washed her hair and dried it before the fire. Now, it shone with silky lights and felt like kitten fur. Her cheeks had vanquished the evidence of her recent ordeal. Her face was unblemished, her cheeks rosy with good health. The deep blue gown enhanced her sapphire eyes, drawing many a hungry stare.

Jack caught her elbow at the entrance to Soapy's gambling house. He asked gravely, "Are you sure you want to go through with this? It isn't too late to back down. You've had some rough experiences lately."

"You know the plan, Jack. I'll be just fine. Besides, I'm not prepared to walk through those wilds again so soon. I'd rather wait for spring and challenge those treacherous rapids in your boat. Chin up, old friend. All I can do is fail to locate those papers."

Jack sighed in resignation. He opened the door and escorted her inside. They hesitated briefly, looking around for a moment. Kathy wasn't prepared for what her vision revealed. She didn't quite know what she had expected, not having been in such a place before. But this was far from her naive speculations!

It seemed as if hundreds of candles and lanterns flooded the room with glittering light. From her vantage point, she saw three entertainment rooms. She was alert to note their differences. To her left, an archway led into a rustic room. It had bare, wooden tables and hard chairs. There was a rough wooden bar the length of one wall. It was apparent men with little money drank and relaxed there. Even the women who served them were older, plumper, or less than attractive.

She half-turned to gaze into the room to her right. Red drapes, which could be closed for privacy, were held aside by golden cords. A deep red rug covered the entire floor, or at least all she could see. Matching red drapes covered the windows, denying a curious eye a view of its occupants. From the attire and behavior of most, that room held the more successful customers this area could claim.

To the far end of that splendid room was a low stage, with a piano and bench, and a branched candleholder on the piano.

The center room, where she was still gracefully poised by the door, was a combination of sights and sounds to stir the senses: laughter, conversation, tinkling glasses, roulette wheels, faro tables, assorted card games, and lovely females fluttering around. Kathy eyed several women. Most were attractive and shapely with seductive smiles and movements to entice wandering hands and eyes. Naturally they wore make-up, but it wasn't brazen as she had been told. Nor were their red dresses that gawdy or revealing. But then again, with so few females around, sexual stimulation didn't require any help from such trappings!

For an instant, Kathy caught herself trying to pick out Michelle. Which flagrant creature had enticed the company and affection of Landis Jurrell? She rebuked herself for such mental wanderings from her plans.

Jack removed her parka and flung it over his arm, along with his. The room smelled of cigars and pipes, their smoke curling upwards to float about until dissipated. To the far end of this main room, a bar stretched nearly the length of the wall, but for a private doorway to the back. Near the right wall was a wooden dance floor where couples were obviously enjoying themselves. The moment Kathy's coat was removed, lecherous gazes fastened to her shapely body and beautiful face. Noting the open-mouthed stares of their companions, other eyes followed their line of entranced vision. Kathy rosed as a hush fell over the main room and all eyes seemed pinned on her. Worse, even the gay music halted.

Soapy was leaning on the bar talking with a man when this strange occurrence took place. He curiously turned to see what was happening. His face brightened, his dark eyes sparkled. She was a rare vision of loveliness and innocence. Her champagne tresses cascaded over her shoulders like a golden waterfall. Secured by a blue ribbon, its lengthy edges mingled with her tawny curls. The gown molded her sensuous curves. In spite of his plans for her, a craving to possess her surged through him . . .

Smith walked forward to greet them, his stride measured and self-assured. He clasped her hand in his and raised it to his lips for a kiss, his mustache tickling her. "I'm honored, Mrs. Jurrell. Please come in. I have a special wine for such a beautiful occasion," he gallantly stated. "Is your husband coming along shortly?"

Kathy extracted her hand from his moist grasp and lowered her lashes demurely. "Landis is busy trapping. He said Jack could give me a look at the notorious Dawson and leave messages about my father."

"Ah, still no luck with your search?" he inquired solicitously.

"No, sir. Jack said yours was a safe establishment. He claims you serve the best food in this wilderness." She had begun her scheme.

Several men rushed forward, wanting to know if this was Soapy's newest find. A scarlet blush suffused Kathy's face, for their meaning was clear. Soapy admonished them, claiming only that she was a dear friend, failing to mention Landis. He insisted on their respect and warned against accosting her. He waved his hand for the music to begin a lively tune. Eventually some eyes returned to their dealings, others remained on her. Several of the women were openly glaring at this undesirable competition.

Soapy led them into the room at their right. He seated

Kathy and called over a girl. "Maura, the very best wine from my private stock and three glasses," he ordered without taking his eyes from Kathy.

Kathy was leery of the way he was staring as he spoke with Jack. She looked around the room, admiring the furnishings and decorations. "I am most impressed, Mr. Smith. This isn't at all what I expected," she complimented him with honesty.

"I know, Mrs. Jurrell. It isn't all bad; am I correct?"

"I must admit you are, Mr. Smith. We just arrived today. I'm anxious to view everything. I wonder if dinner will live up to Jack's words."

"It will. How long will you be staying in Dawson?" he asked.

It was time to begin her daring strategy. She glanced away and softly replied, "A few days. Until . . ." She halted to snare his undivided interest.

"Until your husband joins you, or orders you home?" he teased.

"Landis won't . . ." She cunningly played her role. "He's too busy to leave home for weeks," she added, hoping he suspected a problem.

Soapy's expression said he knew Landis wasn't busy or at home. His grin told her he caught her sly hint at marital troubles. "When do you leave for America?" he asked, falling into a trap he didn't suspect.

"The first thaw," she responded, then flushed at her seeming slip.

Soapy let it pass. "I had hoped you'd come to accept my offer."

"From the looks of your arrangement, I see no urgent need for my meager talents. Is your pianist good?" she debated as if declining.

"I'm sorry to say I have none. I designed this room

412

myself with such a pleasure in mind. However, I hadn't found the right woman to enliven it, until I met you. I promise you protection, respect, and a great deal of money. Why should Landis object when he's so busy?"

"You flatter me," she replied warily. "But I hardly think this a proper place to work. I'm married," she reminded him.

"As you wish, but please call me Soapy or Randolph. Mr. Smith sounds so formal. Gads, it makes me sound old." He laughed.

Soapy and Jack conversed for a time, then Soapy left Jack with Kathy to dine on an excellent fare. Such began three days of feigned sight-seeing, while Soapy besieged her at every turn to accept his job. Each time, Kathy refused, but appeared to waver in doubt and to look troubled. To avoid suspicion, they posted messages about her father. For now, she hoped her father wouldn't appear; she needed this time for her charade.

They dined again at Soapy's with Kathy trying to parry his questions about Landis and her future plans. She pretended to attempt to conceal sadness and dismay, but guilefully and subtly exposed them. If Soapy knew too much, he would believe her marriage had collapsed and she was alone and vulnerable, needing help and money to get home to America.

Her answer came when he coaxed, "You needn't be embarrassed, Mrs. Jurrell. I know you left him weeks ago. I don't blame you. If you need a job to finance your search or trip home, it's yours for the asking," he stated bluntly.

As if shocked, she inhaled sharply and stared. "My personal life is none of your concern or business, Mr. Smith," she informed him.

"I suppose not, but the offer stands," Smith didn't

back down.

Kathy wisely and politely refused him again, but he reasoned and entreated her to accept. When she told Smith that Jack needed to leave and she had to go with him, Smith instantly coaxed her to remain a few weeks and allow Jack to come back for her, listing what her gains would be in Dawson and blackening what her existence in Skagway would be until the spring thaw. As if nervous and reluctant, Kathy finally agreed to try it for a few weeks.

"If I don't like this job or Dawson, I'll have to quit. Is that agreeable? And no more questions about my personal life." Her voice was even and soft, but her expression serious and pure. Soapy would suspect something if she waltzed in here begging for a job. It was also manadatory to present a ladylike, very married visage at all times to prevent overly friendly advances from Smith and the other men.

"Do these ears deceive me? Are you saying yes to my offer? Surely my luck has changed," he exclaimed on what he viewed his victory.

"You appear to be a man who makes his own luck," she told him.

"When I listed your qualities, I forgot wit and intelligence. So few women possess so many rare qualities. Welcome to Soapy's."

"Please remember this is only temporary," she reminded tensely.

"I have discovered my undesirable reputation serves me well. It prevents trouble and disloyalty. So, I didn't take the time or energy to correct their mistaken impressions. I hope you don't believe all rumors."

She mused pensively, then said, "Men don't reach such heights of wealth and power without stepping on others while climbing to it."

Soapy believed she was referring to Landis. She fooled him completely. "Your insight astounds me, Kathryn; if I may call you that. You are indeed rare. My business will flourish once you begin your work."

"First, Mr. Smith, there are some conditions to be agreed on before either of us makes a final decision," she hinted.

"Conditions? Ah, a woman with a head for business. Do you have no flaws at all, Kathryn?" he mirthfully taunted.

The wine arrived and was served. Kathy lifted her glass, but Soapy halted her. "We must toast our new venture."

"Not until we agree on its terms," she murmured insistently.

"Then list your 'terms' for me," he encouraged, intrigued.

"First, a question. Do I receive a set salary?"

"A salary of fifty dollars in gold nuggets per night, payable at the end of each week. And any tips you receive are yours to keep."

"If I hadn't sampled a taste of the living expenses here, I would think your offer most generous. As I recall you saying, you earn seven to nine thousand dollars nearly every night. I would think that one hundred dollars and tips would be fairer." She looked collected, but was apprehensive.

He stared at her with undisguised appreciation. "Done," he agreed.

"Not so fast, Mr. Smith. I also want my meals and board paid. Plus, I insist on your most trusted man escorting me to my boarding house each night when I finish. This is a dangerous area."

She waited to see if she had demanded too much. He eyed her critically. "You drive a hard bargain, Kathryn. Most of my girls earn less than half of what I just agreed to pay you. But, your talents are unique."

"If I stay to earn money for my passage home this spring, I can't use that same money to survive here. I'd be no better off here than in Skagway. I told you, I'll only accept this job until the spring thaw."

"You are most intelligent. Perhaps I would be wise to make you my partner," he jested, his eyes sparkling with amusement.

"Your confidence pleases me, sir. But I've had my fill of your territory. You see, my motives for taking this job are most selfish."

"Not selfish, Kathryn, smart."

"I would require a few days to practice first. I haven't touched the keyboard in months. I wouldn't want you to lose business instead of gaining it. If I come to work for you, I will do a good job. My job will only include singing and playing the piano. Do you ever have trouble here?"

"I have several men positioned around to keep peace. They won't allow any customer to approach you. However," he began, noting her sudden rigidness. "If you would like to join some of the better class for dinner or wine, please feel free to do so. I think they would find your company most enjoyable. As to your demands, consider them all met."

She stared at him, then feigned a sigh of relief. "Thank you, Mr. Smith. I shall do my very best."

"Did you really think I would refuse your terms?" he asked, fooled by her crafty act.

"Yes. But I must have those terms, or I would be wasting my time here. If it's all right, I'll start in three days. By then, I should have my fingers limber and the tunes

416

down. Do you have any music to go with that piano? How did you get it here?" she abruptly asked another question before he could reply to her first one, recalling the trail between here and the Lynn Canal at Skagway.

"By steamer. The entire Yukon is easily navigable during the summer months. You should have seen them delivering it and those mirrors over the bars. I stood over them with a whip, daring one man to falter," he playfully alleged.

She smiled in amusement. "I'm sure that was a sight to see. Does business go on all day and night? I prefer to practice in private."

"We don't open until noon. But you will only play in here during the evenings. Say off and on between seven and eleven?"

"I'll try it. Can I come in and practice between nine and noon?"

"Fine. The men are usually cleaning up then, so someone will always be present. Plus, I live in back. There is one demand I must make. If I'm to pay for your room and meals, then you must live in my boarding house. Just so you don't feel cheated, all my girls live and eat free. I have an especially lovely room recently vacated. You can move in there tomorrow."

"Someone quit?" she asked, her surprise lucid.

"No, one of my girls met with an accident, a fatal fall. Too bad, Michelle Darney was my prettiest girl," he casually remarked.

Someone stopped at the table and caught Soapy's full attention, denying him the look on Kathy's face at that incredible news. Michelle dead? Was that why Landis was so full of rage? She bristled.

Jack nudged her and shook his head, warning her of her reaction. She quickly masked the emotions churning inside of her. Live in Michelle's room? Sleep in the same bed where they . . .

When Soapy's attention returned to her, she was patiently waiting for him to finish his conversation. From her serene look, the news meant nothing to her. He assumed she didn't know about Michelle and Landis. Should he tell her and test her reaction? Not yet.

"Mr. Smith, unless you are most adamant, I would prefer to stay where I am. I don't mean to sound . . . haughty or judgmental, but I don't think I care to live with . . . your other girls. I'm a married woman, and they're . . . all single."

Deceived by her reservations completely, Soapy smiled. If he was to gain control over her, she had to live where he told her. Evidently she needed this job and money, giving him an advantage over her. "If I'm to cover your expenses, my dear, I must choose the place and meals. I can promise you the house is strong and warm. I have women who clean it, do the girls' laundry, bring their baths, and serve their meals. You will be pampered and protected there. I really must insist."

A worried look flashed across her lovely face, but not for the reason he imagined. She was trapped. It was either accept or lose the offer. As she was thinking, he added, "The other girls won't bother you in any way. I'll see to that myself. And you will have the best and largest room there. Michelle was my favorite girl; I was most lenient and generous with her. She didn't have any family, but she did have a fellow who dropped in frequently to see her. He and Michelle were very close for a long time; he was most upset by her sudden death," he hinted.

Kathy was prepared for his words, allowing her to conceal her true emotions. "If Michelle was your favorite, I'm sure her death also upset you. Please accept my condolences. This seems to be a dangerous land here. Jack and I were attacked by wolves on our way up," she tactically altered the subject, careful to make no inquisitive remarks about Michelle or Landis. Soapy was testing her feelings just as surely as it was snowing outside! Did he doubt her and her claims?

"You mean I almost lost my new pianist before she played one song? Tell me about it," he coaxed. As she and Jack related the terrifying details of their misadventure, Soapy was thinking about something else. If she had any love for Jurrell, she certainly hid it. Not a jealous light had flared in those exquisite eyes. She hadn't even been curious about Michelle's looks, if she knew about Michelle and Landis. Also, a woman in love wouldn't accept a room shared by her husband and his past whore. Perhaps she was afraid of a fierce and aggressive man like Jurrell. Perhaps Jurrell had demanded something in exchange for loaning her his name. She was well-bred, and a woman like that avoided enterprising rogues like Jurrell. But the point was, Jurrell was attracted to her. Only a jealous or spurned man would react the way he had that day at Log Cabin.

He paused in his mental roamings to ask a question to attest to his attention. She went on with her colorful account, fully aware his mind was somewhere else. A woman like Kathryn Hammond was a challenge to any man, Soapy thought. Jurrell wouldn't take to being denied what he desired. Soapy knew from his eavesdropping that day at Moore's tent that Landis had falsely married the vulnerable girl, then tried to convince her she owed him for his generosity and help. The question was, how could Soapy entice Kathy's interest in Jurrell without being obvious? Soapy had to distract Jurrell from snooping in his own affairs! He couldn't very well extol Landis's virtures and prowess. He had to get them together for his plan to work. Maybe Landis himself would conceitedly aid his cause! If Soapy flaunted her before his senses every time he came in, Landis would eventually fall into the trap so carefully prepared.

Elegant gowns and jewels would enhance her beauty. Soapy had plenty of those in the storeroom. Surely she wouldn't mind being adorned like a queen for business purposes. This might be more difficult than anticipated since Jurrell had her frightened of him. But it would work; Landis was half-snared by his phony marriage. When Landis turned on his charms, which he would, the plan would be put into action . . .

They talked for a while longer, then Soapy arose to leave. He smiled and kissed her hand. "Farewell until tomorrow, my golden treasure," he murmured. Too bad I need you for more important reasons than my own desires, he mentally added. But if his deadly scheme failed, he would still have Kathy to himself.

"Well? How did I do? I was quivering from head to toe," she confessed to Jack when they were alone.

He eyed her in amazement. "I wouldn't have believed it if I hadn't seen it with my own eyes, Kathy. You charmed the socks off of him. You handled every minute with perfection, especially when he hinted about Landis and Michelle. Will it bother you to take her room?"

"Yes, but that can't be helped. We've come too far to back down now. I wonder what happened to her."

"A fatal fall, he said. Be careful, Kathy. No chances. If he even hints at suspecting you, you're pulling out. Agreed?"

"Yes, Jack. I hate to say it, but I'm glad she isn't around.

I'm not happy she's dead, just not here now. Do you think that's why Landis has been so moody and harsh? Was he in love with her?"

"I honestly don't think so, but I can't answer for him. I almost wish she was still here. Then you could see she's no competition for you. No doubt she would have hated your guts. You aren't forgetting; he married you, not her. I wonder what Landis will say when he sees you working here," he mused aloud.

"I pray he won't come here causing trouble and ruining everything."

"He's too proud. He's had time to settle down by now. Even if he still doesn't trust you, he wouldn't embarrass himself by appearing the rejected . . . husband."

"We're in this together," she mildly chided him.

"Don't you think we should tell Landis what you're doing? That way he can't say or do anything to mess it up," he fretted.

"Absolutely not. He'll know, if and when it succeeds. Not before. Promise me you won't say a word to him."

"I promise, but I don't like it."

They slowly exited after saying goodnight to Soapy and meeting several of his more prestigious customers. They were thrilled to hear she was coming to work. Jack escorted her to her room, then went next door.

Kathy stood before her fire in deep thought before starting to undress. She slipped into her flannel gown and snuggled under the clean linens and blankets. "Well, Kathy, it's do or die," she whispered nervously to herself, shuddering violently at the last word. Tomorrow night she would be sleeping in Michelle's bed. God, how she dreaded that end of this deal. Tears began to ease from her closed eyes. For the first time since that night in Skagway when Landis had confronted her truculently, she allowed the healing tears to flow freely. Yet, other speculations kept nagging at her mind. If Landis was trying to uncover evidence against Smith for his Mounty friends, had that been his connection to Michelle? He had alleged there was no love between them, but why visit her so often? After all, he hadn't needed sexual appeasement with a wife willingly supplying it! Still, how could Michelle not love and desire him? Perhaps he had only been using both of them for pleasure and business. Did he honestly believe Kathy was a thief? Now that Michelle was lost to him, would he seek to bewitch her again? If so, did she have the willpower and desire to repel him? With this lethal game in progress, she must, if only to safeguard their lives.

Kathy was tormented by her defeats. Why would no one, except dear Jack, help her? Why did the famed Mounties, except Trace, appear devious and threatening? Who and what was Landis Jurrell? Where was her father? Except for Skagway, the only friend around was Ben. Frustration and sadness plagued her, for nothing seemed to go right. How could little Kathy unmask the insidious Soapy, or merely recover one demanding file? She had won a cover job; but with Smith in residence, how could she safely snoop around? She wished she were a powerful man, then she could solve her many problems and protect herself. Were her cruel father and her traitorous husband worth these hardships and anguish?

Nineteen

Jack and Kathy lingered over breakfast the next morning. To avoid suspicion and to strengthen her protection, it was decided Jack would come to Dawson each Friday. At the first hint of danger or failure, Jack would take her to Skagway. When their separation couldn't be stalled, Jack arose to speak words of good luck and goodbye. Kathy told him not to worry. He chuckled and vowed he would anyway.

She stood on the roughly planked sidewalk, watching his steady retreat. She had secured his promise to take it easy for the next week. She didn't know much about scurvy, but it must be a tormenting disorder. She sighed, knowing it was time to head for Soapy's. She prayed she could pull off this reckless farce. My God, she was here alone!

She gingerly headed across the trampled street, covered with a frosting of white slush and dark mud. There was no way to protect her shoes from damp and dirt, but she carefully lifted her skirt-tail to insure its cleanliness and beauty. Luckily, few were about this early, offering her only stares and no advances. She stepped on the porch of Soapy's gambling house and knocked on the thick door.

A man answered it. He was a porcine fellow with muttonchops and heavy jowls. He smiled in a friendly manner and invited her inside. She entered and stepped aside for him to close the door.

"Mr. Smith said I could practice the piano this morning. I'm Kathryn . . . Jurrell," she said, the name bittersweet on her lips.

"I was expecting you, ma'am. If you need anything, just give me a yell," he responded in a respectful manner.

"Thank you, Mr. . . . ?" she asked.

"Harkins, Luther Harkins. Soapy's real pleased you've come to work for him. We don't get many ladies around these parts."

"I'll be here until noon if that's all right, Mr. Harkins."

"Soapy said you was to have whatever you wanted. And you can call me Luther," he entreated affably.

"Thank you, Luther."

She entered the room, removing her parka and lay it over a chair. She mounted the steps to the stage and walked to the piano. Her fingers lightly traced over the splendid instrument. She smiled. She sat down on the bench and straightened her skirt, then stared at the ivory keyboard. Kathy apprehensively wondered, can I really do this? She inhaled several times, then ran her deft fingers over the keys. Not bad, she instantly decided. Only one key was off tune; the low "C" was slightly sharp. Relieved and impressed, she grinned. After all, how many of these rough people would realize the difference? She skillfully began to run the scales; beginning at low "G," she finished at high "G." To test her dormant talent and to settle her nerves, she played a medley of tunes from childhood. Then, she bravely attempted a relatively easy sonata by Chopin.

She smiled at her success and ability. Perhaps this job wouldn't be impossible. She lifted the stack of music from the top of the piano and scanned it. She laughed softly to herself; playing one concert piece was harder than playing all of those combined! Confidence filled her as she began to pick out the first few. Within an hour, she had ten songs flowing like rich honey from the musical honeycomb.

Time passed as she gave each one a try, dismissing several songs because of their risqué wording. Finally, she started to sing one appealing lay in a muffled voice. The words came forth a little hoarsely due to her recent battle with nature's elements. Still, with more practice, she could adequately carry out that end of their bargain. She tried other songs, finding the right key to complement her voice.

Around eleven, she halted. She placed her hands on either side of her hips, fingers clasping the edge of the bench. She leaned back to relax her muscles, sighing in pleasure. "Some water or coffee to wet your throat?" Soapy spoke from behind her.

She jumped, then turned to find him leaning against the doorframe, watching her appreciatively and intensely. "I didn't see you there, Mr. Smith. I hope I'm not disturbing you," she remarked, recalling his residence.

"Not at all. These ears have hungered for such sweet notes. You underestimated yourself; you are most talented, not a bit rusty. Do you still feel you need three days of practice?"

"If for nothing else than to learn these new songs," she responded.

"If you're ready to take a break, I can see you to your new home. I'll have Luther bring your belongings over. That way, you can get settled and rested before tonight."

"Tonight?" she echoed. "But I won't be ready to play for two more days," she asserted softly.

"I still want you to come over for dinner tonight. By the time you play Wednesday, they will be chomping at the bit to hear you. You could use the next few days to get to know some of our better patrons. Might help to ease that stage-fright. We're not savages, Kathryn."

"You're right. But I feel strange being in Dawson alone," she voiced her reservation. "Harriet gave me a small gun; I hope you don't mind."

"Not to fear, you won't need it. You can sit at my table with me. I'll introduce you as they come in. With you sitting in here, it might encourage some of those penny-pinchers to pay for the right to enter this room."

"I don't understand," she mused aloud. She didn't like the idea of his being her escort. But how could she avoid the man she was duping?

"It costs ten dollars just to be seated in here. That keeps out the undesirables. The food and drinks are also higher. You see, only the best can enjoy your music. I'm going to start closing the curtains each night. I've kept them opened to entice men who can easily afford to dine in here. But the denial of your beautiful face as you play will drive them wild. I think I'll raise the entrance fee to twenty dollars. That should halt the same people from filling the room every night."

"But they can hear me from out there," she reasoned on his contradictory logic. He sounded awfully obsessive to suit her.

"If you heard an angel singing in the distance, wouldn't you seek a view of her face? If they see you, they'll pay for the privilege."

"But won't that cut down on profits? How many men can afford such a treat?" she debated. "I'm here to earn

426

money, sir."

"Don't worry; you'll earn plenty," he vowed smugly.

He held her parka while she slipped into it. He escorted her to Paradise House. He had sent Luther to fetch her packed bags from her boarding house. With concealed reluctance, Kathy entered Michelle's old room.

As with her first glimpse of Soapy's gambling house, she was astonished. There was a four-poster bed in one corner, flaunting a floral coverlet. Near it was a small table with a decorative lantern. She swept past the only window with matching curtains to admire the clothes chest in heavy pine. On the adjoining wall, she noted two doors on either side of the fireplace. She ignored them for the present to move her intrigued gaze to a cushiony chair in soft French blue. In the left corner, her eyes absorbed a corner desk with a wooden chair, another lantern sitting upon it. Toward the left center of the room was positioned a small eating table and two chairs. No personal possession of its previous inhabitant could be sighted.

Soapy walked to one door and opened it, pointing out an ample closet. He opened the other one and called her attention to a private closet for bathing and dressing. On one wall, there was a lengthy cabinet for placing toilette items, over it an oval mirror. Suspended from the ceiling were two lanterns, one on either side of the mirror. Beneath the cabinet, there sat a colorfully decorated chamber pot which brought a rosy flush to her cheeks. Before another wall was a large, oblong tub, long and deep enough to submerse herself. She brightened at that luxury. The remaining wall was the stoned side of the chimney, allowing for heat. Again, no personal items were in view.

The center of the floor was covered by a blue and beige

floral rug. The entire area was spotless and hinted at great expense. Evidently this Michelle had been highly prized, perhaps overly pampered. She couldn't help but wonder why. Soapy didn't appear to be a man who indulged his employees.

"Well? Is it suitable, Kathryn?" he inquired.

She met his amused gaze. "The room is charming and cozy. I am most pleased, and relieved," she courteously remarked.

"Aren't you even curious about the former occupant?" he asked mischievously, twirling his mustache.

"I have found it best not to broach subjects of a personal nature to others. It also serves to prevent their intrusion into mine," she smiled.

"Aren't you wondering if I was in love with her?" he fenced.

"I would never ask anyone such a rude question," she parried.

Soapy insisted on clarifying the matter of Michelle, "The answer is no. Jurrell didn't steal her from me, if you're thinking that's why I despise him. Michelle loved all men. She was spoiled and willful, a wicked flirt. She wanted men to love and pamper her. Jurrell was the only one she couldn't beguile. Being Michelle, she couldn't admit even to herself that he was unattainable," he nonchalantly revealed.

"I don't understand . . ." She halted to gaze quizzically at him.

"You're Landis's wife. I don't want him demanding you quit because of his personal quarrel with me. He's a proud man. I sort of stretched the truth to tarnish his image. I wouldn't want to force you to side with either of us. Your husband was never in love with Michelle."

"Why are you telling me such things, Mr. Smith? What

he did before we married doesn't concern me. I don't wish to discuss this."

Soapy chuckled in unsuppressed humor. "I just didn't want him coming here and making me look childish. May I ask why you split up?"

"No, you may not. Let it rest, or I'll quit this moment," she announced, hoping her face wasn't betraying her inner turmoil.

"Evidently you two had a terrible misunderstanding. If not for our differences, I might like him. I must begrudgingly admit that he does have certain merits. At times, I wouldn't mind being in his boots."

She eyed him skeptically. What was he implying? "I thought you hated him," she stated, knowing she should reveal some natural curiosity, since he seemed determined to press the subject.

"In all honesty, I suppose I do. I just wanted to make sure that news wouldn't change your plans. I'm not so certain Michelle didn't arrange her own fall," he mysteriously speculated. "Or Jurrell."

Appalled, Kathy inhaled sharply. "You think my husband had something to do with it?" she asked, mistaking his meaning.

"Absolutely not. I meant, Michelle was one to use certain things to her advantage. A fall and injury might call his attention back to her. She had been most upset after his last visit. No doubt he told her about you and his surprise marriage."

"But the fall was fatal. Surely you're not insinuating suicide because of our marriage?" she asked, distressed.

"I don't think so," he replied noncommittally. "But she was furious after his last visit, about six weeks ago. She told one of the girls he wasn't planning to visit her again. Naturally she didn't take that in stride. Michelle was a spiteful creature. I wouldn't put it past her to seek revenge. To threaten suicide is a desperate way to regain lost attention." He laughed, then added, "There was no way she could make him jealous with other men. He isn't the jealous type. I would imagine he fiercely dislikes being pushed into a corner. Could be he dropped her to pursue his own wife."

She gasped in shock. "Surely you jest! I hope you don't think I'm partly responsible for her death." Six weeks ago? her mind echoed.

"Sometimes our emotions have ways of defeating us. Jurrell was an excellent catch, quite wealthy and influencial here."

"I find this conversation most distasteful and dismaying, Mr. Smith. None of this applies to me or my work."

"I only wanted to fill you in, Kathryn, in case one of the other girls or customers drops a nasty remark. I wouldn't want you upset or hurt. I can assure you that was my sole intention for speaking so bluntly and persistently. I apologize if I overstepped myself."

Kathy flinched inwardly. What and how much did Smith know? If he was as well-informed as she imagined, he knew many of the problems between them. Unless Landis had spitefully maligned her, Soapy couldn't know about their life together. She would stand on Soapy's ignorance of her foolish actions. If she lied, he would be suspicious.

"I appreciate your concern. As I said earlier, my private life is my own business. But, it's no secret that Landis and I met and married quickly. We didn't take time to get to know each other. We both realized we had made a mistake, and we parted. He's refusing to help me search for my father, so Jack and I are trying to find him. Either way, I leave for America at first thaw. Landis has nothing to say about where I go or what I do. Your quarrel with him doesn't include or interest me. I hope that sufficiently satisfies your curiosity, for I'll say no more."

Luther came with her luggage. She mentally assessed the length of time it had required to retrieve it. Had he searched it?

"I'll leave you now to unpack and rest," Soapy said, "and see you for dinner around seven. I'll send Luther over to fetch you. I wouldn't want anyone to offend or frighten my new star on her first day."

"Thank you, Mr. Smith."

Luther set her luggage on the bed and hastily left, to await Soapy outside. Soapy soon joined him. "Anything, Luther?"

"Just clothes and underwear. No jewels or papers."

"Make certain Jurrell knows she's here as soon as possible. I want to see how quickly he takes my bait." The two men walked away. "Keep an eye out for Blitch. The way she acted, I think she's too taken with him."

Kathy unfastened her packs and gazed inside. Luther had been most careful, but it was obvious he had searched her bags. Since nothing was missing, she would let this offense ride. She hung her dresses in the closet, then placed her other garments in the chest. She took her toiletries into the bathing closet and lay them on the cabinet. She glanced at herself in the oval mirror. She instantly chided herself for wondering if Michelle was prettier than she was.

She set the packs on the floor of her closet. She walked around for a time, imagining Landis spending time with another woman in this room, making passionate love to Michelle in that very bed. She flung herself upon the bed and wept softly. Would he never cease to torment her? Even amidst these haunting facts, she discovered herself seeking his manly odor on the clean linens. How her traitorous body ached for his touch; how her ravaged heart pined for his love. She berated herself for such destructive emotions. Adding this treacherous secret to his previous actions, she knew it could never be right between them again. She must forget him. But why was it so impossible, so agonizing? The trying day taking a heavy toll on her emotions, she fell asleep.

Someone was shaking her gently on her shoulder. She opened her sleepy eyes and looked up. She was momentarily confused about her surroundings and the strange woman who was leaning over her. "Soapy said ta bring ye bath water, ma'am. He said Luther wuz ta come fer ye 'bout seven. Ye wuz sleepin' sa peaceful, I hated ta wake ye up. It be nigh six now."

"Who are you? How did you get in here?" Kathy blurted out.

"Ye left tha door unlocked, ma'am. I be Silly Nelle. I takes care of Soapy's girls. If ye be needin' a thing, ye send fer Silly Nelle."

Kathy pushed herself to a sitting position, studying the coarse creature from beneath lowered lashes. The woman appeared to be in her forties, short and plump. Her garments were heavy and full, but nearly colorless from endless washings. Her crinkled hands were chapped, excessive redness and creases indicating harsh work and weather. As she met Nelle's simple expression, the woman smiled warmly, enhancing the laugh-lines near her sparkling blue eyes and almost non-existent lips. Nelle's hair had once been light brown, but now it was drab and mingled with gray. There was a jagged scar across her left cheek, drawing Kathy's inquisitive eyes to it.

"Ye be won'ering 'bout me scar?" she stated matter-of-factly, giving Kathy the impression she wasn't as simple-minded as she pretended. "I'll tells ye 'bout it. Don't bother me none. Helps keep tha sourdoughs away. Got it when me late husband, God rest 'is soul," she quickly added before continuing, "wuz fightin' a claimjumper. Ole Nelle jumps right in ta he'p. Got clobbered. Me dear man wuz kilt. I been workin' fer Soapy since tha' time. He be a kind man ta ole Nelle. Don't let none of them greedy men git ta me. I cooks, cleans, an' sees ta his girls. Ye need any wood, water, or clothes washed, an' old Nelle'll see it's done."

"You've never worked in his saloon?" Kathy asked, immediately sorry.

Nelle puffed up with pride, not anger. "Not Silly Nelle. Tha good Lord puts me 'ere ta take care of one man. He be gone now, so old Nelle sees ta herself. I gots ta be starvin' afore I does tha' kind of work." Her expression was friendly. Kathy warmed to her instantly.

"That's most admirable, Nelle. But why didn't you go back home after your husband's death?"

"Na way er money. 'Sides, ain't got na family nowhere. I be happy 'ere. Soapy takes good care of Silly Nelle. I gots me own room, hot victuals, an' clothes on me back. Better 'an most 'round 'ere."

"He sounds like a good man, Nelle. I shall enjoy working for him."

Nelle shook her head of flying hair. "Ye don't be tha kind ta work in no such place, ma'am. Ye husband be kilt, too? Ye got no money ta git back ta ye family?" Her genuine concern touched Kathy.

"Oh, I'm not here to work like his other girls. I play the piano and sing," she hastily explained to the displeased woman.

"Ye be doin' tha' first. I know Soapy. He'll be after ye ta

433

do more soon. Ye too pretty an' gentle ta ruin yeself. Ye best leave afore he has ye trapped 'ere lik' old Nelle an' tha others. Soapy likes money, an' he be seein' ye ta earn him plenty more," she warned, leaning forward as she whispered, as if fearing to be overheard.

"He'll be wasting his time, Nelle. You needn't worry. I'm leaving in a few weeks, just as soon as I earn enough money to catch the first ship to America. I would die before becoming a harlot!" she forcefully vowed.

"'E'll ne'er allow tha likes of ye ta leave. Ye best make friends with some pow'rful men, like them Mounties. Soapy's afeared of 'em. 'E'll find some way ta keep ye here," she warned again.

"I thought you just told me how kind he was to you," Kathy debated.

"He be kind ta ole Nelle' cause he needs me ta see ta his girls. But he ain't kind ta them. Once they comes, they don't ne'er leave, not alive, anyways. When Soapy gits ye, death be tha only way ta git free. Ye best keeps ye door locked. Them bad girls brings men o'er 'ere. Ye don't wants nobody sneakin' ta ye room."

"I'll be very careful, Nelle. Thank you for the advice and warnings. But I must stay a few weeks. I need the money," she stated, happy she was only half lying to this affable woman. It was suddenly clear to Kathy that Nelle was feigning her dull-witted state for protection and survival. How sad she was trapped here like this.

"If ole Nelle had any money, she'd give it ta ye ta leave."

Kathy smiled and embraced the tender-hearted creature. "You are a wonder, Nelle. You're my first friend here. I'll remember all you've told me." Kathy thought it best not to mention her husband.

The woman giggled and remarked, "I ain't had no

434

friend afore. Ye be differ'nt, Miss Kathy. Ye be special. Tha other girls treats ole Nelle like she wuz trash. Ye be needin' anythin', ye calls Nelle."

"I will, Nelle. But I'm not here to be waited on or pampered like the other girls. I can do most of my own chores. I'm certain you have more than you can handle."

"I has he'p some days. If'n one of them girls makes Soapy mad, he punishes 'er. She hasta stay 'ere 'til tha whippin' don't show. Soapy make 'em he'p me then, added lickin', he says. I'm 'posed ta work 'em 'til they's glad ta obey him an' git back ta playin' o'er there." The woman noticably tried to cover her slight burr and rustic dialect.

"You mean he beats the girls here?" Kathy stated incredulously.

"He don't calls it that. He says he's like they's papa an' hasta punish 'em when they's bad. Most 'em afraid ta cross 'im. That Michelle weren't! I knowed she wuz headin' fur trouble. She been actin' up fur weeks. Onest I heared him threaten ta smash 'er face if'n she didn't behave. She wuz a mean un. Spoiled like a brat." Nelle laughed. "She had 'er due."

"Nelle, that doesn't sound very kind to speak of the dead that way," Kathy softly rebuked her. "Was she mean to you?"

"I don't be meanin' 'er death. She wuz after tha' Jurrell chap. Couldn't stand it 'cause she didn't have 'im 'round her little finger like tha rest. I seen tha' gurl pitch fits after he'd leave. She shorely wanted tha' man somethin' fierce. I'm glad she didn't git 'im. 'E's ta good fur tha likes of 'er."

"But I thought Landis and Michelle were . . ." She couldn't complete her sentence, blushing and feeling madly excited.

"Oh, he came ta see 'er ever' week. But he wuz ta strong ta handle. That crazy gurl wanted ta marry 'im. Kin ye imagine that? Ye called 'im Landis; ye knows 'im?" Her eyes glowed with affection.

"Yes. He's the most infuriating man alive."

"Ye be seein' 'im all wrong, Miss Kathy. He be tha kindes' soul I knows. He makes ole Nelle laugh an' feel good. He sneaks me gold nuggets when he's 'ere. If'n I had more like 'im, ole Nelle could leave."

"I don't understand. I was told Michelle and Landis were very close, maybe in love. You make it sound as if she was after him, but he wasn't interested in her. Why did he keep coming to see her?"

"Ye has a mind as pure as snow, Miss Kathy. He be a man," she hinted, as if that should tell Kathy of his only interest in Michelle. "Michelle weren't like them other girls. She could pick an' choose her men. Them others go with any man who has tha gold ta pay fur their pleasures. Michelle didn't sleep with no rough prospec'ors. She took care of Soapy's rich friends, them chaps who could afford tha best. But I thinks she did more'n tha' fur him. She plays up ta 'em an' steals theys secrets. That's why ole Soapy let 'er have 'er way so much. She be va'uable property." She looked as if divulging a national secret.

"You mean she was spying on Landis and others?" Kathy probed, intrigued by this first clue, sensing she could trust this plain woman.

"Others, yep. But Mis'er Jurrell ain't nobody's fool. I bet me week's wages she told 'im more'n she learnt. 'E came fur news, not love. She wuz actin' mighty scared them last few days afore she took tha' fall. I 'spected Soapy uncovered her. I heard 'em fussin' one night. She wouldn't tell 'im 'bout Jurrell's visits, claimed he didn't talk none. Soapy don't lean ta lies. He wuz madder than I

436

ever seed 'im. If you askt me, I bet she wuz runnin' away when she fell an' kilt herself."

"You don't think Mr. Smith had anything to do with her fall, do you?" she pressed, clearly worried.

Nelle actually went white. "Don't be saying nuttin like tha' 'round 'ere. Soapy's a dangerous man. Ye don't cross 'im. Ye ever seed them iron knuckles of 'is? He kin crush a face with 'em. Ye best askt no questions. Soapy don't like nosy people."

"Do you think Landis was using Michelle to spy on Soapy?"

"He be my friend, an' I don't says nuttin' bad 'bout 'im."

So, that Jurrell charm had worked on this woman, too! Her slips had given Kathy something different to ponder. Perhaps Landis had only been using Michelle. What if Michelle found out? Would Landis kill her to silence her? Would Soapy? What secrets were so critical that Michelle had been slain because of them? Perhaps this self-appointed mission was far more perilous than Kathy had imagined. Should she pull out now? She couldn't; somewhere in this deadly maze was the truth about Landis Jurrell.

"Ye won't be tellin' nobody what I said?" Nelle asked warily.

"Certainly not. We can look out for each other. It will be nice to have a friend I can trust and talk to. We'll keep our talks a secret from everyone," she promised, smiling radiantly. Knowing Nelle would discover her identity, Kathy felt compelled to enlighten her to hold her trust and loyalty. But just in case Nelle was on Soapy's payroll in another facet or recklessly babbled, Kathy told her it was a mock marriage for her protection. Nelle grinned and stated she bet it wouldn't remain that way. Nelle was relieved and delighted by their marriage.

"I best git ye bath water. Ye be careful o'er there."

"I will, Nelle. But you also be careful over here."

The tub was filled with warm water. Kathy hurriedly bathed, knowing time was passing swiftly. She dressed in her red gown and brushed her long hair, allowing it to curl and fall softly around her shoulders. Nelle returned to see if she needed anything else, informing her Luther was waiting for her. Kathy smiled and thanked her.

Kathy slowly devoured her supper, hungry after missing lunch. The talk was light and genial. Soapy left her several times to speak with friends or to settle disputes amongst gamblers. As the evening passed, she was introduced to many local people, male and female. Sometimes they would approach Soapy's private table or Soapy would take her over to theirs. It didn't take long to realize she was sparking great interest and anticipation. Soapy was cunningly flaunting her like delectable food before a starving man. Although she resented being displayed, she reluctantly accepted it.

She knew she was revealing concern and tension, so she guilefully remarked to him once, "I'm so nervous, Mr. Smith. What if they don't like my music? What if they hiss and boo? I'm inexperienced."

He grinned. "Don't worry. They'll love anything you play. I'll give you five dollars for every catcall. See how confident I am?"

"I just hope I don't disappoint you or them. But what do I have to lose with an offer like that?" she quipped.

"Nothing," he replied, a glow she didn't like filling his eyes.

As Soapy had vowed, those next two days went smoothly. She practiced each morning, then rested each afternoon. She witnessed leering looks and noted how several patrons just bearly restrained their mouths and hands. Soapy had warned everyone she was "hands off." Knowing Soapy, the warning was respected, for now anyway. But what about Soapy himself, she fretted.

The morning of her scheduled first appearance, Kathy practiced for one hour. She returned to her room to wash and dry her hair. Nelle took special pains to assist her, delighting in this fresh and natural girl. After lunch, Kathy rested for several hours.

She was just about to dress when someone knocked on her door. Feeling safe, she opened it. It wasn't Nelle or one of the other girls, girls who had been avoiding her and casting hateful looks in her direction. They had nothing to be jealous of, for she didn't plan to take any of their business! Luther and Soapy were standing at the door, several wooden boxes on the floor. Nelle came up to join them.

"Yes, Mr. Smith?" she hinted in bewilderment. "I was just about to dress. You did say seven o'clock?"

"I meant to send these earlier, but I was busy," he began, confusing her even more. "I'm going to loan you some fancy gowns and jewels while you're here. Naturally they'll remain with me when you leave. Nelle can help you dress; she'll press anything with wrinkles."

Kathy dreaded to look at his choice of clothes. Luther brought the crates inside and opened them. Soapy lifted several gowns and gave her a closer look at them. Her eyes widened in astonishment. "They're beautiful. I really couldn't borrow such elegant and expensive gowns," she politely declined. "I wouldn't risk damaging one." What wily enticement was this?

"The gowns go with the job, like food and shelter. As you can see, not a single one is cheap. As to the jewels, you'll pick them up each night in my office, then return them before you leave. I wouldn't want to endanger your life or safety by tempting some desperate thief."

His office? That would give her a safe way to look around. Kathy knew she couldn't refuse. What did it matter? He was right; the gowns were exquisite. Since he wasn't trying to give them to her, it made it simple for her to agree. "Thank you, sir. I shall be most careful with them." Her first stroke of luck!

Soapy and Luther left Nelle and Kathy going through the crates. "They be lovely, Miss Kathy. Which 'um ye be wearin' tonight?"

Kathy abruptly asked, "Were these Michelle's?"

"No, Missy. She be green if'n she knowed 'bout these."

Kathy sighed in relief. Evidently Soapy had been collecting them for another purpose and person. Several gowns caught her appreciative eye: an emerald, a deep sapphire, and a lush scarlet. Her mother had worn gowns like this, but she never had. She decided on the sapphire gown: it had the fewest wrinkles. The skirt possessed flowing lines to attest to the changing styles. The stamp of the French was on it: it was striking and feminine, but proper and delicate. If only Landis could see . . .

Kathy dashed such dreams and traced her fingers over the soft satin. She tested the strength of the matching lace from bodice to throat, from shoulder to hand. It couldn't be old, for the material was supple and the style too new. Satin ruffles adorned the tail, while lace ruffles and tiny pearls were secured near the throat and above the breasts. The satin was sensual and soft, possessing a hardly noticable rustle.

Kathy freshened up and fixed her hair while Nelle worked on the wrinkled gown, frequently heating the iron's surface by placing it on the wood stove. Kathy piled curls on her head and allowed several shorter ones to dangle over her ears. It was a romantic style which suited the elegant gown. Nelle returned to help her into the dress. Ready just in time, she went to join the waiting Luther.

His brows lifted with admiration. He smiled and swept off his floppy hat. She flashed him a warm smile. Catching up her dress, she followed him across the busy street. When one roughly clad prospector surged forward to take a closer look at the vision in blue, Luther knocked him aside and warned him to keep his distance from "Miss Kathy."

Kathy joined Smith for a light meal before she was scheduled to begin. She accepted the proffered glass of wine with his merry suggestion it would calm her nerves. When she was ready, he approached the stage and announced her name, saying she was there to bring enjoyment and culture to this harsh wilderness. Kathy gracefully arose and took her place, the room utterly and nerve-rackingly silent.

She skillfully played several agreeable tunes which the people readily recognized, drawing smiles of pleasure and stares of awe for her beauty and talent. After one mellow and hauntingly sweet song, she played other lively tunes. Then took a short break, following roaring applause. She smiled and curtsied, thanking them for their attention and gratitude. It wasn't a fancy recital, but it was fun.

She sipped one glass of wine before taking her place once more. This time, applause preceded her playing. Soon, she mentally closed out the entire room and concentrated on the music. After her second break, she dared to sing several songs. The room fell silent, as did the other two. Men listened with teary eyes as she sent forth silvery peals of a lovely ballad which reminded many of home and family. Noting this melancholy effect, she played a spirited song. These songs and music unfamiliar to her, she had to use the sheets on the piano.

When one man came up to her, he requested a favorite ditty. She smiled ruefully and told him she didn't know it. He named another song; she smiled and complied. After that, others made requests. During one happy song, the audience clapped to the rhythm. She selected one she thought they should know and invited them to sing along. Her winning smile and bewitching aura charmed them. To her surprise, the evening passed swiftly after her first break.

When Luther came to escort her to her new home, the crowd booed him and begged her to stay longer. She smiled and invited them all to return tomorrow night. Soapy was pleased by her talent and congenial manner and complimented her on her way out.

Nelle was waiting to help her undress, but didn't linger at the sight of Kathy's fatigue. One distressing fact had come to light earlier: Soapy's office was nearly impenetrable, and a deadly obstacle to Kathy's scheme. Exhausted, Kathy was asleep the moment her head touched the pillow on the tormenting bed.

Twenty

Those following two days were spellbinding for Kathy. She realized what it was like to be artistically popular, deeply appreciated for her own abilities. It was a heady feeling to have people pay highly to sit practically hypnotized while she played and sang each night. She had been fondly received by the town's upper class. Often, she was given many tips of gold nuggets. When she appeared embarrassed to accept them, Soapy placed a metal plate on the piano to prevent her from having to take the needed prizes from the sweaty hands of admirers. Very few made requests without dropping something into the plate. She knew the folly of keeping the money in her room, placing it in the local bank that third day, adding her first week's wages to it, withholding only a small amount for emergencies and for tipping Nelle for her extra work.

The woman had tried to refuse, but Kathy insisted. Through teary eyes, Nelle had concealed the nuggets in her bosom. She had fondly embraced Kathy and bussed her cheek. Friday and Saturday nights had produced added strain, as Kathy feared Landis's arrival. When he failed to come, she assumed it was due to news about Michelle. Or perhaps he had heard about Kathy's work?

She discounted her last thought; he would relish antagonizing Kathy again. She could not forget the menacing tinge to his voice when he had snarled vows of revenge, when she was surprised he hadn't dragged her off to Log Cabin to be further harassed for answers she did not possess.

She spent part of Sunday seeing the town with Soapy, unable to decline, and late with Nelle. How she wished she had a book to read. When she mentioned that to Soapy, he took her to his office and suggested she borrow one of his. She thumbed through them and selected a volume of poems by Browning. She thanked him and allowed him to escort her home around noon, wishing she had been given some time alone in his office.

Late that afternoon, Jack came to visit. She squealed when Nelle told her who was out front. She forgot her parka to race outside and hug him fiercely. "I've been frantic with worry over you. You didn't come Friday night. I was afraid you'd taken a turn for the worse, but you look much better."

"I'm just fine, Kathy. Some business came up. It won't happen again. But I needed the money," he contritely explained.

"You need money? I'll loan you some," she hastily offered.

"No need. I made plenty guiding two fellows upriver to check out new trapping grounds. Things going all right?" he probed anxiously.

"Almost too good. They love me. I've earned a small fortune this week alone. I put it in the bank," she rapidly informed him.

"That's smart. Any trouble?"

"They guard me like a treasure. Everyone's been so wonderful. I can tell they appreciate me. They seemed to brighten up after my arrival. It must be awfully lonely and difficult up here."

"That's the price for seeking gold, Kathy. How's the act going?"

"The one on stage or the one I'm playing?" she teased, relieved and excited to see a friendly face.

"Both," he stated succinctly, then grinned.

"Both are going perfectly. I'm moving slowly and carefully. I think Soapy would give his right arm if he could persuade me to stay here. Business has steadily increased. We've stolen a great deal from the other places. Two of their owners have offered me jobs with more money. Soapy quickly told them we had an iron-clad bargain. Lucky for me, he made it appear impossible for me to leave his employ. But I haven't dared look around this early or ask any probing questions. I'm never alone over there."

"Has Landis been in yet?" he unwillingly asked.

"No. I worried he might show up Friday or Saturday. I did learn about him and Michelle; it sounded as if they were spying on each other."

"How did you learn that?" he asked incredulously.

"The woman who lives here and takes care of Soapy's girls told me. She and I have become friends. Of course it doesn't help that she adores Landis and thinks he can do no wrong." She gradually related their many conversations, then added, "Soapy has also dropped several hints about them." She went on to tell Jack of their talks. "I almost got the feeling he's pushing me on Landis. You think he has plans of enticing me to spy on him, to take Michelle's place?"

"It's my guess Smith's hoping you'll be in a position to innocently pass information to him. Or he could have hopes of passing phony information to Landis through

445

you. You might give Smith's ruse some thought. You could learn something from both men."

"Surely you jest! I couldn't fool Landis," she mildly protested.

"Sometimes the best way to get a man's attention is to ignore him. I have a feeling Landis will try to charm you once he sees you here. It's a good cover if he presses you. Make him think the initiative is his. Just do it slowly and reluctantly. Use those feminine wiles you women possess."

"I'm not like that, Jack. I'd never pull it off."

"What have you got to lose?" he devilishly challenged.

"Myself. I don't trust me around him. He's much too cunning and disarming. Besides, Soapy might have another motive in mind. Landis is a threat to me and this mission. If I weakened, Soapy would surely find some way to use it against me, and perhaps against him."

"Do what you think best, but don't hem yourself in. You might find need of Landis's prowess and influence one day."

"I hope not; I'm too indebted and bound to him as it is."

"You're freezing. Let's go eat at the hotel where we can talk."

"Why not? You staying the night?"

"With a friend on the edge of town. I'll be leaving at first light. I'll be back Friday," he promised.

Jack and Kathy made their way to the hotel and sat down. After being served, they ate, then talked. Jack was impressed by her acceptance and progress. Kathy told him everything said and done since his departure.

"When you get the jewels and return them, is Soapy there?"

"Yes. Why?" she inquired, hearing something in his voice.

"Just don't get any heroic ideas. If he caught you snooping around his office, he might arrange an accident for you. I don't like the mystery around Michelle's." His gaze clouded in worry.

"I won't nose around unless he's gone, which he hasn't been. I fully plan to come out of this thing alive and healthy."

"Any news about your father?" he mentioned an ignored topic.

Kathy sighed. "No. Soapy put a notice on the wall near the front door. The men are passing the word along. Half of them want to impress me by locating him. Looks as if I'm getting lots of help with that problem. If Jake is around here, he'll soon know I am, too. If he even cares," she muttered, starting to believe he wasn't or didn't.

Jack tried to encourage her, but he failed. "It sounds hopeless, Jack. I think the only way I'll find him is with his help. What if he knows about me? If I got into trouble or danger, do you think he would come to my aid?"

"Don't you go doing anything crazy to get Jake's attention!"

"I was referring to Landis's threats, if I fail here."

"Landis won't harm you. I think he's mad because you left him."

Jack walked her home and left. Kathy read before falling asleep to dream of Landis and to have nightmares of Soapy and Michelle.

Three days were lost in music and madness. Her popularity increased, as did the number of guests in the room where she played and sang. It wasn't unusual for the noise and action to halt in the other rooms during a particularly lovely number. The patrons had become accustomed to her presence and smiles. She talked with many guests. So far, no one had dared to offend her in any way. But Luther or Soapy was always nearby to make certain of that promise. Wisely, Zack was ordered out of sight.

Many songs were now committed to memory. Her confidence and poise had grown each night; she had gradually relaxed and blossomed under this admiration and affection. Adorned in Soapy's jewels and gowns, she sat on the stage as a regal queen, entertaining her adoring realm. She had wisely and politely refused dances and dinners with many eager men. Even their rustic minds comprehended she was vastly different from the other girls here. Within those first ten days, all knew she was wed to Landis Jurrell and was a lady of fine breeding.

On Wednesday night, Kathy was heading to Soapy's office to return the borrowed jewels when his voice caused her to pause and listen outside his cracked door. Her leather slippers had muffled her approach. Her suspicions about Soapy were confirmed—but she still didn't understand his motive.

"Jurrell hasn't been in since she's been here?"

Luther replied, "Not yet, Soapy."

Kathy tensed. Did he suspect her ploy? Was he waiting and hoping to catch them in some dangerous charade to unmask him? His next words eased those doubts, but inspired more intrigue and fear.

"I saw the way he eyed her at Log Cabin. If that wasn't jealousy and fury, I don't know beans about making money. I've made certain he knows she's here. He should be furious that his little possession is working for me. I've got to find a way to get those two together. He ought to see her as the challenge of a lifetime. I know their marriage is a farce. Dang it, Luther! I'll bet she's attracted to him. She's just too proud and frightened to admit it.

But Jurrell can't work on her resistence if he doesn't come around. I need Jurrell captivated by her. She's a damn good distraction."

"Don't worry none; she won't be able to resist him; she did marry him. Look at how he got to that heartless bitch Michelle."

"The little fool was crazy to fall in love with him. I warned her many times. He wouldn't give a damn about a female like her if she didn't have something he wanted. If anyone can get him, it's Kathy."

"Jurrell's smart. He might not fall for a woman working for you."

"He don't have to. All I need is a long game of catch-me-if-you-can. It'd be best if he does fall for her, but it really doesn't affect my plans. Let me know when he shows up. I'll snag his interest; he can't resist a challenge. When I laugh in his face and boast of how he couldn't hold his own wife, he'll try his damnedest to prove me wrong. She'll weaken."

"You're a sly one, Soapy. But I really hate to see her hurt."

"Sorry, Luther, but we don't have room for mushy feelings."

When it sounded as if they were about to wind up their talk, Kathy slipped back down the hallway. She began to head for Soapy's office once more, humming to signal her second approach. She halted and knocked at the door. Soapy called for her to come in.

She did so. She unfastened the extravagant necklace of emeralds and diamonds. She removed the bracelet and earrings and passed them over the desk to Soapy. "It seems to be going very nicely, Mr. Smith," she stated to exit on a light note, her pulse racing.

"I couldn't be more pleased, Kathy. Business is up for

us and down for others. We had every table filled in there tonight. Which gown are you wearing tomorrow night?"

She mused, then replied, "I think the velvet crimson gown. I haven't worn it yet. Perhaps the diamonds to enhance it?" she suggested.

He opened his desk drawer and withdrew a large box. He opened it, the lid denying her a view of the inside. Yet, from the number and variety of gems she had worn so far, she knew there was a huge fortune inside that box. "I think this will do better," he responded, holding up a stunning necklace of large rubies surrounded by sparkling diamonds.

She took it in her hand. She stared at it, her blue eyes wide in amazement. "It's magnificent. It will certainly do the gown justice."

"You do those gowns and jewels justice, Kathy. If I was a smart man, I would use them to entice you to drop Jurrell and marry me. I'm afraid I'm too selfish to share myself with anyone or anything."

She warily stated, "I think that was partly a compliment and partly a softened insult. I'm glad you have no such intention; I can't be purchased for any price. Do you have a hair comb or clasp, say with diamonds? I might wear a special style to go with the dress."

He grinned and dipped into the box once more. He pulled out several of both. "Take your pick," he offered.

Kathy studied each one. "I think this one will be fine," she murmured, the subject artfully changed.

"Perfect," he concurred.

"Good. I'll pick them up tomorrow evening as usual. Goodnight, Mr. Smith, Luther." She turned and walked out.

A man passed her. She paid little attention to him. He was dressed in furry pants and parka, in a big hurry.

When she realized Luther wasn't following her, she headed back to remind him of his escort duty before another talk ensued. She heard only one alarming sentence before she fled, to wait out front while she composed herself.

Her hands were suddenly cold and shaking, her heart racing madly. She could feel the warm flush on her cheeks. She didn't know which emotion held dominance: apprehension, fear, or excitement. She realized she would be wearing the most beautiful gown in the lot. She walked to the nearly deserted bar. She asked Monte for a glass of white wine while she was waiting for Luther to see her home.

She stood chatting with the freckle-faced, red-haired man of about thirty while she sipped her wine. He was relating tales of past big games and suspenseful fisticuffs when Luther came to join her. He hastily apologized for keeping her waiting, fearing she had gone on alone.

She playfully chided him, "I wouldn't go out without my sturdy bodyguard. Monte was spinning yarns for me while I was having some wine to relax." She set the empty glass down and asked, "Ready?"

She pulled on her parka and followed him outside. The night was clear and cold. Hardly a breeze could be felt, masking the below freezing temperature. The music from the other saloons had mellowed with the late hour and decrease in customers. The ice-matted streets were mostly deserted. She glanced around, seeing the curls of gray smoke leaving the wooden shacks and heavy canvas tents. The stars were brilliant; the moon was full. It was a lovely night for romance.

She bid Luther goodnight at the door, nodding to the night guard inside the front room. As she made her way to her room, a door opened and a man came out. Kathy avoided his smelly body and foul breath, clinging to the wall to prevent any contact with him or his leering gaze. He spoke to her, but she pretended not to hear. Enflamed by her, the man reached for her wrist and halted her departure.

She yanked on it, but failed to break his tight grasp. "Take your filthy hands off of me! I'm a married woman!" she shrieked at him.

"Come on, Miss Touch-me-not, just a little kiss for Charlie. You been driving me crazy for days. I got gold-dust. I'll pay any price you name. Just one night with you," he lecherously pleaded, seizing her around the waist and jerking her stiff body to him.

She screamed, "Let me go this instant, you vile scoundrel!"

The guard was at her side in moments. "Take your hands off Mrs. Jurrell if you want to see another sunrise," he coldly warned.

"She ain't no better'n them other girls! She teases us ever' night with her smiles and prissing. I offered her good money."

"Mrs. Jurrell don't see men. She's under Soapy's protection. You don't want to tangle with him or Jurrell, do you? They'll kill you if you lay one finger on her. Git before I do it," he growled seriously.

When the guard cocked the hammer of his gun, the man grumbled and cursed. "You best guard her good. One night some man ain't gonna take no for an answer! Ain't no place for a married woman. Jurrell oughta kick her butt," he threw over his shoulder as he stalked out.

Kathy swayed against the wall and breathed raggedly. She smiled sheepishly at the guard and thanked him for his help.

"No need," he said. "Soapy says you don't see nobody unless you want to."

She walked to her room on trembly legs. She closed her door and locked it. She could hardly unbutton her gown with her shaky fingers, laying it over the chair and slipping into a gown. She stood by the fire before crawling between the chilly covers. This situation was unpredictable; a wedding ring offered no protection. Then she thought of what she had just overheard: Soapy was having Landis watched! Why? He was arriving tomorrow! She was grateful for this prior warning. But why did Soapy want to push them together? What did he hope to accomplish?

What should she do? Say? She was being adorned and flaunted before Landis for some malicious reason. Like a golden challenge, she humorously concluded. If that tawny gown which sparkled like gold in the sunlight wasn't so sexy, she would be tempted to wear it tomorrow night! That phony Landis letter and Soapy's words on her marriage fused; somehow he knew the truth.

After what happened tonight, Kathy thought, the gold gown wouldn't be a wise choice. The crimson gown was perfect, a blending of propriety and subtle seduction. If Soapy was eager to have her entice Landis, she might accommodate him! But very deceptively, she decided. Landis had once called her his golden torment. He hadn't even begun to suffer for what he had done to her! Treachery could run in two directions! He had never faced a futile challenge before. Let him taste some defeat! Nothing would taunt his monstrous ego more than a ravishing prize he couldn't possess! Tomorrow . . .

Kathy stirred around ten o'clock the next morning. She threw back the covers and hopped out of bed, thrilled by the thought of this heady game. As was their arrangement, Nelle brought her breakfast around eleven. She told the woman she wished to bathe early and wash her hair. She showed Nelle which gown she was wearing tonight. Nelle fondled it and sighed dramatically. "Ye'll be an angel, Mrs. Kathy," she declared, tweaking Kathy's cheek.

Kathy told her what happened outside Darlene's room last night. Nelle was outraged. "Ye best have Tom see ye ta ye room each night," she advised in that motherly tone of hers which she now used with Kathy.

"That might be a good idea. I was petrified," she confessed. "How do they allow such horrible men to touch them? Some nights, many men! Total strangers! It's disgusting and sinful."

"They be bad, Mrs. Kathy. I's glad ye'll never git caught in tha' trap. Ye still be plannin' ta leave in two weeks?" she tested.

"Yes, Nelle. I plan to leave soon. By then, I'll have nearly four thousand dollars in the bank. That's plenty to see me safely home."

Nelle didn't want to frighten her, so she didn't ask what Kathy would do if the bank was robbed. In her years here, it had only happened once. The Mounties had caught the robbers and returned the stolen money. If they had gotten away, the bank wasn't responsible for any losses over one hundred dollars. That was why Nelle hid her money behind her chimney.

By seven o'clock, Kathy was dressed in the stunning cherry-colored gown and ready to confront Landis Jurrell for the first time since that fateful night in Skagway. She took one last glance in the mirror. The gown fit as if made for her. The neck dipped in the front, but not at the loss of any modesty. There were gathers across the shoulders, revealing several inches of creamy flesh.

The arms were snug to the wrist, where ruffles fell softly over the back of her hands. A heightened waist-line drew attention to her softly curved bosom. The skirt gracefully drifted to the floor to inspire a vision of small waist, shapely hips, and fluid movements. There were no other embellishments or distractions. The gown was beauty in simplicity, yet elegantly styled to seize attention. With the necklace, the effect should be perfect. What if Landis changed his mind?

She turned her head to the right. Cutting her intensely blue eyes to the left, she travelled the wealth of tawny curls hanging there. She repeated this action to the left, eying the hair secured above her right ear with the diamond comb. The diamonds captured the lantern light and glittered brightly. She faced the mirror, pinching her cheeks to give them color. Pleased, she headed to join Luther.

This gown was the only one with a matching cape which flowed to the floor. Kathy had it secured around her throat and was holding it clasped together. Even though the distance between here and the gambling house was short, she knew she would be chilled without her parka. Still, she defiantly refused to prevent the full effect of this set.

Luther smiled and motioned for her to accompany him. He made a funny remark about the men's eyes bulging out tonight, amusingly vowing he would have to fight off some adoring fan before he brought her home. Her silvery laughter teased the ears of the rigid man concealed by dark shadows not far away. He stiffened in annoyance, but remained where he was. He watched her seemingly float across the street with her dedicated guard, her ruby gown daintily held up. Even at that distance and in nothing more than moonlight, her beauty assailed him. She wouldn't get away so easily tonight, he vengefully resolved. She owed him, and he planned to collect. She wasn't any better than these other women.

Kathy followed Luther inside and down the hall to Soapy's office. He handed her the ruby and diamond necklace. She put it on, her fingers trembling at what she would face tonight, adding earrings. She tossed her cape on Soapy's chair and said she was ready.

Luther grinned in pleasure to be the first to see her tonight. "I never seen you so beautiful, Mrs. Kathy," he sincerely complimented her. Soapy sat in pensive silence, his own loins aching to possess her.

"Thank you, Luther. Frankly I feel a wee bit nervous in this particular gown. You can see its color a mile off," she fretted.

"Their eyes will be popping out of their heads when they get a look at you. Maybe you best not smile or talk with anybody tonight. I sure would rather hear you sing than fight off men."

When Kathy walked through the front room where roulette and faro tables were noisily busy, men halted their games and talks to stare at her. A man caught her arm and said, "Got a minute, Kathy?"

"I'm late, sir. Please unhand . . . ," she was saying politely, but firmly, as she turned to scold him. Her gaze widened in surprise, then softened as she smiled into the gentle eyes of Trace Blitch.

"Trace!" she squealed in pleasure and relief.

His gaze appreciatively walked over her. He sighed and remarked, "You look lovely, Kathy. Landis is a lucky man." She smiled and thanked him.

Trace was dressed in full uniform, distinctive and impressive. He removed his low, broad-brimmed hat and

fluffed his brown hair. His scarlet jacket nearly matched
her gown. He was wearing dark blue pants with a bold
yellow stripe down the sides and his black knee-boots
shone. The uniform was clean and crisp. He dangled the
hat strap over his left arm, leaning indolently against the
bar.

"My, but we look dashing tonight, Mounty Blitch. I
do hope this isn't an official call; I have a job impatiently
awaiting me. Been saving any maidens from hungry
wolves?" she ventured with a merry sparkle in her eyes,
wanting all men to see she had a powerful friend.

"Most maidens don't live in these parts, ma'am. Those
who do don't bravely head out into the wilderness. You
all right since your little escapade?" he inquired, sending
her a genial smile.

Trace was a most likable person, easy to converse with
and pleasant to be around. His rugged good looks and
stalwart frame gave arresting qualities to his splendid
dress. "Just fine, thanks to you," she freely confessed,
smiling innocently into his dancing eyes.

"I'm always eating alone. Any chance of you joining me
for some wine and dinner later?" he hinted, his respect
and admiration shining.

"I would be honored. After all, you did save my life. In
fact, to show my appreciation, I'll treat you to a table in
my room, and to the wine of course," she offered. It
would be nice to share company with a good friend for a
change. For certain, a Mounty offered plenty of protection from two-legged wolves! And perhaps he had news
of Landis.

"I really can't allow a lady to pay for my treat," he
declined.

"I insist. You can be my protector again tonight.
Besides, the other girls will be terribly envious of me,"

she playfully teased.

"I accept. From the way you look tonight, you'll need one," he roguishly responded. "But the girls won't mind; they know I'm off limits. Mounties aren't allowed the privilege of marriage. Regulations state we must be single. So you see, nothing to fear."

She laughed softly. "Why do Mounties have to remain single?"

"Curious as a cat? We lead dangerous lives. We travel over the territory. We can't afford distractions. What Mounty could keep his mind on his work with a wife waiting at home?" he murmured seriously.

She nodded, her flowing curls falling enticingly over her shoulders. "What a shame. Shall we?" she invited.

Soapy walked over and crisply stated, "I believe you're late, Mrs. Jurrell. Do you mind starting now? I am paying you for four hours each night. The customers are getting restless in there."

She glanced at Smith. His expression was one of thinly veiled irritation. Why? She instantly knew; Jurrell was the man he wanted her to notice, not Trace. Was he here yet? She dared not look around. She smiled contritely and murmured, "I'm sorry, Mr. Smith. I stopped but a moment to greet an old friend. You recall, I told you how Trace saved my life. He literally pulled me from the gaping jaws of several ravenous wolves."

"Do you mind waiting until your break to profusely thank him for merely doing his job?" he suggested tersely.

Kathy flushed, embarrassed by his rudeness. Lights of anger gleamed within her sapphire eyes. "You will get your money's worth, Mr. Smith. I will stay until I have played for four hours. I keep my word to everyone. I had no intention of cheating you out of a single minute," she softly scoffed, wanting him to notice her vexation. "Trace, will you follow me?"

"Mr. Blitch hasn't paid to enter," he brazenly announced.

She fumed noticably. "I invited him to join me. I'll pay for his table and anything he desires to drink or eat. I owe him my life, sir. Plus, we're friends," she smartly informed him.

"I see. Then by all means, take him to your table and get busy."

"Perhaps we should end our association tonight. I cannot play when I'm upset; and you, sir, have deeply upset me. I've been most cooperative and generous with my time. Many nights I've stayed to play extra songs for your friends, or have you conveniently forgotten? I do not appreciate being embarrassed. You were rude to me and Trace," she reprimanded him boldly. "Perhaps this should be my final performance," she threatened seriously.

Smith wisely backed down, the action nettling him. "I'm deeply sorry, Kathy. Of course you're right. I had other things on my mind. I should not have taken my irritation out on you. It will not happen again. If you wish, you may begin at seven-thirty."

"That won't be necessary. Our talk can wait until my break."

She took Trace's arm and led him to her table. After he was seated, she coaxed, "Order whatever you like. I'll be back in one hour. Don't worry; Smith's earning too much money to fire me. Besides, I don't care."

Kathy went to the stage and took her place. She played a variety of songs: soft and romantic tunes, lively ballads, and one funny melody. She sang with some, others only the moving strains of the piano were heard. When the hour was over, she headed to join Trace. He was grinning broadly at her spunk and beauty. He arose to seat her, then reclaimed his own chair. Wine was waiting for her.

He filled their glasses. "You did say one hour. You are very punctual, Mrs. Jurrell. Smith mad at you or me?" he speculated aloud.

"Both. He doesn't like me to fraternize with male customers," she declared in a smothered voice, hating to lie to him.

"I think he dislikes having Mounties in here. Makes him nervous."

"You didn't say, here on business or pleasure?" she probed.

"Both. Business is a secret; the pleasure's checking on you."

"Here to see if I'm in danger again?" she jested.

"Nope. Just to make sure you're all right," he replied honestly.

"As you can see, I'm just fine. Excluding the episode with wolves, I can usually take care of myself."

"How long you planning to work here?"

"Only a few more weeks," she readily confessed.

"Have you learned anything?" he inquired, no hint of suspicion or accusation in his mellow voice, purposely not mentioning Landis.

Her smile vanished and her eyes clouded. "Not yet. I'm leaving soon. I don't care very much for your land or its people."

"But most of them are Americans," he corrected her mildly.

"I know. I wish you luck in controlling them. Too bad you can't order them to leave the Yukon."

"Most of them, I wish I could," he stated with a laugh.

"Before my boss pounces on us, I'll get busy. See you next hour."

As she began to play, Soapy was furtively watching his moody foe. Kathy had strolled past Landis without noticing him. While she had been chatting with Blitch, Landis had been drilling his stormy glare into her. Landis had turned in his chair to watch her disappear. Three times he had gotten up and peeked through the red curtains, but hadn't entered or revealed himself. Blitch was an unforeseen interference, Soapy raged inwardly. How dare Blitch show up on this night of all nights in full dress! Kathy had to be intrigued by the dashing Mounty who had saved her life, probably feeling greatly indebted to him, as with Landis. Something had to be done . . .

Landis was feeling and thinking much the same. He wanted to surprise Kathy, shock her with his sudden arrival. He didn't want anyone to overhear their reunion. He was furious at her for endangering her life. How dare she tempt fate's wolves! Or behave like a single woman!

Worse, he was now viewed as a heartless rogue, while Trace was a knight in shining armour! The note by the door hadn't gone unnoticed, nor the reports of her avid search. He had been told countless times she had nothing to do with any men. Considering their last contact, she would do well to even speak civilly to him! Thankfully, Trace was a Mounty first and last, as Landis had once been. Landis would find no rival in the Mounty. Only now did Landis realize he had angered, hurt, and confused Kathy—emotions which matched his own.

Damn, she was exceptionally stunning tonight! His loins had tightened just viewing her. To be so near without being able to touch her was sheer agony. He missed her. He wanted her. She had been eating at him

461

for weeks, as a vicious disease trying to painfully devour him. He had resisted coming until he could stand it no longer.

But another scheme nagged at his keen mind. Soapy had been cunning, but Landis wasn't fooled. Was Kathy working for Smith in another facet? Their alliance was curious. Jealousy filled Landis and his fury rose the longer he sat there fuming.

Was Kathy another pawn like Michelle? Had Kathy heard those false rumors about himself and Michelle? Probably Soapy had flooded her ears! That was another false black mark against him. Landis pushed thoughts of Michelle from his mind. He hadn't asked her to help him. She had volunteered. He didn't want any woman, except Kathryn Hammond Marlowe!

The waiting unbearable, he entered the red room. Kathy's back was to him. He swaggered to the stage and dropped two gold nuggets in the plate. "Do you know 'Beautiful Dreamer,' my talented wife?"

Kathy tensed briefly, recognizing the stirring voice. She had been expecting him, but he caught her unprepared. She steeled herself to meet his mocking gaze. "I'll sing it just for you, dear husband." She bravely gazed into smoldering eyes as she softly sang the romantic and compelling song. When she was finished, she locked gazes with him and purred sarcastically, "I hope you got your money's worth."

He grinned beguilingly. "I always do, Kat; I always do."

Twenty-One

"You're stunning tonight. Such expensive clothes and jewels. Seems I have lots to learn about my own wife. I'd be careful around Dawson, Kat. Beauty and riches are a rarity. Men kill for them."

"Thanks for the flattery and warnings," she said. "The gowns and jewels belong to Smith; they go with the job. I don't get to keep them. But you needn't fret over my safety; Mr. Smith makes certain I have a guard at all times," she casually remarked to pique him. "Plus, I carry an intimidating last name," she scoffed insultingly.

"By all means, continue. You are indeed talented in more than one area. I'm positive you have half the town bowing at your feet," he murmured huskily, his eyes alive with mischief and pleasure.

"You underestimate me, my beloved husband. I would venture it's ninety percent of the entire area," she smiled audaciously.

"I'll never underrate you again, Kat. You've been quite an education for me," he retorted.

"Too bad it was a most unpleasant experience and such difficult lessons," she stated meaningfully, glaring into his merry eyes.

"Very little of the time. How have you been? I heard about your tangle with the wolves. Seems you have a penchant for tempting danger and being timely rescued. Too bad I wasn't around."

She eyed him coldly. "What are you trying to pull, Landis? You couldn't care less if I fatally confronted either kind of wolf."

"You're wrong, Kat. You're still my wife, legally, that is," he informed her, then chuckled at her look of anger and rebellion.

"I owe you nothing. Rest assured the challenges weren't planned. Both times I assumed I was safe. But it does strike me odd two gallant knights appeared just in the nick of time. Do you think I should repay Trace in the same manner? A Mounty as a husband makes a more powerful protector," she rashly taunted to bait him, smiling sweetly to fool any witnesses.

He bristled and frowned, but kept silent.

"Get away from me; I'm busy," she caustically warned.

"See you later, Kat; I wouldn't want to miss your show."

He swaggered off, joining Trace. Kathy inhaled several times to calm herself. Soapy inquired, "That husband pestering you?"

Kathy turned and looked at him. "He seems to have forgotten we're separated," she claimed softly, needing to guard their lives. "I need the protection of his name, so I've tried to keep our troubles a secret."

Her implication was clear and vexing to the scheming Soapy. "What did he want?" he asked.

"He asked me to sing a song, so I did."

Soapy chuckled. "Why, Mrs. Jurrell, I do believe I see a spiteful streak in you," he mockingly declared just above a whisper.

"From observations, spite is a luxury people can't afford," she unwittingly quoted Landis. "I best get busy or the customers will complain."

He smiled and nodded, walking over to speak with Landis. Kathy focused her full attention on her music, performing at her best, needing to show Landis she wasn't as shallow as he thought. Alarmed, she hadn't considered how to handle tonight. Their marriage was a fact, so how did she get around it? It was dangerous whether she behaved as a wronged wife to Soapy or as a wife delighted to see her husband for the other males.

When Landis had joined Trace, his friend had smiled cautiously. "Don't tell me you're still teasing that sweet wife," he chided.

"She thinks I was. But I was trying to apologize and flirt with her. She's really mad at me," he stated, admitting to his romantic intentions. He would deal with this annoying situation head on. He cursed his stupid rantings at Log Cabin after Kathy's departure.

"You've got nerve, Landis. I couldn't face her if I had acted like you did," Trace brazenly retorted, nettled with his friend.

"But you aren't like me, Trace," he responded.

"Something leads me to think you're in love with her; and you know the regulations only too well," he said to the undercover Mounty.

"You know the old saying, 'rules were made to be broken'—or at least sidestepped. Am I wrong in suspecting you're also falling for my wife?"

"Also?" he echoed the intentional slip. "You worried I'm moving in on your territory? Funny, I'd swear I saw a gold band on her finger."

"Competition makes for a more exciting challenge," he tested.

"She's a nice lady, yours. I wouldn't want to see either of you hurt," he averred.

"Abuse my own wife?" Landis murmured lazily.

"Let's not have a scene. You'll both be embarrassed."

465

"You eying my place as protector?" he calmly fenced.

"Protector? You? The only thing you've done is hurt her. If you're still seeking revenge, I suggest you put it aside for tonight."

"Did she tell you that?" Landis probed, leaning forward to rest his arms on the table, his piercing gaze on Trace's rankled expression.

"She didn't have to. From knowing her and hearing your reports, it's obvious to even a fool. She's innocent. One day soon, you'll be sorry."

"I know she's innocent. But I think she's being used by someone. I just have to discover if it's Smith, the American government . . . or Jake Hammond."

Trace also leaned forward. He was all ears to Landis's logic. "You know something I don't, Clint?" he quietly probed. "Can I help out?"

"I'm working on a clue. The problem is to get Kat to trust me. You read those initial reports on Hammond; he isn't here to flee family responsibilities. Question is, why is Jake ignoring Kat? Plus, Smith's up to no good. He's flaunting Kat in my face like she's forbidden candy. He made sure I've been getting reports about her. Tonight, he dared me to risk another rejection by chasing her skirt-tails. Keep a sharp eye on him and Kat. Why did she come to work here? Something's going on. I've got to find some way to talk to her, to make her see what she's gotten involved with."

"She'll avoid you like a blizzard. I know she hasn't heard from Jake yet. But Smith was mighty nasty when he caught her with me earlier," he admitted unwillingly, sensing Landis was withholding something.

"He's afraid you'll mess up his plans," Landis voiced smugly.

"You implying I should step aside and let you move in on her?" Trace teased his fellow officer. His eyes twinkled with new life.

"Either nicely, or I'll make it an order," he jested in return.

"You want her enough to pull rank on me?" Trace continued.

"For now. Later, I'll see about settling our private mix-up."

"She'll never trust you. You're wasting your time." Trace's voice waxed serious, his grin fading. Was this intrepid Mounty feeling painfully trapped between two loves: Kathy and his career?

"We can't let her share Michelle's fate. In spite of everything, I'm not going to let anything happen to her," Landis resolved confidently.

Before they could continue their conversation, Soapy walked over and informed Landis, "I hope you don't unsettle my little singer with your irascible nature. Husbandly rights go only so far."

"How much is a table in here?" Landis inquired.

"Twenty dollars." Soapy and Landis exchanged probing looks.

"My little woman's mighty expensive, Soapy. You sure you can afford to keep her?" he quizzed, handing him the money.

"She doubled my business. She earns every nugget I pay her. In return, I protect her from undesirable characters."

"I'm delighted and relieved to hear you take such good care of my wife. I would hate to end her amusement here by taking her home."

"Husband or not, if you cause trouble, I'll have you kicked out. That is legal, isn't it, Mounty Blitch?" he asked to nettle Landis.

"It's your place, Soapy. You make the rules in here. As long as you break no laws, I won't interfere," Trace icily concurred.

"Thanks, Trace. Nothing like the support of a Mounty friend. Which table did I just purchase?" Landis growled humorously.

"The best in the house," Smith wickedly pointed to the next one. "Kathy won't quit. Eat your heart out, Jurrell; it's gonna be a long, cold winter." Soapy flashed him a sardonic smile and strolled off.

"See what I mean, Trace? A husband should sit with his wife. Why put me next to her?" His ebony eyes danced with wild speculations.

"Why take it?" Trace asked, frowning. "She's leaving in less than four weeks. Don't cause her any more trouble."

"She's returning to Skagway? Why so soon? She's earning a fortune here," he mused thoughtfully, this news disturbing.

"She's earning money to go back to America on the first ship."

"So, she's returning home," Landis murmured as if surprised. "That means Soapy and Jake have to make their moves soon. Think you can arrange to stop in a few times a week to keep an eye on her?" Landis asked, stunning Trace. "I need to check on someone."

"I'm not going to spy on your wife," he defied Landis's words.

"I meant, keep an eye on her safety," he snapped.

"But that's all I'll do," Trace persisted stubbornly.

Kathy left the stage and walked over. "I believe that's my seat, Mr. Jurrell," she sweetly informed him as he arose.

Landis seated her. "Have a pleasant evening, Kat. I'm enjoying your performance," he murmured into her ear, his double entendre clear.

"I'm not enjoying yours," she objected softly, glancing up at him.

"Can I help it if my wife has me so smitten I hardly know what I'm saying or doing these days?" he teased her, hands on her shoulders.

"I know. And you have a strange way of revealing your affections. Would you excuse me; I'd like to rest my throat."

"Of course." He turned and sat down beside her, their chairs touching. Dismayed, she stared at him. He flashed her a beguiling grin.

"Did you pay for that table?" she whispered.

"You don't expect me to miss your finest act? You're like a pesky mosquito, always buzzing around and biting, but impossible to quash," he whispered in her ear to unnerve her.

She puffed up. "I can promise you, you've cruelly swatted me numerous times. After our last meeting, I wisely gave up my greedy appetite for your distasteful blood," she whispered in return to mock him.

He placed his arm along the back of her chair and leaned very close to murmur softly, "I guess I'll just have to find some way to return your lost appetite. What do I have to do? I find myself missing you something fierce," he hinted.

She glared at him. "You're wasting your time, Jurrell."

"Am I?" he challenged unflinchingly. "As far as I can tell, you're still locked in with me." Their gazes fused and clashed.

She turned her back to him and lifted her glass of wine. Landis tapped her on the shoulder. He touched his glass to hers and murmured, "To my golden torment, may she cease to resist and torture me."

Kathy seethed at his conceited determination. She touched his glass and toasted frigidly, "To my tarnished knight, may you never gild yourself again at my expense." She drained her glass, her stormy eyes never leaving his obscure ones, wanting to remove his searing arm.

"You really hate me, don't you?" he questioned.

"Whyever would you think such a terrible thing, dear husband?"

She turned her back to Landis. Trace was grinning playfully. "Tell me what you've been doing since our suspenseful adventure," Kathy forced her attention on their friend. Landis Jurrell was like a perpetual tide, always coming in and out of her life. No, he was a stormy wave, cruelly tossing her around and threatening to drown her.

"Just trying to keep the peace. Seems like all the excitement is around here. Perhaps I should stop in more often."

"I wish you would. It's good to see a friendly face."

Trace winked at her, then mischievously said, "We did spend several days and nights in Pete's cabin. I didn't know it was so nice to have a woman around. If I'm not careful, my days in service are numbered. Some lucky lady might trap me into marriage. Despite the tales of us dedicated Mounties, we aren't unattainable. A woman like you comes along rarely. Landis is surely a lucky devil." Trace wanted to enlighten his friend to his good fortune and perilous position if he didn't change his tactics. They were a perfect match; sadly Landis didn't know how to treat a good woman.

"I have to perform again, Trace." She went to the piano and played a provocative and amusing ballad, her hypnotic eyes on Landis's broad back.

I came to a land with dreams in my heart;
I met a true love who wasn't so smart.
I gave him my love, but he sent me away;

Choosing his freedom for another lonely day.
His hair was like deerskin, so sleek and brown;
His eyes blue as heaven as he left me for town.
Denying all else, I flew to his side;
Casting away modesty and even my pride.
He gazed into eyes with love all aglow;
Seeing his loss as cold as the snow.
Taking my hand, he dropped to his knee.
My love's yours forever, if you'll marry me.
So I ask you, my friends, isn't he so smart?
To take me to wife, and give me his heart.

Landis turned to watch her. When she finished, she sent him a taunting smile. His face was stern and his eyes turbulent. He downed the glass of whiskey and left. Kathy watched him swagger out, suddenly feeling very empty and sad. She finished her night and was escorted over to Paradise House by Trace. He bid her goodnight and left.

She spoke to the guard. Tom nodded and returned his gaze to the yellowed paper he was reading. Kathy walked to her room, unlocked the door, and went inside. She closed and leaned against it, sighing in fatigue and loneliness. First she tossed the cape over a chair, then she slipped out of her gown and shoes and followed them with her undergarments.

Standing naked by her chest as she retrieved her flannel gown, a soft chuckle came from the shadows of her bathing closet. She whirled in fear to confront her unknown threat, holding the crumpled gown before her. "Who's there?" she asked in a quavering voice, her gun out of reach.

Landis casually stepped into the light of the fire. "I wanted to talk, Kat, alone. We have an unsettled matter or two."

"Get out of my room," she scathingly warned, cautiously holding her voice low. If caught, how would she ever explain this? Landis could ruin everything with his arrogant meddling! "I'll call the guard."

Before she realized what was taking place, he had struck as lightning: gagging and binding her, crushing her in his steely arms. He lifted her squirming body and tossed her on the bed. When she attempted to jump off, he pinned her down with a knee in the small of her back. With speed and agility, he was out of his clothes and boots. He turned her and pinned her beneath his naked body. Her gaze burned with leashed anger and passion.

He chuckled in amusement. "I'm not going to ravish you, Kat. I'm going to free you and remove the gag. Considering how we're dressed," he hinted roguishly, "if you scream, you'll create an embarrassing scene. Aren't you forgetting we're married? Just a lonely husband visiting his beautiful wife after a lengthy separation? Before you seek help, I would think about the consequences." He removed the gag and untied her hands. He captured her wrists as she attempted to slap and claw his mocking face.

"You had everything planned, didn't you? Say what you must and leave me alone." She struggled to pull free from his painless grip.

He released his hold, but kept her imprisoned beneath him. "Get off of me," she seethed quietly. "Put your clothes on. I'll hear you out." She didn't like the intoxicating sensation of his burning flesh against hers. It stirred too many yearnings and memories to life, and she was much too conscious of his stimulating sensual prowess.

"Not until I'm finished. That way, I can trust you to keep your word. You wouldn't want anyone to catch us like so," he gestured to their position. "This is a complex predicament." His finger toyed with a curl as his burning gaze flickered over her, his face close to offer safe communication.

"Spit it out, Jurrell. I'm very tired. If it's about those damned reports again, I'll scream," she vowed in frustration, his virile body warm against her chilled one, his manly odor assailing her warring senses.

She was stunned when he calmly agreed. "I believe you, Kat. In fact, I think you've told me the truth all along. I want to apologize for the way I acted in Skagway. I know my behavior was unforgivable. I'm sorry for hurting you." His hand drifted to her cheek, caressing it ever so lightly. His fingers trailed over her lips, inspiring tremors.

His touch and actions disturbing, she slapped away his hand. He chuckled, not the least put off. "I'll never forgive you. An apology is nothing but empty words, like you. I detest you and all you've done. Leave."

"Not so fast. You don't know what you're risking. Soapy is deadly. It's time I put some sense into that lovely, stubborn head."

"You think you're the one to do it?" she scoffed.

"I care about you, Kat, more than you realize. I know I've made plenty of mistakes where you're concerned. You'll get hurt, Kat. Believe it or not, I want you safe and happy. Why are you here?"

"I don't believe anything you say, even on a stack of Bibles."

"Are you doing this to spite me?" he ventured.

"No. As soon as I've earned enough money, I'm going home to America," she said. "If you try to stop me, I'll kill you. You have no right to hold me here." She grimaced in torture as he shifted, their bodies gluing together.

"You might try, but I'd have to stop you. I couldn't have you going to jail for slaying the man you love in a vengeful fit of rage."

"I'm positive they'd believe me justified," she snapped, failing to deny his mention of love. She bravely and rashly locked gazes again.

As his finger began to draw tiny circles on her neck and chest, he asked, "Tell me something: why is Soapy throwing you at me?"

She inhaled sharply. How did he know? All she needed were more suspicions to ruin her scheme! "What are you jabbering about? Your imagination is wilder than mine. Throw a wife on her own husband? I don't trust you, Jurrell."

He misread her reaction; he assumed she was shocked at that fact, or she truly doubted his conclusion. "I depend on my instincts every day, Kat. For some reason, which I haven't deciphered yet, he's using you to get to me. I think he might want to persuade you to spy on me," he surmised aloud, his hand stopping all movement as it cupped her chin.

"Keen instincts and sharp wits, yet you view me a thief and worse? Your logic baffles me. Get you? I already have you. Stay away from me; Smith thinks we're separated and I'm leaving Alaska. Since you two are enemies, it seemed best to play the wronged wife to work here. What could I possibly learn from you that would interest Smith? No," she quickly declared. "Don't say anything. Then, you can't accuse me of dropping any innocent slips. Do you think I'm working with Soapy against you?"

"Not yet, but you might be enticed to go along with this new scheme, just to avenge yourself." She gaped at him; he looked serious.

"Since he doesn't know I have reason to spite you, where would you get this ridiculous idea? I told him we'd married too hastily, and we're planning to correct our mistake. I've played the perfect married lady here." To rankle him, she tenderly cuffed his chin, then smiled.

"Don't let him use you. It's a deadly game," he warned gravely.

"Like it was for your precious Michelle?" she sneered coldly.

"You're partially right. She was feeding information between us. But she was spying on him for me, not the other way around. Just for your information, I've never slept with her. To clarify that, I've never made love to her. We pretended to be fond of each other to cover our meetings. She was working for the Mounties. I was her contact with Bill Thomas. Another thing for the record, it wasn't my idea. She went to Bill with it, and I agreed. Soapy knows the Mounties. She hoped her aid would make me indebted. I didn't love her or want her, Kat. This is my first visit to this bed."

Kathy was skeptical of those admissions. "Is that why she met with a fatal accident? When her ruse failed, she was going to tell Soapy about you two?"

"If you're asking me if I had anything to do with her death, the answer is no. It'll be proven Soapy killed her. When she kept telling him I wouldn't drop any hints, he realized she was making a fool of him. She was after his personal papers. The Mounties were going to take her to safety and pay for her help, give her a new beginning. I don't want you getting involved. He could kill you, too. Damnit, I can't allow you to get hurt!"

"Then why are you here? If he discovers you were here tonight, he'll think I've lied, that I'm spying on him. If you were concerned about my safety, you wouldn't be endangering it," she sneered, then revealed Nelle's statements and the words overheard in Soapy's office to prove he should stay away.

"He'll smugly think his plan is working. I had to see

you, Kat. I needed to explain. Trace said there wasn't any news about your father yet. I'm sorry. I have been looking for him, like I promised."

"Is that why you came? To beguile me into locating Jake for you, or to spy on Soapy? Why are you and the Mounties so intrigued by my father? You haven't changed. You're still trying to use me. It won't work. Aren't you afraid I might tell Soapy about you and Michelle?"

"No. If I can trust you, that means he can't. People he can't trust get themselves killed." He dropped a kiss on the tip of her nose.

"I can take care of myself. I've changed a great deal recently. But you have a point," she reluctantly agreed.

"Has he said or done anything else which might sound suspicious?" She told him about the confrontation tonight over Trace. "What about Trace, Kat? Are you falling for him?"

Surprised, she gaped at him. "Don't be silly. We're just friends."

"It didn't sound like it earlier," he reminded her of her deceit.

"I did that just to pique you. He knew I was only teasing."

"You're a prize, Kat. Don't play with his emotions. He's a fine man. Lonely men get crazy ideas when you're around. I should know."

"I'm not leading him on. That's the first time I've seen him since Pete's cabin. I'm not cruel and heartless, Jurrell." She then responded to his questions about her hazardous trek to Dawson. "Surely you aren't jealous?"

"Damn right, I am. I shouldn't have driven you away, Kat. Is it too late to change things?" he boldly ventured, capturing her head between his hands and forcing her to look into his eyes. "Ben said I'd be sorry," he added, to test her reaction to Ben's name. If she heard him, she ignored it.

"I'm going home soon, and I hope we never meet again. So if you're here to coax my help, you're wasting your time and energy. Have you learned anything about the missing reports?" she inquired, praying he would say yes and she could end this precarious act.

"No. But I think Soapy's in on it," he rashly remarked.

"So, that's it! You want me to check, then recover them? You utterly astound me. I'm almost tempted to work for you, just to find those papers and end all contacts between us. But I'm not eager to get killed to appease you. Even if I miraculously succeeded, you would probably think I had them all along. Please feel free to search my room before you leave. As you can see, I have nothing to hide. Let me up; I'm freezing."

He chuckled, then pulled the covers aside and eased them under the blankets and quilt. He pulled her into his arms and murmured, "Is that better? Nothing like shared body heat. And I've sorely missed yours."

"You're despicable. Please, Landis; I'm so tired. Won't you leave now?" she suddenly pleaded, even as she automatically gravitated to his warmth. This contact was agonizingly sweet.

"I've really messed things up for us, haven't I?" he pressed, caressing her cheek, strong fingers roaming across her silky arms and back.

She looked up into his somber gaze and replied sadly, "Yes. You very successfully ended all hopes of us staying together. Relax, Jurrell, your priceless survival has been safely insured at my expense."

"It does have a price, Kat, a costly one. That's the problem. I want you and what I have now. But I can't have both, and you're demanding a hasty choice. You have no idea what I must sacrifice to keep you."

"You needn't concern yourself over a decision which no longer exists. I forbid you to come near me again. You're quite safe and secure in your mysterious world. But one day, it's going to get awfully cold and lonesome there. Maybe another Michelle will come along, one a little brighter and less greedy."

"I'm going to do anything necessary to hold you, Kat. When the time comes, you'll understand everything," he mysteriously hinted.

"No, Landis, I won't 'understand everything.' I won't be around. You've had plenty of time to make a decision. I offered you everything I possessed, and you struck out at me as if I were your worst enemy. Too much happened. I can never forgive you or be your wife again."

He rolled to lie half off her body, holding her gaze. "You're saying, even if I tell you everything, you still won't change your mind? You won't give me a chance to earn your love and forgiveness?" he challenged, relieved he hadn't said, even my real name. She was driving him wild.

She fought to restrain her tears and cravings. "Love and forgiveness can't be earned like money, Landis. Like you once told me, everything has its price. I can't afford yours."

"But, Kat, I had reasons for what I did," he argued in self-defense. But how could he make her understand without telling her the whole truth? For once, Landis was unsure of himself, cursing his secret Mounty code which was wreaking havoc on their lives.

"You can justify or excuse your behavior all you wish, and it changes nothing. Let me go, Landis; it won't ever work between us."

"Why?" he coaxed, seductively pressing his taut frame to hers.

"I loved you and trusted you. You betrayed me and

what we had shared. All for some stupid papers I never saw! Maybe they are critical. Maybe you did have reason to suspect me. Maybe you wanted to hurt me so deeply you would be safe from being attracted to me. I don't want to know why. Let it be, Landis; it's over."

"But I need you, Kat. Maybe I was striking out in self-defense. But I was attacking my own pain and disillusionment, not you."

"You're wrong, Landis. If you loved me, you would trust me. You had to despise and mistrust me to do what you did that night. I saw the look in your eyes; I heard the tone in your voice. I'll never forget them. You don't want or need me, Landis; you want Jake and Soapy. If you have any decency or conscience, you'll leave me alone. You said you wanted to protect me enough to share your name. If you do, then you'll want what's best for me. That isn't you, Landis, and we both know it."

"What about me, Kat? I can't just walk away from you."

"You did that weeks ago, Landis," she accused softly.

"Then let me walk back, Kat," he entreated.

As with Alaska's awesome glaciers, Kathy remained frozen and immovable. "No. Not now or ever. It could never be the same between us, and I cannot accept things the way they are. You ask too much."

Landis captured her face between his hands and tenderly plundered her mouth. Her world careened madly, demanding to give wondrous flight to her straining emotions. Her enflamed body throbbed to give free rein to the fires which dangerously raged within it. If she yielded now, all would be lost. She forcefully steeled herself against response. She could not permit her perfidious guide to mislead her again, to treacherously shackle her with the gyves of powerful love and enslaving passion. To prevent her defeat, she kept reminding herself of his past betrayals and of his beguiling ways. Ben had alleged Landis loved and wanted something else more than her; Landis's words implied at least as much. He was using his sensual prowess to weaken her will, to selfishly prove he still had power over her.

She remained rigid beneath his onslaught of kisses and caresses. She attempted to seal her lips against his mouth's invasion, but he deftly pried them apart with his own. She was tempted to bite his exploratory tongue, but feared he would cry out in pain and alert others to his presence here. She needed to halt this blissful madness, until his sole choice was her. Her icy hands went against his broad shoulders to push him back. As a solid oak, she couldn't budge him. His golden flesh burned against her hands.

He was aware of her lack of response and resistence, but refused to give up so easily. He nibbled at her ears, feeling a slight tremor run through her body. With renewed hope, his lips seared a trail to her breasts. As his mouth left one for the other, the warm moisture there chilled the taut peak. She helplessly shivered, praying for strength to reject him.

She pushed against his forehead to dislodge his mouth which was perilously pervading her senses. When she realized she was no match for his great strength, she seized a handful of ebony hair on the back of his head. She pulled gently at first to warn him of her impending action, gradually increasing the pain and pressure. "You can prove you're physically stronger than I am, but you'll be raping your own wife. And I'll see that your Mounty friends learn the truth about their intrepid hero," she warned between tightly clenched teeth, desperation and fear lacing her shaky voice.

Landis leaned back and gazed into her impassive

features. Evidently she was insensate to him now; or so he assumed, unaware of how deeply she was struggling to appear apathetic and remote. "You mean it, don't you?" he asked incredulously, his body aflame with need. Had he actually lost her?

"I've never meant anything more. If you think you can swagger in and delude me, you've never been more mistaken. Get out, Landis."

His voice was hoarse when he spoke. "I want to make love to you, Kat. I need you tonight more than I've ever needed anyone. Do you really hate me so much? Did what we share mean so little to you?"

"You can't 'make love' without love. Sex isn't love. As to sharing, just what have you shared with me? Nothing but trouble and pain."

"I suppose you have a right to be bitter, Kat. But . . ."

She cut him off, "Yes, Landis, I do; and I am."

"Look me in the eye; swear you don't want me," he challenged.

Their gazes locked, seeking and pleading. She inhaled raggedly. "You taught me what passion was. I won't try to pretend you don't have a physical effect on me. I'll even confess it's difficult to refuse you. But I would despise myself if I surrendered. I won't become your legal mistress, or your spy, or your magnet to draw Jake into the open. Stop using me!"

"I don't want you for any of those reasons, Kat," he vowed, novel fears gnawing at him. "I want only you. God, I'm sorry I messed things up."

"You're only trying to ensnare me with your charms," she scoffed, praying he would halt this torment. "But I fear your magic has already vanished."

He studied her fathomless eyes for a time. Kathy compelled herself to deny the warring emotions emblazoned upon his somber face. He was a master at deception; she couldn't fall for this cruel ruse. She bravely stared back at him, barely managing to conceal her turmoil.

He rolled off the bed and stood up, his back to her. He reached for his clothes and jerked them on. He sat down to pull on his boots. Afterwards, he remained there for a short time, shoulders slumped, hands resting on thighs, staring at the floor in silence. Kathy fought the urge to reach out to him. Too many pains and secrets. Perhaps one day . . . No, it was foolish to live for golden dreams.

He turned and looked down at her. His voice carried a strange inflection as he murmured, "I wish things could be different. If you had come a year ago or a year from now . . ." He left his statement unfinished. "I can't vow to leave you alone; I wouldn't keep it. Will you make me some promises?" he asked.

She rolled to her side, facing the wall, remaining mute. Landis went on, in spite of her silence. "Will you swear to be careful around Soapy? He's dangerous, Kat. Don't get any crazy notions of meddling in his affairs. Get out of Dawson as soon as possible. If you need money, I'll give it to you, no strings attached. Don't turn to some other man just to spite me. You'll regret it some day. You'll both get hurt in the process. At least try to forgive me. Don't increase your hatred and bitterness. Last, if you need anything at all, promise you'll stow that pride and resentment to send for me. If there's any trouble, I'll come to help. I swear it. Anything or any help at all, Kat."

Still, she didn't answer him. "I'm not leaving until you make those promises," he vowed, his eyes slipping down her nude back.

Desperately needing to end this tormenting scene, she replied crisply, "I'll be very careful around all men. I'll be leaving Dawson and Alaska, so I don't need or want your money. I couldn't accept any if I were destitute. I would never use men in coy games. My pardon to you depends solely on whether you leave me alone. Lastly, I don't need your help or protection; I won't become indebted to you again. We're even; and I plan to keep it that way. Now, leave; I'm exhausted."

The gaps in her promises left tiny rays of hope. "Goodnight, Kat Jurrell," he murmured sadly, his heart and body aching. He knew he had to leave quickly, or he might forcefully seduce her.

"Goodbye, Landis," she responded, the word painfully ringing with chilling finality. "Thanks for the brief use of your name."

He walked to the door, going cautiously so as to not alert the guard. He gingerly opened it; all was quiet outside. Forgetting one point, he closed the door and soundlessly turned to add it.

Kathy had instantly buried her face in her pillow and given way to muffled sobs which tore at his heart and guilt. "No, Landis, it isn't that easy," she vowed softly into the darkness. "Whatever it takes, I'll get you out of my life," she cried in anguish, "I can't take this constant warring anymore. I just want to be free and happy again."

Just as he was about to go to her, her last words halted him dead in his tracks. "I hate you, Landis; I hate you. I'll never forgive you for what you've done, never . . . God, I wish I had never met you."

Tears glimmered in his eyes. His body trembled. He felt as if some mythical hand had plunged savagely through his mortal flesh and bones to grasp his heart and agonizingly squeeze it. He comprehended the intensity of her sufferings—for he shared their depth and potency.

As she wept into her pillow, he furtively vanished into the glacial night. Kathy needed time and distance. Much as he dreaded granting them, he would. He was suddenly frantic to complete his present missions, to give him the means to confess all, to earn her forgiveness. But how would she feel when he destroyed her father, when he revealed the marital ruse?

I can't lose you, Kat Marlowe, his heart cried out. One day you'll hear the truth, whether you want to or not. I can't allow you to leave without knowing it. If or when you walk away from me forever, it won't be with any secrets between us. Just a few more months, love, that's all I need . . .

Kathy turned on her back and stared at the firelight dancing on the ceiling. She wished he had not made such statements; she wished she had not seen his expressions or heard the tones in his voice. She was so confused. If she could only trust him. Damn him for making it impossible!

Could she walk away and never look back if there was even one ray of hope? So many betrayals haunted her: her father's, her love's, her own body and heart's. In a way, she even felt betrayed by her mother's untimely death. Was that the crux of this complex and racking episode in her life? Too many disillusionments and sacrifices too quickly, all seemingly intertwined? Who, what, and where was her father?

"I love you with all my heart and soul, Landis Jurrell, no matter what you are. Even after all you've done, God help me, I desperately need you. But I can't think about you until this matter is settled. I must prove certain things to both of us. If only you had said, Kat Jurrell, I love you, just once with a verity I couldn't deny . . ." She pulled the covers tightly to her neck, crying softly until relenting slumber claimed her.

Twenty-Two

Landis came to Dawson several times during those next two weeks. Sometimes, he remained in the center room of Soapy's where the gambling wheels and tables were positioned. Often he would halt his conversation or game to stare thoughtfully at his hands or glass while Kathy was singing. When she walked through the center room going to or from her performances, his gaze would longingly lock on her and trail her until out of sight. He noted how long she stayed in Soapy's office, fetching or returning expensive jewels. Most assumed Landis was missing her and trying to entice her home.

He sporadically ate in the red room, for appearances, he told her. A few times, he had blocked her path to force her to look at him and hopefully smile and speak, making their meeting appear accidental.

When this happened, Kathy would reluctantly meet his searching gaze and speak politely, then hastily retreat before he could engage her in any conversation. A few times when he was in the red room, her gaze would be helplessly drawn to him. Again, she would quickly avert her turbulent eyes when she comprehended her action. When he was present, she was apprehensive and quiet. She found concentration difficult.

Soapy furtively observed them, disturbed by Kathy's fierce resistence to Landis's pursuit; that was what the cunning rogue was doing! He was making sure she and other males were aware of his claim. His gaze was like a tender and stirring caress; his eyes were mockingly playful. Evidently that hundred-dollar bet that Landis couldn't win her back again had done the trick!

The puzzle was Kathy, who looked anxious, even frightened. Landis was unnerving her. It was obvious she was fiercely attempting to ignore him and his charms, and she was having an uncomfortable time of it! Kathy was definitely attracted to the puissant tower of strength and good looks; she was just too proud to submit, or Soapy mistakenly assumed. Her distraught mood told Soapy his plan would eventually work.

Only once had Smith called attention to Kathy's troubled state, for he didn't wish to draw attention to his observation and interest. One night when she came to his office, he glanced up and remarked lightly, "You seem distracted when Jurrell's here. Do you want me to refuse him entrance? Why not stop this pretense of a marriage?"

Kathy gingerly responded, "Half the men here watch me, so that wouldn't be smart. I also think it unwise to order him to stay out; he is my husband. Besides, he seems to have lots of friends. He could entice their business from us if you repel him."

"You've got a point there, Kathy," he shrewdly concurred, pleased the argument came from her lips instead of his, calling her by her first name as he had been doing lately. "I think you're making a mistake to publicly avoid him. People might get suspicious."

She gasped in mock astonishment. "I hadn't considered that angle."

"While you're here, I think that's wisest," he advised.

"I only agreed to stay for six weeks; they're almost over. I miss my friends and home. It's so cold and uncivilized here. By spring, thousands of new gold-seekers will be coming to the Yukon. I want to go home."

"We'll miss you, Kathy. You've been great for this town; the people really appreciate what you've done for them. So do I; you've increased my profits by leaps and bounds. You could become a rich, independent woman within a year. I know the terms of our bargain, but I will try to persuade you to stay longer," he mirthfully informed her.

She smiled deceptively. "You've been a good boss, Mr. Smith. You've kept your promises. I want to thank you. And Luther, too; he's been very kind to me. I just feel so out of place here. I'm not pioneer material," she commented, drawing out the conversation with hopes of unmasking some vital clue about those papers.

"It isn't so bad here, Kathy, once you get used to it."

"Maybe not for men. But it is for a woman. I'm tired of being frozen. It's so dangerous I can't go for a stroll without a guard. I don't mean to sound ungrateful, but I don't like living in a house filled with . . . your girls. And prices are so outrageous I can't afford not to accept your hospitality. I miss my own social class; I miss the elegant dinners, the shops, the theaters, and many other feminine pleasures. Dawson might have those things one day. I suppose this sounds frivolous and childish to you."

"Not at all, Kathy. I understand your logic and feelings."

He was apparently falling for her reasons to leave when the time came, which she hoped would be soon. "I'd like to become a concert pianist when I return to America. This job has whet my appetite for performing. I'm enjoying myself. But I'd rather be playing real music in a warm concert hall to people who appreciate it. If I played a thirty-page sonata here, I would be heckled off the stage. This kind of music is fun, but it isn't me."

"You see, it was a great idea to come to work for me. Now, you have some experience. I have every confidence you'll succeed."

"Thank you. I want to ask you something," she hinted, then inquired about alterations on the striking gold gown to make it wearable. When she explained her intentions, he fully agreed.

"I have the perfect necklace to adorn it, a large emerald on a gold chain," he remarked on her plans to trim it in green satin. He could envision the tawny haired beauty in a golden gown in a gold town.

"I think you know more about jewelry than most women."

"Perhaps I'll select a special piece for your going-away present."

"No, I couldn't accept such an expensive gift. It would only encourage robbers along the way. After my experience with the wolves, I much prefer a safer journey back to Skagway. But thank you."

"A little less richer, but safer," he jested, chuckling.

"Thank you for the gesture. Goodnight, Mr. Smith."

By Friday, the golden dress was ready to wear. Kathy and Nelle were overjoyed by the result. Kathy was eager to see Jack tonight and walked over early to meet him for supper. He couldn't believe how dazzling she looked. Landis wasn't around; she was relieved—and disappointed. She didn't tell Jack about Landis's nocturnal visit to her room, but she did relate his numerous visits and curious behavior.

"How can he . . . Trace!" Jack called out in surprise when the smiling Mounty came forward to join them. "Good to see you again."

The two men shook hands and began a genial conversation. Trace was stunned by Kathy. He had been in and out several times, but tonight she was different. There was a glow on her face; she was vivacious and enchanting. Landis was surely eating his heart out!

When Trace questioned her glow, she announced her departure. His smile vanished. "We'll miss you, Kathy. You brighten up this place."

"I've been telling her that," Soapy added, smiling at her over Trace's shoulder. "Maybe you two can convince her to stay longer."

Kathy laughed genially. "No way, my friends. Living here is like being in a frozen prison. I've served my time, thank you."

"You'll be sorely missed," Trace murmured affectionately.

Kathy responded, "I'll miss all my new friends, too."

"We're planning a party here the last night if you two want to come," Soapy unexpectedly announced.

Kathy was surprised. "That's very thoughtful and kind." Kathy watched Smith's retreat, pondering his increased attention.

"My last night, I'll buy champagne to toast our new lives."

"You're getting mighty cocky with all the money you're earning," Jack chided her. For once, Jack selfishly wished Kathy was Dory.

"Trace, could I ask you a big favor? You can refuse, and I won't be upset," she ventured mysteriously.

"Anything, Kathy," he hastily agreed before hearing her out.

"It's about the money I've earned, nearly five thousand dollars. I was wondering if you could take it to Log Cabin for me on your next visit. I'll give it to you secretly, so your safety will be insured. If anyone's watching me,

JANELLE TAYLOR

he'll think I'm leaving it in the bank. I'll let it be known I won't be carrying any. I'm afraid someone might rob us after we leave Dawson."

"You mean Soapy? That would be a cunning ruse to keep you stranded and working here. Naturally I'll help. I'll leave it with Sergeant Thomas, then you can claim it on your way back. I might even be around to escort it and you to Skagway, if Landis isn't available."

She smiled warmly. "What would I ever do without you two?"

The plans were made. Kathy left to sing her first selection, "Beautiful Dreamer." She sang and played other melodious songs. Resigned to end all of her futile quests, she was calm and spontaneous tonight. She had no choice but to halt her daring charade; she was denied any opportunity alone in Smith's office. By now, he had surely burned an incriminating file. Her father hadn't appeared, and Landis intimidated her. Obviously she was wasting her time on all three men and causes.

She looked out at the audience. They also seemed in gay spirits. She coaxed, "How about if everyone helps me with these next few songs?"

They clapped in approval. From "Long, Long Ago," they went into "Oh, Susannah," then "Camptown Races." Someone called out, "Let's do 'Wait 'Til the Sun Shines Nellie'!" She happily complied, as did the customers. Afterwards, she slowed the pace and mellowed the mood with "Jeannie with the Light Brown Hair." After her break, she asked, "Anyone here from the American South? Any die-hard rebels?" she mirthfully added. To her amazement, four hands were raised. "Good. You four help me with this tune," she entreated. She played the song through one time, then began to vibrantly send forth the stirring words to "Dixie Land." True to Southern tradition, the men joined her, their

490

deep voices nearly drowning out hers. Those who didn't know the words began to clap in rhythm to the beat. Once wasn't enough; they were compelled to sing it again. The new merriment enticed several men from the other room. One newcomer asked, "Do you know 'Carry Me Back to Old Virginnie'?"

She smiled and nodded, then easily complied, bringing tears to his homesick body. She skillfully sent forth the lovely strains of the "Blue Danube Waltz," then took another break.

Soapy came in to say how much everyone was enjoying himself. "You really know how to loosen up customers. They're so homesick now, they're buying twice the number of drinks to doctor their pains."

"I didn't mean to make them sad, Mr. Smith; I was trying to make them happy. Maybe I should tone it down a little?"

"Not at all. It gives them a kick to sing with you. If you don't mind, I'd like to hear 'Beautiful Dreamer' again."

"I'll do it first," she agreed, alarmed by his heated look.

The envious Molly came in to ask Trace to dance with her. "You don't mind sharing him for a while, do you, Miss Kathy?" she sneered. Her green eyes glittered with hostility and jealousy. She would be glad when this creature was gone! Kathy couldn't claim any female friends here, except that dull-witted Nelle! All the girls hoped Kathy would cross Soapy and wind up like Michelle, that other hateful witch with sea-water eyes and sultry blond hair.

"You'll have to ask Trace, not me," Kathy responded politely.

To avoid spoiling tonight, Trace agreed to the dance. Alone at last, Kathy and Jack quickly refreshed their imminent plans . . .

As she sipped her wine, a husky voice asked from

behind her, "May I request a special song, Mrs. Jurrell?"

Kathy nearly chocked on the liquid. She looked up into Landis's twinkling eyes and entreating expression. "Name it. If I know it, I'll sing it," she acquiesced, eyes easing over his handsome facade.

"'Love Comes From The Blue,'" he answered casually.

She tensed. "That's rather a new song. Where did you hear it?"

"The place didn't make an impression, but the song did," he responded lightly. "Do you mind singing it for your lonely husband?"

"You have been most polite. I suppose that deserves a special song," she sweetly remarked, actually smiling up at him. "If you wish, you may join me for a glass of wine—one glass," she stressed.

He looked stunned by her invitation. He sat down before she could withdraw it. She turned and called the serving girl over, asking for another glass. It was brought quickly, and she poured the red fluid with grace. She handed it to him; he was still staring quizzically at her.

She smiled. "I asked you to sit down a moment to tell you something. I didn't want to draw more attention to us than you've already done with your incessant staring." He chuckled and smiled, shrugging casually.

"I'm sorry, Kat. I didn't realize I was annoying you."

"The name is Kathyrn, not Kat," she corrected. "That isn't why I wanted to speak with you. You recall our talk your first night here?" He nodded, and she went on, "I thought you should know I think you're right in your assumption. As to why, I haven't the vaguest idea. Let's halt our silent war; I don't want any trouble before I leave. Is that agreeable to you?"

A pensive frown appeared briefly on his arresting face, but was hastily covered with a genial smile. "Agreed."

When she sighed in relief, he asked, "Kat, are you worried about something? Has Soapy said or done anything to frighten you? Please let me get you away from here."

She didn't meet his probing gaze, but she shook her head. "Then why this sudden offer of truce?" he softly demanded. What had her frightened?

don't have time to explain; Trace will be returning soon. If you want the truce, fine; if not, fine. I'm just tired of the strain and the stares. It's causing gossip and speculation. I think it would be best for both of us if we appeared . . . as loving mates until this farce is over."

"Mates?" he echoed, grinning with undisguised pleasure.

"Only for appearances, Mr. Jurrell," she burst his bubble.

"How long are you planning to punish me?" he questioned seriously. "We're both miserable. Is it so hard to . . ." Trace's return cut off the remainder of his words.

"Landis, what are you doing here?" Trace asked, his gaze going from his friend to Kathy. Something was in the wind . . .

Landis chuckled falsely, then winked at Kathy. "We just decided to make a fresh start, old chap. Perhaps we should drink to it."

"About time, don't you think?" Kathy caught his hint and responded.

Landis smiled and drained his glass. He set the glass down by hers and playfully murmured, "A man of his word, one glass."

"I'll remember," she parried, a smile flickering in her eyes.

He headed for his table. He sat down and called the serving girl over to give his order, brandy tonight. The girl smiled enticingly at him to irritate Kathy. It was only minutes before the brazen Molly was asking Landis to dance. He shook his head and said something to her. She laughed flirtatiously and caressed his chiselled jawline. Landis captured her hand and spoke with her again, chuckling softly when he finished. A petulant look twisted Molly's ruby red mouth. It appeared she was miffed. It was also clear she was sending out seductive signals even a blind man could read!

Kathy tried to ignore the distracting vision before her stormy eyes. The cocky scoundrel! Did he think her truce handed him a victory? How dare he carry on like this in front of her! What would people think?

As Molly stalked off, Landis caught sight of Kathy's intense observation. Could that be jealousy and fury in those turbulent and beautiful blue eyes? He grinned at her and shrugged roguishly, deliriously pleased.

Trace shook her arm and teased, "You aren't listening, Kathy."

She pulled her gaze from Landis's and asked, "What?"

"I asked you to dance," he repeated. "Will Landis mind?"

"Fine," she rashly agreed, sending Landis a taunting look.

Trace held her chair for her to get up, then escorted her into the adjoining room to dance a lively polka. She was breathless and laughing when she returned. She refused to even glance in her love's direction, taking Trace's seat to place her slender back to him.

Landis chuckled underbreath. He left for a moment to speak with the musicians. Shortly he returned, grinning devilishly at her as he passed by her table. Kathy smiled at him, her displeasure lucid.

When she returned to the stage, she did Soapy's request first. After numerous songs, it was time to break once more. Before she did, she stated casually, "This ballad was requested by my husband who twice saved my life. For you, Landis," she said softly, then sang it without taking her eyes from his. Just to pique him, she repeated the refrain twice:

When loves comes from the blue,
It calls out to me and to you.
When loves imprisons your heart,
Nothing can tear you apart.
So, you dreamers, please be true;
When loves comes from the blue.

She stood up gracefully and bowed as they applauded, all except Landis. He sat there dumbstruck, staring at her, desiring her wildly. Did she even recognize the truth in that haunting melody?

As she seemingly floated down the two steps to the floor, Landis went into action as they had planned. He gently caught her arm and insisted, "I believe this dance is mine. If you refuse, you'll cause a nasty scene."

"No, I won't," she debated, dreading yet savoring contact with his skin.

"Dance or cause a scene?" he quizzed.

"Either," she retorted, holding her voice low.

"I will, if you don't dance with me," he warned playfully.

"I don't dance with customers," she pertly informed him.

"You dance with Trace, then refuse your husband?" he teased.

Soapy was standing in the archway, mentally prodding her. From the corner of her eye, she noted Smith's eager expression. She sighed dramatically for both men's benefit, then flippantly agreed, "Very well, Landis. But just one dance. I need my energy to perform."

He grinned and sent Soapy a look which said, "I told you so."

As they approached the dancing area, the musicians softened the music and slowed the pace. When she realized it would be a slow dance to a romantic song, she nearly refused. "You afraid to be close to me, even in public where you're safe?" he taunted her.

"Why should I?" she sassed him.

"Why indeed, Mrs. Jurrell?" he ventured huskily.

"You stop that this minute, Landis Jurrell," she warned as he swept her into his arms and onto the polished floor.

"You must admit, love; I've been on my best behavior for two weeks. I do have a black image in your mind that sorely demands cleaning," he whispered into her ear, clasping her too close for comfort.

"That would require more time than I have left here. You amaze me, Landis," she stated, smiling saucily.

"How so, love?" he inquired, gazing down into her upturned face. His hand tightened on hers, his eyes engulfing hers.

"Please don't damage the hand; I do need use of it to work," she chided. "And my name isn't 'love' either."

He threw back his head and chuckled. "Praytell, what's so amusing?" she demanded, stiffening in his disturbing arms.

"You, Kathryn Jurrell. I just realized the tables have turned. Now, I'm doing the chasing and you're doing the fleeing. I wonder why."

"I don't believe we're playing the same game anymore. You're a very skilled dancer. Is there nothing you can't do?" she snapped, vexed at his near-perfection. Her pulse was racing madly.

"It isn't a game, Kat. And thank you. I usually manage to stay off the toes, but I don't get much practice. I wish I could accomplish all I set out to do. If I could, you would be in my cabin right this minute," he impulsively stated, emphasizing each word.

"If I didn't believe your threat about causing a scene, I would slap that smug leer off your handsome face. You're damn good at everything, and you know it," she gritted out just above a whisper.

"Your confidence in me is most inspiring, love," he murmured.

"As if you need anything from me, including my approval."

"Oh, I need and want plenty from you, love," he boldly hinted.

"Like what? My help with two matters involving two men?"

He leaned back to look at her. "No, Kat. The last thing I want is you involved with anything risky. I just want the chance to prove you're wrong about me. I once gave you that same opportunity," he huskily reminded her. "Don't I deserve the same generosity?"

"So I'll naively fall victim to you again? What's the matter, Landis; you hurting for a new mistress?" she taunted him.

"I didn't have an old one," he snarled in exasperation. "I don't want you for a legal mistress, Kat. But I do want you."

She feigned surprise. "If it isn't a little ole job as legal mistress or spy, whatever could you possibly want from me, sir?" she purred in a heavy Southern drawl, eyes wide and falsely innocent.

"You would be shocked to learn the answer to that question, young lady. I can promise you, you'll know within the next few months."

She met his steady gaze and insouciantly whispered in that same borrowed accent, "Alas, my dashing guide, I dreadfully fear I shall never learn the secrets of your treacherous heart. To my great dismay, sir, I shall be safely ensconced in America before you realize I'm gone."

"You've been wondering about me since the day we met, Kat. Too scared to hang around to hear the truth? Afraid I'll prove you wrong? In a few months, everything about me and my business will be in the open. Then, we can decide what to do about us," he added, enticing a strange look to her eyes, one she quickly vanquished. How he missed those lucid eyes which were clear and honest!

"Us? There is no 'us' to keep me here. Your many secrets didn't come between us, Landis; you did."

"There is an us, Kat. Are you dead set against living with me?" he calmly delivered his probing question, his eyes impenetrable.

"Live . . . with you?" she stammered in disbelief, her traitorous heart racing wildly. "We tried that before. You must be crazy."

"I'm not asking right now," he promptly corrected her, noting the stricken look on her face. She quickly lowered her head and inhaled slowly. As she released it, she lifted an impassive face to him.

His own heart was thudding heavily. He had spoken too soon and too bluntly. He tried to extricate himself without doing more damage, "I'm still not in a position to think of our future. If I did ask you to come home in a few months, what would you say?"

Her answer was cautious. "I won't be here to answer, Landis."

"Stay, Kat, at least until June," he coaxed tenderly.

Her eyes darted about as she pondered this insanity.

498

What was he trying to pull? Was he afraid she was taking those cursed reports with her? Was he using this cruel ploy to stall until he could recover them? This seemingly sudden change of heart alarmed her. She levelled her gaze on him. "Tell me, Landis, what do you expect in exchange for this promise? The reports? Evidence on Soapy? My father's head?"

He sighed heavily. "I thought I'd given you time to vent some of that bitterness and mistrust. Evidently I was mistaken. I'll take you to your table. I'm not going to beg anyone for anything, not even you."

"Is this the spot where your blackmail is supposed to panic me into submission? Is this the moment I'm supposed to confess how much I've misjudged you, how sorry I am, how much I love you? Oh, yes, I almost forgot; I'm probably supposed to swear I'll do anything to settle this misunderstanding between us. Which do you want to hear first?" she scathingly attacked him, so softly and sweetly that no one was aware of the storm brewing between them.

She could read the rising fury in his intimidating gaze and feel the tension mounting within his towering frame. He growled softly, "I would settle for an 'I love you.'" His embrace tightened noticably.

"Agreed. I love you," she stated flippantly.

"I've beaten men for a lesser offense than you just committed, Kat. Be forewarned, wife, you'll hear the truth before I allow you to sail. But I promise you, I'll never beg for your love. If another offer is ever spoken between us, it'll come from those enticing lips."

"Don't hold your breath. You'll expire first. You've pulled some brutal tricks before, but none could ever compare to this one."

She smiled sweetly and pulled free. For other ears, she stated, "Thanks for the dance, love. If you'll excuse me, I have some singing to do." She turned and gracefully strolled away.

Landis followed after her, then claimed his chair and tossed down two brandies. The remainder of the evening was passed in phony gaiety for her and moody silence for him. Finally, Landis got up and left. Kathy finished her evening's performance and was seen back to Paradise House by Jack and Trace. The night cold and windy, they didn't linger to chat.

Kathy slowly undressed, cursing the unlucky golden dress. She wouldn't wear it again! She pulled on her flannel gown and angrily brushed her hair. She turned back the covers, but the bed seemed exceptionally cold and empty. She yanked the heavy quilt off and spread it out before the fire. She lay down and curled toward the warmth it radiated. She had half expected to find Landis waiting for her, ready to verbally attack her for her actions tonight. She never stopped to wonder how he had gotten in that other night. She assumed she had carelessly left the door unlocked. She had double-checked every day since that one. Another time, it might not be Landis waiting for her! But tonight, she wished he was.

She restlessly flipped to her back. She didn't even realize she was crying and the tears were now easing down into her tawny hair, which was fanned out around her head like a golden halo. Why did she feel so utterly miserable, so alone, so frightened? Why did her heart plead for any crumbs of affection from Landis? Why did her body ache for his? What had he done to her? She felt like an opium addict who had been cruelly denied that anesthetizing, euphoric white powder.

Her eyes finally closed. She drifted on a tranquil ocean. Landis's unique odor assailed her slumbering senses. Her eyes fluttered and partially opened. They fused with eyes as dark as night, as compelling as a bottomless ebony pit. He was half-kneeling beside her; one knee touched her hip and one foot braced near her shoulder. He bent forward and reached down to stroke her silky hair, still damp near her temples. How angelic and vulnerable she looked. His finger ever so lightly removed the baffling tear stains, then tenderly moved over her parted lips.

She couldn't look away or think clearly; she didn't want to. If she couldn't have him in reality, then she would take him in this beautiful dream world. She lifted her arms to beckon him. His shirt was missing. Her eager hands touched his taut sides, then slipped up his chest to savor the feel of his hard muscles and its furry covering. Unable to reach past his heart, she raised up to clasp his broad shoulders and pull him down with her, sighing peacefully.

Her hands explored every plane on his face. She was like a thirsty soul drinking in life's sustaining fluid. One hand encircled his neck and the other went behind his head, fingers wandering into black hair. Her movements entreated his lips to hers, searing them together. Her arms went around him, clinging fiercely to his muscular body, fearing this tormentingly exquisite fantasy would vanish. She prayed she wouldn't awaken as she sampled the sweet nectar of his mouth. There was a desperation and urgency in her kisses and caresses. She almost savagely ravished his intoxicating mouth. When he leaned back to stare into eyes glazed with smoldering passion, she honestly pleaded, "Love me, Landis, please love me. I need you." That was far more than Landis needed for encouragement. His mouth closed over hers and sent any lingering awareness off into oblivion.

Twenty-Three

Landis's lips deftly and hungrily captured Kathy's. It had been so long since they had come together! The last time, both had been left frustrated and depressed. In this heady moment, nothing mattered to either except total possession. Tonight, passions soared and hearts pleaded.

He covered her face with kisses, then trailed them down her throat. His agile fingers unbuttoned her gown and opened the bodice to bare her ivory flesh to his greedy senses. His lips roamed her breasts to tease each protruding peak. She moaned as he ignited and fanned her molten passions. She didn't halt him when he removed her gown and bloomers; she moved to assist their departure. His pants joined his shirt and boots beside the quilt. He imprisoned her in his possessive embrace.

His hands tantalized her quivering flesh, mutely demanding its response to his loving assault. Slowly one hand drifted over her flat stomach, causing it to tighten momentarily. It sought another peak to caress, driving her mindless with achingly sweet sensations. Their height of passion too great to be restrained, he eased between her willingly parted thighs, slipping easily into her moist paradise to explore, conquer, and claim it.

As he entered and withdrew several times, he feared

he would instantly explode and be unable to carry her over that mountain she was rapidly scaling. He briefly halted his stimulating movements to cool his overheated ardor. He drank love's nectar from her lips and breasts, inspiring her to writhe beneath him and feverishly grind her blond forest against his black one.

He whispered words of caution, but she was too captivated with desire to heed them, her senses ardently absorbing him. He gingerly began to move within her once more, his manhood teasing the tense nerves there. The moment he knew she was approaching the summit, he increased his plunges, driving her over the crest to go spiriling downward into the peaceful valley on the opposite side. His pattern set, he couldn't have halted his own eruption if his life had depended on it. Tossing all cares to the winds, he sailed after her, joining her upon that tranquil sea of contentment.

When all was spent, he rolled aside. Kathy curled against him, snuggling her face next to his heart. He closed his arms around her, resting his jaw against her silky head. His leg was over her thighs, holding her pinned to his languid frame. His fingertips slowly trailed up and down her spine. She sighed happily and cuddled even closer, her eyes closed dreamily.

Thus they lay enraptured, until his voice dashed the arresting spell. "Will you stay until June, Kat?" he murmured against her ear.

Reality couldn't have been more stunning than if he had tossed icy water on her naked body. She tensed. Her head slowly and fearfully leaned away. She gazed into his smiling eyes. The color drained from her face. "My God, you're real. I thought I was dreaming."

His hand covered her mouth, warning, "Sh-h-h, you'll wake someone."

When he took his hand away, she gaped at him in disbelief. "How did you get in here? I thought I locked the door. How careless can I be? Anyone could have come in here." Her terrified gaze flew to the door. "Did you lock it when you sneaked in like some thief?"

"You didn't leave it unlocked, Kat. I have ways of entering any place I choose," he misled her, afraid to confess he had a key, knowing how that news would strike her. He wound a curl around his finger.

She asked sullenly, "Then why don't you use that skill to search Soapy's office? You can surely accomplish more there than here."

"I'm not so sure," he murmured, grinning. "He has guards everywhere."

But Kathy was all too aware of those guards. Her gaze fell to his bare chest and widened. She moved slightly to glimpse their positions. "You vile snake, how dare you steal into my room and seduce me while I'm sleeping!" she accused, punching him near his heart. "You don't own me."

He smothered a cough. "I'm innocent of that charge, madam. You seduced me. I only came to talk, but you begged me to make love to you. What was I to do? Refuse my wife when she reached for me and pleaded, 'Love me, Landis; please, love me. I need you'?"

She was about to hotly deny his claims when she vividly recalled saying those exact words. Fiery patches flamed on her pale cheeks. "I didn't . . . know what . . . I was saying. I . . . thought . . . thought you . . . were only a dream," she sputtered. "You knew I was groggy; you took advantage of me, and you know it. What happened to 'in name only' and our truce?"

"I plead guilty as charged, madam. You were utterly irresistible. I couldn't help myself. No jury in the world would convict me once they saw the stunning evidence," he teased lightly, waving his hand over her naked body.

"It isn't a crime to make love to one's wife."

"You're a beast, Landis. If you insist, I'll take half the blame."

He infuriated her when he readily concurred, "I insist. You wanted me as much as I wanted you. You shouldn't lie around so seductively, making a man forget himself, especially a lonely husband."

She sent him a scowl. "Speaking of forget, why did you come here?"

"To apologize for being an ass again tonight. I pushed you into a corner; I should have known my fiesty Kat would come out hissing and clawing. I won't do it again. I'll give you all the time you need to make your decision." He leaned over to tease a taut peak with ivory teeth.

"Stop that! What decision?" she asked in bewilderment.

"Whether or not you'll remain here until June?"

"There's no decision to be made. I'm leaving the first of April."

"I meant, will you stay willingly or will I have to force you?"

"You're threatening me with arrest again?" she asked incredulously.

"If you leave me no choice," he lazily answered.

"You wouldn't dare," she murmured, doubt in her eyes.

"I'm afraid I would, Kat, if you make it necessary."

"But it isn't necessary," she argued. "You could hold me here . . . until even Hell freezes and I couldn't hand them over. I am innocent."

"I know. That's not why I'll force you to stay."

"If you mean until you locate Jake, that could also be forever."

"But that's not the reason either." He sensually kissed her shoulder.

Exasperated, she entreated, "Then, would you mind enlightening me? I haven't the foggiest idea what you're talking about."

"Yes, you do, Kat. The truth, remember?" he prodded.

Comprehension and puzzlement battled for first place in her eyes. "You'll arrest me to keep me here for your monumental revelation?"

"That's about the size of it. You'll be the first to know when the time is right." His self-assured aura and arrogant stare sent chills over her. It was stunningly obvious he was serious, but also highly enflamed with passion.

"I don't crave your secrets. You might recall from that investigatory letter, I have friends in the highest American offices. If you dare bring false charges against me, they'll fight you. How will your precious Mounties and Canadian Government feel when your phony arrest causes an international crisis between our two countries? I think you'll be most humiliated to have everyone learn you forced an unwilling woman into marital captivity because she rejected you," she made some threats of her own.

It was his turn to scoff, "You wouldn't dare. I know you, Kat. You wouldn't publicly humiliate yourself like that. We have enough problems with your blasted country and people; we don't need any more."

"Then don't create one, Landis. Don't arrest me," she stated.

"Why do you keep saying, arrest? How would I have the power to arrest you?" he asked curiously, poised for her answer.

"I didn't mean you personally. I was referring to your influence with your lofty friends at Log Cabin. Even if they go along with this absurd idea, their careers would be devastated. Somehow I can't see a proud and indomitable Mounty agreeing to such foolishness."

"It would probably surprise you what Mounties would do to get their man," he snapped, while gently biting her chin.

"But I'm not 'their man.' And stop distracting me. If you know I don't have the reports, does that mean you've found them?" she realized what he had said earlier, her expression so lucidly honest he couldn't deny it.

"No, I don't have them; but I will. Have you heard any of Soapy's men mention . . . Never mind! Are you staying or not?"

"No," she replied simply.

"You'll just get on that dang ship without ever learning the truth?" He watched an unreadable array of emotions cross over her face.

"Your 'truth.' What makes you think it will change anything? Will it justify what you've done? Will it magically heal all the wounds you've brutally inflicted? No secret is that powerful."

"Nothing will change your mind about me?" he insisted. He grinned seductively and murmured, "Not even the fact I love you? Or this?" he hinted, wildly ravishing her mouth until she almost gasped for air. "Or this?" he continued, circling her breasts with a moist tongue until she trembled with fiery desire. "Or perhaps this?" he whispered into her ear as his hands skillfully roamed her lithe body, setting wildfires wherever his flaming hands touched.

"You're a tormenting devil, Jurrell. You know my weakness for you and you're exploiting it," she sultrily admonished him. "If only you were as susceptible to my charms," she hinted provocatively.

"That's the trouble, Kat; I am," he huskily confessed, captivated by his own game. "Why did you bewitch me? I want you so much it hurts." She fused her searching gaze to his pleading one. "Love me, Kat; please love me," he entreated, pulling her tightly against him.

She leaned back to look into his eyes, unable to deny the emotions emblazoned there. "I'm here, Landis; all you have to do is reach out for me," she helplessly surrendered, kissing him and clinging to him.

All problems and misgivings cast aside, they joined in fierce and fiery passion. In the golden afterglow of contentment, he refused to release her from his powerful embrace. She chided him, "Must you hold me so tightly; I can't breathe. I'm not going to vanish, my love, unless you force it."

"Every time I see you, Kat, I fear it will be the last time. Promise you'll wait around until I can explain everything," he coaxed. "Don't desert me, Kat."

"What secret could be so powerful to excuse all you've done and said? If by some miracle, you're sincere; then prove it. If you love me and trust me, tell me everything tonight; I'll leave with you the instant you finish," she challenged, feeling confident and secure after his claims of love and display of uncontrollable passion. "Give me reasons to stay."

He tensed and studied her defiant expression. He sighed heavily. "I can't, love. If you truly love me, then you'll trust me a while longer, you'll wait until I'm free of this business."

"I can't, love," she mocked. "It's now or never. The choice is yours."

"No, Kat, it isn't. I gave my word on something long before we met. I'm not free to halt now. All I'm asking is for you to wait here until I can settle this prior agreement," he urged.

"That day in Dray's cabin, you said it could be years before you would be free of this secret obligation. Will it truly be over by June?"

A smile creased the corners of his eyes and mouth. "What do you know about that! I'm lying here emptying my guts bargaining for something I already have. Admit it, Kat; you don't hate me or want to abandon me. You never have. You still love me," he stated confidently.

Landis made a terrible mistake in judgment, pressing her to a wall once more. "Do I, Landis?" she questioned.

Her tone and look caused dreadful doubts. "You're driving me crazy, woman. Do you love me and want me or not?" he demanded, unnerved.

"That remains to be seen, doesn't it?"

"I won't let you leave here," he repeated in firm resolve.

"If you think I'm a fiesty cat now with sharp claws, you haven't seen me at my best. If you hold me with force, you'll have a caged tiger on your hands. That can be dangerous to a man in your position. Divorce me or become committed to me. I'll even give you two weeks to decide."

"I did it again, didn't I? The cornered tigress," he jested.

"You do seem to possess a knack for bringing it out."

"All right, Kat, have it your way. For now," he added.

He stood up and began pulling on his clothes. When dressed, he looked down at her. She had pulled the edge of the quilt over her body, concealing all except her head from the eyes up. He gazed into them. "When it's feeding time, my wild tigress, will you call me?" he jested mischievously.

She shoved the quilt down past her mouth. "If I ever get that hungry. But there does seem to be a wide selection of meat around here."

He dropped to his knees and yanked her into his arms. His mouth seared hers, leaving her breathless when he pulled away. "I'll kill any man who touches you. You're mine, Kat, mine. I'll never let you go." With that startling statement, he slipped out.

She gaped at the door in stunned silence. He was such a mercurial man. Why did he toy with her like this? He called her Kat; but he was the tomcat and she was a tiny mouse. He didn't have to worry; he was the only man she wanted! If he loved her, why couldn't he reveal the secrets which were tearing them apart? Why no reply to her two-week offer?

It was mid-afternoon when Landis convinced Nelle he needed to see Kathy privately. She grinned with pleasure, reading the tenderness and determination in his eyes. She told him all the girls were at Soapy's getting new orders, all except Kathy. She told the eager man his wife was in Michelle's old room. He smiled, that fact known to him. Kathy had been right last night; it was time to settle two vital matters; love and marriage!

"Keep an eye out, Nelle. I don't want anyone to know I've seen her. Understand?" When she nodded, he instructed, "Knock on the door if anyone comes in." He would snatch her before anyone was the wiser! If she needed proof of his affections and intentions, he would damn well supply it! It was time for Kat Marlowe to discover herself!

"Don't forgit 'bout that guard nigh tha front door," she reminded.

He headed down the hallway for Kathy's room. Just as he was about to turn the corner, muffled voices halted his tracks. He started to retreat hastily, but recognized both voices. He furtively peered around the corner. His heart drummed madly; fury washed over him. Kathy was in Trace's arms! He was holding her against him. Her face was turned in the other direction. They were whispering almost too softly for him to hear their words. Trace lifted her chin and looked into her eyes. "Don't worry, Kathy, I won't let him come near you again. When I get to Log Cabin, I'll settle this matter once and for all. If need be, I'll kill him."

He kissed her forehead as she raggedly murmured, "I don't know what I would do without you to rescue me, Trace. He terrifies me."

"Let's go inside. We need to talk. I'll tell you what I plan to do about him." With his arm around her shoulders, Trace led Kathy into her room, fearing to release her lest her shaky legs collapse.

Landis fingered the revolver at his waist, fury building to a perilous level. He balled his fist and jammed it into his other hand. He was tempted to kick that door down and justly slay both of them. What a fool he was! She definitely carried Dory's evil blood and wanton cravings! He was flooded with comprehension for Ben's past decision to desert his family. He turned and walked back into the fragrant kitchen, fearing his dark rage.

Nelle looked up from her baking. She wondered at the black scowl on his face. "I changed my mind. This isn't the time to complicate matters. She'll be leaving soon. I'll see her then. Promise you won't tell her I was here," he wheedled. "I want to surprise her later."

Nelle smiled and agreed, then Landis slipped outside.

In Kathy's room, Trace was attempting to comfort the distraught Kathy. She had completed her revealing story about Marc Slavin. She was still crying, rubbing her bruised wrists where Marc had grabbed her. "I thought he was gone, Trace. I had no idea he was lurking around here. If you and Jack hadn't come over, he would have killed me."

"I'll take good care of him, Kathy. Jack's holding him down the street. I'm taking him to Log Cabin now. Sergeant Thomas will deal with his assault on you. He won't bother you again."

"It petrifies me to think he's been near Dawson all this time. He's probably been watching me, just waiting for the chance to get me alone. He's crazy, Trace. I've never seen such hatred in anyone's eyes. He threatened to get even with Landis, too. You've got to warn Landis."

"When I see Landis, I'll tell him what happened today. You feeling better now?" he asked with genuine concern for her state. He held a cold, wet cloth to her finger-bruised throat, infuriated by Slavin's attack.

"That's twice you've saved my life. I'm indebted to you, Mounty Blitch," she murmured, then shuddered. "I wish Landis were here."

"You best get some hot coffee and over to that fire. You've had quite a scare, young lady. I'll be back in four or five days. I'll send Landis up."

"Thanks, Trace. You're a real friend." She snuffled softly.

He smiled. "You are, too, Kathy. See you later."

She opened the door and let him out, waving goodbye.

Jack, Trace, and the bound Marc Slavin headed for Log Cabin. With Marc cursing and fighting them, it took three days. After their arrival, the crafty Marc convinced them they had insufficient evidence to hold him. He boasted of how it was Kathy's word against his, that he could prove she was a whore, that he could prove Jurrell had forced her to marry him. He loudly proclaimed his American citizenship and elite family wealth and status. When neither Jack nor Trace could visually vouch for Kathy's charges, Bill Thomas was forced to set him free, compelled to protect Landis over Kathy by keeping attention away from him. Thomas said Kathy would have to personally come to Log Cabin to register a complaint against Slavin. When Marc sneered she would never bring charges against him, Trace almost slugged him. He warned Marc he would kill him if he ever went within ten miles of her. Jack and Bill added their serious threats to Trace's.

While Jack furtively trailed Marc to see where he would head, Trace set out for Dawson again: the round trip required five days. He ranted over Clint's actions and sympathized with the girl who was wed to Landis Jurrell, a man who didn't exist. What a cruel deception!

Landis appeared once during Trace's absence, the third day after his departure. He entered Soapy's saloon during Kathy's performance and sat down at her private table. It had taken two days alone in his cabin to risk seeing her. Even watching her on the stage, his fingers itched to get around her throat in that high-neck dress that concealed it.

Should he arrest her and keep her under wraps for a while? No, he couldn't risk that. He mentally scoffed, the sly vixen had planned her strategy well! His fury returned as he realized how dangerously close he had come to telling her everything. Odd, if Soapy or Kat had his file, they already knew his identity, so why this daring scheme? If Kat knew, would her purpose be revenge? Senseless revenge, since they were wed. As if his defeat wasn't enough for them, she was picking Trace's brain, too! Had Trace touched his wife? Doubtlessly she never expected Jake to be here. What a family team they made! Ben had been away two weeks. Landis wondered if he would find the false information lying in wait for him in the secret hole.

When she left the stage, she was surprised to see him sitting there. She smiled radiantly as she approached him. He masked the turmoil seething within him. "I didn't expect to see you so soon," she teased, unaware of his tightly leashed temper, wanting to race into his arms.

"Didn't you?" he huskily debated. "I don't give up so easily."

"Determination and perseverance are two of your

better traits?"

"Among other things," he hinted, testing to see if she was still pursuing him now that she had perfidiously bedazzled Trace.

"I'm glad," she stated warily, smiling apprehensively.

"Are you?" he pressed, something oddly intimidating in his tone.

"The game's over. What are you terms, Jurrell? I yield."

"The game isn't over until the last card's played. And I seem to have it, a lovely Ace. You forget those lessons I gave you when you were living with me?" His obsidian eyes glowed ominously, his reaction stupifying her.

She paled. He hadn't spoken where anyone could overhear, but his words and tone astounded her. He was certainly in a foul mood tonight. She didn't help matters when she innocently asked, "Have you seen Trace yet? He has something to tell you." She didn't want to go into that horrible event here. She anxiously waited for him to coax, let's go home; she would instantly agree on any terms. She could hardly control herself.

"Yep, I saw him before I left. I was around until late afternoon," he lazily responded, watching her closely. "I have business here today."

She looked at him strangely. "You're only here on business? Why didn't you stop by to see me before you left? I'm surprised you didn't rush over. I believe you vowed to kill any man who touched me?"

"What makes you think I was interested in Trace's news?" he casually questioned, intrigued by her look of unconcealed anguish and rising anger. Was she trying to get them to battle over her, to kill each other? Was that Soapy's satanic plan? Disbelief filled her eyes; her face drained of color.

"What? You don't care that he . . . I . . . I see," she

faltered, her lips trembling. She was straining to keep her poise and temper. "Well, I should say I'm surprised and disappointed it doesn't bother you; but I shouldn't be. You really had me fooled, Jurrell. You had me believing you really cared. That's a funny joke, isn't it? Now that your pretense is dropped, what now? Ready to reclaim your borrowed name?"

"Who knows, Kat? I haven't decided what to do about you. I think you should keep the 'Jurrell'; you surely earned it. I might find some use for you. You can bet I'm more dangerous than Soapy, or equally so."

Threats? "I don't doubt that at all. If you've come here tonight to badger me, go ahead. Maybe that's just what I need, to see you viciously ripping me apart again. Take your bloody name and go to hell."

"Cut the victim act, love; it won't work on me. You deserve everything you get. I have no intention of freeing you or embarrassing myself. One look at a ravishing woman in tears and they would think I'm a spurned man bent on spite. What did you tell Soapy?" He didn't have the time or clear wits to analyze her words or curious behavior.

"Why would I discuss such a horrible thing with him?"

"You are working for him, aren't you?"

Losing his meaning, she replied, "You know I do."

"No, Kat. I mean working for him in another way."

"How dare you! I've never told him anything."

"I could care less what you do, unless it involves spying on me. Is that why you pretended to be asleep the other night? Did you really think I would fall for such a silly trick? I'll admit you're good, Kat. But I've seen the best operate. Michelle was one of the best. Soapy figured a beautiful, wily vixen might succeed where she had failed miserably. Did you marry me before or after going to work for him? Have you given him the bad news yet? If so, I hope he treats you kindly. He does seem to like you more. Or were you hoping to have another shot at me? I'm available tonight," he wickedly hinted, "if you lack a man to work on."

Kathy was gaping at him. He couldn't be saying such things and meaning them, but he was and did. "I have other plans in motion," she lied to cover her torment. She had to flee him immediately.

She stood up to leave. She paused and leaned over, fusing her gaze with his. She whispered, "I would never do anything to endanger your miserable life. I tried to avoid you and resist you. You see, my dear husband, I was hopelessly and recklessly in love with you. You've earned another victory. Add it to your record." She turned and left.

She went to Soapy's office and told him she wasn't feeling well. She asked if she could leave early, promising to make up the lost time tomorrow night. When he asked why she was so upset, she was too distraught to be cautious or afraid. She struggled to master her tears and tremblings. She tried to leave before an emotional collapse.

He cursed and seethed underbreath. "It's that Slavin, isn't it? I should have killed him before Blitch could get him out of my town. If they release him, I will. You want to talk a while?" he probed for information, wondering if this Slavin's attack was the crux of her resistance to Jurrell. Too bad his own man Tom didn't get to Slavin first!

"I really don't want to discuss it, Mr. Smith. It was a terrifying experience," she softly refused, cheeks rosy on a pale face.

"Kathy, it happened several days ago. Why are you so distressed tonight?" he suddenly asked, thinking her state baffling.

"Landis . . . is outside," she said faintly.

Soapy's eyes glittered. "Is he forcing you to go home?"

"No. May I go to my room now?" she asked in a small voice.

"What's he doing here? Why isn't he punishing the snake who attacked his own wife?" he snarled, knowing something was amiss.

"I'm not his wife anymore. Please, may I go now," she pleaded, as if he was holding her captive, too upset to think clearly.

"You go on, Kathy. I'll have a little talk with Jurrell."

"No!" she shrieked, terrified. "Please, Mr. Smith, don't cause any more trouble for me. We're still married, and he'll be furious. I'll be gone in another week," she pleaded, actually fearing Landis would lay a wild story on him and cause her more anguish and trouble.

"All right, Kathy. But I'm placing an extra guard at the house until you leave. When you're here, someone will be at your table every night. He won't bother you again," he promised, furious with Landis for thwarting his plans, but Kathy assumed the "he" was Marc.

Kathy smiled faintly and thanked him. She removed the jewelry and handed it to him. She went to find Luther to take her across the street. She headed straight for Nelle's room. The woman was surprised when she pleaded to sleep there tonight, then understood when Kathy related her terrifying episode with Marc. Nelle was briefly tempted to tell her Landis would protect her from that animal. Recalling her promise to him, Nelle didn't mention his visit the other day . . .

Twenty-Four

In spite of Kathy's plea, Soapy headed to confront his foe. He stalked to Landis's table, a menacing air surrounding him. "I want to see you in my office, Jurrell. We have some talking to do," he commanded icily, then turned to walk off, assuming the curious Landis would follow him.

Soapy walked around his desk and sat down. Landis dropped into a chair and leaned back, his body flexible and his gaze indifferent. Soapy boiled inside. "You want something?" Landis controlledly asked, unruffled.

"I believe there's a matter of a hundred dollar bet to settle. You ready to pay up tonight?" Soapy abruptly asked.

Landis saw the hidden pitfall in Smith's supposedly cunning ruse. He unflinchingly stated, "What makes you the winner?"

"By default," he clipped out smugly, his satanic mind plotting.

Landis mulled over those words, having difficulty comprehending them. "How did you come to that absurd conclusion?" he fenced. "If memory serves me, I am married to the girl in question."

"Winning would be impossible now," he stated coldly, his scornful stare drilling into the impenetratable eyes

518

of Jurrell.

Landis's sharp wits were quickly taking in Soapy's irritation and the insinuations behind his words. "Did the little woman tattle on me?" he playfully fenced with the less skillful man.

"Only after I insisted. She was so distraught she couldn't even continue tonight. I won't have you upsetting her. Take your business elsewhere from now on. She told me how you made her feel obligated to you. Rescuing her from one villain doesn't give you the right to force another one on her. The way you two men have abused her, she'll probably swear off all men!" he lied, his eyes flashing fires of revenge.

These statements registered, but Landis didn't have time to analyze them. Soapy's truculence baffled him. He probed for more clues to this puzzle. "How does that make you the winner?"

Soapy flared at him, losing his temper at the sight of Landis's composure and arrogance, "Stay away from her, Jurrell."

"Seeing as I'm her husband and you're only her temporary boss, don't you think your warning a bit absurd?" he taunted.

"You won't be her husband long," Smith sneered.

"Only if I agree to release her from her vows," he debated.

"She despises you; she's terrified of you. There's no way you can keep her against her will. You lose, Jurrell; admit it."

"Twice in the last week, she's offered to come home," Landis stated.

"You don't say? She's a real lady, Jurrell. There's damn few of those left, and none around these parts. She sees you as the Black Ogre. Even with your charms and skills, you couldn't win the bet before she leaves. You too proud to admit defeat? Tastes mighty sour, don't it?" Smith crowed his victory.

"That doesn't make me the loser in our bet," he announced.

"You're an arrogant bastard. Our little joke has gone too far. I should have realized you would do anything to win. But somehow, I hadn't pegged even you that low and despicable." He fumbled in his top drawer. "If it's a matter of pride and obstinance, take the winner's fee; the bet's cancelled. Stay away from her," he fiercely declared, tossing the money across the desk.

Landis looked at the money, then stared at Soapy with that piercing gaze of his. "What's the matter, Smith? You decided you want her for yourself and the competition's too stiff?" he taunted.

Soapy laughed, his evil smile twisting his lips into a contemptuous sneer. "I'm not a fool, Jurrell. The only man who stands a chance of winning Kathy in these parts is Trace Blitch. He's the only one bright enough to woo her with manners and patience."

"My wife is pursuing another man?" he mocked Smith. "If he can take her away, she isn't worth having," he said to fool Smith.

Soapy shook his head in disgust. His whole plot had fallen apart because of Jurrell's character. The insolent bastard was too dedicated to his only love: the Mounties! You'll lose, you arrogant liar, he mentally swore.

Landis watched a mocking smile appear on Smith's face which sent his rage fleeing. "Is this jealousy I detect in the immovable Landis Jurrell?" Smith taunted. "Take the money and go. Game's over. Blitch is the real winner, or soon will be. Perhaps I should encourage that relationship. Blitch'd make Kathy a fine husband. If she stayed, she could still work for me while she waits for him. Since she earns so much money and enjoys this job, Trace shouldn't mind sharing his wife. Don't appear your name helps her much, but who would dare insult the wife of a Mounty?"

"Mounties can't have wives, Smith," Landis told him.

"Ah, yes, I'd forgotten that silly rule," he murmured, glimmers of amusement flickered in his cold eyes.

Soapy grinned at the impassive man across his desk. "'Course Kathy inspires a man to tempt much, doesn't she?" Smith teased. "You don't think she's worth Trace's sacrifice?" he probed for some clues. "You married her."

Lusty laughter rumbled from Landis's chest. "I've met lots of Mounties, Smith. I've yet to come across one who would surrender everything for any female." Did Soapy know the truth? Why this change in strategy?

"I'd imagine she's the one female who could inspire a Mounty to reassess his life and values. If Kathryn Hammond was available and attainable, what intelligent Mounty wouldn't question his options?"

"You forget, Smith; she's Kathryn Jurrell. I hear they turn in their hearts in exchange for that uniform. Most men think it's an honor to be selected by the North-West Mounted Police."

"You sound envious. Your lifestyle and character suit their rules. Why don't you join? Aw, you aren't single," Smith taunted.

"I'm afraid I'm too spoiled and self-serving. I prefer going my own way and having to account only to me. Besides, a man doesn't join them; he's picked. Or so I've been told," he alleged.

"It's late. Take your winnings and get out. I don't want to see your face in here again. Savvy?" Smith abruptly ended their talk.

"I understand you clearly, Smith," Landis said smugly. "Keep the money. I don't take things I haven't earned. I'll take my business somewhere else, my wife too."

"I'll make sure you don't. I've placed extra guards around the house and her at all times. You won't be able to come near her."

"My, my . . . Aren't we the protective father all of a sudden," he scoffed sarcastically. "Kat working on another debt of gratitude?"

Incensed, Smith slammed his fist down on the desk as he jumped up to verbally attack Landis. "I'm the one indebted to her. She's bringing in over two thousand extra dollars a week. If my help can repay her, I'll see to it. I wish you would try to injure her; it'd give me a legal excuse to have you shot! My men will be on alert, Jurrell; one mistake, and you're a dead man," he warned, utterly serious.

Unaffected by Smith's wild threats, Landis slowly stood up, stretching his lithe body. "You should know by now, Smith; I know how to take real good care of myself. You send any of those wolverines of yours after me, and you'll be missing some hired hands. I even sleep with one eye open. You get any foolish ideas about arranging another phony accident for me, I guarantee it won't sit well. I'll go for the throat of their leader."

Late that night, Landis stealthily slipped into Kathy's room while the guard was carelessly dozing. He was alarmed to find her bed still neatly made. Soapy was being cautious and calculating. Was he keeping her at the saloon, under his sharp eye and within easy reach? Landis was befuddled and unnerved by their curious conversation. Things just didn't add up. Why had Kathy been crying? Why those confessions? Why comply with Smith's orders? His acute senses were spinning. He clenched his teeth in painstaking concentration until his jaw ached.

He sat down on her bed. Being a skilled guide, he returned to day one since coming here and step by step covered the winding trail to this point in time and place. He didn't like the way the evidence was stacking up. He defensively halted his probing mind from racing down another path, dreading to reach a final destination. Somehow, he had to force accurate answers from her! Or from Trace and Jake.

As surreptitiously as he had entered, he left. For two nerve-racking days, Landis tried to get to Kathy. True to his threat, Soapy and his guards made it impossible. She didn't return to her room each night.

Landis altered his course of action. If he couldn't get near her, a friend could; and he should when he heard Kat was in grave danger. For certain, Smith would use any excuse to kill Landis, so he dared not storm in and drag her out, wife or not. If Smith told Kat he was Marlowe, both would realize she was free of him. Landis needed Ben's help; then, he needed to check in at Log Cabin and talk to Trace. Landis left Dawson as soon as he'd made his decisions—missing Trace's arrival by another trail.

Kathy was relieved to see Trace on this fairly sunny Saturday. They ate lunch in the largest hotel, then talked. When he informed her of what happened with Slavin, she stared at him. Panic joined disbelief in her eyes. Her voice was strained when she asked, "How could they turn him loose? He was going to murder me, Trace. He's dangerously insane. Where is he now?" she asked in rising alarm.

"Jack's following him to see where he goes. I wish I could hang around until you're ready to leave, but I can't.

If he does show up here, Jack will be on his tail. You be very careful and alert. He's mad, but he's not dumb. He's been warned to stay away from you."

"Idle threats, Trace!" she scoffed. "He's been given countless warnings, including several beatings. He isn't afraid of any of you; don't you see that? He's obsessed with revenge. Tell me, Trace; will your outstanding Mounties arrest him when he finally kills me?" she scornfully challenged. Stars above, her own husband wouldn't help her!

"I know this makes you lose respect and faith in us. But we can't hold him. He's an American. Unless we can present a strong case against him, it'll cause trouble. I wish your government would lend us some assistance with the criminals they're dumping on us. The least they can do is send an agent to check out this situation. He won't harm you again."

"Landis made that same promise twice, for all the good it did. He could care less what Marc does to me," she accused hotly.

"Did you and he have another quarrel?" Trace asked.

Kathy refused to answer, but told him about Soapy's intensified protection and her gun. "I'll be perfectly safe until I leave."

Trace wisely didn't press her for clarification. They discussed his promise to take her money to Log Cabin, then headed for the bank, which was open every day except Sunday. Shown into bank president Dobb's office, the elderly, keen-witted man joined them. He smiled at Kathy and shook hands with Trace. He sat down behind his desk and looked at them.

"I have the money ready, Mrs. Jurrell. I gathered it in the largest American bills I have to make it easier and safer for Mounty Blitch to leave without notice. We'll carry out the rest of your plan when I come to dinner. We'll make certain everyone thinks you're leaving without it."

"Thank you, Mr. Dobbs; you've been most kind and helpful."

Trace concealed the money inside his waistband. As Dobbs walked them out, he stated in a distinct and slightly raised voice, "I'll be happy to hold your earnings until you send your friends back for it."

"Thank you, sir. I don't think it would be safe for a woman to travel alone with so much money. Good day, Mr. Dobbs."

Trace walked her to the boarding house and said farewell. "I'll try to get back. If not, I'll see you at Log Cabin or in Skagway."

Kathy thanked Trace for his help and friendship before he left. When she went to work early that evening, she headed to Soapy's office for two reasons: the jewelry, and news about Marc to aid her departure ploy. She knocked and was invited inside. Soapy halted his writing when he witnessed her distressed state. "Is Jurrell out there?" he asked, assuming that the reason of her emotional upheaval.

"No. Trace came to see me. He had some alarming news. The Mounties didn't arrest Marc. I'll finish out this week, Mr. Smith, then I'm getting far away from this savage land," she informed him.

"They actually turned him loose?" he said in surprise.

"Yes," she stated.

Soapy came around his desk and stood near her. "Don't worry, Kathy; my men will guard you. He'll skulk around until this dies down."

"I hope you're right," she said doubtfully.

He smiled. "I know so, Kathy. He'll bide his time until

he thinks you feel safe. By then, you'll be heading for America."

He led her to the oversized sofa, seating her. He gave her a glass of sherry. "You relax a little while, then go to the back room and freshen up. I think I'll have a look around before you go out there."

He left. Kathy sank against the sofa back and inhaled raggedly. She had to pull herself together. She was safe for now; neither man could get to her with Soapy's men on alert. She would do as Soapy had instructed, this one time. She would delight in leaving this place.

She pushed up her limp body. She reached for her shawl, having brought one to ease her chill. The shawl fell behind the sofa. She futilely leaned over the tall back. She went to the end and stuck her leg behind it. She sighed in annoyance. She got down on her hands and knees and squeezed into the tight area between the sofa and wall. She grasped the shawl and was ready to back out. Alone! Was this the chance she'd waited for? Until now, she had never been alone in here.

The door opened and Soapy stormed inside. Noticing her absence, he snarled to Luther, "We've got to figure out Jurrell's coded report!" He fumed.

Kathy froze, keeping her presence a secret. As the precarious pieces of the puzzle which had hurled her to this town fell into place, she almost laughed hysterically at the ludicrous timing of her elusive victory; it was too late to matter.

"Damn that infernal redbird! He thinks he's so cunning! But I know who and what he is!" Smith claimed smugly.

Kathy came to full alert. Would she finally learn the truth about Landis? But what did Smith mean, who he was?

"Now, I've got this trouble with Kathy! I was tempted to try and keep her, but I think it's best if she leaves as scheduled. Her problems are drawing too much attention from her Mounty friends—or she foolishly believes they are. That bastard ruined my plans for them! If he had fallen for her, I would have him right where I wanted him."

"It was a long shot, Soapy. After Michelle, it's no surprise he didn't trust Kathy," Luther reasoned to soothe his riled boss.

"He's a damn fool, Luther! I gave him too much credit for intelligence and instinct. Any imbecile can see Kathy doesn't have the wits and daring to do anything illegal or risky! Marlowe wanted her, all right, but only for one of his missions! I stole something I can't even read! Hell!"

"Think he was trying to get her to work with him like Michelle? You think that's why he pretended to marry her?" Luther asked.

"No way. He knows I wouldn't trust her. He was just trying to win that bet we had; he was determined to earn my hundred dollars. That phony marriage has something to do with her father. I wanted him to fall in love with her; all he wanted was to use her!"

Kathy was stunned, tormented, and confused by what she was hearing. She listened intently. She wondered what was supposed to happen if they had fallen in love; Soapy didn't expound right away. Luther's next question and Soapy's glacial, affirmative chuckle sent chills and tremors over her body, alerting her to her great peril.

"If she had agreed to spy for him, would you have gotten rid of her, too? Two accidents would look mighty suspicious."

Soapy's wintry chuckles answered. Accidents? her reeling brain asked. Cold-blooded murder! She had to escape! But how?

If she possessed the slightest doubt of Soapy's insidious nature, his next words removed it. "Kathy wouldn't be a problem. A neat fatal robbery on her return trip to Skagway," he stated coldly.

"She won't be taking her money along," Luther debated.

"What about an evil desperado on the trail who hasn't heard her plans? Some men murder and rob just for survival," he reminded.

"I like Miss Kathy, boss. I wouldn't want to see her harmed." He added almost ruefully, "She's been kind to me, gave me real respect. She was always talking to me and thanking me. She's a real lady, a heart of gold."

"Don't go getting sentimental on me, Luther," Soapy coldly chided.

"I ain't," Luther declared sullenly, worried about Kathy.

"I've got to decide what to do about these reports," he returned his attention to the problem at hand. "I can't risk holding them."

"Why don't you lure Marlowe here? Torture the information out of him," Luther suggested, terrifying Kathy.

"I could carve a Mounty into little pieces and he wouldn't talk, especially Sergeant Clinton Marlowe. I can tell, he don't give a shit about her. If only Marlowe had fallen for Kathy, then . . ." He paused to think. "A man in love, even an iron-willed one, would never stand by and watch his love sliced to ribbons. Pain wouldn't matter to him, but witnessing hers . . ." He didn't have to complete the petrifying scheme. He salaciously licked his dry lips, envisioning a sexual torment.

Kathy feared she would burst into screams or be sick. She did neither. She remained stiff and silent, bombarded with these revealed clues.

"I wonder when Marlowe's going to tell Kathy that Landis Jurrell doesn't exist. Mounties can't marry, so he can't have no future plans for her. Marlowe wouldn't end his career for a woman, surely not one he's used. When she hears the truth, she'll be glad she hasn't played his wife in bed. That little license isn't worth the paper it's written on. Open the safe and put these reports back," he ordered. "Here, put this jewelry in, too."

When Luther knelt before Soapy's large desk, Kathy could see where the safe was cunningly concealed. Her face resting against the cold floor, she watched Luther release a hidden catch under the edge of the desk. A panel opened, revealing a small and sturdy safe.

Soapy announced, "I'm going across the street to see Tinsley. You take care of this matter, then keep an eye on Kathy."

Soapy left as Luther began to work the combination. "Three times right to six . . . Two times left to twenty-eight . . . One time right to seventy-nine . . ." He pulled the door open and placed the jewelry and reports inside, then closed the door and twirled the lock. He snapped the wooden panel shut, then left.

Kathy remained where she was. She questioned this twist in fate. But the mind-staggering quirk was the combination which she could never forget. How could she? It was her date of birth: 6/28/79. Summoning her courage, she left her hiding place. She peeked around the corner of the office door. No one was in sight. She hurried to the girls' private room, went inside and exhaled in relief when she found it empty. She went over to the bed and sat down, a bed used only for sickness during working hours. Soapy would permit a short rest, but not any time off to recuperate.

So many facts and clues were spinning around in her mind. Should she leave now and forget everything? Was it all some terrible mistake? Landis's words kept running through her mind. It couldn't be true . . . Was that the great "sacrifice" and "choice", her or his Mounty career?

She deliberated on her perilous situation. The key to locking the door forever between her and Landis was now within her reach. Dare she risk using it? Landis hadn't lied or exaggerated about one thing: Soapy was lethal and relentless. But if Soapy hadn't lied, her life and love were cruel shams. How could she extricate herself from these dangers? Soapy would kill her if he suspected she knew such things; if her love was an undercover Mounty, Landis might, too . . .

Yet, the vision of being the one to hand that file over to Thomas was overpowering, temptation beyond resistence. Landis would discover she had daringly risked her life to end their involvement. She tried to imagine his expression and reaction to learning she had not only saved his file, but also his life. How would he explain his deeds? So, Landis Jurrell was really Clinton Marlowe . . .

America . . . Safety . . . No more terror, anguish, or sacrifices . . . No more traitorous love or self-betrayals . . . No rightful husband . . .

Home, that was the answer. There wasn't time to think and plan. She must force herself outside and through her performance. She must act her normal self until help arrived. Jack, that was the only person she could trust. If Landis had tricked and used her and if he was a Mounty, Trace was in on those deceptions. That fact alone inspired a strange calmness and courage in Kathy, perhaps a defensive numbing to all emotions until she was on that huge steamer gliding down the Inside Passage to Seattle and freedom. She went to the mirror. She washed her face and brushed her hair. She pinched her pale cheeks to add color. She smoothed the lines of her gown and adjusted the rubies at her throat. She balled her left hand, wanting to snatch off the treacherous gold band. She walked out.

Luther was leaning against the wall. He straightened as she came out. "I was about to ask Molly to check on you, Miss Kathy. You feeling better?"

"Yes, Luther," she murmured, deceiving him most convincingly.

Later in her own room, Kathy was a little apprehensive about her shutters being securely nailed shut. This town was constructed of wooden shacks and buildings which would burn like paper if there was a fire. She locked her door and shoved the chair under the door knob to add security. Soapy had placed a guard at each outside door; they were to watch all means of entrance during both day and night. Kathy might have appreciated this security if she hadn't learned his motives and sinister nature! Now she felt trapped by Soapy, too.

Monday night, Ben Weathers showed up in Dawson. He was extremely worried about Kathy. Somehow, he had to get her out of this trouble. Landis had come by the cabin to explain matters, then left for Log Cabin on business. Ben frowned, recalling Landis's words as he left, "I'm going to stop at each settlement between here and there. If Jake's here—by damn, I'm going to locate him and make him get her out of Dawson! The irresponsible bastard's going to get his own child killed looking for him!"

Kathy was already singing when Ben arrived. He sat down with some acquaintances to have a drink and to listen to her. She was really talented. So beautiful and innocent . . . trusting and vulnerable . . . She had received some painful blows in life, all undeserved.

He was talking with Hawkins, the engineer for the new railroad, and banker Dobbs. They conversed on how the railroad would benefit this area. Hawkins verbally fretted over the problems they would encounter with the local Indians and Eskimos, not to mention the staggering conditions and dangers his men would work under. Henry had planned the route, but Hawkins would be in charge of the actual work and crews.

When Hawkins laughingly mentioned Soapy's hints about helping the Americans find men and money for the imminent war with Spain over the independence of Cuba, Ben said, "That should be interesting to witness, considering Smith's wanted on criminal charges in several states. He's so sly and stubborn, he might pull it off. That's one way to earn a pardon."

"Any news about that conflict, Ben?" Dobbs inquired.

"A couple of tenderfeet told me it looked like war. Trouble's been brewing for years. McKinley and Alger sent an American warship into the Havana port; they were hoping to prevent the loss of American lives and property. The last news was that the Spanish sank the ship and killed everyone aboard, with over two hundred men lost. He said it happened early February. From what I understood, the Senate's meeting this month to decide its course of retaliation. I might be encouraged to go home if it comes to war," he somberly hinted, knowing he would have work to do. Why was his timing always wrong, controlled by dire fate?

As Kathy left the stage, she saw Ben. She walked over to him, wondering if even he could be trusted. Ben stood up and smiled fondly. "I haven't seen you in ages," she told him.

"How could I go all winter without seeing you?" he

playfully responded, perceiving a newborn reserve and wariness in his daughter.

"You having good luck this year?" she asked.

"My luck could definitely be better," he confessed gravely.

"Mine is improving every day," she murmured sadly.

"How's that, Kathryn?" he pressed.

"I'm leaving in a week. I'm going home to America."

"Where will you go after you arrive?" he questioned.

"I'm not sure yet. Someplace warm and safe," she added.

"I'd like to write you once in a while, Kathryn, just to see how you're doing," he hinted, needing to know where she'd be.

"When I get settled, if I ever do, I'll write you," she vowed.

"Just send it to Mrs. Pullen and I'll pick it up when I'm in Skagway," he suggested. "You don't seem awfully excited about going home," he remarked.

"I don't have a home anymore. My mother sold our house before we started searching for my father. I'll decide what to do later. I guess that's the good thing about a new life; you can start from scratch."

"You've had a rough time here, haven't you?" he queried. A look of haunting sadness filled her eyes. "It won't be so awful next year. I hear from newcomers that the American Congress has finally taken notice of us. They're working on laws now, including a homestead law. That should bring families here, instead of just countless men and fleeing criminals. It sounds like the Mounties will soon receive help from our side."

"Mounties," she repeated distantly.

"Something wrong, Kathy?" he gingerly probed to draw her out.

"No, Ben," she said unconvincingly.

"Has Landis been in lately?" he asked.

Her eyes seemed to freeze into chips of blue ice. "No."

To see how she was faring in her futile search for him, her father, Ben asked about it. Kathy's eyes darkened with resentment as she told him exactly what she felt about her traitorous and selfish father. She added that her quest was over, that she didn't care about ever finding him anymore.

"Why did he leave home, Kathryn?" he asked.

"I don't know and I don't care. I have work to do."

"For your own peace of mind and happiness, Kathryn, I pray you'll hear him out when you find him." he stated, watching her intensely.

Kathy wouldn't say anything else before taking the stage.

Ben fretted over her coldness and bitterness. How can I break your heart or make you believe me? he thought. Dory had only prayed for the return of her lover, Morgan Reynolds. All these years she never told you one word of truth! How can I ever hurt you? Isn't it better to let the lies stand? My trusting child, are you so hurt that you don't even realize you're the spitten image of me?

Tuesday morning, Kathy went to the saloon to practice as usual. She wanted to make certain all was set for her departure. She nodded to the guard as she entered. The barkeeper was in the back room counting liquor stock. No one was around. She headed for Soapy's office; it was empty. She went to ask Monte where Soapy was this morning.

He told her Soapy was in a meeting with some other men at the bank; he shouldn't be back for a couple of hours. Kathy returned to his office, staring wistfully at his desk. Did she dare take the file? Did she owe Landis anything, even his life? She couldn't help but hope he hadn't deluded her. He had offered the Jurrell name for protection, and it had succeeded. He had made no attempt to get her to spy on Soapy. What if it wasn't true? But if he was a Mounty, that explained many statements and actions. How to whisk the file away? Steal it and hide it in her chamber pot! This could be her only chance . . .

She locked the door and hurried to the front of the desk. She dropped to her knees. She found the catch and released it. She twirled the dial and opened the door. She lifted two files, glancing at both. She recognized the sprawling script of Landis on one; how could she ever forget seeing it on her pillow that heart-rending morning at Log Cabin? Worse, she mentally matched Soapy's to that mysterious letter that had misled her back in Skagway! She trembled. Thinking there might be evidence against Soapy in his personal papers, she seized them. She didn't consider taking the jewelry as a cover for theft. She closed the safe and locked it, then shut the panel door and fastened the catch. She concealed the files under her flowing shawl. She went to the door and peeked out. All seemed clear. She headed for the front entrance. The door opened before she could reach it— She nearly fainted. A man walked in. She just gaped at him, helplessly wishing he were Landis . . . or Clinton . . .

Twenty=Five

"Hurry, Jack," she anxiously whispered, racing to him. "Hide these and get out. Don't fail us. Sneak out a side window; there're guards at all doors. Please hurry," she fearfully coaxed, passing the two files to him.

Stunned, he asked, "You got them? He'll kill you, Kathy!"

"They were locked in his safe. I shouldn't be able to get them out. Leave before you're seen. Follow our plan, Jack," she demanded.

"The guards are talking out back. No one will know I was here."

He concealed the files and slipped out. Kathy hurried to the piano and started her practice session. Shortly, Monte came to see if she wanted any coffee. She smiled and sighed, "I would love some, Monte; thanks."

He returned carrying two cups. He handed her one, then sipped from his. "I love to hear you play, Miss Kathy. We're gonna miss you," he voiced the words she was hearing frequently these last days.

"I'm going to miss all my new friends, Monte," she chatted, masking her tension with her newly acquired skills at deception. They discussed her times here and her future plans. Talking with Monte was easy, especially

536

since she was telling the truth. It would soon be over. She was feeling calmer, even slightly confident. It had almost been too easy—but too late.

"I think I have two workers loafing on the job," Soapy remarked as he walked into the room, eying Kathy from tawny head to foot.

"Taking a justly earned break, boss," Monte responded with a chuckle. "We've been working hard, haven't we, Kathy?"

"I was learning a couple of new songs for my last night. Monte thought I was banging too much, so he brought me some coffee to rest his poor ears."

"I have some papers to put away. I'll join you two in a minute," Soapy informed them, turning to leave.

Monte asked if he wanted coffee. "Laced with brandy," Soapy responded. "Join me for a farewell lunch, Kathy?" he halted and invited.

"Can we eat at the hotel?" she replied politely.

"I don't own it yet, but you deserve a nice going-away meal."

She murmured, "Thank you, Mr. Smith."

"You've been in high spirits since Sunday. I'm glad you're feeling better. I was worried about you last week."

She forced herself to give credit to this despicable man, "I have you to thank, Mr. Smith. I appreciate all you've done for me," she stated with convincing sincerity, wanting to spit the bitter words from her mouth.

When he left for his office, Kathy braced herself for a stormy return. She was playing and singing a new melody when he rushed from his office, shouting for his men. The guards and Monte instantly responded. Kathy halted. She turned, her brow lifted inquiringly at his hysterical tone and enraged prancing. He screamed for her to come forward.

She responded, joining the others who were staring at him in bewilderment as well, all silent and still. They waited to learn what offense had been committed and by whom. Smith was dangerously furious, but Kathy didn't feel threatened, for no one had seen Jack come or go with the papers.

"I want to know who's been in my office this morning," he coldly demanded, glaring from one person to the other, his lips twitching.

The guards had entered the office for their rifles from the gun rack, their normal routine. Monte had placed his stock report on Soapy's desk. Kathy told him she had glanced inside to see if he needed to see her. She added Monte had told her he was out, so she started practicing.

"Who came in while I was gone?" he snarled in rapidly rising fury.

The two guards hadn't seen anyone. Monte had been in the storage room. Kathy said her back had been to the center of the room.

"None of the other girls or men came here while I was out?"

All four people shook their heads. "You're all saying you were present while I was being robbed, and none of you saw or heard anything!" he shouted, his temper unleashed, a pulsing vein standing out on his forehead.

"Robbed?" they all shrieked in unison, gaping at Smith.

Smith drilled his gaze into each person's eyes in turn. They all appeared stunned by the news. "The money and jewels?" Monte inquired.

Smith's face went livid and his body tense. "That's the crazy thing! They weren't touched! Just papers were stolen!"

Disbelief was shared by all. "They didn't take those

538

jewels?" Kathy asked incredulously. "But they're worth a king's ransom!" She dared not let the word "papers" cross her lips for fear of guilt clouding her eyes.

"So are those papers!" Smith yelled at her.

She shrank back as if he had struck her, inhaling sharply at the ferocity in his voice and slashed across his rage-distorted features. "You don't have to attack me; I'm not a thief," she retorted angrily.

Monte spoke up in everyone's defense, "Boss, you keep everything in that locked safe. None of us could break into it."

"Safe?" Lewis echoed. "I've never seen a safe in your office."

"It's hid . . ." Monte began, but Smith harshly silenced him.

"If one of you saw anybody leaving and returning, speak up now." He paused. "It wasn't a ghost!" he snarled.

"Monte?" Soapy accused.

Monte nervously cleared his throat. "I can't answer for these two," he stated, nodding to the two guards, "but Kathy hasn't left."

"Kathy?" Smith prodded, trying to terrify her with his gaze.

"I saw Lewis when I came in. Monte was in the storeroom. We talked twice. I'm certain he didn't leave at any time."

"Lewis?" he continued, his expression tight and his face red.

"I didn't see either Kathy or Monte leave, even for a minute. Every time I checked the sides of the building, I called out to Tom and he was there." It didn't occur to him to mention those few minutes of conversation when he and the other guard were loafing.

"Tom?" he prodded the last man.

"I can't vouch for Kathy and Monte from my position out back. Like Lewis said, boss, we call out every little while to make sure the others are all right. I didn't see or hear anyone come near the saloon."

Smith spoke clearly and controlledly, accusing, "One of you is lying through your teeth. With guards posted and two people inside, how do you suppose someone walked in and robbed me, then left without anyone seeing him? It ain't possible," he sneered. "Luther!" he shouted.

The sturdy man came rushing from the office. "Yes. Soapy?"

"Get my men and Molly. Sit down and don't move," he commanded icily.

"Listen, boss, if you think I . . ."

Smith tersely cut Monte off, "Shut up and sit down! Nobody's leaving here until this place and each of you are thoroughly searched."

Kathy gasped in astonishment. "You wouldn't dare search me!"

"I'll have Molly do it for me," he replied.

"You expect me to submit to such an outrage! Pray tell, where would I hide papers?" she scoffed. "Do you hear any papers crackling? This is unforgivable, Mr. Smith. How dare you accuse me of theft!"

"I'm not accusing anyone, Kathy. I plan to clear each one of you in turn. Just relax," he said.

Lewis and Tom both argued against the possibility of getting into the safe mentioned by Monte; Monte said the same about himself and Kathy.

The men and Molly arrived, wondering what was taking place. Soapy commanded, "I want this entire building searched from top to bottom, inside and out.

Search these men. Molly, you make certain Kathy has nothing on except her clothes and that look of anger."

Smith's jest brought smiles and laughter from nearly everyone. Kathy glared at him, not the least amused. Soapy revealed the robbery to the newcomers. He described what he was missing. "There's a thousand dollar reward for finding it," he enticed. The treasure hunt began.

The men were searched in Smith's office, another man with each at all times. Kathy went to the back room with the devilishly happy Molly and undressed. "As you can see, I have nothing to hide," she said.

To antagonize Kathy, Molly took an absurd amount of time to check her clothes, leaving Kathy standing naked getting chilled. Vexed, Kathy seized her clothes. "Considering the size Soapy described, Molly dear, it's obvious to even an imbecile they aren't in my clothes! I'm not going to stand here freezing just so you can be spiteful!" She began to dress.

"I'll tell Soapy you refused to let me search you," Molly warned.

"He isn't a fool, Molly, he'll see your hatefulness. He's terribly upset by this robbery. I wouldn't tangle with him if I were you."

They left when Kathy was dressed. She returned and sat down. Molly entered, glaring at Kathy. "Well?" Soapy asked for her report.

"She didn't have nothing, except the best looking tits and arse I've ever seen, including mine," Molly crudely announced before the men.

As Molly started to reveal more, Kathy was on her feet instantly to deliver a stunning slap to Molly's smirking face, sending her backwards to land roughly on her seat. "You filthy-mouthed piece of trash! Open it once more

541

and I'll give you the most unladylike beating of your miserable life!"

Molly shrugged indifferently and kept silent.

Smith came forward. He grabbed Molly by the arm and yanked her to his chest. "If you ever act like the feather-brained slut you are in front of me again, I'll make you regret the day you were hatched. Don't ever presume my authority! And keep your vulgar mouth shut!"

"She's trying to get me into trouble," Molly vowed petulantly.

"Molly, my harlot, I was standing outside the door. I heard every word spoken. I don't tolerate liars or troublemakers," he murmured in a deceptively calm voice, then brutally slammed his balled fist into Molly's face as she pleaded for mercy. Kathy was too stunned to move or speak. Smith shoved Molly toward the door, shouting, "Get out of my sight and my house. You're fired. My women don't act and talk like cheap trash."

Even with a crushed and bloodied face, Molly raced to fall on her knees to plead with him.

"You won't have trouble finding another job around here," Soapy remarked. "Charlie, see that she's out of my house within the hour. And make sure the guard knows she's not allowed to go back in."

"Please, boss, no one will dare hire me if you throw me out. I'll starve and freeze," she wailed fearfully, a pitiful sight.

"You know my rules—and the punishment for breaking them."

"I was just mad at her. Everybody loves her. Ya'll act like she's a queen. I was only teasing her," she confessed.

"You idiot! She's a lady, and she behaves like one. It isn't her fault if you're jealous of her. Haven't you girls learned anything from her? That's why I brought her here, to teach the rest of you some manners! She's done a lot of teaching, but no one's learning. I'm surrounded by dunderheads! If the others won't hire you, you'll find some way to survive with thousands of starving men around," This conversation was for Kathy's benefit. Her reaction to his uncontrollable beating had shocked her delicate senses. Soapy didn't want any bad reports taken back to Skagway to be given to newly arriving girls. He was witnessing fear and repulsion in her sapphire eyes. That wasn't any way to end their pleasant relationship.

At last, Kathy was allowed to leave. As she swept past Soapy, he caught her arm and halted her to say, "I'm sorry about this, Kathy. But those papers are critical. A lot of people would be interested in getting their hands on 'em. Please don't take it personal."

She coolly met his entreating gaze. "I'm afraid I do 'take it personal,' Mr. Smith. I realize I haven't been here very long and you don't know me well, but I resent being treated like some common criminal. The facts speak for themselves. How did I know you had a safe? How could I break into it? Where could I have put your papers? Your actions and innuendoes have spoiled my last days here. I'm glad I'm leaving this awful place."

When Kathy entered the boarding house, for the first time the girls flocked around her, pressing her for answers. Kathy related the news of the robbery, Soapy's actions, and Molly's punishment. While she had their undivided attention, she announced, "And you should all be happy to know I'm leaving after Friday's show." She turned and walked to her room.

Nelle knocked on the door the minute it closed. Kathy opened it, smiling to find Nelle there. The two discussed the intimidating scene at Soapy's saloon. Nelle was flabbergasted to learn how Kathy had been treated, and was angry and sympathetic.

It seemed forever to Kathy before Friday arrived. She sang and played as usual each night. But she was distant and formal with Smith. As promised before this catastrophe, she did a magnificent job during those four remaining nights. She knew Soapy was still carrying out his personal investigation into the daring theft. Thankfully, no one had seen Jack that morning, at least no one who was around to report it . . .

Friday night, Kathy dressed for her last performance in Dawson. She sang all the regular numbers and the two new ones. Jack had arrived as scheduled. Luckily she had seen him in time to get their stories to match about their last known meeting, the week before the theft.

During her breaks, she related the events following the robbery. He was dismayed to hear of her treatment, but was very proud of how she had handled matters. When she ended her night's work, the applause continued to ring for fifteen minutes. She shook countless hands and accepted words of farewell and good luck. Nugget after nugget was pressed into her hands. She realized what she had been bringing to these lonely people. She smiled so much her cheeks ached. At last, she reached Smith's office. She handed him the jewels and said a crisp goodbye.

"I want you to have this as a remembrance of your time with us," he stated, handing her a gold chain with a single diamond droplet.

"I can't accept this, Mr. Smith."

"Please, Kathy, isn't there some way to thank you?"

She thought for a moment, then replied, "Just words."

"If you ever change your mind, Kathy, you'll always have a job open here," he offered, handing her her final wage.

"Goodbye." She prayed she wouldn't see him again.

Jack walked Kathy to her room to see her safely locked

in, then left to join a friend. Knowing what she would face along the trail tomorrow, Kathy went to bed, the chair propped under the doorknob.

Kathy couldn't have imagined what was taking place with Landis to the south. Landis had reached Log Cabin late Thursday evening to find Trace Blitch in conference with Bill Thomas. A report was due soon on Jake, so he kept silent about his personal suspicions. He had assigned Mounty McLorey to guard his precious love. Recalling the last time he had seen Trace, he greeted him coolly. Both Trace and Thomas stared at Landis in puzzlement. This whole mission was going crazy!

"Don't mind me, just continue as you were," Landis mumbled sullenly as he sat down, boring his gaze into Trace.

"Anything up, Clint?" Bill questioned in mild irritation.

"Nope!" he growled like a hungry bear. "Continue," he said.

Trace watched Landis closely as he stated, "Bill and I were discussing Kathryn Jurrell. Do you still want to sit there?"

Landis stiffened and frowned. "This seat's as good as any about now. What about my wife, Mounty Blitch?" he prodded.

"Have you been drinking, Clint?" Bill quizzed his odd behavior.

"Not yet, but I plan to very soon," Landis drawled lazily. "You care to join me, Mounty Blitch?" he invited.

Trace glanced at him. "Is something annoying you, Sergeant Marlowe? I sense bullets heading my way. Is it me? Or just a nasty mood and fatigue?"

Landis glared at him. "The name's Landis Jurrell

around here, Mounty Blitch," he caustically reprimanded his befuddled friend. "I suggest you recall that at all times, even during amorous circumstances."

Bill and Trace observed him. He was trying to score some point. But what? Why? "Amorous what?" Trace asked in total confusion.

"You know what I mean," Landis scoffed, his eyes stormy.

"No, Landis, I don't know. Mind explaining?" he hinted,

"Kathryn Jurrell," he stated concisely.

"What has she got to do with this?" he asked curiously.

"For your sake, I hope you haven't told her anything."

"Kathy hasn't asked me any questions, and I haven't dropped any information. If you think I've flirted with her because I know you two aren't legally wed, you're wrong. I hate what you did to her, but it's none of my affair. What are you implying, Clint?" he demanded, standing up.

"You saying you haven't dropped any clues during your visits to her?" Landis furthered the mystery rather than cleared it.

"Of course not!" Trace snapped indignantly, stiffening.

"Not even when you stole into my wife's bedroom Saturday?"

Trace's face filled with enlightenment. "You saw me go in?"

"Yep!" he stated succinctly, his expression accusatory and glacial.

"So that's what has you riled! You're bloody jealous over an official visit! I was just comforting her. She was distraught, in tears. Or didn't you take the time to notice?" Trace angrily snarled, provoked.

"The old maiden-in-distress routine?" Landis surmised insultingly.

Trace's anger rose. "What was I supposed to do? She was hysterical, terrified. You couldn't blame her after Slavin attacked her and tried to kill her moments earlier! She was shaking like a leaf during a storm. If Jack and I hadn't arrived just in time, she would be dead right now. I arrested Slavin and brought him here. We couldn't hold him: insufficient evidence. Plus, he threatened to blow your cover. I went up again to check on Kathy and to bring her earnings here. She plans to pick them up on her way home. You can imagine what she felt and thought when I told her we let Slavin go free. Kathy and I are friends, Landis, just friends. She could hardly fall for me when she's already helplessly in love with you. Everyone knows it but you! When are you going to stop harassing her? She isn't spying on anyone. She's just a young girl, alone and troubled. She turned to me and Jack because we offered her help and friendship which should have come from you."

"Slavin attacked her? I saw her later; she didn't say anything. Let me think," he demanded, easing into moody reflections of that day.

He had mentioned seeing Trace. Naturally Kathy had assumed he knew about Marc! When he recalled their conversation, he grimaced at what she hadn't said clearly and what he had implied. He didn't like the way he was thinking and feeling. He frowned as he realized how brutal he had been. Now her confusion and anguish made perfect sense to him.

"When is she leaving Dawson?" he asked, his tone vastly altered after his deliberation, concern lining his face.

"Sunday. Jack's picking her up to head for Skagway. She's leaving on the next ship out. Why, do you care?"

"Where's Slavin?" he asked, his voice and eyes frosty.

"Jack's keeping an eye on him until Sunday."

Landis met Bill's intense stare. "You should have found a way to hold the bastard. She's in danger, and you know it, Bill. Why didn't you send word to me?" he demanded, filled with anguish.

"Your cover," Bill remarked, slightly vexed by Landis's tone.

"From now on, give her whatever she needs," he added sternly. "I'm heading for Dawson at first light."

Bill commented, "I think you're forgetting something, Sergeant Clinton Marlowe. I give the orders around here. You're in my territory. You haven't the rank to change them. Your cover's vital; you can't blow it."

"We've been friends a long time, Bill. I was asking as a personal favor, not issuing orders." He was tempted to inform both men he would soon be in full control of the entire area, but didn't. Later, when things were neatly tied up, he would tell them he was resigning from the North-West Mounted Police to accept the appointment of Commissioner of the Yukon Territory from the Governor-General of Canada, which amounted to territorial governor, a position which offered power and excitement and the freedom to move about as he chose. Most of all, it didn't require the Mounty rule of being single . . .

At first light Friday morning, Landis left Log Cabin to head for Dawson and the truth. If he really pushed himself, he could arrive Sunday about midday. If she left early, he would pass Kathy on the trail between Stewart and Dawson. "Sharpen your teeth and claws, my Kat; we'll fight until this is settled!" he murmured, eagerly hitting the long trail toward his love.

*   *   *

Saturday morning began with a flurry of activity. Nelle brought Kathy lots of hot water for one last bath before starting out on the trail at nine o'clock. Kathy pressed her last week's wages and the golden tokens of friendship and gratitude into Nelle's quivering hand. "I want you to have this, Nelle. Someday, I hope you escape this horrible land, too. I love you, Silly Nelle. I'm going to miss you something fierce. If I had enough money, I would take you along as my chaperone. Please take care of yourself. You've done so much for me here."

Nelle stared at the money: nearly seven hundred dollars in money and gold. "I can't, Kathy. Ye be ta sweet an' givin'."

"I've already sent my money home last week with Mounty Blitch. If I carry it with me, someone will rob me and maybe injure me. Please keep it so I'll be safe on the trail," she wheedled.

Nelle understood what she was doing. She cried. "Ye be an angel. Silly Nelle won't e'er forgit ye."

Kathy hugged her. "Go hide the money while I finish dressing."

Just as Kathy was dressed and packed, Soapy came over. She was surprised and distressed to see him. "I was just about ready to leave, Mr. Smith," she remarked with feigned courtesy.

He looked at her with a rueful expression. "I'm sorry, Kathy. But I'll have to inconvenience you for a moment."

She was perplexed and alarmed. "I don't understand."

"You're the only one leaving Dawson since the robbery. I'm afraid I'll have to search you and your possessions before you go."

"Surely you jest! We've been all through this," she argued.

"Do you object to my search?" he challenged.

"Yes, I do. But I doubt I could stop you."

Kathy sat down while Soapy checked her packs, then searched her entire room. Nelle promptly answered his summons. "Nelle, I want you to undress Kathy and search her for any papers."

Nelle gaped at him. "Search Miss Kathy?" she asked again.

"I know you're slow-witted, Nelle. But that order is clear."

"Miss Kathy?" she asked uneasily, eyes large and wary.

"It's all right, Nelle. Do as he says," Kathy agreed.

When Soapy stepped out, Nelle was about to say something, but Kathy placed a finger to her lips, then motioned to the door. She grinned and winked at Nelle. "Just do as he says, Nelle, and avoid trouble," she stated, smiling conspiratorily.

Just so Nelle could tell the truth, Kathy stripped and proved she had nothing to hide. She pointed out her clothes, which contained nothing. She redressed, then opened the door. "May I leave now, sir?"

"Nelle, did you find anything?" he demanded in an ominous tone to frighten the presumedly dense woman.

Nelle played her part well. "I didn't see nuttin', Soapy. I felt 'er clothes; weren't no papers or anythin'. Only a little gun in 'er pocket."

"Look at me, Nelle. Swear she's carrying no papers."

Nelle looked confused, but complied. "I swears, Soapy."

"Satisfied, Mr. Smith?" Kathy indignantly asked.

"For now. However, I do plan to search Jack's things, too."

She gasped in fury and annoyance. "I don't believe this. Have you even considered the possibility someone stole them during the night, right under your nose? When was the last time you saw them?"

Kathy's cunning ruse partially worked and Soapy began to think. He hadn't seen the papers since the afternoon before. They could have been taken during the night! Still, he would make sure Kathy and Jack didn't have them.

When Kathy and Soapy joined Jack on the front porch, Jack was rankled as Soapy's demand to search his belongings. At first, he adamantly refused. He and Smith argued. Kathy broke in with, "Please, Jack, let him so we can leave this awful place."

The note of exasperation in her voice made him yield. "Make it quick, Smith. We've got lots of walking ahead," he snapped.

Soapy's search revealed nothing except a personal journal of Jack's daring adventures and exploits in Alaska. To Kathy's astonishment, Soapy fluctuated between relief and annoyance that the missing reports and papers weren't with them. Smith bid them a hasty farewell, heading to his office to give Kathy's ingenious suggestion some thought.

By ten o'clock Saturday, April third, Jack London and Kathryn Jurrell were heading for Skagway, by way of Log Cabin. Jack had rented a dogsled and husky team, but the melting snows hindered their speed. Jack knew they were being followed those first two days, but said nothing. Kathy was delighted when he told her where he had hidden the reports and papers: within a mile of Log Cabin!

Whoever was furtively trailing them made no appearance. The rivers were still icy this far north, so they were forced to take the overland route. The dogs were strong and sleek. Kathy marveled at their agility and strength. She enjoyed this swift and carefree journey.

Saturday night, Jack and Kathy spent the night with a friend of Jack's, within five miles of Landis Jurrell . . .

Sunday dawned as the warmest and brightest day since winter had swooped down on this wilderness. Landis arose to head northward, while Jack and Kathy departed southward. Just past Whitehorse was when the blond adventurer relaxed. His tension subsided along with that keen instinct which warned: danger. Their ghost had vanished during the day; no doubt to report back to Soapy that nothing unusual was taking place with them.

Sunday night would find Jack and Kathy camping within easy reach of Log Cabin on Monday about mid-day. By Tuesday night, they would make Skagway. By Wednesday, Kathy would be on a ship, while Jack headed for Stewart to profit from the spring rush up the Yukon for one last time before leaving himself. That was their plan to date . . .

Landis entered Dawson shortly after lunch on this promising Sunday. Confident in his prowess, he headed for the boarding house to get his wife. He was surprised to see the guards removed. Odd, since he hadn't seen Kathy on the trail. Maybe she was staying until Monday. He walked to the back door and knocked. Nelle answered it, smiling broadly at him. She glanced outside, then invited him to enter.

His first query was, "Nelle, did you tell Kat I'd been here?"

She replied, "Ye said ta say nuttin'. Nelle keeps 'er word."

He had hoped Nelle had accidentally dropped that clue for Kathy to mull over. Before he could say anything, she rushed into a flurry of talk, revealing the events in Dawson and Kathy's abuse.

"What was taken, Nelle?" he warily asked.

"Tha bloody thief didn't tak' na money 'er them fancy jewels. All's missin' wuz 'is papers. He's madder 'an a wolv'rine in a trap!"

Landis wondered if Jake had done it. "How is Kathy, Nelle?"

"Poor lass. An' right atop tha' Slavin animal attacking 'er right under me nose! Did ye hear how he tried ta kill 'er, right in there?" she stressed, pointing toward the hallway to Kathy's room. "I thanks God Mounty Blitch saved 'er. If ye'd come sooner tha' day, ye coulda been 'er hero to ye wife," she stated romantically.

"So do I, Nelle," he responded enviously.

Nelle chuckled. "Ye shoulda stayed or taked her 'ome. When he took tha' wild animal off, she stayed in me room for days, afeared ta sleep in hers. Had ter'ble dreams."

That news caught him unprepared: sleeping here with Nelle those nights! She grinned slyly. "Ye be frettin' fur nothin'. She spoke ye name in 'er sleep," she informed him, reading his jealousy.

"My name?" he entreated for confirmation, smiling.

Nelle grinned and nodded. So, the battle wasn't lost yet! "Where is she now? I need to see her. Like it or not, she's coming home today."

Nelle looked distressed. "She be gone since yesterdee."

"She left Saturday morning?" he asked in dismay, that would put them a day and a half beyond him. Still, Jack couldn't travel as fast with Kathy as he could alone. He would catch up with them soon.

"Ye know wha' she did? When she left, she gave Nelle nigh seven hundred dollars, all 'er money from tha' last week."

"You really liked her, didn't you?" he asked. He smiled, thinking what a good housekeeper Nelle would make for them. Too, Kathy would need help with their children and company when he was away, for he planned lots of children with Kathryn Marlowe.

Before she could answer, Soapy Smith stalked in. "I was told you were in here. How dare you come into my house!"

"I came to take my wife home, but Silly Nelle tells me she's already left," he informed the astounded Smith.

"Take her home? Your wife?" Smith scoffed tauntingly.

Landis's grin was mocking, and his dark eyes were mysterious and playful. "About time, since she wasn't safe or happy here."

Smith glared at him. Jurrell certainly was in a cocky mood! Did Jurrell have both sets of papers? Smith might be tempted to think Jurrell and Kathy had been in this theft together! There was no way she could have opened the safe or gotten the papers out of his saloon!

Smith laughed at his foe's self-assurance. "Hell will freeze over before Kathryn Hammond goes home with you. Since ships anchor nearly every day now, you'll never lay eyes on her again. She couldn't leave fast enough after I told her about our bet. She left convinced that you were after her for only two reasons: to use her and to best me."

Landis was riled by Soapy's lies, as Smith knew he would be. A dark scowl lined his handsome features and settled ominously in his ebony eyes. "You play dirty, Smith. What else did you tell her?"

"Only the truth, Jurrell. You wanted to use her like Michelle!" he retorted in uncontrollable ire.

"How did I use Michelle?" Landis scoffed.

"We both know! But Michelle was greedy, wasn't she? What did she do, demand marriage in exchange for evidence against me?"

"Is that why you killed her, afraid she would offer me your secrets? You don't fool me for an instant, Smith.

But why would I be interested in your secrets, 'evidence' you called it?"

Smith laughed heartily. "You think I killed my best harlot?"

Landis scrutinized him closely. "Who else?"

"Since you have no proof I had anything to do with Michelle's death, I suggest you stop making wild allegations."

Landis alertly noticed Smith never denied a hand in Michelle's death. Landis also knew Soapy was lying about badmouthing him to Kathy. Soapy had wanted them together. Some day he would know why. Yet, Landis feared Soapy had darkened his image after their last talk. "I'm going after Kat. You'd best pray it isn't too late to catch her," he icily warned, thinking it safe now to expose his feelings.

"Catch her for what?" Soapy sneered, as if impossible.

"I don't plan to lose her; she is my wife," Landis stated.

"You mean you do love her?" Smith asked in disbelief, a look of thwarted revenge etching his harsh features.

"Why else would I marry her?" Landis sarcastically sneered, unaware of offering Soapy a second chance at victory.

Soapy couldn't suppress his pleased smirk. He quickly concealed it, bursting at the seams to gloat, but knowing that unwise. It was imperative to prevent Kathy from leaving Skagway!

Landis shrewdly observed the curious emotions which flitted over Smith's face. He fiercely scolded himself. He had to get to Kathy before Smith tried!

Landis drilled his trenchant gaze into Smith's ecstatic one. He warned with a truculence which caused Soapy to think twice about his imminent plans, "Don't go near her, Smith. If anything happens to her, there'll be no place for you to hide. You'll be begging for the sweet mercy of death before I finish with you."

Smith glared hostilely at him. No, you'll be the one begging to tell me anything to save your love from me and my men . . .

The look in Smith's eyes sent chills of warning and worry over Landis. "Mark my words, Smith, you're a dead man if you try to use her to get to me," he threatened, as if reading Soapy's mind.

"You've heard my safe was robbed," Soapy abruptly changed the subject. "Wonder how I'll get my papers back," he mused. "Any chance you know something about them?" he asked casually.

"Why would I be interested in your papers?" Landis coldly reasoned.

"Odd, those were Kathy's exact words when I questioned her. I wonder what the thief would be willing to trade for their return."

Landis came to full alert. "You think my wife took them?"

"I think you did. I wonder what I have that you might want in exchange for them," he said.

"Even if I did have them, nothing. But I'll make certain the thief learns I'm willing to pay to get my hands on them. Once I have them, your days are numbered, Smith."

"You're talking more and more like one of those Mounties. Why don't you join up? From what I see, they can use the help. But I wouldn't be so quick to decide I have nothing you want. In my opinion, you'll be coming around to see me very soon. If you'll excuse me, I have some work to do. Don't forget, Jurrell, bring my papers with you when you come next time," Smith meaningfully suggested.

When Soapy returned to his office, he sat down and stared into empty space. Perfect timing was the key to unlocking this riddle. Someone knocked. Piqued, he shouted angrily, "Who's there!"

A malevolent stranger walked in, smiling sardonically. He stopped before Soapy's desk, placing his palms on it and leaning forward, his shaggy brown hair falling over his forehead. His impenetrable green eyes fastened to Soapy's quizzical face. A diabolical grin curled his lips.

"You want something?" Smith asked of the stranger.

"No. You do," he insidiously hinted, a cruel sneer on his lips.

Soapy studied the crude man. "What might that be?"

The nefarious stranger drew himself up to his full height. "Your missing papers, and Kathryn Jurrell. I can get you both for a price," he boasted, his eyes gleaming satanically. "After you finish with her, she's mine," he stated with an evil coldness which was greater than Smith's.

Soapy smiled knowingly. "Name it," he said agreeably.

Monday morning saw Landis heading out of Dawson for Skagway, full steam ahead. All he could think of was getting to Kathy as quickly as possible. Little did he suspect the obstacles which would be placed in his path . . .

Monday afternoon, Kathy and Jack were at the clearing to Log Cabin. Beneath her parka, Kathy held the incriminating packet clutched to her aching heart. When Jack had retrieved it from its hiding spot and placed it within her hands, they had trembled with suspense. As the Mounty headquarters loomed in sight, she tensed in anticipation and dread. She knew what would end the moment she handed these papers to Sergeant Thomas.

She was relieved and tormentingly sad at the same time. Fate had begun to draw her adventure in early September of 1897; by mid April of '98, it would painfully and indelibly end as she sailed home.

Jack pulled on the leather harness straps to halt the dog team. The huskies obeyed the tug upon them, the sled coming to a slow stop. Jack apprehensively questioned, "You want to do this alone, Kathy? I can wait here with the dogs."

She drew in a deep breath to steady her nerves, then slowly expelled it. "If Landis is here, you can return it later. I want to be out of Alaska before he finds out. If you don't mind, I would prefer to handle this alone. I will give you half of the credit," she said.

"You took all the risks. Be careful in there," he cautioned.

"I will, Jack. One thing, no matter what I say, will you back me up?" she asked mysteriously, eyes wide and appealing.

"If you lie about something, you want me to agree?" he questioned.

"Yes," she murmured, still concealing her agony.

Jack tended to the animals as she slowly approached the door. She paused before knocking, dreading to begin this final leg of her journey home. A Mounty opened the door and invited her inside.

"I'm Kathy Jurrell; may I speak with Sergeant Thomas in private, please?" she politely requested, holding her slender body erect and proud.

"I'll see if he's busy, ma'am," the man responded.

Within moments, he was leading her inside Bill's office. Bill stood up instantly, smiling at her and offering his hand. He stated amiably, "It's nice to see you again, Mrs. Jurrell. What brings you here today?"

As if oblivious to his gesture, she sat down before his

desk. "We need to talk privately, sir," she remarked, her darting gaze and edginess displaying her tension and wariness. She didn't trust these Mounties; what if they used this theft against her? Or held back her escape money?

"Certainly," he agreed, assuming the motive was her money. He told the Mounty to shut the door as he left.

Kathy falteringly began, "Is . . . Landis here?"

Bill hesitated noticably before answering. "I'm afraid not. He left for Dawson on Friday. I'm surprised you two missed each other. I was under the impression he was going after you. Even if he heads right back, he won't arrive until Wednesday or Thursday."

"Before I pick up my money and leave, I wanted to ask if there was any word at all on my father," she questioned.

Bill frowned slightly before shaking his head. "I'm sorry we can't be of more help to you; I'm afraid I can't turn your father over to you," he regretfully half-lied to her, warily observing her.

She sighed heavily. "I see. I want to thank you for holding my money. If I miss Trace before my departure, would you thank him for me? He's been most kind and helpful during some trying moments."

"I just wish you weren't leaving with such a distasteful opinion of us. Landis was furious with me for not holding Slavin, but my hands were tied. We've got greedy politicians on both sides anxiously seeking any crisis to stir up more trouble. Slavin's from a wealthy and prestigious American family. He had a spotless reputation and record, and Jack and Trace can't testify to witnessing your attack. You see why I had to release him?" he rationalized his action, shifting uneasily in his chair.

Kathy stared at him as he spoke. "Landis witnessed two violent assaults; is his word also worthless?" she refuted him.

Thomas grimaced; an investigation would be detrimental at this time. He said, "Jack was trailing him. Slavin headed into the North Country. You'll be gone before he knows you've left. As to Landis being a witness for you, a husband's testimony would be viewed as biased. I'm sorry to be so blunt. But without firm evidence, Slavin's arrest could lead to trouble for all of us. But if you insist, I will ferret him out and follow your wishes."

"All I ask is that you keep him clear of me until I leave."

"Agreed. I'll get your money," he stated, starting to rise.

"There's another matter of utmost importance, sir," she intimated, and the Mounty sat down again. "I'm not sure how to begin. I find myself in a complicated position. Are you certain Landis won't return sooner?" she asked.

"You have some problem involving Landis?" he speculated.

"Yes, a very big one." Kathy witnessed Bill's reaction closely.

"I'm afraid I can't help you there. I don't meddle in his private affairs," he declared crisply, hoping to halt any intimate confessions.

"But you can help me, sir," she protested.

"No; I'm sorry," he stated more firmly at her insistence.

"It's business, sir; 'critical,' I believe he called it." To test Bill's depth of knowledge, she began, "Some papers were stolen from him; he accused me of taking them. No matter what I said or did, I couldn't convince him I was innocent. He threatened to arrest me and hold me here until the papers were found," she informed him.

"Arrest you!" Bill repeated in disbelief. Had Landis

recklessly revealed himself? "Just how did he plan to do that?" he asked.

"He was going to convince his Mounty friends to handle it for him. He was determined I couldn't leave Alaska until those papers were recovered. I suppose he was going to bring theft charges against me."

"I don't see what how that affects me." Bill said, confused. "He doesn't have sufficient evidence to warrant an arrest. Besides, you are his wife."

She controlled her warring emotions as she began her enigmatic tale. "As you know, I've been working for Soapy in Dawson these past two months," she gingerly began, then gave details of the robbery episode.

"You saying you think Landis took them?"

"Landis didn't steal them; I did. I only went to Dawson to win Soapy's confidence so I could return those papers. While I was at it, I also stole Soapy's private papers with the hopes of providing you with evidence against him. If that's illegal, you can return them. I hope you don't have to arrest me, since I am returning Landis's reports." She waited anxiously.

Bill was openly gaping at her. "You broke into Smith's safe and robbed him?" he asked. "Does Landis know about this?"

"No, sir," she stated, drawing the packet from beneath her parka and handing it to him. "I was afraid if I handed them over to Landis, he would think I had them all along. If you can arrange it, I would prefer he doesn't know about this until after I sail for America. I know he said they're critical, but I'll be gone in a few days. So there won't be much delay."

"But how did you do what none of my men have been able to do?" he demanded, mildly vexed this slip of a girl had succeeded on her own.

Kathy related her daring adventure. "If you doubt my

word, Jack is waiting outside. I came to look for my father, but things went awry. Since there is nothing for me here, I wish to leave now."

Bill opened the packet and glanced over both sets of papers. His guarded gaze met her lucid one. "Did you read any of this?" he inquired, his tone of voice carrying a strange note, forgetting they were in code.

She related the talk overheard in Smith's office. "I never looked inside. Landis told me that you can't reveal what you don't know. Too, I wanted to remain able to honestly swear I have never seen his papers."

"Then you have no idea what's in here?" Bill pressed.

"No, I do not. I didn't even look at Soapy's. They could be worthless for all I know. I took them on impulse," she confessed.

"I can assure you they are priceless. The culprit will finally pay for his grievous crimes. He's a swindler, a whoremaster, a murderer, and a thief. You've just handed me the evidence we need to put him down. He must be wild with rage and fear. The pompous brute was so conceited he actually recorded every foul deed he committed. I might add, some of your lofty American officials are implicated in collusion and fraud. Some nasty favors were being exchanged."

He glanced at several more notations in Soapy's papers, then laughed in ecstatic satisfaction. "We've got him now. You're a brave girl, Kathy. You've done us an enormous service. Saying thank you is hardly sufficient," he almost reluctantly admitted, cognizant of the power of these two files combined, envisioning Landis's reactions. "How can we repay you?"

"The only thanks I want is for you to keep this matter a secret from Landis until I'm gone. Soapy might get suspicious if we're seen together. Both our lives would be in jeopardy. Promise?"

"Why?" Bill confusedly protested.

"I insist, sir, he can't know until I'm gone," she persisted.

"I don't understand, Kathy," he stated, having shifted to her first name during this conference. "You're not in trouble for this."

"You don't need to. Just take my word, it will be best for both of us." She reminded him of Soapy's lethal scheme to get them together. "Landis claimed those papers could cost his life. In view of his need for secrecy, I doubt even I would rise above them in importance."

"I'm sorry to hear that," he said.

Kathy stared at Bill, then at the folder in his light grasp. She licked her suddenly dry lips. Several tremors swept over her, and her respiration ragged. The real Landis was contained within that file. She had held his stunning "revelations" in her hands and never read them!

She suddenly sat up straight and gasped to fool him, "There isn't anything in there to get Landis into trouble with you, is there?"

"No, Kathy. This report is safe with me. I'll see that it's returned to him. I can promise you he hasn't done anything illegal."

A pain knifed her bruised heart; she had her answer. The reports were in code; therefore, how could Bill know what they said, unless . . . She fought against the tears which threatened her poise.

"If you have no further questions, sir, I would like to take my money and go home." She stared down at her wedding band.

"It's hidden in my cabin; I'll get it for you. Make yourself at home. There's coffee over there on the stove." He got up and left.

As she took an envelope, Kathy's gaze returned to the

files. As with Soapy's papers, she impulsively jumped up and grabbed them before she knew what she was doing. Just as she was about to scan the contents, she caught herself. She severely scolded her reckless intent. No, she couldn't do this to herself. She couldn't become more confused or risk selfishly vindicating him. Besides, they were in unreadable code.

She walked around the desk to lay them down as Bill had left them. Just before the papers touched the desk top, two words on the file which Bill had been avidly studying when she had entered struck her sight. She snatched up the file. "Jake Hammond"!

She tossed the other two now-forgotten files to his desk. She stared at the one held tightly in her quivering grasp. A Mounty file on her father? A thick one, at that! She compulsively opened it. Page by page, she hurriedly and incredulously scanned the shattering information.

Emotionally devastated, she sank into Bill's chair. Her father was right here all the time! He truly was spying for the American government! The Mounties knew all about him! They had lied to her, used her, deceived her! Had they been patiently and covertly waiting for her to lead them to her father? Did they plan to arrest him? Had Landis known all along? Was there no treachery too great to use? Did Landis possess no conscience, no mercy, no morals, no principles, no guilt?

Kathy angrily grabbed Landis's file. She glared at the coded messages which she couldn't read. Was it his report to Bill about her and her father? About his monstrous triumphs over her? She asked herself when Landis had started spying on her—probably the moment her name slipped from her lips. Rage flamed within her. All his rantings about Kathy being the spy and betrayer had been cunning ruses! The notations in Jake's file had clearly inspired his motives. But nothing gave the Mounties the right to abuse her in such a malicious way! Landis had obviously used the marital sham to keep her close. Her father had chosen suspenseful adventure and fidelity to America over his family. He had accomplished much during his self-centered, selfish, arrogant twenty years! But his successes at her expense tore at her ravaged heart. He was courageous, loyal, and daring: qualities he had never shown to her! Hostility and anger joined bitterness and disrespect in her. Her father's secret career had ruined her life, here and in America. If she hadn't been Kathryn Hammond . . .

Her teary eyes flickered over the last page. He had reported to his American agent two months ago: from the Yukon Territory! That told her all she needed to know. Kathy flipped over the final, torturous page. There was a picture, face down, with his name on the back. If they knew his identity, why use her to get to him? Had this file just arrived?

She stared at it, daring herself to turn it over. Her hand was shaking so badly she could hardly lift it. She held her breath as she twisted her wrist to present the image of her unknown father to her wide, anguish-filled eyes. Her lips and chin quivered. Tears rolled down her ashen cheeks. Agony gripped her heart. Now, she comprehended Landis's invitation to his cabin and why he was so positive she had stolen his reports.

At last, she didn't have to wonder about Jake's appearance or new identity. At last, she knew her mission here had succeeded—and failed. Landis had gone for blood; now she knew why. The photograph seemed to explain everything. Her heart thudding painfully in her chest, she stared at the image of her traitorous father . . .

565

Twenty-Six

Kathy was dazed by this staggering pervasion of facts. She mechanically returned the pages to their folders. She went to the stove, then picked up a cup and poured herself some strong coffee, adding sugar to it. She walked to the side window and pushed the curtains back to gaze out.

When Bill entered his office, he found her standing there in deep thought, sipping coffee. He called her name twice before she heard him and responded by turning to face him. She appeared tired, emotionally and physically drained. She came forward to sit down, as he did. Something was distressing her. "Here's your money, Kathy," he stated, passing her the leather pouch.

She leaned forward to accept it, thanking him automatically. Rising gracefully, she remarked mechanically, "I'll leave now. Goodbye."

Bill studied her heart-wrenching look and somber mood. "Are you positive you don't want to hang around until Landis gets back?"

"No, Sergeant Thomas. He loaned me his name and twice saved my life; now, I've repaid him in full. I'll accept your gratitude for him."

Bill wondered what to say or do, fearing she would

leave before Landis had the chance to clear up matters. It would be a shame to end their relationship in this bitter way. Trouble was, Clint had revealed affection and responsibility for her, but he hadn't vowed love. In spite of Clint's obvious passion for her, Mounties couldn't marry. Bill assumed Clint wouldn't surrender to the callings of love and passion at such a high price. But Landis did need to reveal their phony marriage and deal with that consequence.

She glared at the money pouch in her left hand and murmured absently, "It's amazing what some men will do."

"Is something bothering you, Kathy? You seem very depressed."

She smiled falsely. "I'm just mentally and physically exhausted, now that it's over."

"What about your father, Kathy? You giving up your search?"

Kathy stared at the floor. This supposedly honorable man was sitting there so deceptively innocent when the truth was within his reach. She restrained the urge to confront him. If Bill discovered she knew the truth, he might be compelled to hold her here. She couldn't allow that for countless reasons. She was crushed and embittered by their betrayals. She had lived with Landis and Ben. She had trustingly confessed her desires, fears, and soul to them. She almost laughed as she cynically wondered if each traitor was spying on the other.

Her father . . . could she even think of Ben Weathers as Jake Hammond? Jake knew her identity. He couldn't even offer her a few crumbs of affection and loyalty, for he apparently had none for her.

My father . . . My own flesh and blood . . . How could you do this to me a second time? I will never forgive you! As for you, Landis

Jurrell, did you have to use my love and steal my innocence to further your causes? Like two rotten peas in the same pod, both men were so much alike! Users! Takers! Deceivers! Betrayers! Self-centered monsters!

At last, she lifted her impenetrable gaze to look at the bewildered Thomas. "As far as I'm concerned, my father is dead; I'll not search for him again."

"Would you like to leave your address with me, just in case we locate him and he wants to get in touch with you?" Bill kindly offered.

She declined. "I don't want anyone to know where I'll be. When you close my file, just note Kathryn Hammond also mysteriously disappeared."

Bill observed her closely at the use of her name. This vivacious and spunky girl had changed greatly and Landis Jurrell was partly responsible. Annoying guilt chewed at Bill. Yet, his hands were bound by duty. He knew what her erroneous assumptions were doing to her. "I'm sorry, Kathy. I wish I could say or do something to ease your pain and sadness. I can't."

"I know, sir," she concurred.

"What about Landis? Your marriage?" he speculated softly.

"There's nothing to keep me here," she remarked dejectedly. She handed him a sealed envelope and asked him to give it to Landis after her departure. Once the pain was gone, she would be fine. She had never felt this confident or resilient, so pleased with her talents and courage—yet so utterly miserable and lost.

Kathy left with Jack. They travelled a few hours, then camped. Tuesday, they would be in Skagway. She prayed a ship would enable her to sail Wednesday. She would pack, then hopefully sell her cabin to Dray as an investment. She would say her farewells to her friends, then leave this land of golden torment.

After extracting another vow of silence from Jack at their campsite, she revealed her meeting with Thomas and the truth about Clinton Marlowe. Jack couldn't believe her stunning news. It enlightened him to many episodes, but infuriatingly clouded others. He couldn't summon any logical debates to her conclusions, and it didn't help the truth when Jack readily concurred with Kathy.

Jack was troubled by the anguish in her eyes and voice. He was aware of her soft weeping several times during the night. When he could bear her pain no longer, he placed his sleeping bag next to hers. He pulled her into his arms to comfort her. His solace was in knowing she possessed the courage, intelligence, and stamina to conquer this bitter defeat and to succeed in her new life. She cried until exhaustion claimed her. By two o'clock Tuesday afternoon, they were approaching Skagway . . . Kathy looked up at Jack and smiled sadly; there was indeed a large steamer anchored in the Lynn Canal . . .

"Don't leave so soon, Kathy," Harriet pleaded with her young friend when they reunited. "You've been gone off and on for months. We've missed you terribly. Stay just another week," she coaxed, afraid to ask about Landis.

Other friends added their pleas to Harriet's. "I've stayed too long. I'm leaving in the morning," she said with finality. Fortunately, all kept silent about Landis, knowing by now it had been a mock union and must be over. Kathy feared everyone except her had known the truth all along . . .

Kathy talked with Dray and made a deal on her cabin. Kathy and Jack embraced. She cried and hugged him fiercely, thanking him for all he had done for her. Jack promised to look her up when he returned to America that summer. She waved as he left, tears still clouding her eyes, sensing they would never meet again. She had been tempted to give Jack her mother's locket as a keepsake, then concluded it was best if they both let their bittersweet pasts die.

Later, Harriet had some time alone with Kathy and tried to convince her to stay in Alaska. Kathy revealed Slavin's brutal attack and release, then added another piece of information to justify her departure: the robbery and suspicions at Soapy's. "As you all know, he isn't a man to have as an enemy."

Kathy noted glimmers of comprehension in Harriet's eyes. "It's finally over now; it's time for me to go home." Kathy related her plans to become a concert pianist and revealed her numerous experiences in Dawson. She left out the truth about her father and her false love to spare both needless anguish.

"What about Landis, Kathy? Does he know about the files and your departure? What about your marriage? Your father?"

"It's over, Harriet; everything. It was only a necessary charade."

"Are you sure, Kathy?" Harriet persisted doubtfully.

"Yes," Kathy vowed sincerely. Tears filled her eyes; she inhaled raggedly. Agony knifed her vulnerable heart.

"You've really had it rough here, haven't you?" Harriet asked, but Kathy was staring unseeingly out the window. Harriet shook her head sadly. There was nothing to say or do for this tragic girl, so she went to her cabin and family.

A terrible thunderstorm savaged Skagway as Kathy completed her packing. She reflected on the farewell supper in Moore's tent, needing to keep her thoughts from other topics. Soapy's papers would tell Landis his cover was blown; he would be safe. Everything was ready except for a bag in which her last items would be placed. Her nightgown was lying on the bed; her clothes for the voyage were across a chair. Strangely, she almost hated to leave Skagway. She was taking a last journey around her cabin when a knock sounded at the door.

She went to it and asked who was calling. The thunder boomed loudly, denying all except one muffled name: Jack. She flung the door open and stepped aside to allow his quick entry from the torrent of rain. She closed the door and turned to see why he had returned.

A wet hand clamped tightly over her mouth and a rain-soaked man pinned her against the door. Her heart raced wildly in panic. Her eyes widened in terror as they stared into those satanic green ones. Her world reeled madly as he malevolently hissed, "I don't think you'll be leaving by ship, Kathy. Soapy and I have some unfinished business with you. After I told him a few facts, he decided he had judged you innocent too quickly. He wants to see you before you join a girl named Michelle." Marc Slavin laughed cruelly as she fainted.

Shortly before noon that next day, Landis pounded insistently on Kathy's door. When she didn't answer, he tried the latch. It was unlocked, so he opened it and glanced inside. The cabin was deserted and chilled. He didn't step inside, denying him a glimpse of the havoc behind the slightly ajar door or a view of her bags at the end of the bed. He closed the door and leaned against it. His gaze reluctantly turned toward the deserted canal.

He stood transfixed. There was nothing he could do now. What a damn fool he had been! He had lost the only woman he had ever loved or wanted. Even if he went after her, she would cover her tracks to prevent any of them from finding her.

Perhaps if he hadn't stopped at Log Cabin to avoid the storm, he could have gotten here in time to stop her departure. He had recklessly assumed he could out-distance her and Jack. Damn, how she must be suffering! he thought in agony. Never had he felt so frustrated and helpless in his entire life.

She had risked her life to clear her name with him. Bill had been caught up in a dispute over a gold-claim after Kathy's departure; Bill hadn't realized Jake Hammond's file had been tampered with until he pulled it out to show to Clint. Then Landis was furious with Bill for letting Kathy leave.

Thinking about Ben/Jake, Landis knew Kathy would never forgive either of them. She surely believed he had known the truth about Jake all along! If she hadn't stolen his papers from Soapy, he would have charged Jake with their theft! But Ben hadn't acted the least suspicious since Landis realized his identity. Evidently Jake didn't know about his hiding place, else Ben would have con-fessed himself after reading that real marriage document left as a test! Where was Ben? Ben hadn't been home since his visit to Dawson. If Ben had confided to Kathy, she wouldn't be running away!

Jake had revealed honest affection and concern for her. What had Jake been feeling and thinking during her stay with them, knowing he wasn't Landis Jurrell? Did Jake think he was cruelly using Kat? Perhaps Jake had hoped Clint would take the responsibility for his vulner-able daughter.

A mortal grief tormented Landis, for she was as lost to him as through death. He fearfully wondered if she would really marry another man, thinking herself free.

After knowing her and loving her, he couldn't imagine life without her. He loved her and needed her. He had discovered his golden dream, to have it become his tarnished torment.

I love you, Kat Marlowe, he miserably thought. What have I done to you? To us? God help me, to myself?

"Landis! Where's Kathy?" Harriet asked in concern.

Landis's startled expression levelled on Harriet's flushed face. "She's gone home; I was too late to stop her," he somberly stated, anguish undisguised in his face and voice. "The ship's sailed. She'll make certain I can't find her. Why didn't she give me time to explain?"

Harriet gaped at him in confusion. "She's not with you? Then where is she?" she shouted in panic.

He stated in anguish, "She's gone. The ship left this morning!"

"That's what I mean; Kathy didn't get on it! Her cabin's a wreck; her bags are still in there! Nobody's seen her since last night. I've questioned everyone; I've looked everywhere. Something's wrong, Landis; she's vanished," she concluded aloud in dread.

Landis straightened, coming to full alert. "What do you mean, she's vanished? She didn't get on a ship?" His heart began to thud wildly.

"No. We've been looking for her all morning. I'm worried. When I saw you standing here, I thought you had something to do with her disappearance. If you know where she is, tell me," she pleaded.

"Her cabin's unlocked," Landis remarked, his keen mind working swiftly. Unlocked? Strange. "Maybe she was hiding from me; maybe she missed the ship; maybe she even changed her mind," he anxiously speculated.

He opened the door and entered. It was then that he saw the concealed bags and her gown. From the looks of the mussed bed, she hadn't slept there. His frantic gaze swept the entire cabin. The floor was still damp and muddy in several places. The table had been shoved against the corner cabinets; a chair was overturned. Landis went over to the table. He leaned over and picked up a torn sheet. It didn't take a Mounty to realize strips had been torn from one end, strips for bindings . . . He bent over again to retrieve a piece of cloth, a pocket from her flannel shirt, probably torn away during a fierce struggle. As he hunkered down to check out another clue, he asked, "Where's Jack?"

"He left yesterday right after he delivered Kathy."

Landis touched his finger to the damp spot on the wooden floor. He raised his shaking hand to stare at the crimson stain, sheer terror washing over him. He held the finger up as he spoke one word, "Blood."

"Smith?" Harriet said in gnawing fear. "Or Slavin?"

Landis appeared deceptively calm. But Harriet saw the deadly lights glowing in his eyes. "I'll kill him," he stated with cold and ominous assurance. "By God, I'll kill him!" he thundered in unleashed rage. He tested other semi-congealed spots of brownish red to assess the length of their presence on the floor: hours old, he concluded in fear.

Harriet nearly went to pieces as she imagined what either man would do to Kathy. "What if she's already dead?" the panicky words escaped.

Landis closed his eyes, trying to shut out the mental vision of his love's broken and bruised body at the foot of some precipitous cliff. Had Smith followed her to Log Cabin and put two and two together? Had he kidnapped her to torture the truth from those sweet lips? Landis couldn't forget Smith's allusions to an impending trade and visit. "I'm going after her, Mrs. Pullen. If he's harmed one hair on that golden head, I'll carve him to pieces!" He needed clear wits. Did Smith have her? Was he waiting for him to come and bargain for her life?

Suddenly Harriet brightened with hope. "Jack was heading inland to make certain no one followed her until she could leave. Maybe he'll see them!" But it was a vast and hazardous territory, and Jack was ailing.

Within twenty minutes on this eventful Wednesday, Landis had enlisted Dray's help and the two desperate men were heading toward Dawson, by way of the Mounty headquarters and Landis's cabin . . .

Twenty-Seven

At Log Cabin, Landis and Dray borrowed two roans, the melting snows making it possible to cover the trails on horseback. They raced out for Whitehorse, their speed and intent urgent. They left the animals with a friend there, then took a boat. The Yukon was still treacherously icy in many places, but it was imperative to get to Dawson before Smith could harm Kathy. Both men were banking on Smith's insistence on seeing her before killing her, or on trading Kathy for Landis's cooperation.

Strong, agile, skillful, and determined, the two men battled the raging waters to rescue Kathy. They beached near Landis's cabin. Dray anxiously remained with the boat, while Landis rushed to his cabin to fetch Ben. They might need an extra man along to assist against Soapy and his cohorts.

Ben was startled when Landis stormed in, glaring coldly. Before Ben could question his fury, Landis shouted, "There's no time for talk, Jake Hammond. Kathy's been kidnapped. Smith will kill her if we don't get there in time to stop him. If you care anything about her, I'll need your help up there. You coming? Or do you still deny your daughter in this moment of need?"

Ben warily studied him. Was this some trick? Landis

sneered, "You traitorous bastard! If she dies, we're both to blame!"

Landis stalked into his room. He jerked open his closet and kicked in the secret panel to the back. He grabbed his Mounty uniform and struggled into it, hands trembling with tension and fear as he snatched a hidden paper. He strapped on his service revolver and seized a rifle. He just might need some convincing authority in Dawson . . .

Watching Landis desperately toss his cover aside, Ben realized he wasn't playing a game. Landis rushed past him and left. Ben yanked the door open and shouted at his retreating back. "Hold up, Sergeant Marlowe; I'm coming with you!" He hurried to his room and grabbed his mackinaw and gun, then hurried to Landis's side.

"How could we do this to her?" he sadly murmured. "God, how I love her, Ben; or should I say, Jake? If anything happens to her . . ."

"I know you won't believe this, but I was going after her this week. My work's over. I love her and need her. She's all wrong about me and what happened. I didn't desert them; Dory left me for another man. She swore Kathy was his child. One look at her and I knew what Dory had done. I tried to tell Kathy the truth, but I couldn't. Even if I had, she wouldn't have believed me. My mission here isn't detrimental, Clint."

Clint stared at him. "Let's go. We can talk later."

They headed back to where Dray was nervously pacing. He stared at the crimson jacket, blue pants, and low-brimmed hat. He shouted in befuddlement, "You can't impersonate a Mounty!"

"I'm not, Dray. The name's Sergeant Clinton Marlowe of the North-West Mounted Police. I'm on assignment here from the McKenzie Territory."

"Jake Hammond of the United States War Department," Jake introduced himself. "Kathy's father, also on secret assignment here."

Dray gaped at them. "You're both phonies?" he accused.

"Let's go! We're wasting valuable time!" Clint ordered.

They jumped into the boat and pushed it into the turbulent river. Soon, they were docking where the Yukon merged with the Klondike at Dawson. They wasted no time getting to Soapy's saloon. The men who knew Clint as Landis Jurrell, stared, thinking he had joined the Mounties, wondering about his wife. Clint nodded and spoke, never hesitating in his tracks. When Luther tried to halt him from heading down the private hallway, Clint forcefully shoved him aside and sneered, "Get out of my way, you scum!"

Without knocking, Clint barged into Smith's office, along with Jake and Dray. Smith looked up, paling at the sight which greeted his wide eyes. "What's the meaning of this!" he shouted timorously.

"You know why we're here, Smith. Where is she?" Clint snarled, his gaze piercing, his stance intimidating.

"I have no idea where Kathy is," Smith shot back before thinking.

"I'll kill you if you've harmed her," Clint vowed with deadly confidence. "I'll ask one more time, where is she?" His towering frame was rage-taut.

Smith fused livid with anger. He stiffened. "I don't know."

Jake raced around the desk and yanked him to his feet. "I'll kill you if you don't speak up, you worm!" he added his threat to Clint's.

"Just who do you think you are to threaten me, Ben Weathers?" Smith scoffed, trying to hide his fear of these furious men.

"I'm Jake Hammond, Kathryn's father," he replied coldly.

"You?" Smith shrieked in utter surprise.

"That's right. Where's my daughter?" Jake demanded.

"I haven't seen her since she left!" Smith answered honestly.

"Who's got her? Where? Speak, man, before I strangle you!"

Clint stormed around the desk and seized him from Jake's grasp. He shook him by the shoulders and snarled, "I'm warning you, Smith!"

"I don't have her! Damn you, Marlowe, I haven't seen her!"

Clint grinned tauntingly at his slip. Smith appeared flustered and frightened. Clint roughly shoved him into his chair and tied him to it. He withdrew his hunting knife and toyed with the blade as he warned, "You have one minute to answer. I know about your plans for us. I'll kill you first."

When Smith opened his mouth to shout for help, Clint slammed his fist across his jaw. Jake grabbed his hair and yanked his head backwards, warning, "Speak, man, before we slit your throat!"

Dray was standing at the locked door with a rifle. He coldly sneered, "Your men can't help you. We leave with Kathy, or you're a dead man!"

"I stole your blasted file, Smith; so I know you're aware of who and what I am," Clint lied most convincingly. "If you think to trade Kathy for the file, you best forget it. We have all the evidence we need on you. Give me Kathy, and I'll look the other way while you escape," he bargained.

"I don't trust you," Smith scoffed. "Besides, I don't have her."

"But you know who does," Clint countered. "You have my word."

"And Mounties never lie, right?" he contemptuously spat. "I doubt Mrs. Landis Jurrell believes that honesty crap!" he scoffed.

Clint drew back his balled fist. He was about to beat Smith mindless if he didn't confess.

"All right!" Smith screamed in cowardice. "Slavin has her! He was going to get my file back for a tidy sum."

"Where is she?" Clint demanded, fear chewing viciously at his gut.

"I don't know! Slavin went after her. I haven't seen her."

Jake yanked his head back again, placing a sharp knife at his throat. "One more lie, Smith, and you've bought it!"

Smith struggled to speak without nicking his neck. "He . . . was taking her to . . . Domino's cabin . . . near Whitehorse. She's . . . probably still alive. I was . . . to question . . . her first."

"If she isn't, you'll answer to us. You can't run far enough or fast enough if she's met with harm," Clint warned ominously.

They decided to deal with Smith later; force and time were essential. It was late Friday afternoon when they shoved the boat into the chaotic water to head for Whitehorse, ignorant they had actually passed within a mile of Kathy and Slavin along the trail . . .

Shortly before noon, another event was taking place far to the south. Marc had been forcing Kathy on since the wee hours of Wednesday morning. Her hands were tightly bound behind her back, restricting their circulation. He had allowed her little rest and privacy, constantly pushing her on through dark and light, his energy coming from hatred and spite.

Each time she had balked at their murderous pace, he had threatened to shove her over the steep precipice to certain death. Kathy knew as long as she remained alive, there was hope for escape or rescue. She compelled herself forward until she thought she would pass out from exhaustion and fear. Marc gave her only enough food and water to keep her alive and walking.

On several occasions, he had roughed her up, relishing her discomfort and terror. But he shrewdly restrained his violence, holding himself in check until they reached their final destination. Then, he promised himself she would pay dearly for his downfall!

Her hands had been untied only twice. She didn't expect rape yet; she knew he was anticipating another place for her torment. By noon Friday, she was too weary to care any longer. He was going to kill her, so what difference did anything make? They had passed many prospectors, but Marc had noticed them first and concealed their presence. It was hopeless.

Kathy ached all over. She was laboring to breathe. Her throat and lips were parched. She was utterly dejected. Even fear no longer pushed her onward. Her hands were numb and her feet refused to take another arduous step. This experience, added atop others, sapped her strength and will.

She sank to her knees, her action yanking the rope in his hand. He whirled and jerked on the leash around her waist. She fell to the slushy ground. Slavin came back to her and painfully seized her shoulders, forcefully bringing her back to her throbbing feet.

"Get up, you bitch! Start moving or I'll kill you!" he snarled.

"Then kill me," she weakly told him. "I can't go on this way. I've got to rest. I need some water."

"You'll rest and get water when we get to Domino's! Get up!"

"I can't," she faintly refused, unable to obey.

He backhanded her across her pale cheek, planting a livid print there. Blood eased from the corner of her lip. She fell backwards into the gooey mush. She curled to her side, yielding to the stitch there. "I can't," she still refused his command, crying softly.

Slavin bent over her, aware she couldn't move on. He cursed her and kicked at her, bruising her shoulder. "Then rest for five minutes! No more!"

He stalked away. Suddenly Kathy was aware of thunderous voices. She struggled to sit up, seeing two burly lumberjacks hurrying toward them.

Slavin shouted, "Halt there! Come any closer and she's dead!"

Kathy's gaze flew to Slavin; he was holding a gun pointed at her. She glanced over at the lumberjacks—Mike and Danny—as she struggled to her knees. "He's going to kill me anyway. Better here than later. If you let him take me, he's planning to torture me first," she told them, swaying precariously.

Mike was straining from cautiously leashed fury. Danny was alarmed. "Let her go, Slavin. We'll kill you first," Mike called his bluff.

"No! She's mine! I'll kill her if you move," he countermanded.

Mike and Danny glanced at each other. They began to slowly move toward Slavin. The frenzied man saw his victory escaping. He fired at Kathy, shouting insanely, "Die, you witch!"

The bullet struck home. Kathy screamed in pain and shock. She was thrown backwards, bright red blood flowing into the melting snow to pool together. She didn't move again.

With a shriek of thunderous rage, both men surged toward Slavin before he could get off another shot. As Slavin retreated, a horrified scream tore from his throat as he plunged over the jagged escarpment behind him. His body was tossed about as it yielded to gravity. It crashed into the icy edge of the river and was instantly swept under by the powerful current, never to see another day.

Mike raced to Kathy. He gasped in alarm as he saw the bloody pool forming near her left side. He hurriedly cut her bonds, roughly massaging her hands to restore their circulation. With Danny's help, he removed her parka. He ripped a bandage from her shirt tail and wound it tightly around her left arm. There was so much blood, and she was so ashen.

He shook her and called her name. No response. He picked her up and headed to their lumber wagon. Mike held her gently in his strong arms as Danny drove the wagon wildly to Skagway and the doctor. They luckily met up with Trace Blitch, hesitating only briefly to enlighten him, then hastily continued their desperate journey.

Trace urged his horse forward, heading to warn Clint. It was late Friday evening before Kathy arrived in Skagway. She was taken to her cabin by Mike, while Danny raced to find the doctor. Harriet and Griff surged forward to check on her. Mike quickly related their rescue.

When the doctor arrived, everyone was sent out except Harriet. Kathy was undressed down to her chemise. The doctor examined the wound, instantly noting the bullet had passed clear through her upper arm. He tested for a break, finding none. Evidently the excessive bleeding was from a severed blood vessel. He placed medicine on the injury, after carefully cleansing it, then bound it tightly to halt the flow of blood.

Kathy was exceedingly pale and weak. The doctor worked on the smaller cut and blackened bruise on her forehead, clearly an older injury. He checked her arms, legs, and ribs for breaks, relieved to find none. Then he placed ointment on several minor abrasions and tested other bruises.

When Harriet continued to press him for information on her condition, he finally halted his work to answer her. "She's suffering from shock and exhaustion. The bullet wound should heal nicely. She's lost some blood. I can't detect any broken bones. She'll need hot food and plenty of rest."

Kathy began to stir and moan. Her lids moved and her eyes opened slowly. She was briefly confused by her surroundings. Harriet fretted over her. Gradually the whole petrifying episode returned. When Kathy asked about Slavin, Harriet explained what happened after she was shot.

Kathy never commented on Slavin's death. Harriet hurried on to explain that Dray and Landis had gone after her Wednesday morning, telling Kathy how frantic they were before heading out to Dawson.

"Dawson?" Kathy weakly echoed.

"They thought Smith was behind this," Harriet clarified.

"He was," Kathy informed her.

"They're so worried. I hope they get here soon to see you're all right."

"I hope not," Kathy countered, assuming Landis was only feeling guilty. If they were in the North County, perhaps she could still leave before their return! She prayed her father wouldn't hear about this trouble and come to see her as Ben. Their guilt didn't concern her! She didn't have the strength or frame of mind to battle either man.

Harriet was surprised by her coldness. Yet, Kathy was in no shape to be troubled with questions. The doctor asked about any pains or discomforts. Kathy moved this way and that, replying to each query. When he was satisfied, he told her he would return in the morning to change the bandage. He warned her to stay in bed and to avoid any unnecessary movements.

After he left, Harriet told her she was going to get some hot soup and coffee and let Kathy know Griff would be on guard outside. Kathy smiled and thanked her, confessing to her great hunger and thirst. Harriet gingerly helped her into one of her gowns, then tucked her in like a child. Harriet fondly patted her hand and left, still in the dark about Landis and Jake.

Griff stuck his head inside as Harriet left. He grinned affectionately and stated, "You rest, Miss Kathy; Griff's right here."

"Griff?" she called. He halted and glanced back at her, his gaze expectant. "Please don't allow anyone to come in, except Harriet and the doctor." When he nodded understanding, she clarified softly, "Please don't let the Mounties or Landis enter this cabin."

Griff looked confused, but agreed. He closed the door. Kathy's face sank into the feather pillow, allowing the salving tears to flow freely. She had to rest and eat; she had to be strong enough to get on the next ship! There was Clint and Jake. Slavin was dead, but the insidious Smith wasn't . . .

Harriet returned with the soup and coffee and remained until every drop was gone. She cautioned herself against asking any distressing questions about anything or anyone. She smiled encouragingly at Kathy before leaving. "I'll bring you a hot breakfast in the morning. If you need anything, send for me. The doctor left some medicine for pain on the table. He said it would make you sleepy. Do you need any now?"

Kathy nodded. "It's throbbing some, but I really need the sleep more than anything." She needed escape from her own mind and heart.

Harriet spooned it out and placed it in her mouth. Kathy swallowed then remarked playfully, "I'm not sure whether to call you Mother or Nurse. Thanks, Harriet, my good and loyal friend."

Within a short time, Kathy was sound asleep. Harriet checked back later, but didn't disturb her. She told Griff to please keep an eye on her. He grinned and promised he would.

Kathy was pampered all day Saturday. Harriet and Griff had difficulty turning away her anxious friends. Mike brought her a small bunch of bright spring flowers he had found during his working day. The other lumberjacks were eager for news of her condition; they didn't seem satisfied by words passed along. They wanted to see for themselves if she was all right. Only Moore and Mike were allowed inside her cabin, telling others she needed to conserve her strength.

Kathy sent messages to the others through Moore and Harriet. When Mike came, she asked Griff to let him inside. She thanked him for saving her life, something done too often in this vast and perilous wilderness. When he told her about meeting Trace along the trail and his intentions, she whitened noticably. When Mike questioned her reaction, she told him she was simply tired and needed to rest.

Griff was the one who accidentally told Kathy a steamer was sailing into the canal. She perked up immediately and told him to fetch the doctor. He did, worrying over her curious excitement.

When the doctor arrived, Kathy came right to the point, "Will I be able to sail tomorrow? The voyage is long; I'll have plenty of time to recuperate."

"You're still weak, Mrs. Jurrell. You've been through a terrible ordeal. You need rest and care. What about your arm? What about your husband?"

"There's a doctor aboard. I'll have meals sent to my cabin. I'll get lots of rest. I'm going," she firmly stated as he helplessly shook his head.

"I strongly advise against it, but I can't stop you," he murmured sternly against her determination and foolishness.

"Will the voyage kill me?" she asked.

"Certainly not," he promptly stated.

"Good! Then I'll be on that ship in the morning."

He observed the defiant jut of her chin and the rebellion flashing in her eyes. "It sails Monday; tomorrow's Sunday," he smugly announced.

"Are you positive?" she debated, suspecting even the doctor of trickery.

"Yes, Mrs. Jurrell. The captain told me himself."

"Excellent. That gives you one more day to see me to good health," she teased to lighten the tension.

"The captain's obviously a friend of yours; he came ashore to check on you and Mrs. Pullen," he remarked.

"Captain Shurling?" she asked.

"Yes, that was his name. He was most upset to learn of your accident and Mr. Slavin's death. He sent his best wishes."

The moment he left, Kathy called Griff inside. She sent him to see Captain Cyrus Shurling about her return passage. In view of his part in her troubles, he agreed to take her home Monday when his ship sailed. Since her last voyage aboard the *Victoria*, he had been more careful in his crew selection. That was wise, as more and more females—a mixture of wives, daughters, sweethearts and hopeful brides—were coming to the territory.

Kathy told everyone goodbye Sunday, since she was leaving early and some would be gone to the timberline. Harriet helped her bathe and prepare for bed, trying one last time to change Kathy's mind—but she couldn't.

Trace was pacing impatiently before Domino's cabin Sunday morning when Clint and the others came riding up to him. He was only mildly surprised to see Clint in his uniform. The men hurriedly dismounted. Trace walked toward them to relate his news.

Clint asked fearfully, "Why are you here, Trace? Is Kathy . . . dead?" he could hardly force the word from his lips.

"Wounded. I waited here because I knew you would pass this way. Domino was kind enough to let me hang around," Trace said.

"Kind, my ass!" Jake thundered. "Smith told us Slavin was bringing her here. Was she hurt badly? Is she inside with that beast?"

"You mean Domino's in on this scheme?" Trace exploded.

"Evidently Kathy didn't know or she would have told you."

"She was unconscious when I saw her. Mike and Danny rescued her; they carried her to Skagway. Slavin's dead," he announced.

"You mean she isn't here?" Clint wailed in agonized disbelief, feeling hindered and thwarted at every turn.

Trace told all he knew. Clint and Jake both sighed in relief. Wounded on Friday, she couldn't be gone Sunday. Pushing themselves, they couldn't make Skagway before Monday. She couldn't be ready to leave before their arrival, but they didn't want to chance her determination to get away.

Trace lingered to arrest Domino as the others rapidly left. All three men were tense and worried. They allowed brief periods to rest the horses and to catch a quick nap, riding in stony silence, wondering what to say.

The *Victoria* issued bellowing blasts, indicating she would be sailing soon. Kathy stretched out across her cabin bunk, her good arm resting over her eyes. She was safely aboard the ship, out of their reach. She was weary from her exertions; her arm ached, refreshing her memory of her horrible ordeal. How strange she was leaving this land in windy April on the same ship which had brought her here early last September.

Shurling had been overly kind to make amends. She had paid him well to guard her privacy. She was plagued by September's golden dreams and April's stygian torments: all born and nourished in this wild frontier where men would give their souls to strike it rich, where honor didn't exist.

Kathy recalled the letter Harriet had pressed into her

hands as she stepped into the boat with Griff. Ben had made Harriet promise to give it to Kathy only as she was leaving for good. Not wishing to inspire questions, Kathy had accepted the letter and stuffed it into her bag to read later.

She wondered if she should open it and risk slicing her heart anew. Jake had placed the letter in Harriet's safe-keeping for such a moment. Did it finally reveal the truth? Could she face what might be written there? No, not yet. Perhaps she would destroy the letter without reading it . . .

She jumped as the horns blasted their signal to leave. She wept for what was, what had been, and what was to be . . .

The men rode into Skagway. Noticing friends standing near the shore, they headed to them. "Where's Kathy? How is she?" Clint spoke up first.

"Is she all right, Mrs. Pullen?" Jake anxiously inquired.

"I'm going to her cabin," Clint said, sliding out of his saddle.

Harriet and the others were staring at Landis in the splendid Mounty uniform. Harriet called out, "She isn't here; she's on that ship."

Clint whirled and glared at it. He and Jake exchanged probing looks. "Let's go, Jake," Clint said hurriedly.

"Jake?" Harriet echoed, staring at Ben Weathers.

"This is Jake Hammond, and I'm Sergeant Clinton Marlowe, Mrs. Pullen. We'll explain later. We've got to stop Kathy."

With Dray trying to explain, Clint and Jake borrowed Griff's boat and headed for the ship. Clint shouted to the baffled Shurling that he needed to come aboard; Shurling couldn't refuse a Mounty. He nimbly climbed the rope which had been tossed over to him. He asked Shurling where Kathryn Jurrell was. The captain studied him a moment. Clint snapped impatiently, "You can't sail until I've talked with her. This is official business. Where is she?"

Shurling didn't want any trouble, so he responded instantly. "Just make it quick. I've got a schedule to keep," he retorted, scolding himself for allowing that troublesome girl aboard again.

A loud and persistent knock sounded on Kathy's door. What now? she wearily mused. She called out from the bed, "Who is it?"

"It's . . . Landis, Kat. I've got to talk to you."

Landis! What was he doing here? They were ready to sail! How had he reached her in time? Why couldn't he let her leave in peace?

"Go away. I don't want to see you or talk to you," she said dully.

"I've already gotten permission from Captain Shurling to break down this door if necessary," he warned seriously. "You're going to hear the truth before I let this ship sail. Open up, Kat."

"No! Leave me alone!" she screamed in rising panic.

"If you force me to kick this door in, I'll take you ashore with me! Just hear me out, then decide if you still want to leave," he coaxed.

"More lies and tricks? Thomas has your reports."

"I know all about the damn reports, Kat! Believe me or not, I found out about Jake only recently. You are going to hear me out!"

"Oh, no, I'm not! I despise you! You and Jake solve your own problems; I'm not involved!" she cried in defiance.

"Shurling is holding this ship until we talk face to face."

Kathy realized they were still anchored. Evidently

Landis had stopped their sailing! She was trapped. She got up and walked over to the door, but didn't open it. "What do you want to say?"

"Face to face," he insisted, trembling in dread.

"I don't want to see you," she panted. "I don't care what you have to say. You're up to something, Landis Jurrell; I don't trust you."

"I can't blame you for feeling that way. I've given you no reason to trust me. Damnit, Kat! I was a bloody fool. Please, talk to me."

"Haven't you done enough to me?" she entreated.

"Too much. I've made countless mistakes with you, Kat."

"I'm going home, Landis. Please go away."

"I can't, love. Just five minutes . . ."

She unlocked the door and pulled it open. "Just five minutes," she warned him. As he stepped inside and closed the door, she stared at him. Her startled gaze went from his touseled ebony hair, to his scarlet jacket, to his dark blue pants with their sunny yellow stripe, to his muddy black boots, back up to the revolver strapped around his narrow waist, and ended its exploratory journey on the low-brimmed hat dangling by its strap from his arm. The uniform fit him perfectly, evincing his broad shoulders and enhancing his handsome looks. He looked splendid, utterly arresting. Her mind screamed, a Mounty can't marry!

"I see you finally decided to wear your true colors. The uniform suits you, Landis, as does the job. Are you arresting me or are you here to torment me?" she sneered, cradling her injured arm.

His keen gaze swiftly took in the bandage, her bruises and scrapes, her pale face, and her glazed eyes. "If Slavin weren't dead, Kat, I would kill him. Are you all right?" he softly and tenderly inquired.

"Surely you didn't halt this ship to inquire about my health?" she scoffed. "I'll be just fine. You go back to work for your Mounty friends; they can make good use of your skills and talents," she insulted him.

"I've been a Mounty since I was nineteen. My name is Sergeant Clinton Marlowe, Clint to my good friends. I was on a secret mission here; that's why I couldn't tell you anything about me. Those reports covered two years of demanding work; that's why I had to get them back. With the added report you bravely supplied on Smith, my work is finished."

"Are you here to present me with a medal?" she tartly snapped.

"You deserve one. I'm here for an important reason, Kat, the truth."

"Do you even recognize it?" she sarcastically taunted.

"You don't want this quick and easy, do you?" he asked sadly.

"I don't want it at all, Landis. I forgot, Sergeant Marlowe."

"I was trained to be wary, Kat. You're different from the women I've known. I was blind, overbearing, and stupid. I treated you badly. I was selfish and harsh. I craved you. I didn't know how to handle such unfamiliar emotions. I honestly thought you took the reports as revenge, or to make me chase after you. I was hurt and angry. I thought you had betrayed me. I took my feelings out on you, and you didn't deserve that. In Dawson, you would turn me away; then, you would respond to me. I was so damned confused and edgy that I reacted violently. After I saw you in Trace's arms that day, I went wild with rage and jealousy; I was afraid I might strangle both of you if I didn't get out of Dawson right away."

He grabbed a quick breath and continued before she could interrupt, "When I saw you two days later, I was reacting from anger. When I told you I had seen Trace, I meant I had seen him in your arms; I didn't speak to him that morning before I furiously stormed out of Dawson. I didn't know then what Slavin had done to you. I didn't know Trace was only comforting you. I was so blind and resentful that I assumed you had dropped me to seek information from him, or perhaps both of us. I forced myself to hurt you as you were hurting me. I wanted to prove to you I didn't care about you either. Later, I saw Trace; I nearly took his head off. Needless to say, he set me straight. Ever since that day, I've been tracking you all over the place. I was always a few days behind you. I've been crazy with worry."

Kathy just stared at him. He pressed his advantage. "When I heard what Slavin did, I went to Dawson. You were gone. I made the mistake of telling Smith I was going after you because I loved you. He put his old plan into motion again. When I got to Log Cabin, the reports were waiting for me. When Bill related your news of Soapy's motives to get us together, I knew Soapy would come after you. Bill showed me the file he had just received on your father; it was evident you had read it. I knew what you would be thinking and feeling. By the time I reached Skagway, I feared you had sailed out of my life forever. Then, I figured out what had happened to you. We struck out for Dawson to rescue you. We beat the truth out of Smith, then went to Domino's. That's when we learned you were shot and back in Skagway. We came as quickly as we could, but you were already on the ship. I've been going mad these last two weeks, Kat."

"Why bother?" she probed, her heart thudding heavily.

"Your father is with me, Kat," he informed her. "When he heard of the danger you were in, he instantly dropped his cover to help me rescue you. You're wrong about us, Kat."

She was wrong? she mentally scoffed. "Your five minutes are up, Sergeant Marlowe," she stated softly, wondering if he would press her.

"I love you with all my heart; I can't let you go . . . ever," he delivered his stunning decision. "You love me, Kat; admit it."

She swayed slightly. He reached for her. She jerked away. "Don't you touch me," she warned.

She walked to the bed and sat down. "I'm still weak. I'm tired, so please go now. I've heard you out. It doesn't change anything."

He came over to her. He dropped to one knee, taking her right hand in his. She tried to pull free, but he wouldn't release it. There were tears welled in her eyes; she turned her face to deny him a view of her anguish. She could never forgive his false marriage to her.

His eyes roamed her features. "Do you want me to beg, Kat? God, I will if you'll only listen. I love you! You're my wife, Kat; I can't lose you. You're the most important thing in my life."

"What about your precious career? Mounties can't marry," she debated his words, words she believed false and cruel.

"I've resigned, Kat. I've accepted the position of territorial governor. The Mounty rules don't apply to that position. That's why I kept trying to get you to wait, to hear me out, to stay with me. I've loved you since that first day I walked into Moore's tent and found you chattering to yourself. When you looked up at me with those entrancing blue eyes, I was lost. We've had countless misunderstandings, Kat. Please stay here and work them out. I promise I won't hurt you again; I swear it."

"You're asking me to stay married to you, after what you've done? You found Jake; what more do you want? I'm not his accomplice."

"You're wrong about your father. While we were travelling in search of you, he told me what happened. Hear him out, Kat. You owe yourself that much. He loves you and needs you. He was coming after you this week. He's already dropped his secret identity. He's told everyone who he is."

"What is this, Landis, some code of honor between you lawmen? I don't want to see or speak with him, or you. Can't you see? It's over, Landis. I keep forgetting, Sergeant Marlowe," she angrily corrected herself.

"Will you force me to arrest my own wife to keep her here? Damnit, woman, I will. You're too stubborn to listen!" he heatedly accused.

"I have listened, Marlowe! You wouldn't dare arrest me on phony charges! And I'm not your wife!" she shrieked.

He imprisoned her head and pulled her lips to his. He crushed his mouth against hers, forcing her lips to part. He hungrily savored her mouth before drawing back. "I love you, Kat. I'll keep you here until I prove it."

"I'll fight you all the way, Marlowe. You have no claim on me."

"I'll force you to discover how wrong you are."

She eyed him warily. "I'm not your wife; Landis Jurrell doesn't exist. If you hold me, I'll let everyone know about your vile deceit."

Suddenly Clint understood. He threw back his head and laughed. He withdrew a sheet of paper from his jacket and handed it to her. "I beg to disagree, but we're

596

very legally married, Kathryn Marlowe. If you don't believe me, read this wedding certificate and check the ship's log. I'm sorry I had to trick you, but you are my wife, Mrs. Marlowe."

Kathy stared at his beguiling grin. "You're lying," she breathed.

"Nope!" he averred. "Read it."

Kathy snatched the paper and read it, her eyes widening. "This is another one of your tricks. Are you forgetting the license I have? I don't trust you."

"Why not?" he reasoned softly, grinning at her. "I said I'd marry you. I merely gave you a phony license; I couldn't reveal myself back then."

"Because . . . you can't be serious!" she argued apprehensively.

"But I am, love. That's why Soapy was confused; he knew I wasn't Jurrell. But he didn't know you were Kat Marlowe. I couldn't lose you, even when I doubted you. I was determined to save you and keep you."

"All right, Marlowe; I'll call your bluff," she sassily stated.

He captured her face between his hands and smiled into her defiant eyes. "I'm not bluffing, Kat Marlowe. It can easily be verified.

"Do you object to seeing your father?" he asked quietly.

She looked at him. "He's here?" she asked fearfully.

"Yes. Please, Kat, just listen to him," he entreated. "We all need to settle everything today. This battle's raged too fiercely and too long."

She turned away from his probing eyes. "I can't, Landis," she stated faintly, old habits hard to break. "You're confusing me even more."

Clint sat down beside her and pulled her against his

chest. "He didn't tell you the truth at my cabin because he knew how much it would hurt you, Kat. I'm not sure you're strong enough to hear it today. Will you agree to hear him out later?" he coaxed her.

She lifted her head. "You know the truth, don't you?" When he nodded, she sighed. "You believe him? You think he was justified?"

"Yes, Kat. He loves you. He was willing to let you leave here before ripping your world apart again. More so, love, he was afraid you wouldn't believe him; he feared you would hate him."

"If you're a Mounty and my father's an American spy, doesn't that put me in the middle of a crisis? Are you going to arrest him?"

He chuckled in amusement and sighed in relief. "That isn't necessary in his case. In fact, he's done me and Canada a big service with his reports and investigation. He isn't our enemy. He's a good man, Kat."

"How so?" she questioned in bewilderment.

"He's been working to unmask some of Soapy's American partners, those I mentioned who're involved in corruption and fraud. He's also been ferreting out some dangerous criminals in hiding here. He's made it clear to your government that claiming any territory here will cause new conflicts. Plus, he was mighty surprised by the power of the Mounties," he listed some of Jake's accomplishments.

"Is there more?" she asked with genuine awe and curiosity.

"Yep, plenty. They asked him to check out the resources around here, to see if Alaska was worth their time and attention. I know he's settled some disputes between the Hudson Bay Company and the Alaska Commercial Company; that rivalry could have been explosive. I must compliment your government for worrying over your prospectors' treatment of our locals. It's clear to us your country isn't looking to cause trouble here or to attempt any takeover. Jake tells me they're setting up a seat of authority in Skagway soon. He vows we'll have their cooperation and assistance with crime and violence. I can promise you, Kat; his work was critical for peace and progress. I must say, I envy him and respect him greatly. He never expected you to show up, complicating his work."

"What about his reason for deserting me and mother?" she challenged.

"I think he should explain that, love. I'm not taking his side because he's a man and a friend, but I do see his logic. I'll admit he handled some matters unwisely, but he did have reasons. Just hear him out, and then decide for yourself. Give us both another chance, Kat," he pleaded earnestly.

When she remained quiet and thoughtful, he said, "I'm going to call your father in, Kat. If the answer's no, stop me now."

When she didn't, he smiled and kissed her soundly, then left.

Kathy sat dazed. Were they honestly married? He loved her?

"Kathryn?" her father's voice called from behind her.

She turned, her gaze slowly roaming over him, staring at the blond hair and blue eyes which matched her own. He came to stand before her. "I know I've hurt you deeply, but I do love you and want you. Did you read the letter?"

"Letter?" she echoed, staring at him.

"I left it with Mrs. Pullen; she was to give it to you if you left. It explains everything, Kathryn. I was hoping you had read it and considered it."

"She did, but I haven't read it. Why did you lie to me? Why did you leave?" she helplessly asked, tears rolling down her cheeks.

"Are you certain you want to hear the truth now, Kathryn?"

"I must," she whispered faintly.

Kathy didn't interrupt as he painfully told his story. When he finished, he stated hoarsely, "I swear that's the truth, Kathryn Leigh."

Little things began coming back to her, slips her mother had made, slips gone unnoticed or unchallenged. No matter how much it hurt, Kathy couldn't deny the honesty and anguish in his eyes. "Please, Kathryn, give us time to talk and get acquainted. I'm finished here. We can go home now. I won't ever leave you again. I'll resign and we'll make a home together."

"Landis, I mean, Clinton and I are married."

"Do you love him?" he asked soberly, wondering what she planned to do about their situation; Clint had tricked her.

She stared at the wall before her. He continued, "I think you two can be very happy. I know I'm partly to blame for messing things up between you two. Do you want to remain as Mrs. Clinton Marlowe?"

"You think he loves me?" she ventured.

"I'm certain of it. But if you don't love him, you can come back to America with me. We'd have to dissolve your marriage."

The door opened and Clint walked in, wondering at the words just overheard. Clint walked over to Kathy and helped her to her feet. She was weak and shaky by now. He held her tightly against him. "Kat? What about us? I love you. Will you stay with me?" he asked again.

She looked at him, at her father, and then back at Clint. The room was very still. "Yes," she murmured softly, fusing her gaze to his.

He smiled ecstatically and whooped with relief, "Let's get going."

Clint held her in his powerful arms and gazed deeply into her trusting eyes as he asked in a clear and vital tone, "You ready to wear this again?" He pulled out the wedding band she had left with Bill.

She smiled at him and murmured tenderly, "Yes."

Clint slipped it on her finger, laughing merrily. Kathy eyed the gold band around her finger and murmured happily, "You thought of everything, didn't you? What if I had refused to hear you out? Would you really have arrested me to keep me here?"

"Absolutely!" he declared honestly. "I couldn't let you leave the Yukon with my heart and soul," he jested, kissing her lightly.

He glanced at the anxious Shurling. "Sorry about the delay, Captain Shurling. Can I get some help with these bags?" he inquired.

Shaking his head in disbelief, Shurling called two men to place the bags in their boat. At the railing, he bid them farewell and even bussed Kathy's cheek, relieved to get rid of the female troublemaker. Clint didn't want to risk an injury to her, so he helped her down the rope ladder. He placed her between his body and the ladder, easing her down slowly and safely. They waved to Shurling as they shoved off from the *Victoria*. Before they made shore, the steamer was underway.

When they landed on shore, Clint picked up Kathy and headed for her cabin, asking Jake to see to her bags. When Harriet misunderstood this situation, she questioned Clint, dismayed by this outrageous behavior.

After all, she was married to Jurrell, who wasn't real.

Clint glanced at Harriet, stating, "She's not under arrest; we're really married. May I introduce Mrs. Clinton Marlowe," he announced to everyone. "Now, I would like to be alone with my wife."

"Clint!" Kathy playfully scolded him, blushing.

He looked down at her and savored the radiant smile on her face. "Sorry, wife. I guess you'll have to teach this wild frontier rogue some manners. We've had damn little time together."

Griff, Dray, and Jake carried the bags to her cabin. Jake ushered everyone out, saying he would explain. Clint closed the door and locked it, when turned to Kathy, inviting her into his protective and longing embrace.

He lifted her and carried her to the bed, gently laying her there. He blissfully tantalized her mouth until she was breathless. He gazed down at her and vowed, "No more golden torments, my love, just beautiful golden dreams for our future. I love you, Kat Marlowe," he whispered huskily.

"Kat Marlowe . . . it has a nice ring to it," she murmured.

She sighed wearily. He studied her pale face and trembling body. "How's the arm?" he asked.

"It's hurting like hell, Mr. Marlowe," she responded saucily.

"Perhaps I should teach you some manners," he quipped.

"That isn't the lesson I have in mind," she shamelessly chided him.

"You better rest, love. You're still weak and hurt."

"Rest?" she seductively taunted him. "I could have sworn you just vowed no more torments. Yet, here you are racking my body with torturous frustration. Have you no mercy, my handsome groom?"

"But you're hurt, Kat." he reluctantly argued.

"Then come and ease my worst pain," she entreated.

"You sure?" he questioned, wanting her so badly his loins ached.

"I've never been more certain of anything in my life. Except . . ."

"Except what, woman?" he pressed curiously, teasing at her lips.

"Except that I love you with all my heart."

He was promptly out of his clothes, then gently undressed her. He placed her beneath the covers and joined her. He gingerly leaned over her and captured her inviting lips. He pulled away long enough to vow, "I love you with all my heart and soul, Kat Marlowe. At last, a priceless treasure is mine alone."

"Nothing's free, Jurrell," she provocatively teased. "Is the price worth it? No more splendid uniform or carefree life?"

"It's definitely worth anything," he concluded.

"But I do like the name Landis Jurrell," she pouted.

"Then we'll name our first son Landis Jurrell Marlowe," he cunningly solved that problem. "Landis was my father's first name, and Jurrell was my mother's maiden name," he quickly explained.

She smiled serenely. "If you don't get busy, Marlowe, there won't be any sons," she hinted, kissing him greedily. "We'll have years to discuss our adventures together. This isn't the time to talk."

"God, how I love you and need you, Kat Marlowe," he huskily murmured again, savoring the melodious sound of her name. Closing his sensual mouth over hers, he skillfully and eagerly fanned golden torments into fiery passion . . .

Historical Epilogue

This author has made every attempt to portray the vivid character and fascinating life of Harriet Pullen with accuracy and detail. Historically, Harriet Pullen left Seattle in September of 1897 to seek her fortune in Skagway. A thirty-seven-year-old widow, she headed for Alaska with only seven dollars in her pocket, leaving her four small children behind until she could afford to send for them. She was a strong and vital female with flaming red hair; she exhibited an adventurous, daring, resourceful, and independent air which rivalled any male pioneer's. Though history has recorded little about this fascinating and courageous woman, she was lovingly labelled "Mother Pullen" and the "Mother of the North." Her hotel, Pullen House, stands in Skagway to testify to her achievements. As in this story, she actually became famous in Alaska and the Yukon Territory for her bravery, endurance, and success. She began her fortune by baking and selling apple pies to the men there; later, she added to her success by actually transporting goods over the dangerous Chilkat and White Passes, braving all conditions and obstacles to make her imprint upon that vast and harsh frontier. As civilization and progress touched Skagway, she built a hotel and restaurant. Dan, one of her sons, was slain during World War I, and she lost her son Chester to a drowning accident. Later, Harriet purchased cattle and a farm to supply her restaurant with fresh foods and meats. A heartwarming legend, Mrs. Pullen can be viewed as a forerunner of equal rights for women and as an inspiration to all. May her memory and achievements be known forever.

Jack London, the famous American novelist, was stranded in Stewart for one year, during 1897-'98. He was a ruggedly handsome blond giant of twenty who fearlessly piloted the dangerous rapids of the Yukon River to carry prospectors to the gold fields. Jack left San Francisco to seek adventure and wealth in the Klondike, but never found gold. As a reckless and defiant youth, he allowed his health to deteriorate greatly in that treacherous environment, eventually suffering from scurvy. History has labelled Jack many things: a loner, a rebellious adventurer, a spendthrift, a serious and forceful man, and a talented writer. After leaving Alaska, Jack spent years travelling and absorbing ideas for his novels. But his later life was tragic: following two unsuccessful marriages and a battle against alcohol, he took his own life in 1916 at age forty. But his experiences in the savage and suspenseful Yukon gave him the insight and stimulation to write many of his best novels, including my two favorites: *White Fang* and *Call of the Wild*.

Other characters who actually lived during that eventful period and location were Moore, the lumberman and Harriet's first boss, and Randolph "Soapy" Smith. "Soapy" was a legendary villain, known for his wild and devious exploits. Several mementos, including his iron knuckles and gambling equipment, are on display in Harriet Pullen's Hotel/Museum in Skagway. Smith's saloon was also restored to its original appearance. Following a dispute in 1898 over how he was handling his recruits for the Spanish-American War, Smith was shot and killed by one of his own men. Even today, when tourists go to Skagway or Dawson, they learn who and what Smith was.

Dawson was destroyed twice by fire: late 1898 and early 1899. It eventually became the seat of the territorial government. The railroad was completed in mid-1900. Although the United States began to evince interest in Alaska during the gold rush, the gold-boom was actually at its historical heights during 1897-'98.

My gratitude to these historical figures who inspired this tale of peril, passion, and *Golden Torment* . . .